George John Whyte-Melville

Holmby House

A tale of old Northamptonshire

George John Whyte-Melville

Holmby House
A tale of old Northamptonshire

ISBN/EAN: 9783337088248

Printed in Europe, USA, Canada, Australia, Japan

Cover: Foto ©Andreas Hilbeck / pixelio.de

More available books at **www.hansebooks.com**

HOLMBY HOUSE:

A TALE OF OLD NORTHAMPTONSHIRE.

BY

G. J. WHYTE MELVILLE,

AUTHOR OF

'DIGBY GRAND,' 'THE INTERPRETER,'

ETC.

NEW EDITION.

LONDON:

LONGMANS, GREEN, AND CO.

TO

THE REV. CHARLES H. HARTSHORNE,

F.S.A. &c.

HOLMBY RECTORY.

———◆———

Dear Sir,

In dedicating to you the following Tale of Old Northamptonshire, permit me to offer you my hearty thanks for the assistance I have derived in its details from your local knowledge and archæological research.

I can only wish I had been better able to take advantage of those resources to which you have so kindly given me access; but I may still hope that, however far I have fallen short of the mark I aimed at, with *you* at least a story will find favour, of which the scene is laid in your own immediate neighbourhood, and the time of action chosen full two hundred years ago.

Believe me to remain,

Dear Sir,

Yours very sincerely,

G. J. Whyte Melville.

Boughton: *February* 1860.

CONTENTS.

CHAP.		PAGE
I.	THE OLD OAK TREE	1
II.	A CAST OF HAWKS	8
III.	THE QUARRY	16
IV.	'FALKLAND'	23
V.	BRIDLED AND SADDLED	29
VI.	BOOTED AND SPURRED	38
VII.	THE REVELLERS	46
VIII.	NEWBURY	5?
IX.	'ROSA QUO LOCORUM'	59
X.	'ANCILLÆ PUDORIS'	67
XI.	MERTON COLLEGE	75
XII.	'NIGHT-HAWKS'	90
XIII.	'FOR CONSCIENCE' SAKE'	99
XIV.	MAN TO MAN	115
XV.	CROSS PURPOSES	123
XVI.	THE QUEEN'S APARTMENTS	137
XVII.	'THE PROSELYTE'	147
XVIII.	'SAUVE QUI PEUT'	155
XIX.	'THE NEWS THAT FLIES APACE'	165
XX.	THE MAN OF DESTINY	172
XXI.	'UNDER SENTENCE'	183
XXII.	'FATHER AND CHILD'	188
XXIII.	'THE TRUE DESPOTISM'	193
XXIV.	'FAREWELL'	201
XXV.	NASEBY FIELD	210
XXVI.	'THE WHEEL GOES ROUND'	224
XXVII.	'HOLMBY HOUSE'	233
XXVIII.	KEEPING SECRETS	246
XXIX.	'THE FALCON GENTLE'	259
XXX.	'A RIDE ACROSS A COUNTRY'	269
XXXI.	'FOR THE KING'	281
XXXII.	'THE BEGINNING OF THE END'	287
XXXIII.	'THE BEACON AFAR'	294
XXXIV.	'PAST AND GONE'	302
XXXV.	'THE LANDING-NET'	309
XXXVI.	'YES OR NO'	315
XXXVII.	'WELCOME HOME'	32?
XXXVIII.	'WESTMINSTER HALL'	327
XXXIX.	'THE MUSKETEER'	337
XL.	'THE PROTEST'	345
XLI.	'A FORLORN HOPE'	354
XLII.	'THE WHITE KING'	363
XLIII.	A GRIM PENITENT	367
XLIV.	'COMING HOME'	376
XLV.	'LOST AND FOUND'	384
XLVI.	'THE FAIRY RING'	391

HOLMBY HOUSE.

CHAPTER I.

THE OLD OAK TREE.

THE Pytchley hounds have had a run. Io triumphe! The Pytchley hounds have killed their fox. Once again, Io triumphe! Not that these are unusual events with that well-ordered and efficient pack, nor that the establishment is more than commonly exhilarated by success; but that such runs as this last do not occur oftener than two or three times in the season, and deserve to be recorded accordingly.

It is a curious mania, that fondness for hunting which pervades the rural population of Great Britain, from the peer to the peasant, and which we alone of all their progeny seem to have inherited from our Scandinavian ancestors—a mania that outlives love, friendship, literature, money-making, all the devices of poor human nature to squander its most priceless possession—time; and which seems to flourish only the more vigorously when the health and bodily strength indispensable to its enjoyment have passed away for evermore. We, too, in our 'hot youth,' were once inoculated with the malady, and its seeds have never since been thoroughly eradicated from our constitution. There *was* a time when our heart used to beat thick and fast at the first whimper of a hound; when the colour mounted to our cheek, and our eye glistened brighter, as we watched the gorse shaking above the busy pack; when the life blood coursed quicker through our veins as we listened for the distant 'View-holloa' proclaiming him '*away!*' and the mad equestrian revel really about to commence. Then it was ecstasy to be borne along at speed by a gallant generous horse, himself giving and receiving the mutual pleasure enhanced by so confiding a partnership; to

B

thread with calm dexterity the rushing cavalcade, and reach, unbalked by restive steed or undecided rider, the spot we had marked out many a stride back for our own. Large, black, and formidable, hand, seat, and eye combined to land us safely on the further side; and *then*, with tightened rein, head up and hands down, to speed away after the streaming pack, good friends and true to right and left, but not a soul between ourselves and the hounds!

Alas, alas! '*post equitem sedet atra cura*,' she can cling even to the sportsman's scarlet, she can keep her seat even over a Northamptonshire ox-fence; but though the good horse carry double, he feels not the extra load, and the rider's heart must indeed be heavy if it can ache at moments such as these.

As the penitent highwayman remarked to the chaplain at the gallows-foot. 'Oh, I repent unfeignedly of my sins, but yet —a gallop across a common! *you dog, it was delicious!*'

So now, though the days of our pilgrimage are in the 'sere and yellow leaf;' though boots and breeches have given way to flannel bandages and fleecy hosiery, whilst gout and rheumatism warn us that wet days and 'wet nights' are equally dangerous to our *physique*; though our quiet cob, once the property of a Low Church bishop, is getting too much for us, and is coveted inwardly by our eldest grandson, who already considers his own Shetland pony 'hardly up to his weight,' we have still a hankering after the golden joys of our youth, still a sneaking kindness for the tops and the scarlet, the crack of the whip, the echo in the woodland, and all the appliances and accessories of the chase.

'What a hunting day!' we remarked aloud to our walking-stick, as we climbed the hill painfully towards Holmby, and stopped to admire for the hundredth time the wide expanse of beauty and verdure stretching far away beneath our feet for many a mile to east and west, dotted here and there with noble standard trees, and shut in by the dark stately woods of Althorpe that crown the rising ground to the south. 'What a hunting day!' a sky of dappled grey, a balmy breeze just wooing into existence the hundred buds and beauties of early spring—a day to have gathered the first peeping violet 'long, long ago.' *Eheu fugaces!* what's a violet, with no one to give it to?—day of beauty and promise, a day such as George Herbert so charmingly describes:

> Sweet day, so cool and calm and bright,
> Sweet bridal of the earth and sky,
> Sweet dews shall weep thy fall to-night,
> For thou must die.

But nevertheless, rather too muggy a day for an elderly gentleman nearly fifteen stone weight to walk up such a hill as that; so we rested on our stick, mopped our heated brows, and leaned our back against the stem of a fine old oak that stands within a stone's throw of the wall surrounding all that is now left of the ancient palace of Holmby. We own to the practice of daydreaming—'mooning,' it is called by the irreverent—and we were soon lost in the long vistas of the past, threading the labyrinth by help of that delusive skein which we are pleased to term history, taking up one end at the period at which we supposed this oak to have been planted; and so winding it gently off from the Wars of the Roses to the jolly days of 'bluff King Hal;' congratulating it on its inland position, which saved it from forming part of that fleet whose thunders helped to destroy the Invincible Armada, speculating on its size and luxuriance in the peaceful time of that crowned wiseacre whom Scottish parasites termed 'gentle King Jamie;' and thinking how fervently its beauties must have been appreciated by his ill-starred son, to whose charge want of veneration could never have been laid as a fault. 'Here,' we thought, 'beneath these venerable arms, under the stately shade, how often has the unfortunate Stuart, the martyred Mon—— Hulloh! what is that?—the note of a hound, as we are a living sinner and a gouty one; but gout or no gout, we haven't seen hounds for a twelvemonth; we must hobble on and have a look at them once more. But stay, there's their fox! —a beaten fox, by all the beauties of Diana!' and forthwith we gave vent to a prolonged and, we rather flatter ourselves, not unmusical yell, which we should despair of conveying to the reader by any other means than oral demonstration. We used to pique ourselves upon doing it rather well, and with one finger in the ear and a rubicund well-fed physiognomy, the effect is, to say the least of it, imposing, if not harmonious. Yes, there he was, stealing along, his back up, his fur draggled, tangled, and black with mire; his brush drooping, his tongue out, his long knavish countenance wobegone and indicative of thorough physical exhaustion, his whole instincts so intent on his pursuers that he scarcely turned aside at our salutation—there he was, dead-beat, and running short for his life, not a covert or an earth within two miles of him, and the best pack of hounds in England running frantic for his blood in the next field. See, he has nearly reached the old oak tree! one, two, three white hounds are through the fence, the rest following, like a stream of water set free from a dam. How they strain across the ridge and furrow, their bristles erect, their sterns lowered, their hungry eyes flaring out upon him with instinctive hate! He is creeping quite slowly now; but as Harmony and Fairplay near him he turns and shows a long, ominous, gleaming set of teeth. Over they roll, all three together. Marplot and Marygold are close upon them, hounds tumble over each other in hungry confusion, a crash is heard in the fence, and Charles Payne is off his horse in another moment and amongst them. A faint strident noise, like that of a smothered saw, grates upon the ear above the stifled 'worry,' 'worry,' of the hounds, and ere Charles, the pink of politeness, has time to touch his cap to ourselves (for he takes us for the parson, and therefore a stanch fox preserver, if not fox pursuer), he holds him high up in air, and with a loud 'Whowhoop' proclaims the conclusion of one of those 'best runs of the season' which occur at least once a fortnight.

Who-whoop! indeed. Three more sportsmen have by this time arrived, one over and the other two *through* the fence, which still hides the rest of the field from our eager gaze. Soon a gate opens, and some half a dozen more, including a couple of black coats, make their appearance. There are a good many still *coming*, and a large proportion of the original field that will never get here at all. No wonder; the pastures of Northamptonshire are full of them: they are scattered all over the country. Those who *have* arrived look wild and heated, and intensely pleased with themselves as they jump off their exhausted horses, and talk and laugh and gesticulate; the while Charles Payne throws the fox to the hounds, with another encouraging 'Who-whoop!' and the clamorous baying of expectancy is exchanged for the 'worry, worry, worry,' of fruition. 'Had a good thing?' we inquire of the first whip, who is appeasing a difference as to a tid-bit between Countess and Caroline. '*Carpital* thing, sir,' replies that affable functionary, whose cap and side are plastered with mud, and who looks as pleased as if some one had given him a hundred pounds. '*Carpital* thing, sir. Brought him from Sulby gorse over the finest part of *our* country; never checked but once, down by Cottesbrooke; never touched a covert the whole blessed while! It's eleven miles if it's a yard, and I make it exactly an hour and fifteen minutes from the time I "holloed" him away till we run into him in this here grass field just atween your reverence's legs. Whoop, my darlings! Worry, worry, worry! tear him an' eat him!' Cigars are lit, congratulations are exchanged, the bay horse and the brown horse and the chesnut horse receive their due share of praise, a reflective flattery somewhat in this wise: 'How well he carried you, old fellow; and what a stiff line! *I was close to you the whole time!*' From different versions and many contradictory statements we gather a tolerably correct notion of the run; and as its glories gradually flood our still enthusiastic imagination, it is with a pang of regret that we reflect we shall never see gallops such as these again.

We were there in spirit, nevertheless; we know every yard of the country, every field and every fence—though we can practise it no longer, we *think* we know every move in the game. We can fancy ourselves astride of a good horse by the side of Jack Woodcock as he views the fox away from the lower corner of the gorse. What a long, wiry, tough-looking animal it is, with a white tag to that handsome brush, which, as he steals across the neighbouring pasture, he whisks in derision, as much as to say, ' Gallop away, my fine fellows! according to your wont; hurry and bustle, and jump and splutter! The harder you ride the better for me!'

' Tally-ho!' shouts our friend Jack, erect in his stirrups. ' Twang' goes Charles Payne's horn from the middle of the gorse. Already the owner of the covert is coming best pace round the corner. Trust him not to lose his start, and to make good use of it when he has got it. In twos and threes the hounds are pouring through the boundary fence; ten or twelve couple are settling to the scent; the rest, with ears erect, are flying to the cry. Now they stoop together with collective energy, and drive along over the grass in all the mute ecstasy of *pace.* A burst such as this is pastime for the gods!

It sobers our imaginary steed, our pen-and-ink Pegasus; he drops quietly to his bridle, and a turn in our favour enables us to pull him into a trot, and to look about us. Seven or eight men are in the same field with the hounds; half a dozen stiff fences and a couple of miles of grass have shaken off the larger portion of the field, but they are even now coming through a bridle-gate not far distant in the rear, and should a check unfortunately occur at this critical moment, they will be up in plenty of time to do lots of mischief still. But no; the pack is streaming on. ' Forward,' says Charles Payne, cramming his horn into its case, and gathering his horse for an ' oxer.' ' Forward!' echoes Mr. Villiers, ' doubling' it neatly on his right. ' Forward!' adds Mr. Cust, cracking the far-rail as he swings over the obstacle in his stride. ' Line!' shouts a Meltonian at an unfortunate aspirant whose horse is swerving to the thickest place in the fence. ' Serve him right!' remarks the Meltonian to himself, landing safely in the next field, while the aspirant rolls headlong to the earth. Jack Woodcock, with an amused smile, slips quietly by to the front. Three or four more men, one in a black coat, enter the field at different points; that quiet gentleman *over*, not *through* the gate. A loose horse with streaming reins gallops wildly after the chase; and the hounds, with a burning scent, are pointing straight for Naseby Field.

And now every man hugs his trusty hunter by the head, and spares his energies as much as possible ere he encounters the yielding soil of that classic ground. Many a tired horse has Naseby Field to answer for, from the thundering battle-steeds of the Cavaliers, led by hot Prince Rupert, to the panting thoroughbreds of Jersey and Allix, and Cooke and Knightley, and the heroes of fifty years ago, who urged the mimic war over that eventful plain. Ay, down to our own times, when, although the plough has passed over its marshy surface, and draining and high-farming have given secure foothold to man and beast, many a sobbing steed and dejected rider can still bear witness to the exhaustive properties of that black adhesive soil, many a dirty coat and stationary hunter rues the noble impulse that *would* follow the fleeting pack over such a country as this after a three-days' rain.

Some of them begin to hope he may have entered the thick holding covert of Naseby Thorns, and that the conclusion of so rapid a burst may save their own and their horse's credit. But a countryman on the opposite hill is holloaing as if his throat must crack. Our fox is forward still; he has not a notion of entering the covert, warmed as he is by the merry pace of the last mile or so.

'No occasion to lift them, Charles,' observes Mr. Villiers, as he lends an ear to the far-off countryman, and points to the streaming pack wheeling with every turn of the scent, like pigeons on the wing.

'Couldn't get near enough if there was. Come up, horse!' mutters Charles in reply, as he bores through a black close-cut hedge, sinking up to the hocks on the taking-off side. There is no chance of a check now; and as the professed jester of the Hunt remarks, ' If he don't stop at Tally-ho, he may go on to Texas!'

The field, that enterprising body, whose self-dependence is so touchingly illustrated at every sign-post, are already somewhat hopelessly behindhand and considerably puzzled by the coincidence of two safe practicable lanes, leading equally in the direction of the line of chase. It divides accordingly into two hurrying columns, neither of which will in all probability see a hound again to-day.

· So, 'on we go again,' leaving 'Tally-Ho Gorse' to the left, and up the hill for Hazelbeech, threading the fine old trees that tower upon its heights, and pointing ever onwards for the wide grassy vale of Cottesbrooke, spread out like a panorama before us, shut in by wooded hills, dotted with fine old standard trees, and smiling beauteous and peaceful in the chequered light of a February sun.

Thank Heaven! a check at last. Pegasus was beginning to want it sadly. He struck that top-rail uncommonly hard, and has dropped his hind legs in the last two consecutive ditches. There are still some half-dozen men with the hounds, but their horses look as if they had had nearly enough, and we are inclined to believe one or two of the riders are beginning to wish it was over. The country for miles back is dotted with equestrians of every rank and every hue. A child on a pony has turned, not *headed* the fox. Charles Payne opines he cannot have entered the gorse with so 'warm a jacket,' as he phrases it; so he holds his hounds towards the plantations on his right. Fairplay whisks her stern about her sides, and drops a note or two to her comrades as they gather to the line.

' Yo-geote, old lady!' says Charles, in the inexplicable language of a huntsman.

'She's always right, that old bitch,' remarks Mr. Villiers, who has just turned Olympian's head for an instant to the wind.

' Twang' goes the horn once more, and away score the hounds through 'Pursar's Hills,' as if they were fresh out of the kennel, and over the wide grassy pastures below, and up the opposite rise, with untiring energy, leaving the foremost horseman toiling a field and a half behind them, till a pause and momentary hover in the Welford Road enables Pegasus and his comrades to reach them once more.

It is labour and sorrow now, yet is it a sweet and joyous pain. Still, we can hardly call that enjoyment which we wish was over; and most devoutly now do we all hope that we may soon kill this gallant fox, before *he* kills our gallant horses. The best blood of Newmarket is but mortal, after all; and Pegasus is by this time going most unreservedly on his own shoulders and his rider's hands.

Down the hill between Creaton and Holywell we make a tolerable fight; but though Olympian clears the brook at the bottom, the rest of us flounder through. We have no false pride now, and do not any of us turn up our noses at gates or gaps, or other friendly egress. Everything is comparative. A country doctor on his fresh hack, meeting us at this period, opines we are going quite slow, but *we know better*; so does Pegasus, so does old Fairplay, so does the fox.

He is not travelling so straight now. Up and down yonder hedgerow the pack turn like harriers, and we think we must be very near him. But see: the crows are stooping yonder over a low black object in the distance. 'Tis the hunted fox, pointing straight for the coverts of Althorpe. He will never reach them, for the hounds are now close upon his track, and they run into him in the large grass field by Holmby House under the old oak tree.

   *   *   *   *   *   *   *

Our dream is over. Hounds and horses and sportsmen are all gone home. The excitement has evaporated, and left its usual depression of spirits behind. We are left alone—all alone—under the old oak tree. What is life at best but a dream? What is happiness but a dream?—fame, honour, love, ambition? Dreams all. The bitterness is in the waking. ·

Let us put the clock back a couple of centuries or so, when the old oak was stately and vigorous as now, his branches as spreading, his stem as gnarled and knotted, his growth as majestic. What a lesson to us creatures of a day, in our short span of earthly existence, is instilled by the comparative duration of these vegetable giants! How they outlive us! How their 'winter of discontent,' unlike our own, is annually succeeded by a spring of promise! How they spread and tower upwards into heaven, whilst we grovel upon earth. *Væ mihi!* 'twere a weary world, my masters, if there were nothing beyond. A weary world! Let us put the clock back, I say, and dream again.

CHAPTER II.

A CAST OF HAWKS.

She was hatched on a snow-topped, bluff-faced cliff, towering over the iron-bound coast of Iceland. The parental eyrie, hundreds of feet above the level of the sea, was strewed with bones and feathers, and all the warlike spoils of her predatory progenitors. Her infancy was fed on blood warm from the living victim, her youth trained in long flights over the dark seething ocean; so her spirit knew not what it was to quail, nor her wing to droop.

But a daring cliffsman, one of those whose pastime and whose profession it is to undertake risks such as quiet men shudder even to read of, made his appearance one clear frosty night at the entrance of her home, and awed her with the immediate presence of the human face divine, never seen before. Well might she be astonished, for the cliff was a sheer precipice, rising perpendicularly from many a fathom deep of ocean, and the eyrie was securely placed some hundred feet or more below its landward edge, a giddy height indeed above the restless sea, heaving and surging down yonder in the darkness. Three strands of a rope in the numbed grasp of a comrade were between the cliffsman and eternity, yet his nerve was totally unmoved, his hand steady, his face not even pale. Quietly he selected the most promising bird from the eyrie; and she, the very essence of whose existence had been freedom, wild as the winds and waves themselves, must be a captive now for evermore.

At first she pined sadly: her bright keen eye grew dim, her feathers lost their gloss, her wings their sweep and vigour. She was breaking her untamed heart, like a wild-hawk as she was, but custom and discipline at length prevailed. Her feminine spirit, half won and half subdued, yielded to the combined influence of kindness and coercion. Ere she reached England in a merchant-ship she would perch contentedly on the deck, sunning herself for hours in the pure sea air. She would take food eagerly from the hand at which she once fought and tore. She was tamed at last, that winsome wild-bird, ready for the lure, and the bells, and the jesses; willing, under man's tuition, to become more than ever an inveterate enemy to her kind.

So they sold her for ten gold pieces to a north-country lord, and the north-country lord being *more suorum*, a judge of horse-flesh, exchanged her away to Sir Giles Allonby for a dapple grey palfrey; and now she sits jessed and hooded, under the old oak tree at Holmby, far and away the best falcon within forty miles of fair Northampton town.

So thinks the falconer standing yonder, with his perches slung from his broad shoulders, and his hooded pupils sitting contentedly thereon, who would wager his new doublet and his Christmas fee on the success of her, the pride of his mews. So thinks the lithe active lad his assistant, in whose grasp those handsome spaniels are straining at the leash, and who clings to his opinion with the glorious tenacity of sixteen. So think those two jolly-looking serving-men who are in waiting, and who seem to have no earthly thing to do save to crack broad English jokes, and to laugh at them with their broad English faces. So thinks fair Grace Allonby, whose nature it is to pet and love every mortal thing that comes within her reach. So thinks good Sir Giles himself, who only yester evening over his claret was loud in the praises of his favourite, and eager to match her against all and everything on the wing.

'Let them come,' said the stout old knight, 'with their purses in their hands. My Lord Vaux, my Lord Montague, my Lord Goring, Colepepper, Carnarvon, and the rest, within fifty miles of this spot—ay, within the bounds of Britain itself—Peer or Puritan, Cavalier or Roundhead—always excepting the falcons of his most blessed Majesty. Let them come with their hawks, every feather of 'em, and "Diamond" shall have a flight at them all!'

It was a glorious morning for the sport. The sky was clear and blue, softened here and there with light dappled clouds; dewdrops sparkled in the sun from thorn and briar, while the earth exhaled new life and fragrance from her teeming bosom, moistened but not saturated with the late genial rain. How blithe and gladsome was the lark's shrill song as he mounted cheerily into the sky, such a speck against that glorious fathomless blue—how soft and mellow the sunlight on the uplands—how sweet the perfume of the free fresh air!—sight, smell, and hearing all gratified at once. What a morning for hawking, or indeed for any manly, vigorous, out-of-door pursuit.

'The knight is late this morning,' remarked the falconer, a man of few words, and whose whole energies were wrapped up in his profession; 'and the wind is changing even now,' he added, with an anxious glance at the heavens, whilst 'Diamond' stirred uneasily on her perch, jingling her bells, and moving her hooded head from side to side with characteristic impatience.

'Drinking the King's health overnight,' remarked one of the serving-men, with a leer at his comrade. 'Liquor and loyalty make sleepy heads in the morning; is't not so, Will? Thou wast ringing chimes in the buttery thyself, lad.'

Will shook his head, as who should say, 'I follow the example of my betters,' but answered not a word; and indeed in those days late sittings, large flagons, and bumper healths were the daily custom of the age; and the strong ale flowed as freely in the hall as did the red wine in the banqueting-room or the dinner-parlour.

But there was a stir amongst the group under the old oak tree; the falconer's eye brightened, the serving-men sprang to an attitude of respectful attention, and the spaniels fawned and whined, and strained in the leash, for a party of three equestrians were approaching; up the hill they swung at a dashing hand-gallop, and cantering over the smooth sward with feathers waving, habits fluttering, bridles jingling, and palfreys snorting, pulled up under the oak, and returned the salutation of their inferiors with the frank courtesy that is always the stamp of good-breeding and high birth.

'What a morning for us, lads!' remarked Sir Giles to the retainers, with a kindly smile lighting up his ruddy countenance, still handsome and high-bred, though marked with many a deep and furrowed line, the inevitable consequence of a hard life spent in much excitement, much anxiety, much danger, and some excess. 'We flushed a brace of herons as we came along the riverside at Brampton; and a fairer flight than one of the beauties made I never wish to see. Ah, "Diamond!" don't know the old man's voice? Come to my wrist, old lass? Soh! Soh!' and Sir Giles caressed the hooded bird, and smoothed her neck plumage with a loving hand as she fluttered sagaciously to take her well-known place on the glove of the old Cavalier.

Sir Giles Allonby was a specimen of the old English gentleman such as no other country but England could produce; such as the troublous times in which his lot was cast brought out in all its excellence, and all its faults. In person he was tall, spare, and sinewy, framed for a horseman, a swordsman, or a sportsman; for success in any bodily exercise demanding strength, quickness, and agility. Field-sports and campaigning had toughened him into the consistency of pin-wire; but the same causes, coupled with a considerable amount of deep-drinking, had hardened the almost feminine beauty of his countenance into a type strangely at variance with the delicate chiselling of its small features, and the mirthful glances of its bright blue eyes. It seemed a contradiction to see that oval face so rugged and war-worn, that well-trimmed moustache and carefully-pointed beard so white, those soft curling locks so thin and grey. The man himself corresponded in his inward character to his outward appearance. Generous, enthusiastic, and chivalrous, he was passionate, prejudiced, and obstinate. Quick to resent insult with blow or sword-thrust, he would forgive and embrace the bitterest enemy who should move a hair's-breadth towards reconciliation; though he would lift his hat on entering a poor man's cottage, and address his dame with as much courteous deference as a duchess, no Cavalier alive was such a thoroughgoing aristocrat in his reverence for what he called 'blood'—not one of his Norman ancestors could have expressed a greater contempt for the puddle that stagnated through the peasant's veins, as compared with the generous fluid that warmed his own; though he would fling his gold pieces about to all that asked for them, he would screw his tenants to the uttermost, nor stop short of what we should now call acts of violence and rapine, to raise men and horses for the king; and when his wife died, whom he had loved with all the unrestrained ardour with which such a nature could not but love a kindly, handsome, gentle, generous woman, although devotion to the crown, which he called loyalty, became the one guiding impulse of his life, Grace herself, his lovely daughter Grace, was second in his estimation to his sovereign, and in that sovereign's cause he would not have scrupled to sacrifice even her, his sweet, dutiful, and loving child.

She is reining in her horse with a graceful but somewhat timid air, and appears not too well pleased at the caresses and attentions of those busy spaniels, to which the steed replies with a degree of playful restlessness not quite agreeable to his rider. Grace is a sad coward, and though she spends much of her life on horseback, like other gentlewomen of her time, she has never acquired the perfect self-possession and masculine ease which sit so well upon her companion, yonder lady, whose long curls are waving in the wind, whose soft blue eyes are deepening and dancing with animation, whose lip and cheek are blushing carnation in the fresh morning air, under the rays of the bright morning sun.

'Give him a gallop, Gracey,' says she, with a ringing laugh at her friend's obvious misgivings. 'Why, Sir Giles himself could hardly ride my Bayard if I let him get as fresh as you do that riotous pet of yours. Silly Grace, you spoil everything you come near. What a tyrant you *will* make of your husband, my dear, if ever you get one!' and she bent her beautiful figure to pat her horse's neck in a bewitching attitude, which was not lost, as it was not meant to be, on old Sir Giles, or the busy falconer, or the grinning serving-man, nay, not even on the lad of sixteen, who gazed on her open-mouthed, with a ludicrous expression of stupified amazement and delight.

Mary Cave dearly loved admiration wherever she could get it. Left early in life to her own devices, brought up chiefly abroad, and transferred from a foreign convent to a foreign court, she had acquired, even in the first flush of youth, a habit of self-reliance and a decision of character seldom to be observed in those of the softer sex who have not passed through the crucible of much pain and much tribulation. Clever and quick-witted, with strong passions and strong feelings, she nursed an ambition which was stronger than them all. She had the knack, partly natural, partly the result of keen observing powers, of detecting at once the mental value, and, so to speak, the moral weight, of those with whom she came in contact; and this gift, so dangerous to a woman, necessarily imparted a harshness to her character, and robbed her of that trusting, clinging tendency which is woman's greatest charm. Young as she was, she busied herself in all the intrigues of the day, and her beauty, her fascinating manners, her extraordinary influence over everything that wore a beard, rendered her a most dangerous enemy, a most desirable and efficient partisan. From her kinsman's house at Boughton she corresponded with the leading men of the Cavalier party, and Lord Vaux himself, in all his wisdom of years and experience of intrigue, was indebted to beautiful Mary Cave for many a happy resource, many a deep-laid and successful scheme.

Every one in the house adored her. The respectful and austere *major-domo*, a condition of whose very existence it was to preserve on all occasions a demeanour of supernatural decorum, would follow her about with his eyes, and dodge after her with flowers and porcelain and choice old glass, and every device he could think of, to win the reward of a word and a smile; and the little page-boy, the lowest of all the varlets in the establishment, spent a whole night on the staircase in darkness and tears, when he heard that ' Mistress Mary was ill at ease, and troubled with a slight cold.'

So she turned and wound them all round her finger—and why not? The lower animals have their natural arms, offensive and defensive; the ox his horns, the tiger his claws, the serpent his guile, man his obstinacy, and woman her beauty : the last is the most fearful weapon of all, and right well does she know its advantages and its use.

Even now old Sir Giles, keen sportsman as he is, cannot but feel that his attention to the business of the day is much distracted by his daughter's friend ; that if ' Diamond ' *could* have a rival in his admiration and attention, it would be beautiful Mary Cave.

She ought to be very happy, speeding along in all the enjoyment of health and power, and conscious charms, and the delightful motion of Bayard's easy gallop. And yet there is a little black imp sitting behind her that no gallop on earth can shake off—a secret sorrow nestling at that proud wayward heart which no triumphs of beauty and influence can stifle or eradicate. Both

girls laugh out merrily as they fly along, but timid Grace Allonby
is alarmed about herself; dauntless Mary Cave is uneasy about
another : the latter's frame of mind is the least enviable of the two.

And now the little party are winding slowly along the brook-
side in the valley down by Althorpe. Many a noble elm and
stately oak nods above their heads, many a patch of sedge and
rushes shakes and rustles to the quest of the busy spaniels and
the long poles of the falconer and his assistants. Far and wide, to
right and left, extends a prairie-like and undulating pasture,
nourishing here and there a few scattered flocks feeding in the
sun. Near one or two small hamlets, a few posts and rails, or an
old straggling overgrown hedge, denote an attempt at cultivation
and enclosure, but the general character of the district is wild,
nomadic, and provocative of galloping.

'What a country for a flight !' says Mary Cave, bringing her
obedient horse alongside of the old knight's well-trained steed,
and loosening the jesses of the hawk upon her wrist, no unworthy
rival to 'Diamond' herself. 'Look well to your laurels to-day,
Sir Giles. "Dewdrop" and her mistress are both bent on victory, and I shall wear the heron's plume to-night in my hair or
never hawk again !'

Even as she spoke the short shrill bark of a spaniel, and a rush
of his companions towards a sedgy, marshy piece of ground,
startled Grace Allonby and her palfrey out of the pleasant mutual
understanding to which they had arrived, and a glorious wide-
winged heron rose slowly into the air, flapping his way with
heavy measured strokes, his long legs tucked behind him, his
little head thrown back, his sharp scissors-like beak protruding
over the distended crop, heavy with the spoils of last night's fishing excursion. Mary's quick eye has caught him in an instant.
Like lightning she has freed her hawk from hood and jesses, and
with the same movement that urges her horse to a canter, ' Dewdrop' is tossed aloft into the air.

Sir Giles is not much slower in his arrangements. Like an old
sportsman, he is methodical in all matters connected with the
field, but 'Diamond' understands her master, and her master can
depend on 'Diamond,' so she is not three strokes of her wing
behind her rival, and soaring at once high into the air, has caught
sight of prey and competitor almost before the heron is aware of
his two natural and implacable foes.

Too soon, however, it strikes him that his position is one of
imminent and mortal danger. With a grating harsh cry, a
' crake, crake,' of mingled discomfort and alarm, he proceeds slowly

to disgorge from his pouch the weighty spoils of his overnight's sport. The dead fish glisten white and silvery as they fall through the sunny air, and the lightened heron, whose instinct teaches him there is no safety but on high, wheels upwards by a series of gyrations farther and farther still, till he seems but a speck in the bright element to the straining eyes that are watching the flight from below. But there is another higher still than he is, and yet another wheeling rapidly upward to gain the desired point of 'vantage.' The topmost speck falls suddenly headlong several hundred feet, past the pursued and his pursuer, down, down, nearly to the summit of a huge old elm, but recovering herself, once more resumes her flight, with even greater vigour and determination that at first.

'Peste! elle a manquée!' exclaims Mary in the language of her youth, while a flush of vexation burns on her handsome features, and she admonishes her steed with hand and rein to make no more 'mistakes' like that last, at a time when earthly considerations should not be allowed to divert his rider's attention from the business going on above. 'Dewdrop' has indeed made a failure, and she seeks in vain to wipe out the disgrace, for 'Diamond' has now gained the vantage point, and swooping down like a thunderbolt, beak and talons, and weight and impetus, all brought to bear at once on the devoted heron, brings him headlong with her through the air, turning over and over in their fall to that green earth from which he will never rise again.

And now Sir Giles is riding for his life, spurring his good horse across the rushy pastures, keen and happy and triumphant as a boy at his falcon's success; whilst Mary dashes along by his side, inwardly provoked, though she is too proud to show it, at the failure of her favourite; and Grace, with fretting palfrey and secret misgivings, follows carefully at a less break-neck pace in the rear.

It is a service of danger to take a heron from a hawk, or a hawk from a heron, even after the most prolonged and exhausting flight. The victim, breathless and stunned though he be, has generally sufficient strength and energy left to make good use of the sharp and formidable weapon with which nature has provided him; and as the thrusts of his long beak are delivered with extraordinary accuracy, and aimed always at *the eye* of his captor, he is a formidable opponent even in the last struggles of defeat and death.

'A fair flight, Mistress Mary, and an honest victory,' said Sir Giles, as he plucked a long shapely feather from the dead

bird's wing, and presented it with playful courtesy to his antagonist. ' " Diamond " is still unconquered, and you shall wear the
heron's plume to-night in your bonnie locks in token of forgiveness! Said I well, sweetheart ? '

' Sir Giles, I might forgive a fault, but I *never* forgive a
failure,' was the laughing reply ; yet to a keen observer the
expression of her face, the curl of her ruddy lip as she spoke,
would have denoted more truth in the sentiment than she would
herself perhaps have been willing to admit.

' I am sorry for the poor heron,' was all Grace Allonby remarked, as they remounted their horses to commence their
homeward journey.

CHAPTER III.

THE QUARRY.

AND a lovely ride they had over the wild moorland and the green
undulations that waved between the wooded hill of Holmby, and
the sweet fragrant valley along which the quiet Nene was stealing
his silver way. Those were the days when the early morning air
was esteemed the best cosmetic for the check of beauty, when
ladies did not sit over the fire till dusk and then flutter out like
birds of night for a gentle stroll to the hothouses, or a half-hour's
saunter in a pony-carriage. Our little party had breakfasted at
daybreak, had been in the saddle since the sun was up, and had
got their day's sport concluded by the time that we of the modern
school would have finished breakfast. There is nothing like early
rising. We have ourselves tried it, and we speak from experience
when we insist that it is profitable, poetical, healthy, and invigorating; nevertheless candour compels us to admit that for its
systematic practice we entertain a cordial detestation.

A lovely ride they had. In front of them extended the rich
valley of the Nene, smiling with cultivation, dotted with trees and
hedgerows, and standard thorns growing stunted and sturdy here
and there, backed by the distant buildings of Northampton and
the light cloud of white smoke that curled above the town. To
their left wide and uncultivated moorlands, with occasional
stretches of vivid green pasture, and many a patch of gorse and
clump of alders, swept away over the rising eminence of Spratton
(on the sky-line of which a string of packhorses could clearly be

distinguished as they neared the little hamlet where they would stop and refresh), and melted into a dim haze of beauty under the crest of Hazelbeech, crowned with a swarthy grove of giant forest trees, frowning down on the sunny valley below; behind them, sharp cutting against the sky, a long level plain, that was ere long to earn its immortality under the name of Naseby Field, showed clear and hard and cheerless, as though its only harvest was to be the gathering of the slaughter; while the towers and pinnacles of Holmby Palace itself shut in the picture in their immediate vicinity. On their right a bank of waving gorse hid all beyond its own wild beauties with its sharp dark verdure, and its little yellow blossoms scattered like the drops of a golden shower over its surface. Sir Giles plucked one as he passed with a sly smile, ' When the gorse is out of bloom, young ladies,' quoth Sir Giles, ' then is kissing out of fashion !' Grace Allonby laughed and blushed, and playfully bid her father ' not talk nonsense;' but Mary Cave, drawing her horse nearer to that of her gentle friend, commenced moralising after her own fashion on the old knight's trite and somewhat coarse remark.

' Yes, Gracey,' said she, smoothing back the folds of her rich brown hair, which shone and glistened in the sun, ' Sir Giles is right.· So it is, and so it has ever been. There is no day in the year when the blossom is off the gorse, from the brightest splendours of July to the bitterest snowstorms of December. There is no phase of life, from the triumph of success to the agony of disappointment, which is not affected by woman's influence and woman's smile. I used to wish, dear, that I had been born a man. I thank my fate now that I am a woman. I have more *power* as I am, and *power* is what I love best in the world. They are only puppets, Gracey, after all ; and if we are but true to ourselves, it is for us to pull the strings and set the figures moving at our will. I saw a pretty toy once at the French Court that was brought there in a box by a certain Italian juggler, in which little dressed-up dolls acted a mystery in dumb show, and the juggler, sitting in his dark corner, managed all the wires, and made each play its appointed part. Grace, I thought to myself, men are but dressed-up dolls after all; it is women that have the strings in their hands, if they will but use them. I have never let one go yet, my dear, and I never will. Confess—is it not delightful to have one's own way ?'

' I should think it must be,' replied Grace, who never could get hers, even with her horse ; ' and yet it must be a great responsibility, too,' she added, with a look of profound reflection. ' I think I

would rather give way, that is, if I *liked* people ; and I don't think
I could like anybody very much that I wasn't a little afraid of.'

Mary's lip curled contemptuously, yet a pang shot through her
too. Was there one before whom her proud spirit would quail
—for whom that eager undisciplined heart would ache with a pain
only known to the strong tameless nature? It is the wild bird
that beats itself to death against the bars of its cage; the wild
flower that droops and withers in the close confinement of a hot-
house. Woe to him whom Mary loved, if he loved her too!
Nevertheless, she laughed merrily as she replied, ' Nonsense,
Grace—*afraid?* I never feared mortal thing yet, and least of all
would I fear a man that professed himself to be my slave ; and
yet, dear, I have my own ideas of what a man ought to be. Mind,
I don't say I know *one* that comes up to them. He should be
proud as Lucifer—not in appearance and demeanour—far from it.
I would have him courteous and kindly to all, gentle and chivalrous and conciliating in his manners, but at heart unimpression-
able and unyielding as adamant. I would have him cherish some
high ambition, to which he would sacrifice all that was dearest to
him in life, ay, sacrifice *me* myself if he loved me to madness ; and
he should smile when he did it as if nothing could make him
wince or waver in his purpose. He must be clever, of course,
and looked on with admiration and envy by his fellow-men, or
he would be no mate for *me*; and he must give way to me for an
instant on no single point more than I would to him.'

Grace opened her large dark eyes with astonishment : she had
her mother's eyes, as Sir Giles often remarked, dark and soft and
full like a fawn's.

' And if you were both so obstinate,' observed Grace, ' and you
loved him so very much, what would you do if you disagreed?'

' I would break my heart, but I would never yield an inch!'
was the reply ; ' or I would break *his*, to hate myself ever afterwards, and love him, perhaps, none the worse for that.'

While she spoke a light broke over Mary's countenance which
softened it into beauty such as struck even her companion with a
new and fervent admiration : but it faded as it came, and her
features soon recovered their usual joyous, careless, and somewhat
hard expression of self-dependence and self-satisfaction.

But Grace's womanly nature, true to itself, recoiled from such
sentiments as these. ' Indeed, Mary,' said she, ' I think it would
be very uncomfortable. If I liked anybody so much, I should
wish him to like me too, and I would give in to him on every
single point, and find out everything he wanted, and try to make

him happy; and if I failed I should not be angry with *him*, but I think I should be very miserable, and I am sure I should sit down and cry. But I should not like him to be such a person as you describe. I would rather have him good looking and good natured, and cheerful, and brave certainly, and I should not mind his being a little hasty, and *very* loyal to the king, and—like my father, in short, but younger, of course, and—don't laugh at me, Mary—I think I should like him to have dark eyes and hair.'

'Oh, Grace, what a child you are!' was the reply; and Mary put her horse once more into a canter, and raised his mettle with voice and hand, turning and winding him at her will, and seeking vent for the exuberance of her spirits or the depth of her feelings —for no mortal ever was allowed to penetrate her *real* sentiments —in the delightful exercise of skilful equitation.

But to give our reader some slight insight into the character of this young lady, still young in years and beauty, though matured in knowledge of the world, we must be permitted to recount a little scene that occurred at the royal palace of Hampton Court a year or two previous to the events we have now taken upon us to describe.

One of the merry masks or pageants which were the delight of our ancestors, and which were keenly appreciated by royalty itself, had just been concluded; the great nobles of the Court had left the Presence; the King himself had retired to his apartments harassed and fatigued with the responsibilities of a ruler, and the many difficulties which in all ranks hedge in the movements of an opinionated man. None but the Queen and her immediate household, with two or three especial favourites and high officers of the Court, were left; and Henrietta's French love of gaiety and natural flow of spirits prompted her to seize the opportunity of relaxing for half an hour the decorum and formality which have ever been distinguishing characteristics of the English Court.

'A game at forfeits! A *cotillon*! and a forfeit for the loser, to be decided by my ladies and myself. Marguerite!—Marie! That will be charming,' exclaimed her Majesty, clapping her hands in the exuberance of her merriment, her keen eyes sparkling, and her little French person quivering with delight at the prospect.

'*Dansez milor! voilà le jeu qui commence!*' and she gave her hand with much dignity to the most accomplished young nobleman of his time, whose air of self-possession and gravity was somewhat at variance with the general mirth and festivity of the other courtiers, and herself commenced the measure, in which all were in duty bound to join.

It was a foolish game, somewhat provocative of levity, and calculated to have given scandal to the Puritans of the time, involving much dancing, changes of partners, and the infliction of quaint forfeits on those who failed in its complicated conditions. A venerable Lady of the Bedchamber was condemned to dance 'a saraband' with a certain future Chancellor, whose forte was scarcely bodily grace or agility. A young maid of honour, blushing to the tips of her fingers, had to receive the homage, offered on their knees, of all the gentlemen there present. And lastly, Mary Cave, then attached to the person of the Queen, was adjudged to stand in the midst of the admiring throng, and accept a chaste salute from an individual of the opposite sex, to be chosen by lot.

'No, sir!' said the Queen, as the future Chancellor, who imagined himself to be the happy man, stepped forward, with a gay and *debonair* demeanour, to exact the penalty; 'it is reserved for a younger man—and a better courtier,' she added, somewhat lower, but loud enough for the mortified candidate to overhear. 'Stand forward, Marie,' she proceeded, laughing roguishly; 'and you, milor! claim your rights!'

It was the same young nobleman who had already been honoured with her Majesty's hand in the dance; who had acquitted himself with the ease and grace of an accomplished cavalier, but with a grave and preoccupied air, as of one whose thoughts were far away from scenes of mirth and revelry, and who now stepped forward with a profound reverence to claim from Mistress Mary Cave a penalty which any other gentleman in the presence would have readily given his best hawk, his best hound, or his best horse to exact.

And this was the only man in the room on whom she would have hesitated for an instant to confer that which was in those times accounted a mere mark of courtesy and friendly regard. She would have offered her cheek to any one of them, from intriguing Harry Jermyn to profligate George Goring, without moving a muscle of her proud cold face; but when this young nobleman approached her with his chivalrous deference of manner, and his simple, courteous, self-possessed air, Mary felt her heart beating, and knew her cheek was blushing, as heart and cheek had never beat and blushed before.

He was her master, and *she knew it.* Slight as was their acquaintance, she had seen and heard enough of him to be aware that his was a strong stern nature, keen of intellect and indomitable of will, which she had no chance of ever subjugating—that his mind was of that superior order which breaks through the meshes of pleasure and dispels the illusions of romance. Her woman's instinct told her that he nourished some lofty purpose, which woman's influence would never be suffered to affect; and simply because she knew it was quite impossible that she could ever win his homage, like a very woman, she would have given her heart's blood to possess it, if only for an hour.

He stepped up to her, slowly and courteously. He did not even take her hand; but he lifted one of the long brown ringlets that fell heavily across her bosom, pressed it to his lips, dropped it, and retired, with another low reverence, and without ever raising his eyes to her face.

He slept calmly and peacefully that night. When he woke on the morrow, his thoughts were of the great Cause and the country's good; of measures and principles, and counsellors—of judicious laws and a happy people; of ancient sages and classic patriotism; a little of his fair young wife, whom he loved with a sober, temperate and rational love;—and he rose to pray earnestly for strength and means to carry out the great work on which his heart and soul were bent.

Her rest was fitful and broken, disturbed by strange wild dreams, of which the central figure was still a slight and nervous form, a keen, dark intellectual face, a compressed and resolute lip—the lip that had caressed her hair. She had detached that ringlet from the rest, and lay with her hands folded over it, and clasping it to her bosom. When she rose, it was to a new and strange sensation—to a wild keen thrill of pleasure, dashed with shame—to a galling feeling of subjection, that had yet in it a dependence most delightful. She would have been torn in pieces rather than confess it even to herself, but she loved Falkland, and it was a changed world to Mary Cave from that night for ever after !

The gambols of one of them are apt to disturb the equanimity of all the rest of the equine race who are within hearing and sight of such vagaries. Nor was Grace Allonby's palfrey, on whom its mistress could never be induced to impose proper terms of coercion, any exception to this general rule of insubordination.

Ere our little party had descended into the valley of Brampton, and reached the ford by which they were to cross the river, poor Grace was certainly no longer mistress of the animal she rode ; and it was with a pitiable expression of helplessness and terror on her countenance, at which even her father and her companion could scarce help laughing, that she plunged into the ford, now somewhat swollen and turbulent from the late rain.

'Father! what shall I do? He's going to lie down!' screamed Grace, as the wilful palfrey, turning his head to the stream, plunged and pawed into deeper water, that already drenched his rider's skirts to the waist. Mary Cave was ere this on the opposite side with Sir Giles; the latter, turning suddenly to his daughter's assistance, checked his horse so fiercely that the animal reared straight on end, and then struck his spurs so deep into its sides that the good horse grew restive and refused to face the water on such terms; and Grace might at least have experienced a very complete wetting, had it not been for the assistance of another cavalier, who, coming up at a smart trot from behind, dashed in to the rescue of the astonished girl, and himself guiding her palfrey to the bank, brought her, with many apologies for his timely interference, in safety to her father's side.

'Well and promptly done, young sir,' said Sir Giles, as, after wringing the wet from his daughter's habit, and replacing her on her horse, he turned to thank the new comer for his unexpected assistance. 'May I enquire to whom I have the honour of being so much indebted?' added the courteous old cavalier.

The stranger reined in his horse, and lifting his hat, made a profound bow as he replied, 'My name is Humphrey Bosville, cornet in Colepepper's Horse, and about to join his Majesty's forces at Newbury. I have orders to proceed to Boughton, with despatches for Lord Falkland. Am I in the right road?'

Mary's eye sparkled and her cheek flushed.

'For Lord Falkland?' she enquired; 'is he, then, expected by Lord Vaux?'

The cornet made another profound bow as he replied in the affirmative; but he too blushed to encounter the glance of those deep blue eyes, and the self-possession with which he had commenced the interview seemed to have entirely deserted him, though he accepted willingly and courteously the hospitable invitation of Sir Giles to his kinsman's house.

'You are just in time for dinner, sir. My lord will be well pleased to see you or any other gallant cavalier. Had we met you an hour sooner we could have shown you as fair a flight as often falls to a sportsman's lot to behold. I can show you now the best hawk in Christendom. But you are in time for dinner, sir; and we will give you a hearty welcome, and drink the King's health after it in a stoup of claret worthy of the toast!'

As they mounted the hill toward Boughton, the ladies, we may be sure, did not lose the opportunity of closely inspecting the

person and general appearance of Grace's new acquaintance; and
truth to tell, Humphrey Bosville's exterior was one of those on
which the feminine eye dwells with no slight complacency.

A trifle above the middle size, well and strongly built, with a
frame promising the vigour of manhood, added to the activity of
youth, our cornet sat his strong chesnut, or, to use the language
of the time, his sorrel horse, with the graceful ease of a man who
has from boyhood made the saddle his home. Like a true
cavalier, his dress and arms exhibited as much splendour as was
compatible with the exigencies of active service—a good deal more
of variety than in these days of Prussian uniformity would be
permitted to a soldier. On his head he wore a wide Spanish hat,
adorned with a huge drooping feather, his buff coat was cut and
slashed in the most approved fashion, and a rich silk scarf of deep
crimson wound about his waist to mark the contour of his sym-
metrical figure. His pistols were richly mounted, his sword of
the longest, his spurs of the heaviest; all his appointments marked
the gentleman and the man of war, dashed with the not inappropriate or unpleasing coxcombry of youth. His oval face, shaded
by the long curling lovelocks so much affected by his party, bore
a winning expression of almost feminine softness, attributable to
his large well-cut hazel eyes—such eyes as belong to dispositions
at once imaginative and impressionable rather than judicious and
discerning; but his high, regular features, straight eyebrows, and
determined lip, shaded by a heavy moustache, redeemed the
countenance from a charge of effeminacy, and stamped on him the
bold resolute character of ' a man of action,' one that could be
depended on when the brave were striking for their lives.

' He is very well favoured, your new friend,' whispered Mary
Cave, with a roguish smile; ' and Gracey, there must be " something in it." Look if he has not got *dark eyes and hair*.'

CHAPTER IV.

' FALKLAND.'

LORD VAUX is pacing his old hall at Boughton, with a scroll in his
hand, on which his attention seems but partially fixed. Ever and
anon he lifts his eyes to the stained glass windows, through which
the noonday light is streaming in floods of crimson, and purple,
and orange; but his thoughts are far from armorial bearings and

ancestral pomp. Ever and anon he rivets them on the polished
oak floor beneath his feet, but still he fails to derive the required
inspiration for his task. Like the rest of his party, the cavalier
is puzzled by the hopelessness of proving ' two and two to make
five.' His fine benevolent head, from which the long hair falls in
clusters over his starched ruff and black velvet doublet, is that of
a philosopher and a sage, one whose natural element is study and
contemplation rather than action and conflict with his kind ; yet
must Lord Vaux calculate men, and means, and munitions of war,
ay, don breastplate and backpiece, and if need be, leave the splendours of his home and the quiet retirement of his study for the
hardships of campaigning—the wild alarums of a stricken field.

He listens anxiously for an expected footstep. Like many
another contemplative nature, he is prone to place dependence on
those who show no hesitation in taking the initiative. He is capable of enthusiasm, generosity, and self-sacrifice, but an example
must be set him for the exhibition of these virtues. Without
some one to show him the way, his lordship would never move a
step in any direction, right or wrong. How many such natures
were forced into the stream of political strife by the exigencies of
the times in which they lived ! How many were willing to suffer
fines, humiliation, and imprisonment for a cause which they
esteemed sacred solely because their fathers did. Old men of
fourscore years were simple and enthusiastic as boys. Lord Vaux,
now past middle age, found himself, at a period of life when most
men are willing to seek ease and repose, involved in all the intrigues of statesmanship and the labours of civil war. Cavaliers
and Roundheads, the two watchwords of party, had set merry
England by the ears. The precise puritan, with his close-cropped
hair, his sad-coloured raiment, his long sword, and biblical phraseology, was up and in the field under the same discipline which
scarce served to control the excesses of his roystering enemy, the
swaggering, dissipated, reckless, yet chivalrous cavalier, whose
code of duty and morality seemed but to consist of two principles,
if so they could be called, viz. to drink, and strike for the king.

Such was the extreme type of either party, and to one or other
must sober men of all ranks or ages more or less incline.

But a step is heard in the outer hall, the tramp of horses strikes
upon the ear, the bustle of servants marshalling an honoured and
expected guest breaks on the stillness of the well-ordered household, and a smile of inexpressible relief lights up Lord Vaux's face
as he advances to greet his guest with all the ceremonious cordiality of an old English welcome.

'I have ridden far, my lord,' said the new arrival, 'to taste your hospitality; and in these times we can scarce promise to repeat our visits to our friends. But, my lord, you seem anxious and ill at ease. You have suffered no affliction at home, I trust? You have no bad news of the Cause?'

'I am indeed harassed and at my wits' end,' was the reply, 'or I could scarce have failed to give your lordship a kinder and more hospitable welcome. But I am, in sooth, right glad to see you; for to your ingenuity and to your advice I must look in my present straits. This is no question of a crabbed Greek reading, or a complicated equation, such as we delighted in happier days to grapple withal, but a serious requirement of men, horses, and money for his Most Sacred Majesty; a requirement that, with all our resources, we shall be unable to fulfil, and yet without which the Cause is well-nigh hopeless. Does Goring think I am like the alchemist we have read of, and can transmute these old oak carvings to unalloyed gold? or does that reckless adventurer believe me to be even as himself? to regard neither honour nor credit, mercy nor justice, and to fear neither God, nor man, nor devil?'

'Goring is a useful tool where he is placed, my lord,' was the reply; 'and we could ill spare him in our present difficulties, though sad it is so fair a cause should require the support of such as he has proved himself. Nevertheless, permit me to look over the requirement. It may be that we can see our way more plainly by our joint endeavours, than when we fight single-handed against that deadliest of foes, an empty military chest.'

As he spoke he took the scroll from Lord Vaux's hand with a courteous bow, and retiring into one of the deep windows of the hall, was soon busily engaged in the perusal of its contents.

Lucius Carey, Viscount Falkland, was one of those men on whom no remarkable exterior stamps the superiority which they enjoy over their fellow-creatures. As he stands in the embrasure of that window, his countenance grave and heated, his dress disordered with riding, his gestures of surprise and vexation awkward and ungainly, the superficial observer would pronounce him to be a mere ordinary, somewhat ill-looking mortal, plainly dressed, and bearing the marks neither of gentle birth nor mental culture. He is short and small of stature, of no imposing port, not even with the assumption of energy and bustling activity which so often characterises the movements of little men. His manner is unaffected and plain to simplicity; he stoops and sways his body from side to side in ludicrous unconsciousness, as wave after wave of thought comes rolling in upon his brain, pregnant with reflection, calculation, and resource. When he speaks his voice is harsh and unmusical, his countenance dark and unprepossessing, for he is labouring in mind, wrestling with a difficulty, and bringing all the powers of his mighty intellect to bear upon the struggle. And now he grasps it—now the colossal enemy is overthrown, and as the words flow smoother and faster from his lips, as sentence after sentence pours itself forth, clearer, and more comprehensive, and more concise, the whole countenance changes as changes the aspect of a winter's day when the sun breaks forth; flashes of intelligence beam from those deep-set falcon eyes, and light up the stern, sallow face. Rapid and impressive action succeeds the slow awkwardness of his habitual movements; the slight form seems to dilate and tower into dignity, as of one born to command, and the whole man is changed, by the mere influence of mind over matter, into a sage and a hero for the occasion.

But the inspiration passes as quickly as it comes. The knot is now unravelled, the difficulty is solved. He has seen his own way to surmount it, and more than that, has explained it to the inferior intellect of his friend, and he relapses once more into the ordinary mortal, while an expression of deep weariness and melancholy settles again upon his features, as of one who is harassed and distracted with the disappointments and heartburnings of life; who would fain cast away shield and sword, and turn aside out of the battle, and lie down and be at rest.

Yet was it not always so with this young and gifted nobleman. His youth seemed to give promise of a brighter future than is often accorded to mortal man. Bred in his father's vice-regal court of Ireland, he enjoyed opportunities of learning and cultivation which were not thrown away upon such a mental organisation as his. At eighteen years of age he was skilled beyond his fellows in all the exercises and accomplishments of the day. He was perfected in the Latin and French languages, and had already shown that energy and perseverance in the acquisition of knowledge which formed so distinguishing a characteristic of his after-life. Added to this, he inherited already an ample fortune, independent of his father—no contemptible advantage at an age when all the generous and liberal feelings are still unwarped and unstifled by the sordid cares of life. He was thus relieved from the many anxieties consequent upon inadequate means, which are too apt to embitter the sparkling cup of youth, and had the more leisure to devote himself to those studies in which he took such delight. Firm and resolute to the verge of obstinacy when a point was to be gained, it is related of him that, wishing to obtain a thorough knowledge of Greek, he absented himself rigidly from London until he had acquired an intimate familiarity with that language, nor could all the persuasions of his friends, nor the intellectual temptations of the capital, induce him to forego the determination on which he had once entered. The same disposition prompted him to marry an amiable and excellent young lady, in defiance of the wishes of his family ; and a generosity, by no means unnatural in such a character, induced him at the same time to offer his whole fortune for the liquidation of his father's embarrassments, he himself purposing to obtain a military appointment in Holland, and win his own livelihood and that of his family with the sword. In this scheme being disappointed, he abandoned the career of arms, and had chalked out for himself a path of study and scholar-ship when the trumpet of civil war roused him from his dream of literary distinction to the absorbing realities of the strife.

He was an ardent admirer of real and constitutional liberty, and although his rigid love of justice and regard to truth commanded the respect of the Court party, as his affable demeanour and genuine kindliness of heart won him the affections of all men, it was only when the throne was really threatened in its justifiable prerogatives, that he declared himself openly and unreservedly for the king. When his part was once taken, Charles had no more devoted adherent, no more judicious adviser, than Lord Falkland, but from that time, from the very date of his accepting office under the Sovereign, a change was observed in the whole temperament and demeanour of the young nobleman. He who used to be so ready of wit, so fluent of discourse, so affable towards his associates, became reserved, morose, and taciturn. His countenance wore an aspect of continual dejection; he neglected his studies, his amuse-ments, nay, his very dress. All things became distasteful to him save ceaseless exertion for the sake of his country. Like some classic patriot, some Roman augur to whom Fate had vouchsafed a glimpse of futurity, he mourned in anticipation for those national woes which he already hoped he might die rather than live to behold.

But even in civil war, in public distress as in private affliction, man must dine ; nay, if he is one of the porcelain vessels of the earth, and has performed since daybreak a long journey on horse-back, he must also dress for dinner ; and therefore Cornet Bosville, when, as in duty bound, he had delivered his despatches, betook himself to the chamber Lord Vaux's hospitality had provided for him, and with the assistance of his faithful trooper and servant,

Hugh Dymocke, proceeded to the important duty of adorning his already well-favoured person.

Dymocke disapproved much of such waste of time. One led horse, to carry his own and his master's change of clothing, did not admit of his turning out the cornet in such splendour as he himself thought befitting, and were it not that he had already discovered the advantages of Lord Vaux's hospitality and the strength of his ale, he would probably have urged upon his master the necessity of proceeding on their journey directly their horses were fed and the tables drawn after the early dinner in the great hall.

'And you must wear the pearl-coloured hose, I warrant me, and the point-lace collar of which we have but one with us, and dripping wet it would be had I pushed on when you bid me, and followed that slip of quality into the river on a fool's errand,' grumbled Dymocke, as he bustled about, unpacking his master's wallets, and vainly regretting certain splendid apparel and a beautiful Toledo walking-rapier which the rebels had eased them of when Waller's horse last beat up their quarters at Tewkesbury. 'They will serve directly, and the quality will be there, rustling in brocade and satins, and what not; eating and drinking of the best, and the King's troops starving, and merry England going to the Puritans and the devil!' added Dymocke, who was in his worst of humours, albeit mollified to a certain extent by recollections of the ale aforesaid.

Bosville answered nothing. He was combing out his long love-locks, and thinking how bright were the eyes and red the lips of the lady who had scarcely looked at him during their short ride, and wishing he had dragged her instead of her companion out of the brook, and wondering whether she would observe him at dinner, and converse with him afterwards; and reflecting, half-unconsciously, on the important fact that pearl-silken hose and a point-lace collar were no unbecoming adjuncts to the exterior of a well-looking young man.

Many years afterwards that dinner was remembered by more than one of the party. Happy Humphrey Bosville, sitting next to Mary Cave, was delighted with the share of attention she vouchsafed to bestow upon him; was intoxicated with the radiance of her smiles, the very atmosphere of her beauty. He could not mark, nor would he have comprehended, the eager, restless glance she flashed ever and anon at the plain, reserved, dark man opposite to them, the pained expression and forced smile that overspread her countenance when she failed to attract Falkland's attention. His discourse was directed chiefly to his host and Sir

Giles Allonby, and he left his lovely neighbour Grace ample leisure to observe the cornet's good looks and pleasant smiles. Three of the party at least were drinking in poison with their canary, laying up for themselves a store of future pain in the enjoyment and fascination of the moment. It is better so ; if to-day must never mortgage to-morrow, what becomes of the fee-simple of existence ? If the death's-head *must* be present at all our feasts, in the name of Bacchus, hide him away under the table, there to remain till next morning at breakfast ! So the party ate and drank, and laughed and talked, and the conversation turned upon the scandal of the Court and the characters of the courtiers, and that prolific theme, the enormities and vagaries of wild Lord Goring.

' A good soldier ! ' said Sir Giles, pledging the cornet in a bumper ; ' and never loses his head, drunk or sober. You re-member what he said of Wilmot's charge at Roundway Down ? You were there ? '

The cornet acquiesced in a modest affirmative, glad that Mary should know he had been present at that engagement, whilst Grace looked more interested in her new friend than ever.

' Rash in council,' observed Lord Vaux, still thinking of his morning's work ; ' and totally unreasonable in his expectations and requirements.'

' A weak assailant,' laughed Mary ; ' he scaled a convent at Bruges, and was repulsed with a broken leg, which gives him that limp you all think so charming. He should confine himself to cavalry operations. It is indeed a forlorn hope against nuns' veils and stone walls.'

' I have heard him boast he never was foiled yet by man or woman,' said Falkland, absently fixing his dark eyes on Mary's countenance.

She blushed all over her face and neck, seemed as if she wou'd have spoken, then turned white and held her tongue; the while Sir Giles proposed a bumper health to his old commander, gay George Goring.

CHAPTER V.

BRIDLED AND SADDLED.

WE once heard a remark drop from a pair of the sweetest lips that ever belonged to a gentle philosopher, of the truth of which we have been the more convinced the more we have watched the vagaries and eccentricities into which its victims are drawn by that affection of the brain called by the wise folly, and by fools love. ' In all cases of attachment,' said our beautiful moralist, ' depend upon it one must be always bridled and saddled, the other always booted and spurred.' Of the truth of this axiom experience has left us not the slightest doubt; but what a lesson does it convey as to the inherent selfishness of mankind, and the insufficiency of any earthly blessing to confer perfect happiness. The one that is ' bridled and saddled' has indeed ' a jade's time of it,' the one that is ' booted and spurred' uses the latter instruments ruthlessly and without remorse. Who would be the loser in the game ? Who would not wish to hold the bridle and apply the spurs ? And yet perhaps there may come a time when it will be unspeakable happiness to feel that we have had all the suffering and all the sorrow, proudly conscious that we have been ' bridled and saddled' all our lives, and are about to die honestly in our harness at the end. Woe to the ' booted and spurred' one then. When the kindly face will be seen never again but in our dreams—when the fond heart we have wrung so often is at peace for evermore—when a world's wealth and an age of longing cannot unsay the cruel word, nor recal the cold glance—when hope is dead, and even wishing a bitter mockery, how much better to sleep peacefully beneath the daisies, wearied with the strife, subdued in the defeat, than to pluck them for a remembrance which shall pass away indeed, but shall leave a blank more unendurable than the pain from which we prayed so fervently to be delivered.

A pair are walking on the terrace at Boughton in the golden flush of a fine September morning ; one is ' bridled and saddled,' the other ' booted and spurred.'

Mary Cave, we need hardly observe, was a lady of no undeviating habits, no precise observer of times and seasons. Some days she would idle away the whole morning in bed, reading her letters, stitching at her embroidery, and wasting her time; on other occasions she would bustle up with the lark—and when Mary was busy, no one in the house, not even studious Lord Vaux himself, could be suffered to remain quiet.

On the morning in question she was unusually wakeful, and this is the more unaccountable inasmuch as her sleep had been fitful and broken the whole night through, disturbed with dreams, and harassed with incongruous thoughts and fancies. Was she overfatigued, poor Mary! with her day's hawking, and the rapidity of Bayard's bounding movements; or was it that hard-fought game at chess played on till nearly midnight in the withdrawing-room, with many a false move, and many a smothered sigh? Why will that image never leave her brain? The studious brow bent over the shining pieces, the slender hand clenched on the board's-edge, the long sheathed rapier meeting the point of its shadow on the polished oak floor, and the weary, weary look on that face when its eyes were raised to hers in the intricacies of the game. Why was he so weary? What was the secret reason of this over-powering melancholy, so different from the characteristic jollity of Sir Giles and the other Cavaliers? Could she ever penetrate it? Could she ever find her way deep, deep into that great, proud, inscrutable heart? Had she already done so? A thrill, keen enough to be painful, shot through her at the thought. Up and dressed, she walked to her window and looked out at the fair, calm, joyous morning, so full of hope and peace and happiness, so at variance with her own torn, restless, wayward mind! The sun was even now a hand's-breadth above the horizon; his light had already tinged the dark tops of the cedars on the opposite hill with a purple glow. Patches of the undulating park were gilded with his beams; a skein of wild fowl, disturbed in their quiet refuge down amongst the osiers, were winging their arrowy flight, clear and distinct, against the pearly grey of the morning sky, flushing here and there into a faint pink tinge. The deer, rising to shake the dew-drops from their flanks, were still in dusky shadow, while the woodpigeon, cooing softly from the topmost branches of a fir-tree, trimmed her sleek plumage in a flood of light from the morning sun. The fragrance of a hundred roses clustered round the basement of the old Manor House, stole in upon Mary, soothing her with associations and memories of the past. What are all the chronicles of history, all the diaries of the most inveterate journalists, to the vivid reality that a simple strain of music, the scent of the commonest wildflower, can conjure up at a moment's notice? Beneath her the smooth bowling-green, that necessary adjunct to every country-house in the olden time, stretched its shaven surface, innocent even of a daisy to mar its level uniformity, while broad terraces, with here and there a rough stone vase, and here and there a standard rose-tree, carried the eye onward into the forest beauties, and wild irregularity of the thickly wooded park.

A spare slight figure was already traversing these terraces, pacing to and fro with swift determined strides, buried deep in thought, and plucking ever and anon a blossom or a leaf, which he crumbled nervously in his hand, and cast aside.

Mary was this morning seized with an earnest desire to tend her roses. She stepped out upon the terrace, her white robe falling in graceful folds about her shapely figure, her brown hair waving in the breeze, her rich ripe beauty glowing in the sun, her proud head thrown back with an air of enforced indifference, her whole gait and bearing stately and majestic as a queen. Yet she trembled as she approached that plain unpretending man; and her voice shook audibly as she bid him 'good-morrow,' and interrupted his solitary musings.

'You are early, my lord,' said Mary; 'and equipped, I see, for a journey. Must we, then, lose our guest so soon? It is not Lord Vaux's custom to suffer his friends to depart after one night's lodging; and you will scarce get leave from any of us to bid farewell at such short notice.'

Falkland was courtesy itself, and the gravest of mankind has no objection to his meditations being disturbed by a pretty woman at any hour of the day or night, so he smiled as he replied:—

'It would need no second bidding for a tired and unwilling soldier to remain in such pleasant quarters, and least of all from you, Mistress Mary, stanchest of loyalists, and kindest and oldest of friends.'

Mary coloured with pleasure, and her eyes shone and moistened while he spoke; her every nerve thrilled to the tones of that harsh impressive voice. 'One more day,' she said; 'we will only plead for one more day. There is still much to be done. I have a long correspondence to show you. There are traitors even about the Queen; and we must play another game at chess! You know I never could bear to be beaten. I must have my revenge.'

How soft and tender was her voice, how irresolute her gestures, how different her manner from that assured self-possessed air with which she addressed every one else in the world! He could not see it; he noticed no change; he was not thinking about chess: his was the great game played on the squares that were slippery with blood.

'It must not be, gentle Mistress Mary,' he replied. 'These are days in which we must all of us put our shoulders to the wheel. Alas! it need not have been so once. You know, none better, how the ruler of the ship has failed to shift his ballast, and to trim his sails. He saw the course he felt it was his duty to steer, and he scorned to turn aside for shoal or quicksand. Yet I cannot but revere the man, be he monarch or subject, who will sacrifice his all to a principle. The die is cast now, Mistress Mary; it is too late to look back. We must throw the helve after the hatchet, and stand or fall together, one and all.'

Her eyes sparkled, though her cheek paled. It was sweet to be thus associated with him, no matter what the purpose, no matter what the result. She would stand or fall, womanlike, with her party, at all hazards; that means, she would follow Falkland, right or wrong. She said as much, and he went on, more as it seemed to himself than to her:—

'Yes, we must stand or fall now. The last appeal, which I would cheerfully have laid my head on the block to avoid, has been resorted to, and by the decision of the God of battles must we now abide. War is surely excusable if it lead to peace. Oh, Peace! Peace! I see her in my dreams, with her olive-branch and her dove-like eyes, and the skirt of her pure white robe dabbled with blood from the carnage through which she must pass. I stretch my arms to clasp her round the knees, and implore her to remain, and she vanishes, and I wake—wake to what? To see merry England devastated from sea to sea, her quiet homesteads smoking, her fertile valleys spoiled and trampled by the hoof of war. Widows and orphans appealing to my Sovereign and his advisers to restore them their lost protectors. Thank God for my countrymen! that the worst scenes of rapine and violence are spared us—that when the fight is over, men cannot at once forget that they come of the same stock, and speak the same language. But how long is this to last? How long will it be ere some unavoidable act of cruelty leads to reprisals, and all the horrors of ancient civil war are enacted over again? What will England be then? Oh, that I for one may not live to see those times!—that I may die like a soldier under harness, and be spared a suffering worse a thousand times than such a death!'

'But these calamities will be averted,' she exclaimed eagerly; for her heart bid her believe that Providence itself would interpose to save such a being as Falkland. 'Another victory or two, and the Parliament must succumb. Cannot Waller be cajoled? Is not Essex wavering? Have we not the wealth and the lands, and the old blood of England, all on our side? Are we not prepared, every one of us, to die if need be in the Cause?' And she *would* have died for it willingly then and there—she would have asked nothing better than to 'seal her testimony,' as her Puritan enemies would have termed it, 'with her blood,' but it must have been with her hand in Falkland's—with her eyes fixed on Falkland's face. Verily, a woman's patriotism is influenced

D

by other than the love of country. Nevertheless, if not sincere
politicians, they are unfailing partisans: and Mary was as stanch
a Cavalier as ever drew a sword.

'And therefore it is that I must away to-day before the sun is
another hour higher in the sky,' said Falkland, with the rare smile
that illuminated his plain features into actual beauty—that found
its way straight to his companion's heart. 'If our forces should
be engaged; if the Parliament should be worsted, or we ourselves
defeated; in either case, Mistress Mary, you would not have me
absent from my post?'

'In either case,' she replied, with her voice trembling, her eyes
deepening and moistening once more, 'in either case, Lord Falkland, I would be the last woman on earth to bid you stay. Ay!—
even if I had *the right*, the last on earth, because—because I——'

She hesitated, changed colour, and stooped to pluck a rose,
which she picked to pieces, unconscious what she did; but she
averted her looks from her companion, and seemed to count the
tender pink petals as they fell noiselessly on the gravel path.
Was he blind? was he totally insensible? was the man marble,
that he could proceed so calmly and unconsciously—

'There must be no reserve; we must cast all into the treasury,
and hold back nothing. It is a small thing that I give my life;
there is more than life to be sacrificed—happiness and home, and
all the holiest affections of a man. 'I leave my duties,' he spoke
musingly and dreamily now; 'I leave my children—I leave my
dear fond wife——'

'Hold, my lord!' interrupted Mary, with an abruptness which,
though it was lost on her companion, was none the less startling
to herself, that her breath came quick and her heart seemed to
stop beating—'Hold! we have but little time before us; let us
attend to the business in hand. I have letters to show you here.'
She drew a packet from her bosom as she spoke, one single missive
detaching itself from the rest, and fluttering unobserved to their
feet. 'Letters from Jermyn; letters from Walter Montague, who
writes like a Jesuit as he is; one from poor Marguerite, your old
partner, my lord, in many a merry dance. There are traitors even
in the Court, there are traitors about the Queen. We want the
clear head, and the true heart, and the ready hand. Read those,
Lord Falkland, and tell us all what is to be done next.'

He took the papers from her hand and perused them attentively.
Again the light from within seemed to break over his whole
countenance; and he returned them to her, quietly remarking,
with an inquiring look, 'There is still a link wanting in the chain,
Mistress Mary. Have I seen them all?'

The fallen missive lay under the skirt of her robe. For an instant she hesitated, and moved so as completely to cover the spot where it lay, then stooped to pick it up, and blushing scarlet, placed it open in Lord Falkland's hands.

'One more,' she said, 'from Lord Goring; here it is. He always writes so foolishly; he is so wild and thoughtless. Do not think—I mean, you cannot suppose——'

Her confusion overcame her completely. He did not seem to notice it. Ere he had perused a dozen lines he gave a little start, and then his port became loftier, his manner more courteous than ever, as he folded up the document and returned it to her, coldly observing—

'This letter is private, Mistress Mary; and, pardon me for the remark, highly characteristic of the writer. I was not aware you knew Lord Goring so well.'

She could bear it no longer; pride, reserve, prudence, decorum —all gave way before the force of that hopeless passionate love, sweeping in its headlong violence over every rational consideration, every earthly obstacle.

'And you think I care for him?' she sobbed out wildly; 'that profligate, that adventurer—that licentious, bold, bad man. *You* think it—that *I* care for *him*. Only say so!—only let me hear it from your own lips. *I*, who have had but one ideal ever since I was a girl—*I*, who have dared to worship the best, the noblest, the greatest of mankind.' She had caught his hand while she spoke, covered it with kisses, and was pressing it almost fiercely against her own beating heart; 'I, who have loved the very ground you trod on for your sake; who have been content to toil and scheme and suffer in the Cause, only to have a share in *your* work, a claim to *your* notice. I, who have loved you—yes, *loved* you, Falkland!—and I tell you so now boldly, for, come what may, I swear from henceforth never to see your face again—who have loved you for years fondly, madly, faithfully—without hope of a return. And *you* think lightly of me at the last. Oh! what will become of me; how shall I ever hold up my head again?'

She burst into tears as she spoke. She clasped his hand with both of hers closer and closer to her heart, murmuring over it fond, broken, unintelligible words: then suddenly drawing herself up, looked him full in the face. 'Falkland,' she said, 'from this hour we never meet again; but for your sake I give myself wholly and unreservedly to the Cause—for *your* sake I devote myself to it, body and soul!'

She swept past him into the house with the stately bearing she knew so well how to assume. The proud spirit bore her up the wide staircase and through the long passages to her own chamber. If she gave way when the door was locked, and she had to wrestle it out unassisted with the one great fatality of her life, what is that to us? 'Verily the heart knoweth its own bitterness.'

We do not assert that from the corner of her window she did not watch him ride away on his eventful and fatal journey; but her oath was religiously kept from that hour, for on earth she never saw Lord Falkland's face again.

And he paced once more up and down the terrace, and thought of the beautiful woman who had so unreservedly cast herself upon his generosity, and so frankly confessed to him her wild and hopeless love. Then he remembered a fond, faithful face at home; and a thrill of pain shot through him as he reflected how he might never see that face again. 'Alas, alas!' he said, almost aloud, 'is it even so? Is there no peace, no happiness on earth? Must there be nothing but conflict and sorrow, and envy and strife, in public as in private. Women's hearts sore and breaking, men grappling at each other's throats. Peace, Peace! must I look for thee in vain, save in another world? Oh! I am weary of the times—God grant I may be out of them ere long!'

They were soon mounted for the journey, and a gallant cavalcade they made. Lord Vaux himself, bareheaded, conducted his honoured guest to the door. Grace Allonby presented the stirrup-cup, at which good Sir Giles took a long and hearty pull. Habit is second nature after all; and in those days men belted on their swords and thrust themselves into their stout buff coats on the eve of an engagement with as few misgivings and as little ceremony as would precede a stag-hunt or a hawking match. Even Grace postponed her tears till after their departure, and accepted the ceremonious farewells of the Cavaliers; and admired the Cornet's sorrel horse, perhaps also the sorrel's rider, as if her father were not bound on a hazardous enterprise, and engaged in a sinking cause.

Ah, we may prate as we will of the *prestige* of success; we may talk of the smile of prosperity, the favouring gale of fortune. It is pleasantest, no doubt, and easiest, too, to ride a winning race; but if we want to see examples of unflinching endurance, brilliant heroism, and superhuman devotion, we must look for them amongst the partisans of a sinking cause—amongst the Bonapartists of 1814; amongst the Royalists of the Revolution; amongst the adherents of weak, chivalrous, misguided Prince Charlie, and amongst the loyal gentlemen who closed their ranks around his ili-fated ancestor, who grudged not to lavish their treasure and their blood in support of a principle which their better sense told many of them, as it told Falkland, it was hopeless to attempt to establish.

Cornet Bosville, however, was absent and preoccupied during all these courteous preparations for departure. To Sir Giles's pledge, which half emptied the stirrup-cup, he gave but a cold return. To Lord Vaux's hospitable entreaties that he would come back at some future time, and improve an acquaintance so auspiciously begun, he replied indeed in an eager affirmative, but left off in the middle of his sentence, and looked about him with the air of a man who is expecting something or somebody that fails to arrive. He was wondering where the bright vision of last night was hid? Why did she not appear to bid them farewell? Could she be watching them from the window of her chamber, and which was the happy window? At least these roses were likely to be her peculiar care, and the Cornet plucked one from its stem and hid it away carefully in the breast of his buff coat. And Grace saw the movement, and wondered why he did it? and blushed as she thought of one or two possible 'wherefores,' and admired the sorrel more than ever. Cross-purposes again. It is well we cannot look into one another's hearts. Would Grace have been pleased or mortified could those soft dark eyes of hers have pierced through the Cornet's buff coat, and point lace kerchief, and Flanders linen, to read the secrets hid beneath those defences? Would the young soldier himself have been gratified had he known which was really Mary Cave's own chamber, and could he have looked through some four feet of stonework and seen with the eyes of the flesh that lady's deep, wild, passionate distress? Why was he not up half an hour earlier, and in the garden, to overhear her conversation with Falkland, and her last long farewell? Would it have altered the whole course of his after-life, and nullified the vagaries which it is the author's province to record?—or is there no such thing as free will; and is the Cornet like his fellows, but a well-dressed puppet in the hands of destiny? Sir Giles is right, after all. He attends to the business of the moment; he returns to the stirrup-cup, which he finishes at a draught; he marshals his own and Lord Falkland's retainers in military order outside the court.

'God bless thee, Gracey! Take care of "Diamond,"' says the old man, in a broken whisper, and with tearful eyes, to his darling; but his voice rings out manly and cheerful the next instant, as he addresses Lord Falkland—'Everything is prepared, my lord. There is no time to be lost; may I give the word to march?'

A trumpet sounds. A small pennon, with the royal arms upon it, is hoisted by an honest English-looking yeoman. Horses snort and trample; steel and stirrup-irons ring cheerily; hats are waved and farewells exchanged once more, and the men ride off to fight and bleed, and the women remain to watch, and weep, and pray.

CHAPTER VI.

BOOTED AND SPURRED.

In the sheds and outbuildings of an old straggling farmhouse upon the outskirts of the quiet town of Newbury, are quartered a squadron of Colepepper's regiment of horse. Chargers are stamping, and snorting, and munching the long yellow straw, of which they pull out and waste at least as much as they consume. Strong well-built yeoman-looking troopers are tramping about in their heavy boots, now in the dairy, now in the kitchen, jingling their spurs, clattering their swords, grinning at their own broad jokes, and making themselves very sufficiently at home. Buxom country lasses, confused yet not altogether displeased by the number and fervency of their admirers, bustle here and there, with scarlet cheeks and laughing tones, and rustic rejoinders to the rustic gallantries of their guests. The good man of the house, one of those prudent individuals who aspire to run with the hare and hunt with the hounds, being a stanch king's man for the nonce, bestirs himself to draw his strongest ale and slice his fattest bacon for the refreshment of the troops. His neighbour, a quarter of a mile off yonder, on the opposite hill, has got wild Lord Goring for a lodger, and he blesses his stars to think what an escape he has himself had of such a visitation, and wonders whether neighbour Hodge has sent his pretty daughters out of the way.

A month or two ago he had a visit of the same description from a few of Waller's godly cavalry, and he reflects that notwithstanding their rigid discipline, long faces, and pious ejaculations, the soldiers of the Parliament were as eager to eat of the best and drink of the strongest as the noisy Cavaliers who are even now turning his house upside down. Nay, the exhortations and awakenings of the former were not confined exclusively to male converts; and black-browed, red-elbowed Joan had administered such a slap of the face to a certain proselytizing corporal as sent him down on the dairy floor with the suddenness and precision of a round-shot. Verily the man of war, under whatsoever banner he fights, is too apt to arrogate to himself the exclusive protection of Beauty; nor whatever might be the shortcomings and back-slidings of the Puritan party, could the Cavaliers be held entirely blameless on this score.

Our acquaintance Dymocke, grave and ill-favoured as is his long weatherbeaten visage, scored with the lines of more than forty years, has yet a dry confident way with him that works wonders with the female sex. Let the daughters of Eve say what they will, there is no man in whom they take such an interest as a confirmed, sarcastic old bachelor. He is a riddle to be read, a rebel to be subjugated; he begins by provoking, goes on to in-terest, and ends perhaps by tyrannizing over them most effectually.

Joan's proselytizing admirer, notwithstanding his cropped hair and hideous orange scarf, was a likely well-looking youth enough, yet she knocked him down without a moment's hesitation when his blandishments became too personal; but to judge by the ex-pression of that determined young woman's physiognomy, such an argument is the last to which she would at this moment resort, even should her colloquy with sly, experienced Hugh Dymocke terminate in as hazardous an enterprise as that which discomfited the unlucky corporal.

'More eggs,' said Joan, returning from a visit to the hen-roost, with flushed cheeks and an apronful of the spoils; 'eggs and bacon and strong ale—better fare than you and your master get at home, I warrant me, and better than you deserve, for all your smooth speeches and come-over-me ways. Get along with you, do!'

The latter ejaculation was consequent upon a practical remark made by Dymocke, with his usual gravity, but which led to no further result than a continuance of the flirtation on the part of the lady.

'Aye, it's all mighty well,' continued Joan, setting both arms akimbo, and looking boldly up at her companion; 'you tell us this, and you tell us that, and you think we're fools enough to believe every word you say. Why now, for all your impudence, you durs'nt look me in the face and tell me you haven't got a sweetheart at home!'

The expression which this flattering suggestion called into Dymocke's face was a study in itself.

'Sweethearts here and sweethearts there, my bonny lass,' was the courteous reply: 'it isn't often such a face as yours comes across us, fighting, and marching, and riding, and conquering from one end of England to the other. There's my master and the Captain as hungry as hawks: let's have the eggs and bacon frizzling on the kitchen fire this minute, and you see, if I'm alive this day week, and taken notice of maybe by the King, God bless him! what sort of a story I'll have to tell you then. Soh, my lass, gently with the frying-pan. There's a face for a wedding-favour!' And with these ominous words the old soldier chucked the aforesaid face under the chin, and bore off the smoking dish in triumph for the repast of the two officers in the parlour.

Cornet Bosville sat and mused in the wide chimney-corner, careless of the noise and bustle in the yard, careless of his servant's ceaseless interruptions, careless of the comrade who occupied the same chamber, and who also seemed deeply engaged with his own thoughts, careless even of his supper, that important event in the military day. He had ridden far and fast since sunrise; he had shared in Sir Giles Allonby's careless jests, and the deep poetry of Falkland's conversation; had listened absently and with equal lack of interest to both. He had reported himself to Colepepper, and been complimented on his diligence, and favoured with the welcome news that an engagement was hourly imminent. His heart did not stir as it used to do at the intelligence. He had inspected his troop with military care and precision, nor neglected to see the good sorrel horse well fed and littered down; and now that the duties and fatigues of the day were over, he sat in the chimney-corner and drew lines on the sanded floor with his sheathed sword, as if there were no other interest or occupation in life.

Humphrey Bosville had insensibly passed the line of demarcation which separates light-hearted youth, with its bright anticipations and merry thoughtlessness, from ardent, reflective manhood, with its deep, absorbing passions, its strong ambition, the vague aspirations, the many cares and anxieties that wait upon a beard. Hitherto life had been to him a thing exclusively of the future, now there was a past on which to dwell and ponder. He had already learned to look *back*. Alas, that sooner or later the lesson never fails to arrive! that the time *must* come when we are too surely convinced by experience that the golden distance before us is but a mirage and a delusion; that for all our discontent and unworthiness while it smiled, we have *had* our share of happiness here; and that, like Lot's wife, we cannot forbear to turn round and gaze yet once upon the city we are leaving for evermore. So we turn and look, and it strikes chill upon our hearts to think, that if we were never really contented there, how shall we be happy in the wide lonely desert stretching far away before us to meet the wide lonely sky?

Bosville's had been no uneventful life, yet hitherto he had borne his part in its stirring scenes and stormy vicissitudes with the frank carelessness of a boy at play. From his earliest youth he had been of a gentle chivalrous nature, which accorded well with his personal good looks and attractive physiognomy. As his exterior was fair and well-proportioned, adapted for proficiency in all sports and exercises, so was his disposition open, ardent, and imaginative, prone to throw itself enthusiastically into the present, but lacking foresight to provide for the future, or reflection to deduce counsel from the past.

He would have been a gallant knight in the olden times of chivalry, true to his God and his ladye love, ever ready to strike for the cause which he espoused, and nothing loth to oppose his single body against a host, if by such an act of self-devotion he could gain honour and renown; but he never would have been capable of assuming a leader's part in a great enterprise. He might have charged alongside of Richard Cœur de Lion, but he never would have made a counsellor for Godfrey de Bouillon. Such a nature in the times in which he lived was sure to embrace the profession that in the seventeenth century as in the nineteenth was esteemed the worthiest of gentle blood. As a matter of course he injured his patrimony, ruffling it amongst the gallants at Court; equally as a matter of course he girded his father's sword upon his thigh and took service in the Low Countries—that happy land, of which it seems to have been for centuries the privilege to afford an arena for other European nations to fight out their quarrels at their leisure.

At the siege of a small town in Flanders the company of musketeers to which he was attached had fired a few detached cottages, from which they had dislodged a superior force of the enemy. A poor little child had been left behind, overlooked in the flight of the inhabitants, and was found helpless and crying amongst the ruins of what had once been its home. The child's mother, regardless of the danger to which she was exposed, was seen frantically waving her arms to her lost darling, and was only prevented from rushing to its rescue and her own death by a couple of stout soldiers who held her back by force. The ground between the hostile parties was swept by a withering cross-fire; Humphrey Bosville seized the child in his arms, and an old halberdier who was near him avowed that the infant ceased crying at once when soothed by that kind face and gentle voice. Coolly, steadily, as if on parade, with measured step and slow, the young officer, covering the infant with his body, paced that deadly interval till he reached the ranks of the enemy, placed the babe in its mother's arms, first kissing the child's wet check, and then, with a courteous bow, the hand of the grateful woman. At the same pace, with the same bearing, he rejoined his own men, unscathed and unmolested. The enemy did not even strive to take him prisoner, but the rough soldiers who saw the deed, friends and foes, gave him a cheer that rose above the rattle of musketry and the thunder of great guns. The action was characteristic of the man. He was brave, generous, and devoted, but there was too much of the woman in his heart. Such a nature is formed to be imposed upon, to be the tool and the cat's-paw of longer heads and less sensitive feelings ; above all, to be made a fool of by that sex which is proverbially addicted to ' ride the willing horse too hard.'

His meditations were interrupted by the entrance of Dymocke bearing the repast which it had cost him such an expenditure of gallantry to obtain, and which he now placed upon the table between the two officers with an expression of fatherly care and satisfaction on his lean long visage which seemed to say as plainly as words themselves, ' What would become of my master—what would become of his friends—of Colepepper's Brigade—of the army—of the King himself—without the experience and forethought of sage Hugh Dymocke ? '

Breaking from a profound fit of abstraction, and drawing his chair to the table, Bosville's comrade proceeded to attack Joan's triumph of culinary skill with all the energy of a practical campaigner. Nor did the Cornet himself, however engrossing may have been the subject of his previous meditations, seem to have lost the appetite which seldom forsakes a soldier living, as the Cavaliers too often did, at free quarters. While the eggs and bacon are rapidly disappearing under the combined trituration of two very handsome sets of white serviceable teeth, and the large brown jug of strong ale is visibly approaching the ebb, we must take leave to introduce to our readers a gentleman of good birth and station, bearing the name of George Effingham, and holding rank as a Captain of Horse in the Royal army.

Cool, brave, and resolute, Effingham had done good service on more than one occasion, when the general laxity of discipline and multiplicity of commanders were creating disorder in the ranks of the Cavaliers. He possessed the rare faculty of retaining his presence of mind and imperturbability of demeanour when all around him were eager, excited, and confused. Nor did personal responsibility seem to affect his nerves one whit more than imminent danger. Such qualities are invaluable to an officer, and Colepepper's favourite captain might have become one of the most distinguished commanders in the Royal army. But Effingham's heart was never thoroughly in the cause. Essentially an enthusiast, one of that class whom persecution too surely develops into fanatics, he was continually reasoning in his own mind on the justice of the quarrel in which he had engaged. His tendency to fatalism bade him argue that the constant reverses sustained by the Royal troops were so many additional proofs that they were warring against the will of Heaven; and the same misfortunes which endeared the cause all the more to Bosville's generous nature, shook Effingham's fidelity, and destroyed his confidence in its justice.

His early life had been spent in study for the law, a profession for which his acute penetrating intellect seemed especially to fit him; but a physiognomist would have detected in the glitter of his dark deep-set eyes somewhat more of wild imaginative powers than is essential to the drawing of deeds or engrossing of parchments, whilst the firm strong jaw, the well set-on head, and bold bearing were more in character with the buff coat than the judge's gown—with the tramp of horses, the ringing of shots, and the wild alarums of a skirmish, than the hushed murmurs of a court or the somnolent dignity of the bench.

He is very dark, almost swarthy, with features of classical regularity, and a stern, fierce expression on his countenance, as of one whom no consideration would turn aside from the path which he had once resolved to follow. A child looking into that set dark face would burst out crying; his frame is large, square, and powerful, his very hand, white and well-shaped though it is, shows a giant's energy and a giant's grasp. Perhaps of all his comrades he likes Humphrey Bosville the best. Their characters are so antagonistic. With the exception of personal courage, they have not one quality in common. Their ideas are so different; there is such trusting kindliness about the one, such harsh defiance in the other, that they cannot but be friends. Woe to the man, though, that crosses George Effingham's path; friend or foe, brother by blood or brother in arms, down he must go, without hesitation and without remorse! He would not turn aside a hand's breadth to avoid trampling down a wounded man in the battle; he would not swerve an inch from his purpose to spare the mother that bore him in the career of life.

'So Essex is marching parallel with our main body,' said the Cornet, setting down the ale-jug with a deep sigh after a hearty pull at its contents. 'Now is the time to bring him to an action, and come down with our cavalry upon his flank. Byron has brought his horse up fresh and ready for work. Our own brigade has rested for thirty-six hours, and will come out to-morrow like young eagles. The enemy must be weary and harassed; now or never is our opportunity. We shall not get such another chance of winning laurels in a hurry. Zounds, Effingham, we ought to gather them by handsful this time!'

'And we shall lose it,' was the reply; 'lose it, as we have lost every opportunity of terminating the struggle at a stroke; lose it, and hold up our hands and bless ourselves, and call a council of war, and say, " Who'd have thought it? " Humphrey, Providence is against us; we are fighting with invisible foes—with careless-ness, supineness, immorality; we are " kicking against the pricks." Laurels, forsooth! what are laurels after all?—weeds, rubbish, refuse, dear to the unawakened heart! And you, young one, what have you to do with laurels? I never heard you talk so before.'

It was true enough. The spark of ambition had, indeed, lain dormant hitherto in Bosville's breast. His daily pay (when he could get it), his nightly quarters, his troop, his duty, his horses, and his arms, had till now been all-sufficient for his wants and interests: this craving after laurels was something new and morbid—a fancy from without, so thought Effingham—not an impulse from within. He said as much.

'You have found somebody to give them to,' continued he, laying his hand on the young man's shoulder, and looking kindly into his face. ' Poor boy, poor boy! I thought you were safe. All alike in the Royal army—all fools together, Humphrey. Listen, lad. I dreamed a dream last night. I pray that my dream come not over true! I dreamed that we broke Waller's column, and were putting them man by man to the sword, when my horse fell, the old black horse, and the charge swept over me, and I rose to my feet light and unencumbered in an instant, and there lay George Effingham on his back amongst the hoof-prints, with his black-muzzled face deadly pale, and his sword in his hand, and his heavy horseman's boots on, and a small round spot on his forehead, as dead as Julius Cæsar, and I stood by him and cared not that he had ever belonged to me. Then a headless figure in a courtier's dress, with a courtier's rapier and ruffles and bravery, came and placed its thin white hand in mine, and a voice asked me tidings of the wife and children it had left, and the cause it had too warmly espoused, and the master who had betrayed it, and I answered it as I would answer you, "Widows and orphans; a failing cause, and a doomed King." Then we were in London, for I could not release myself from the grasp of that thin white hand, and perforce I followed where it led, and we paused at the Tower Stairs, and the river was running red with blood, so we took boat and ascended to Whitehall, and the river was red with blood there too, and the thin white hand grasped mine so painfully that I woke. Read me my dream, Humphrey Bosville; expound to me my vision, and I will confess that there is wit even below the buff coat and embroidered belt of an officer of the Royal army.'

'I can read no dreams,' answered Humphrey, his face kindling and his eyes sparkling; 'but come what may, if all the rivers in broad England must run red with the blood of the Cavaliers, if I alone am left and they lead me out to the slaughter, as long as they don't bind my hands I will fling my hat in the air before every canting Roundhead of them all, and shout with my last gasp, "God and the King."'

A melancholy, pitying smile stole slowly over Effingham's countenance. A kindly glance, painfully at variance with his stern, harsh expression, shone out from his deep eyes. Again he laid his hand upon Bosville's shoulder, and leading him to the open window, bade him look forth and listen.

The night was already dark, save for the glimmer of a few stars faintly twinkling in the solemn sky. All nature was hushed in peace and repose, but from Goring's head-quarters on the opposite hill the night breeze bore the sounds of wassail and revelry, the stamping of feet, the jingling of vessels: all the riotous sounds of an orgie, with a loyal chorus shouted out at intervals in no inharmonious tones.

'And these are the men,' said George Effingham, 'with whom we are content to cast in our lot—with whom you and I must perforce be content to triumph, and content to die!'

CHAPTER VII.

THE REVELLERS.

'HOLD, Goring! Twenty gold pieces—fifty, if you will! 'tis au even main and chance. I set the easter!'

The speaker was a boy of some eighteen summers, tall and graceful, beautiful as Absalom, and, in his present frame of mind, reckless as Lucifer; his eyes shining, and his face pale with wine, his long silken love-locks floating disordered over his point-lace collar and embroidered doublet, his belts and apparel all awry, a goblet of canary in his hand, and on his face the wild joyous gleam of a spirit that has never known misfortune or reverse. Goring smiled pleasantly—winning or losing he could always smile pleasantly—could betray a woman or run a man through the body with the same good-humoured expression on his handsome, dissolute face.

''Slife, Frank,' said he: 'you've the devil's luck and your own too. We can't hold our way with the young ones, can we, Sir Giles? Nevertheless, fifty, my boy, if you will: just to oblige you this once.'

In a hand white and soft as a lady's, he shook the box aloft, and the imprisoned cubes leaped out to mulct the young *roué* of fifty gold pieces for the benefit of the old one. The boy laughed, and drained his glass to the dregs. What cared he for fifty gold pieces, with the inheritance before him—the golden inheritance of hope, that seems so inexhaustible at eighteen?

'Once more!' he shouted, flinging a heavy purse upon the table; 'one more set, Goring, and then for another smoking bowl, and another roaring chorus that shall rouse the crop-eared knaves in their leaguer out yonder on the hill; and bring them down by daybreak on the nest of hornets we have got ready for them at Newbury.'

'Softly, my lad,' interrupted Sir Giles Allonby, laying his heavy hand on the purse, which Goring seemed already to look at as his own, 'you've had gambling and drink enough for one night; you'll have a bellyful of fighting to-morrow, or I'm mistaken. Take an old soldier's advice; turn in with your boots on, all ready for the *reveillée*. Get a few hours' sleep, and so be up and alive to-morrow morning at daybreak. I was young myself once, lad, but I never could keep the bowl trundling all the game through as you do; I never could burn the candle at both ends, and ride all day with Wilmot, to rest myself by drinking all night with Goring.'

Trust him to be snug and sober at this very minute,' said the .atter worthy, between whom and Wilmot, rivals in ambition, dissipation, gallantry, and war, there was a smothered grudge of many years' standing. 'Wilmot's fighting, and drinking, and lovemaking, must all be done by the square. Why, he never could fly a hawk in the morning if he had heard the chimes ring never so softly over-night.'

'Give the devil his due, Goring,' observed Colepepper, a grim old officer, with a scar on his cheek that lent a sardonic expression to his whole countenance, and an inexhaustible power of absorption, such as the handsome lad at his elbow had got drunk in trying to emulate. 'I've seen him fight as well as here and there one. *You* haven't forgotten Roundway Down; and as for drinking—when Wilmot really turns his attention to drinking, he is a better man by two bottles of sack than any one here at this table.'

'Granted,' said Goring, in perfect good-humour, and still fingering the dice-box, as if loth to lose the chance of another cast. 'All I maintain is, he can't do both. Give him two days of leisure to sleep it off, and he'll empty a hogshead; put him in a corner where he can't run away, and he'll fight like a devil incarnate.'

'Run away is a debatable expression, my lord,' said one of the guests with a grave tone, that at once silenced the clamour and attracted the attention of the rest of the party. 'The phrase, as applied to my friend, smacks somewhat of offence. I take leave to ask your lordship what you mean?'

'I mean what I say,' answered Goring, still assuming his pleasant smile, though it deepened and hardened somewhat about the lines of his mouth. 'I always mean what I say, and say what I mean.'

Goring was one of those gentlemen who opine that there is no dishonour so long as the sword is ready to maintain that which the lips have spoken, and that a slander or a falsehood can only affect the character of the man who utters it when he is not prepared to vindicate it by shedding of blood. It is an ignoble creed, truly, and an unchristian-like, yet on its basis are founded many of those sentiments which we so falsely term the essence of chivalry.

'Hold, gentlemen,' said Sir Giles, 'remember our compact when we sat down. Goring only means that Wilmot is a practised tactician. You think so yourself, my Lord Byron: is it not so?'

Goring was the most placable of men when nothing was to be gained by animosity. He stretched his hand to Byron—'I said

he'd fight like a devil, Byron, and I meant it, when he can't run
away; and how *can* he run away, surrounded, as he takes care
to be, by a guard of honour of " Byron's Blacks?" 'Faith, I
doubt if your fellows have ever been taught how to go to the rear.'

'Enough said, my lord,' answered Byron, completely appeased
by the compliment, and wringing Goring's hand with a hearty
squeeze, whilst the handsome face hereditary in his family shone
with an expression of gratified vanity. 'The Blacks are ready
for work at any time; another bowl to our " Next merry meeting
with the Roundheads." What say ye, gentlemen—we haven't
drunk the King's health yet?'

'Another bowl, by all means,' shouted the young Cavalier,
already half-sobered at the prospect of more revelry ; 'and Byron
shall superintend the making of it, and we'll have our host's pretty
daughters in to dance a measure, and one of the Black trumpeters
to play us a *couranto*. Hurrah!'

Lord Francis was indeed burning the candle at both ends, and
seemed as determined to make the most of his life as though he
could have foreseen how short would be its term; as though he
could have looked into the future scarce one brief lustre, and
beheld a dismounted nobleman selling his life dearly at Kingston-
upon-Thames; brought to bay by some dozen Roundhead troopers,
with his back against a tree, striking fiercely and manfully at
them all, scouting the bare notion of surrender; dying gallantly,
hopelessly, and devotedly for the King; a true Villiers, 'prodigal
of his person' to the last.

'The pretty daughters are gone to bed,' said Goring, whom
the immediate prospect of an engagement with the enemy had
placed in an unusually amiable frame of mind, and whom a residence of twenty-four hours in the farm had made completely
familiar with the intricacies of the establishment and the habits
of the inmates. 'It is hardly worth while to disturb their beauty-
sleep for such a performance as you propose. Let us fling a
couple more mains, Frank, while the bowl is getting ready. You
ought to have your revenge.'

Lord Francis seized the dice-box, nothing loth, and whilst the
two are occupied in the strangely-fascinating alternations of hope
and fear which render gambling so attractive a pastime, it is
worth while to examine the person and attributes of that distinguished officer of whom so many stories were afloat; whose
devotion to the King was more than suspected, yet who did such
good service in his cause; whose character for consistency was so
often impugned, yet who never failed to carry out any measure

on which he had thoroughly determined ; whose general life and
habits were esteemed so profligate, and yet who commanded the
confidence of his master—a royal example of propriety—and the
obedience of his officers, of whom perhaps it would be unjust to
make the same assertion.   A man, in short, whose every quality,
good or bad, had been called in question, save his courage, and a
greater portion of whose life had been devoted to establishing the
converse of the proposition which states that ' faint heart never
won fair lady ; ' although, in justice to Mary Cave, we think it
right to insist that, much as she may have appreciated his admiration, and freely as she returned him compliment for compliment,
and gallantry for gallantry, she had never for an instant bowed
her haughty head or turned her wilful heart towards wild George
Goring.

As he sits now, the gayest of that gay party, the stanchest
reveller amongst all those hard-fighting, hard-drinking Cavaliers,
thirstier than old Colepepper, more thoughtless than young Lord
Francis Villiers, who would suppose that handsome well-combed
head to contain a mass of intrigues and state-secrets of which the
simplest and least guilty might bring it incontinently to the block ?
Who would believe that kindly smile to mask a nature that never
knew pity nor remorse; that never had the generosity to forgive
an injury, nor to forego an advantage ; that never spared a woman
who trusted it, nor a man who crossed its path ? Already verging
on middle age, he looks bright and fresh and debonair as the
youth whose money he is rapidly winning with that easy smile.
It requires a keen observer to detect in the little wrinkles about
the eyes, the deep hard lines around the mouth, years spent in
dissipation and indulgence, years of reckless profligacy and fierce
excitement and bold defiant crime.   He is beautiful still, in all
the prime of man's beauty, with his noble head and his white
smooth brow, and his soft eyes, and the long curls of dark silken
hair that fall like a woman's round his oval face.   He is beautiful
in his manly, vigorous figure, on which his rich uniform sits so
becomingly, which is formed alike for strength, activity, and
grace, despite the limp habitual to its gait—a limp which, as
some of his fair admirers think, does but add to the distinguished
ease of his bearing, and the origin of which is a mystery whereof
a thousand rumours are afloat.   He is beautiful still, but it is the
beauty of the tiger or the panther ; the outward beauty that
strikes upon the eye and commands the admiration of the vulgar,
that seldom wins a heart worth the winning, and if it does, too
surely breaks it, and flings it scornfully away.

E

There he sits, keenly intent upon the game, yet noting every jest that passes, joining in every laugh that rises amongst his guests, sipping his wine at intervals, and bowing courteously to the young nobleman whose gold he wins with such graceful ease. Goring is the Mentor to whom has been entrusted this young Telemachus, and these are the Circean draughts of pleasure in which he would initiate his mother's son, were it to conduce in the remotest degree to his own advantage. He is playing the great stake himself; he has a high command, a proud position. Any day may make or mar him, may raise him to the pinnacle of ambition, or leave his saddle empty, and his title gone to the next-of-kin. Has he not enough to risk? enough to interest him? Can he not leave untouched that half-fledged ruffler of the game? No! there are a few broad pieces still left at the bottom of the purse, and he must have them all!

'One more glass of canary,' says the tempter, filling his antagonist a bumper with his own white hand. 'One more main, Frank, my lad, just to give you a chance; and then for the fresh bowl of punch, boys, and a rousing health to the King! Who knows where we shall be this time to-morrow?'

The glass was emptied. The main was called, and flung; the purse was emptied; and Goring, with a careless smile, swept the young man's last Jacobus from the board. He was quite cool and sober; he had no excitement in the game, felt no devil roused in him by the debauch. He was simply in his natural element, in the atmosphere of vice which was most suitable to his temperament and his constitution. To rob a friend of his money, to cajole him of his mistress, to finesse him out of his life should he presume to make objections—such were merely 'the customs of society,' 'the ways of the world;' they suited one like Goring admirably—the game was adapted to his style of play, and he generally rose a winner. What could be better? He would be the last to wish the rules altered.

God help us all! And yet this man was once a laughing, frank-hearted child—once clasped his little hands and said his prayers at his mother's knee!

The scene was worthy of the actors. A long low room, with a stone floor, and a wide chimney, in which sparkled and smouldered. the embers of a wood fire, a few rough deal forms, over which the heavily-booted Cavaliers straddled and lounged in every variety of attitude; a wide, high-backed, carved-oak chair, the farmer's especial throne, in which was established the giver of the feast; a coarse rickety table, on which clattered and jingled every

description of drinking-vessel, from the deep stone jugs and black
jacks of the farm itself, to the tall gilt goblets and massive silver
flagons, richly chased and burnished, which formed the moveable
canteen, perhaps the spoils of the Royal officers, and which had as
yet escaped the melting-pot, sooner or later the destiny of such
convertible valuables. All this seen through clouds of tobacco-
smoke, for the Virginian weed was even then in universal use,
although it must be confessed but as the handmaid of debauchery,
whereas she is now the domestic companion and consoler of many
an honest man's hearth. Amidst her floating vapours could be
discerned the graceful figures of the Cavaliers, manly and soldierlike, wearing one and all the nameless stamp of high-birth and
refinement of manners conspicuous even in the licence of a camp
and the freedom of a drinking-bout. Here sat chivalrous Byron,
with a calm contented smile smoothing his well-cut features,
somewhat flushed with wine. His thoughts were of the pleasantest
—of his stanch, well-mounted troopers—of his new peerage, so
lately won by the sword—of the dream of ambition opening so
auspiciously on the daring soldier and devoted Loyalist. There
reclined old Colepepper, with his scarred cheek and grim war-
worn face, his elbows resting on the table, his spurs jingling
against each other as he mused on cavalry tactics, and supplies of
food and forage, and the remounts preparing in Yorkshire and the
horse-breeding counties for his brigade—dry topics, which he
took care to moisten with repeated applications to the goblet at
his hand.

There was Sunderland, the young and gentle volunteer, attached
as aide-de-camp to the King himself, and who, coming to Goring
with despatches, had been prevailed upon to remain and partake
of his hospitality. There was Carnarvon, the jovial kindly-hearted
gentleman, the ornament and delight of the Court, the finest
horseman, the best hawker, the keenest sportsman of his day, the
adept at all manly exercises, the lancer, the swordsman, the racket-
player, the traveller in strange countries, who had breathed himself with the most skilful fencers of France, had flung the jereed
in 'Old Castile,' had smoked his chibouque with the Grand Turk
at Stamboul, listening with breathless attention to his neighbour,
Sir Giles Allonby, whose thoughts and whose discourse, far from
the present scene of revelry, were resting on merry pastures and
blue cloudless skies, and hawk and heron, and hood and jesses,
and all the delights of the noble science of falconry.

'So the match shall be made, good my lord,' said Sir Giles, as
sober as a judge, notwithstanding his potations, and prepared as

usual to back 'Diamond' against all and everything on the wing.
'The match shall be made for fifty gold pieces a-side; and I pray
you to my kinsman's poor house of Boughton, where we will
entertain you to the utmost of our humble means, and I will show
you such a flight as shall delight your eyes in the pastures of his
Majesty's royal domain at Holmby, where I have had licence to
fly my hawks since the days of his father, God bless him and sain
him! for a discreet sovereign, and as good a sportsman as ever
sat, albeit somewhat insecurely, in a saddle.'

The subject was sure to interest Carnarvon, passionately attached as he was to all field-sports. 'I have heard that gentle
King Jamie loved a good horse well,' he replied; 'but I always
believed he piqued himself most upon his skill in the chase, and
his knowledge of all the secrets and science of the noble art
of venery.'

'Horse and hound, hawk and horn, nothing came amiss to King
Jamie,' was Sir Giles's answer. 'He could follow a buck, and
take a buck, and carve a buck, ay, and eat a fair portion of a
buck, provided it were washed down with a huge allowance of
canary or a tubful of claret. Oh! the times that I have seen at
Holmby, my lord, when the King came down to hunt the stag
over the Haddon moorlands; and we rode all day, gingerly enough,
for it was not to be thought of that we should outstrip his Majesty;
and caution, between you and me, my lord, was a chief ingredient
in his royal character. He had it for his whole family, I think;
but then we made up for it by drinking like Dutchmen at night.
None of your grand entertainments such as delighted his ancestors;
none of your boars'-heads, and peacocks dressed in feathers, and
such dishes of state; but a reeking haggis—by St. George, a
villanous compound!—and a capon or so, with a few confections;
but washed down, mark me! by wine such as you never drink
now-a-days. I sometimes think the Parliament has spoiled the
liquor, as they spoil everything else. And then for company,
myself and poor Archie Armstrong, and two or three hard-headed
Scots lords, to whom nothing came amiss. You have been in
many countries, Carnarvon, and drunk with men of many nations;
can you tell me why a Scotchman, who is a native of a cold
climate, is always so confoundedly thirsty? But the King's delight
was in what he called a "cozy bit crack" with a few kindred
spirits, unawed by his son, whom he respected, or the favourite,
whom he feared; who could drink, for that matter, like a fish, as
all his family can, witness this boy here, who will have old Colepepper down under the table now before he has done with him!

But to return to the nights at Holmby. I have seen Archie Armstrong so drunk that he could not sit upon his horse to go out hunting in the morning, and once he tumbled out of his saddle into the Nene, and when we set him up by the heels to dry, with the water running out of his boots into his neckerchief, and the King rode laughing fit to split his sides, and asked him, " How is it with thee, gossip? Methinks at last thou hast liquor more than enough ! " he replied, sawing the air with his hand, as if deprecating all further hospitality, " Enough, gossip ! I thank thee. Enough. I'm for nae mair this bout—neither het nor cauld ! " The King laughed that you might have heard him at Northampton; and, 'faith, Archie was a ridiculous figure as you should wish to see. But here comes the punch; so now for one rousing health, and " Confusion to the Roundheads ! " After that, we have no more to-night, gentlemen, neither hot nor cold ! '

As Sir Giles spoke, neighbour Hodge entered the room, bearing aloft in person a huge bowl of the steaming compound, which was greeted with a shout of welcome by the Cavaliers, and soon went the way of its predecessors, amidst boisterous laughter, strange oaths, clapping of hands, stamping of feet, snatches of many a wild ranting chorus, and all the discordant jubilee of a debauch.

And yet many an anxious heart far away was aching for these revellers; many a little child had been taught to pray that very night for their welfare; many a fond lonely woman was weeping and watching even then, picturing to herself the beloved one, not flushed and swollen with wine, but calm and hushed in peaceful sleep; and many a one there present ere the same hour to-morrow would be down, stiff and stark, with a white rigid face turned upwards to the stars of Heaven.

Falkland, too, heard the dying shouts which concluded the nightly festivities of his comrades. He, too, had been awake and astir, but his vigils had been like those of some ancient knight who shrives himself and guards his armour ere the dawn of his great enterprise.

He had watched and prayed and pondered, long and earnestly, looking intently at one bright star shining conspicuously amidst the glittering diadem that crowned the sweet autumn night. He was purifying himself for the struggle, arming for the fight,— preparing his spirit unconsciously for the great unknown.

And one at Boughton was gazing fixedly at the same star, and praying her heart out, womanlike—not for herself, but for *him*.

CHAPTER VIII.

NEWBURY.

' How much longer are we to stand here idle, mowed down by round shot and exposed to the fire of those crop-eared citizens?' exclaimed Bosville, as the sorrel pawed impatiently and shook his bridle, whilst the men of his squadron murmured audibly behind him at an enforced inactivity, always so trying to the undisciplined troops of the Cavaliers.

' Steady, men!' was George Effingham's reply, as he confronted his little band, carelessly turning his back to the sharp fire poured in upon them by the Parliamentary artillery, admirably served, and in a commanding position, from which they had got the range of their enemy to a nicety. ' Steady for a few minutes longer. *Our* time will come directly. I never knew Prince Rupert keep us so well in hand as he has done to-day. "He laughs best who laughs last," Humphrey; and the game is none the worse for being played according to rule. See the pikes are deploying into line even now, and here comes Sunderland at a gallop with orders.' Effingham's eyes were beginning to glitter, and his dark face to pale a shade or two, as was customary with him when the moment of action had arrived.

They had waited for it long enough. The day was already beginning to wane, and Colepepper's Horse, with a strong support of ' Byron's Blacks,' had been held in reserve so carefully, that they almost feared they were destined to have no share in the stern conflict which they could themselves behold waged by their comrades with the Parliamentary army.

Essex had taken up a strong position on an eminence called Bigg's Hill, disposing his troops in stationary masses as though unwilling to assume the offensive, and trusting to the well-known imprudence of the Cavaliers to attack him on ground most dis-advantageous to their principal arm—a fiery and impetuous cavalry. The King's troops, on the contrary, had it at their own option to give or decline battle; and their obvious tactics would have been to draw the enemy, if possible, from his stronghold, and whilst manoeuvring on the plain, to fall upon him with their cavalry. The older officers saw this at a glance, and Goring, smart and debonair as though turned out for a review, detached Sir Giles Allonby with a handful of veterans whom he could trust, to make a feint, followed by such a retreat as should tempt the Parliamentary leaders into a general advance of their whole line.

The old knight acquitted himself admirably of his duty. But, alas! the manœuvre succeeded only too well. The Roundheads detached a party of veteran horse to check him. A strong body of foot advanced to the assistance of their comrades. One or two headstrong young Cavalier officers, without waiting for orders, engaged the cavalry regiments they commanded. Prince Ruperts never sufficiently Fabian in his tactics, was nothing loth to offer the main body of his horse, and was soon to be seen conspicuous in the van leading a succession of those brilliant headlong charge, which have made his name proverbial as the bravest of the brave, and the rashest of the rash,—charges which *must* succeed triumphantly or fail irrevocably, and to which, in their undisciplined impetuosity, the slightest check is too apt to prove fatal. Notwithstanding their advantage of position, notwithstanding their superior discipline and numbers, the Roundhead horse gave way before the furious onslaught of the enemy; and the day must have ended in a triumph for the Royal cause had it not been for the unexpected steadiness and gallantry with which the pikemen stood their ground,—a gallantry the more surprising both to friend and foe, inasmuch as it was displayed by the hitherto untried trained bands of London, whom the Cavaliers, as was natural, held in unbounded derision and contempt, and in whom even the Parliamentary veterans had no great confidence as the champions of a doubtful day.

'The knaves stand fast with their yard-measures in their hands,' quoth Goring, wiping his bloody sword on his horse's mane as he re-formed his brigade, and brought them once more into position, after leading them through and through a column of the enemy's horse, striking fiercely to right and left, like the veriest trooper, the grim smile deepening on his countenance at every blow.

'Those pikes will turn the tide of the action yet, my lord,' was Sir Giles's reply, as the experienced eye of the veteran detected the diminished ardour and failing horses of his own cavalry. 'Zounds,' added the old Cavalier, 'it shall never be said his Majesty's troops were turned by their own tradesmen. If they *would* but deploy into line! One more effort, and we might be amongst 'em.'

Goring laughed. 'Opportunity, you know, Sir Giles, opportunity is everything, both in love and war. The happy moment has at length arrived; and here comes Sunderland with orders.'

In effect, even as he spoke, the young Lord Sunderland rode up at a gallop, glancing eagerly at Colepepper's reserve, in which

Effingham and Humphrey Bosville were deploring their inactivity.
As he pulled up at Goring's side with a courteous bow, he
delivered his message. 'You will form the remains of your
cavalry, my lord,' he said, 'upon Colepepper's reserve, and advance with the whole up the hill. The pikes are even now
deploying into line, and the Prince bids you——'

Goring was drawing his girths a hole tighter; his head was
bent down to his pistol holsters, but he looked up quickly as the
young Earl's voice ceased, and saw that a round shot had taken
him off his horse, and that the intelligent, ardent messenger of an
instant back, so full of life, and spirits, and gallantry, was now a
ghastly, mutilated mass that would never speak again.

'I suppose he had nothing more to say,' observed Goring, drawing on his glove, and patting his horse carelessly on the neck, as
he turned to Allonby with a calm, unmoved countenance. 'Sir
Giles, form your regiment on my left. We will advance at a trot
up to yonder brushwood, and there I will give the word to charge.
I think we can pay the reckoning yet.'

In the mean time the trained bands, who had already sustained
the attacks of the Royalist cavalry with such determined obstinacy, and whose long pikes, held by strong English arms, and
backed by stout English hearts, formed a bristling hedge of steel
which not even the King's troopers could break through, were in
the act of making a flank movement to acquire a position more
favourable than that which they had already occupied. Prince
Rupert's eagle eye, ever quick as lightning to detect an advantage, saw their wavering line, and seized the opportunity to order
up his reserve for one last desperate effort. The rise of the hill
was against the horses; a minute sooner and they would have been
in time, but ere the cavalry could reach their steady, resolute foes,
they had again become a stationary mass of resistance, hedged with
steel, and pouring forth a deadly, withering fire, that enforced the
Royalists to return, emptying many a saddle, and bringing many
a curled head to the dust. Old Colepepper stormed and swore in
vain. The most he could accomplish was to make an orderly
retreat; and as Humphrey Bosville, with tears of shame and
indignation in his eyes, brought his troop back in good order to
their appointed position, Effingham quietly observed, 'Another
point in the game scored up against us, young one. Another
opportunity lost! Laurels, indeed, Humphrey! better gather a
handful of weeds, and lay your head down here on the turf, and
be at rest!'

In another instant he had darted like lightning from his men, and was engaged hand to hand with some half a dozen of the enemy's cavalry, who, like meaner birds about a hawk, were besetting the gallant Earl of Carnarvon, and hemming him in on all sides with their swords. That officer had got detached from his own men, and was now returning, alone and on a tired horse, through the scattered troopers of the enemy. Strong, athletic, and a practised swordsman, he had already emptied more than one of his opponents' saddles; but he was exhausted and out-numbered, and George Effingham's assistance came too late.

He had received a pistol-shot, which had broken his bridle arm, and deprived him of all control over his failing steed. Still, his fine horsemanship, and thorough use of his weapon enabled him to hold at bay the troopers in his front; but, alas! a sword-thrust from the rear had run him through the body; and as George Effingham cut down the successful assailant, and took the Earl's horse by the bridle to turn him out of the press, the life-blood was welling up through the rivets of his breastplate, and saturating the stout buff-coat with its frothy crimson stains. Courteous and gentle to the last, he thanked Effingham for his services.

'I am bounden to you, comrade,' he said, sinking forward on his horse's neck; 'but it is too late. I am hurt to the death, for all my cunning of fence. I pray you leave me, and save your-self.' Even as he spoke he fell heavily from his horse; and Effingham, with many a shrewd blow and many a hairbreadth 'scape, fought his way back to his own men.

Night was by this time drawing on : and as its dark mantle fell over the combatants, neither Cavaliers nor Roundheads could boast of a decided victory. The gallant trained bands bivouacked on the ground they had held with such stubborn valour ; and although they made an orderly retreat at daybreak, pursuing their line of march for the capital, and regardless of the harassing attacks made on their rear by the indefatigable Prince Rupert, with a thousand musketeers and such of his cavalry as were not incapacitated by the action of the previous day, they could scarce plume themselves on having gained any positive advantage over their opponents.

Humphrey Bosville and George Effingham slept under the same cloak, the sorrel and the black picketed close to their feet. Their squadron formed a strong outpost of Prince Rupert's ad-vancing column, and they were to be ready for the pursuit with the first dawn of the morning light. Goring returned to his quarters at the farmhouse on the hill, doubtless to receive a hospitable welcome from neighbour Hodge and his pretty daughters. Old Colepepper and Sir Giles Allonby waited on the King with their respective reports of losses and success. A few hours reconcile the survivors after an action to anything and everything that has befallen. There are rations and forage to be issued, men and horses to be accounted for, reports to be drawn up, misadventure glossed over and successes made the most of; and then, when the fatigues of the day are past, the exigencies of the morrow provided for; 'tis but another day gone by, after all, and the conquerors and conquered lay them down,

> The weary to sleep and the wounded to die.

So the trumpets sounded the *reveillée* blithely ere the first streaks of the morrow's dawn; and Effingham's squadron were up and mounted, and filing slowly over the ground of yesterday's hard-fought struggle in the early light of the soft autumn morning. Above their heads the heaven breathed of peace and beauty and holy calm; the birds were singing in the copse and hedges, the sheep bleating on the distant hill; but below their feet the very bosom of mother earth was torn and scarred by the fierce struggle of her wayward children. The ground occupied by the enemy was indeed vacant, for Essex was by this time in full and orderly retreat; but the traces of the conflict were but too apparent in broken wagons, dismounted guns, turf poached and trodden by dinted hoof-marks and scored with wheel-tracks; worst of all, in helpless bodies of men and horses, lying as they fell, the dying and the dead.

Bosville shuddered as he gazed; a man must indeed be inured to war who can look unmoved on such a scene. Effingham's eye dilated as he touched his comrade's arm, and pointed to a heap of dead who had evidently made a gallant attempt to storm an orchard surrounded by an old blackthorn hedge, and been shot down man by man as they came up.

'The apples in the orchard are hanging ripe from the bough, but the harvest of death is already gathered and carried home,' said Effingham. 'Humphrey, we are like the Assyrians when they came up by thousands against the might of Judæa, and lo! an unseen arm smote the horse and his rider. Have not these been kicking against the pricks? Verily the Lord is against us!'

'I saw them charge over this very ground yesterday,' was the young soldier's comment, 'and a nobler feat of arms I never witnessed, nor a finer fellow than the officer who led them! It was not Byron, for Byron was on the right with the rest of his Blacks, and would have turned their flank had the crafty Roundhead not placed a field-piece at the angle of the orchard. I could not recognise the officer at that distance, but I saw him put himself at the head of a handful of cavalry, and lead them twice up to this old straggling hedge, and twice they were repulsed by the deadly fire of the musketeers who lined it. The third time he leapt his horse into the orchard, and I am certain I saw him fall some twenty paces before any of his men. By St. George, there he lies!—man and horse under that large tree. Let us go in, Effingham, and see who he is!'

The two Cavaliers dismounted, and walked reverently and slowly up to the corpse. He was lying away from his dead horse, on his back. The charger had evidently fallen riddled with bullets at the same instant that his rider was struck. The corpse was stretched at length, its right hand still grasping its sword, and an ineffable expression of peace on its pale upturned face. Yes! in the midst of war he had found it at last. No more bitter misgivings now—no more weary longing and harassing anxiety— no more aching heart and sickening hopes and fears for Falkland. There he lay, the good, the generous, the gifted; born to be the ornament of a Court, the pillar of a state, the hope of a nation; and there he lay, shot below the girdle by some obscure musketeer, himself perhaps all unconscious of the deed. Many were the good and great men that joined the Royalist cause—many a noble heart shed its blood for King Charles; many a wise head plotted for the Crown; many a stalwart arm struck its last to the war-cry of ' God and the King;' but there was but one Falkland, and the morning after Newbury he was found a corpse.

The tears started to Bosville's eyes.

'Let us send back a party to bury him,' said he. 'The Prince will willingly spare enough men for such a duty as this.'

Effingham was not listening to him. 'The King had better have lost his right arm,' was his reply. 'Verily, the Lord is against us!'

CHAPTER IX.

' ROSA QUO LOCORUM.'

NEWS travelled but slowly in the days of which we write. It was already a week after the battle of Newbury, and the quiet party at Boughton had as yet no particulars of the fight. Rumours had indeed arrived that a great action had taken place, but as each narrator coloured his own account according to the political opinions he professed, both the details and the result remained wrapped in uncertainty. Some maintained that Essex had gained a complete victory, and was marching for London in the full tide of success, having dispersed and almost annihilated the royal army; that the King himself had fled, and that his best generals having been either killed or taken prisoners, nothing now remained but an unconditional submission to the terms of the Parliament. For this crowning mercy, it was argued by those who adopted so decided a view of the case, thanksgivings ought to be rendered, and the downfall of the man Charles celebrated by a solemn festival: others, again, and these garnished their version with many strange oaths, and showed a strong disinclination to discourse upon this, or any other topic, dry-lipped, avowed that the Parliamentary army had sustained a complete and unequivocal defeat, that the Royalist cavalry had, as usual, covered themselves with glory, and his blessed Majesty, whose health they were always prepared to drink on their knees, or indeed in any other position, having thrown a garrison into Donnington Castle, so as to command the western road to the capital, had retired in triumph to Oxford, whence he would impose the most stringent and humiliating terms on his vanquished enemies.

Grace Allonby and Mary Cave listened alternately to these conflicting statements with anxious faces and beating hearts; the former daily expecting some assurance of her father's safety, the latter vibrating between a sensation of crushing shame, as she recalled her last interview with Falkland, and all the tender misgivings of a woman for the safety of the man she loves. And yet the days dragged slowly on, in their routine of quiet occupations and homely duties. The women worked at their embroidery, and tended their roses, and rustled softly about the house, as if all were peace both within and without, as if life had no interests, no anxieties, beyond the taking up of a dropped stitch, or the nipping of a faded rosebud.

They were, however, much together; kindred hopes and fears seemed to draw closer day by day the links of friendship which had always bound these two dissimilar characters, and whilst Grace Allonby looked up to her more energetic friend for protection and consolation, the weary spirit of Mary Cave seemed to rest upon her gentle companion, and to derive a soothing, purifying influence from her sympathy and affection.

They were sitting together on a stone bench that terminated

the terrace on which Mary's last interview with Falkland had taken place. A soft, cloudy atmosphere dimmed the rays of the sun, struggling at intervals in downward sheets of light; a gentle breeze moaned through the adjacent woods, claiming here and there its first autumnal tribute in a crisp yellow leaf that floated noiselessly down to the sward. The last roses, already overblown, drooped their heads over the two women, shedding their petals thick and fast, to the insidious wooer that stole so softly across the distant meadow, and over the trim lawn, to win their perfume and waste their loveliness, and kiss them and pass on. There was music in the whispering breeze, and beauty in the dying roses, but it was a sad sweet music that seemed to mourn for the past, and a beauty that spoke of disappointment and decay. Each of them gathered one of the flowers, and placed it in her bosom; each seemed to have some association connected with these autumn roses, some strangely-mingled memory of pain and pleasure, of hope and longing, and shame and sorrow, for Grace blushed scarlet, and Mary's blue eyes were filled with tears.

She brushed them hastily away, and turned her head so as to hide her face from her companion; she was ever ashamed of such womanly weaknesses, and indeed seldom gave way to her emotions, whatever might be their nature.

'Another day, Grace,' she said, 'and no news yet from the army. Oh, it wears one's heart out to sit waiting here when men are in their buff-coats and breastplates, up and armed for the King. I would I were amongst them, Grace, to take my share of danger like the rest. *C'est l'homme qui se baste, et qui conseille*; but as for us poor women, what are we good for but to clog their energies, and distract their attention, and weep and watch, and eat our own hearts in solitude?'

'You did not always say so, Mary,' replied her companion. 'I thought men were the puppets, and we were to pull the strings. Have you changed your note so soon about our power and influence, and why?'

The proud look stole over Mary's face once more. 'Yes, Grace,' she answered, 'ours is the dominion, if we only knew how to keep it. It is our own fault if we lose the upper hand. It does not answer to pull the rein too tightly, and so to break it once for all; nor is it judicious to let the so-called lords of the creation discover how necessary they really are to our happiness. To do them justice, they are wonderfully obtuse on this point, and, in this single instance, strangely prone to underrate their own value. And yet, dear, I sometimes think that ours is but a tinsel royalty, after all—a fairy splendour, that is visible to the dazzled eyes of those only over whom our glamour is cast; that the real power, and wisdom, and glory is not with us, and the time may arrive at any moment when our subjects wake to find this out for themselves, and then all that was life to us is but a dream to them, a dream from which they do not even sorrow to be aroused; a dream at which they can smile when it is recalled to them, and yawn out some vague sentiment, half poetical, half philosophical, of indulgent pity on their own past folly, and self-congratulation that it is over at last for evermore. They are not quite ashamed of it, neither do they wish it had never existed, but they talk of it (as even the best of them will of their boyhood's extravagancies) with a sort of melancholy triumph, and comical self-pity and self-sympathy. "I was very fond of that woman once," they will say, without a particle of the feeling left. The woman does not speak so, but she carries her heartache about with her in silence, and every time his name is mentioned the old wound smarts and bleeds afresh.'

'And do you believe there is no constancy?' answered Grace, in whose opinion her companion's thorough knowledge of such matters was deserving of the most implicit credence, and who felt much more alarmed than she would have been one short month ago at these discouraging views of the relations between the sexes. 'Are men all alike, and all equally heartless and variable?'

'God forbid,' was the reply; 'and yet, Grace, in all I have seen of the world, and you know that my girlhood has been passed amongst the gaieties and intrigues of a Court; well, in all I have seen, I can recall scarce one single instance of an attachment that has lasted more than two years. You look astonished, Grace, but it is so, nevertheless. They are nearly all alike, and differ only in degree from wild Lord Goring, who says that he requires a week to conquer, a week to triumph, and a week to weary, after which he allows himself a week's repose, meaning simply a rotation of hard drinking, and the beginning of the next month finds him prepared for fresh follies and fresh duplicity.'

'What a monster!' remarked Grace, lending an ear, nevertheless, with unconscious interest, to the escapades of wild George Goring.

'And yet, Grace,' proceeded Mary, looking back dreamily, as it were, into the past, 'there was once a time that even Goring was ready to sacrifice his fortunes, his ambition, his life, and indeed his all, for a woman. She was my aunt, Grace, and once I think she loved him well. It was a foolish story. He hoped to win her against all obstacles, and with his energetic nature, his courage, and his recklessness, I cannot comprehend why he failed. But so it was. During his absence abroad, where he was serving to win distinction only for her sake, others came between them, and she was lost to him for ever. It was years ago, my dear, and she is a cold, proud, stern woman now, but I think she was not always so. They say she used to be a sweet-tempered, loveable, and beautiful girl; they say she would have made Goring a good and happy wife. I have heard one person affirm that even he would have been a different man had she belonged to him; that it was not his nature always to be bad amongst the worst; that everything good and gentle in him changed in a day. But he who said so judged all men kindly, and saw everything through the clear atmosphere of his own pure, noble mind. There are few like him. But to return to Goring. I know that even after all hope was over, even at the foulest and blackest stage of his career, when my aunt was thought to be dying, he threw up his command, he returned home with a stain upon his courage, he lost his dearest chance of distinction, to be near her; and when she recovered he was heard of wilder and wickeder than ever. There is no doubt he loved her fondly, and like a fool; and yet listen, Grace, to what I heard with my own ears. After a long absence, Lady St. Aubyn returned to Court. They had not met for years, not since I was a child, and at the time I speak of I was a grown woman, in attendance on the Queen. I was standing close to Harry Jermyn and Goring when my aunt was announced. I knew the story, and I watched the latter's face. It never altered in a muscle. I could have forgiven him if he had turned red or pale, or had even lost for an instant that hateful smile which seems to jeer at everything good and bad. No, he passed his hand through his long curls, and touched Jermyn with his elbow— "Egad, Harry," said he, "how these red and white women alter. Would you believe it, I once run my best friend through the body for a light jest about that one? And now look at her, my boy! She's an old woman, and a fat one. Faith, and almost an ugly one too. Well, its lucky there are plenty of young ones always coming on." And this is the way men can talk of us, Grace; but not all—not all; there are a few, a very few noble hearts that a woman might be proud to win, or failing to win, might be proud to worship in silence and lifelong pain.'

'Are there?' observed Grace, absently, for her attention was occupied by an advancing horseman, mounted on a sorrel that even at a distance she seemed to recognise. Perhaps she was

thinking, 'is this one of them?' perhaps she was speculating, with
the prospective power of imagination, 'will this one ever care for
me? and having cared, will he ever laugh, like Goring, and say,
"how these women alter," and "how fat I am grown?"' The
horseman was accompanied by one servant, a tall spare figure,
mounted on a stout useful palfrey, the spoil of some Parliamentarian whom Dymocke had deprived of his charger by the usage
of war. It was indeed Bosville who was rapidly approaching the
park, and the hearts of both women beat fast, and their cheeks
turned pale, for he would have news of the great battle, and the
Cause, and the King, and Sir Giles Allonby, and Lord Falkland.

The young man reined up his horse at the door and dismounted,
the reeking sides of the sorrel and the marks of disapprobation
visible upon Dymocke's lean visage sufficiently denoting the speed
at which he had been travelling. He gave the rein to his servant,
and advanced to greet the ladies, with doffed beaver and slow
dejected step. His dress was disordered and travel-stained, his
face bronzed by exposure, and now suffused with a deep blush,
and his countenance bore a saddened expression that was ominous
of bad news.

Grace jumped from her seat. 'My father!' she exclaimed,
with clasped hands and eager face.

'Sir Giles is safe, Mistress Grace,' was the reply; 'he bids me
commend him to you, and hopes soon to see his daughter once
more.'

Grace burst into tears, and covered her face with her hands,
Mary Cave meanwhile remaining pale and cold as the stone
balustrade against which she leaned. And yet she dared not ask
the question that was nearest to her heart.

'And you have obtained a victory, a great victory?' she said,
with lips that blanched and grew rigid while she spoke.

'A victory, indeed,' was the Cornet's reply, 'and a triumph for
the Royal Cause. I have despatches here from the King himself
to my Lord Vaux. I pray you give me leave, ladies; I must
hasten to deliver them.'

'And they are safe!' exclaimed Grace, with her eyes full of
tears; 'all safe! those that rode away so full of life and vigour
such a short time ago, and whom we thought we might never
see again?'

The Cornet's face was very grave. He needed not to speak.
Ere a word had crossed his lips Mary Cave knew the worst. Is
it not so with all great griefs? with all those important moments
upon which turn the destinies of a life—nay, it may be of an

eternity? What is it that tells the sufferer there is no hope, whole seconds if you count by the clock, whole ages if you count by the racked and tortured heart, before the decree has gone forth? Do you think the prisoner at the bar does not know the verdict before the foreman of the jury has delivered the thrilling word 'Guilty?' Do you think we are so constituted that by our physical organs alone we can become conscious of outward facts? Is there not in acute mental anxiety another and independent sense of prophetic nature? Who has not suffered has not lived. Is it better to vegetate in contented ignorance, or to pluck, Eve-like, at the tree of knowledge, and taste the wild, bitter flavour of the fruit? Alas! the lesson of life must be learnt by one and all. Happy those who profit by it. Give them place; let them take their proper station at the head of the class; but pity the poor dunce who is smarting in his ignorance, whose hot tears are falling thick and fast upon the page.

'We have bought our victory at too high a price,' said Humphrey; 'some of the noblest heads in England lie low at Newbury. Carnarvon, Sunderland, Falkland, have met a soldier's death and found a soldier's grave.'

Mary spoke not a word. Her beautiful features took a set meaningless expression, like a mask, or like the face of a corpse. There was a dull stony look in her eye, like that of some dumb animal.

Suffering pain and nerved to endure, her head was thrown proudly back till the muscles of the neck started out in painful tension. It seemed strange to see one of her cast of beauty so metamorphosed. Unbending physical resistance and acute stupi-fying suffering combined, seemed so out of character with her ripe womanly loveliness, her soft undulating form, her rich brown hair. She who was formed to love, and laugh, and command with the imperious wilfulness of a spoiled child—it was sad to see her there, with a hard defiance, even of her own breaking heart, stamped upon her brow.

She questioned Bosville again and again, unwavering and pitiless towards herself, she learned every particular he had to tell, she shrank from no incident of the action, no harrowing detail of Falkland's last charge, or the state in which he was found; and then with quiet grave courtesy she thanked Humphrey for his narrative, and walked once more up the well-remembered stairs with the stately step and queen-like gestures that became her so well.

She had been a changed woman one short week ago, when her

chamber door had closed upon her after that interview which she could never forget. She was changed again now; but it was a change that would influence her till she was at rest in her grave.

Bosville followed her with his eyes as she stepped gracefully away, but with his body he accompanied Grace Allonby into the house, that he might deliver his despatches, as in duty bound, to that young lady's kinsman. Now that the first anxious inquiries were over, that Sir Giles's safety was ascertained, and the victory of Newbury—for as a victory it was claimed by the Royalists—placed beyond a doubt, they talked, as young people will, of lighter and more mirthful matters—of the Court at Oxford, of the last jest made by Wilmot, and the last new fashion introduced by Harry Jermyn, of the Queen's caprices, and Prince Rupert's retorts uncourteous, of the thousand topics which come so readily to the lips where the deeper chords of character have not yet been sounded, and which make a dialogue between a young gentleman and lady, both of them well born and well bred, so sparkling and agreeable, that we despair of conveying its purport to the reader through the medium of our staid and sober pen.

Arrived at the threshold of Lord Vaux's own chamber, Grace bid her companion 'Good-bye,' with a half laughing, half formal courtesy. He turned as he closed the door for another glance at his guide. Oddly enough, at that very moment Grace turned too—it always does happen so—and as she tripped away to decorate her person in her own chamber, she felt happy and light-hearted as a bird. Of course it was the news of the great victory at Newbury and the safety of good Sir Giles that created this wondrous change in his daughter's spirits.

Mary Cave was on her knees in the adjoining apartment. The struggle was over, the wild sickening feeling of despair alone remained, but the great agony had passed away, and a flood of tears had brought that relief to the overcharged heart and the overstrung brain which alone saves the sufferer from madness. There are some natures that are at once utterly prostrated by sorrow, that make no effort to resist it, and yield at the first attack; such know nothing of real misery. It is the proud unbending spirit that has defied a thousand storms, which falls with a crash at last.

Mary had been accustomed to conquer, had marched in triumph over the necks of a host of captives; hers was no meek yielding disposition, that clings where it attaches itself, and finds a pleasure in self-abasement and self-sacrifice. No; she was one of those wild birds that must be tamed, and subjected, and re-

strained, to stoop to the lure by a stronger will than their own ;
and she had found her master long ago. Hopeless though it was,
she had fixed her love upon Falkland : though he could never be
hers, there had yet been a vague unacknowledged link that bound
them together ; and now even this was broken, and he was dead.
Dead ! the irrevocable, the fatal word, before which all other
griefs seem so trifling, all other breaches so easily repaired, all
other sorrows so open to consolation. Never, never to see him
more ! It was a dull, stony, stupifying sensation. She was
so glad, so thankful she had told him all before he went away.
There was no shame now, no self-abasement, no womanly pride
to come between her and the loved one in his cold grave : and
Mary's tears welled up afresh, thick and hot, and the band that
seemed to have compressed her heart to suffocation grew looser,
and she rose from her knees with a firm resolve in her brain, and
a giant's strength growing up in her steadfast will to struggle and
endure.

CHAPTER X.

' ANCILLÆ PUDORIS.'

GRACE ALLONBY inhabited a pretty little room overlooking the
terrace we have so often mentioned, and stored with the many
knick-knacks that, even in the days of which we write, were
affected by young ladies to ' keep them beautiful, and leave them
neat.' Albeit the act of prying into such a boudoir may be
deemed an impertinence, yet must we claim the historian's privilege to be at all times in all places, and take a peep at Grace
undergoing the various tortures of the toilet at the hands of her
handmaid Faith, a pretty Puritan, whose duties as the *soubrette* of
a Cavalier's daughter are continually at variance with her conscientious opinions—a mental conflict which imparts to that
damsel's conversation and general character a degree of acidity
foreign to her real nature. She is combing and brushing her
lady's hair with merciless energy, and those long dark masses fall
over the white neck and bosom with a luxuriance of which the
maid is prouder than her mistress. Yet is she reflecting even
now, while with a turn of her skilful hand she adjusts a jetty
ringlet, holding the comb meanwhile between her teeth, how the
crowning beauty of Absalom was a delusion and a snare ; and
how, though a woman may be permitted to retain her abundant

tresses, the long love-locks of the Cavaliers *must* be wicked, they are so very becoming.

'Is the young officer from Newbury going away to-day, Mistress Grace, or doth he remain all night?' asks Faith, with an air and accent of the utmost simplicity.

It is a strange coincidence, but Grace is thinking exactly the same thing. A shower of ringlets falls between her face and the mirror, so she blushes under them unseen; nevertheless her neck and shoulders crimson visibly, and Faith, although a Puritan, deduces her own conclusions. Like a thorough waiting-maid, however, she proceeds, without pausing for an answer—

'He is a likely young gentleman enough; of a fair countenance, and a gallant bearing too, as becomes a soldier. He cannot be as bad as the rest of them, Mistress Grace, or he would hardly have left them by his own desire to come here to our quiet place, where he knows nobody and can care for nobody.'

'He goes where he is ordered, Faith,' replies Grace, very quietly, and with a certain air of enforced dignity; 'he is a brave and good officer,' she adds, her voice trembling a little, 'and has been sent here with despatches by the King himself.'

'I know what I know,' resumes Faith, with some asperity. 'When it came to a question of who was to leave the army, and ride alone—leastways, him and his servant—through the ranks of the rebels, that's to say the Parliamentarians' (Faith catches herself up rapidly as she recollects her political and religious principles), 'facing dangers and what not, to come here to Boughton: —nothing would serve Captain Bosville—for a captain he is and will be when he gets his due, as them that knows and told me is not misinformed—nothing would serve him but down he goes on his knees before the King—I wonder he wasn't ashamed to do it; and says he, "Your Majesty," says he, "where the treasure is there will the heart be also; and my sorrel," says he—that's the one he rode here that's got two fore-shoes off now in the great stable—"my sorrel can do the distance in half the time of e'er another in your Majesty's army; and my servant," says he— that's good Master Dymocke, a worthy man and a right thinker, though backsliding for the time—"my servant knows the ways by track and ford, and none other; and we crave leave to enter upon the duty, and so to kiss your Majesty's hand, and God be with you all." And with that,' continued Faith, now almost breathless, 'they up and saddled, and never drew rein till they rode in at our great gates, and as Master Dymocke says, "faint heart never won fair lady," and "the labourer is worthy of his hire."'

Grace listens well pleased to this somewhat improbable story; drop by drop the poison is stealing gently into her veins. It is sweet to hear his name already; soon it will be sweet to talk of him even to an uninterested listener; then will come blushes and confusion, and a strange wild thrill of pleasure; and then the reckoning must be paid for happiness thus taken up at interest. The lonely hours, the weary days, the sore heart, and the wan face, that never blushes now, but only contracts with a sickly smile and turns whiter than before. Is not this the course of ninety-nine love-tales out of a hundred? Poor fools! wasting your treasure for that which is not bread.

But Grace is busy fastening a rose into her bodice, and Faith is still training the long tresses into two bewitching curls.

'They can't go to-night, Mistress Grace,' says the latter, answering her previous question for herself. 'After such a ride as that, both man and beast are entitled to rest and refreshment, as Master Dymocke says; and moreover, there's one of them as wouldn't be dragged from here by wild-horses except his duty for the King required him. Poor blinded creature! I know what I know.'

'And is it the master or the man that is so wedded to a place he has only seen twice in his life?' asks Grace, half amused in spite of herself, although her heart is beating somewhat faster than usual. Faith is at once overcome by an access of propriety.

'Oh, madam,' she replies, 'it is not for me to make free with the young gentleman's thoughts; and as for Master Dymocke, though a worthy man and a personable, his gravity and his experience puts him beyond all such vanities. Only there's some talk of their staying here for a convoy and a guard to take us all on to Oxford, where may we be preserved from the temptations of a Court!' adds Faith, piously. 'And now, madam,' she concludes, with a finishing twist to the curls and a toss of her own head, 'I have made a clean breast of it; I have told you all I know, and of what may come of it, whether for good or for evil, I wash my hands.'

With which solemn admonition Faith folds up her lady's things, smoothing them into squares with unusual accuracy and precision. She is evidently waiting to be further questioned, but in this she is disappointed, for Grace Allonby is in more hurry than common to attend upon her kinsman downstairs; and it is with trembling steps, and breath coming quick and short that she proceeds to the great hall, where she already hears the voices of Lord Vaux and his lately arrived guest.

Captain Bosville, as we must call him now—for Faith's information, however obtained, is perfectly correct, and his captain's commission is already made out and signed by the Sovereign— has performed an elaborate toilet, and one that even less prejudiced eyes than those of Grace Allonby would pronounce to be most becoming. His long love-locks, curled and perfumed with the greatest care, droop over a point-lace collar, fitting high and close around the throat, but falling back in dazzling width over his broad shoulders. His velvet doublet, richly embroidered, and fastened down the front with tags and loops of gold, is slashed at the sleeves, so as to display the fine texture of his cambric garment underneath, and fitting tightly over the hands, admits of the broad wristbands being turned back so as to exhibit the whiteness and symmetry of those members to the greatest advantage. A ruby clasp fastens his doublet at the throat, a fellow stone, of equal size and radiance, is set in the pommel of his sword. These, too, will ere long be converted into men and horses for King Charles; meantime they are very dazzling, very beautiful, and very useless. A wide rustling scarf, stiff with embroidery, crosses his breast, and is gathered into a huge knot over his left hip, where it meets the broad baldric that sustains his long straight sword. His lower man is clothed in loose velvet pantaloons, reaching somewhat below the knee, to meet the wide wrinkled riding-boots, pushed half-way down the leg, and forming with their high heels and heavy massive spurs a somewhat warlike termination to the festive air betrayed in the rest of his costume. Add to all this a handsome face, embrowned by exercise, and wearing the keen forcible expression which all men of action insensibly acquire, and we arrive at a general effect, which might indeed make sad havoc in a heart already predisposed to look upon it with favour and affection.

Nor was Grace Allonby thrust upon an unequal war unfurnished with those weapons, both offensive and defensive, which women know how to use so skilfully. In the days of the first Charles a lady's dress much resembled that of the present era. There was the same display of confident beauty above, the same voluminous series of defences below, as though the attack must be provoked only to be repelled. There was the same costly taste for jewellery, the same magnificence of texture and gorgeousness of hue in silks and satins—nay, the very arms, bared nearly to the elbow, were overhung by a cloudy, graceful fabric of muslin or lace, or whatever it is which suits so well with a white skin, a handsome hand, and a rich bracelet, and which is to-day so much affected by those who are possessed of any or all of these advantages. Grace Allonby's light girlish figure borrowed a graceful dignity from the ample folds of the heavy brocade she wore—low at the bosom, and descending to a peak or stomacher, the upper part of the body was distinctly and beautifully defined ; whilst the spreading skirt, falling in massive plaits from her slender waist, added that majestic sweep and volume which ladies consider so necessary to complete the finish of their costume. Her hair, undisfigured by powder, which had not yet come into use, curled in graceful clusters over her ivory forehead, and did Faith credit for the manner in which she had dressed and disposed it. The girl wore a double row of pearls tight round her neck, and pearl bracelets round her wrists. Sir Giles had not fought and foraged many a long year without obtaining some valuables to bestow upon his darling ; and those very pearls were a gift from lavish and ill-judging King Jamie for a deed that had required a silent tongue, a ready hand, and a heart stouter than most men possessed. So Sir Giles was asked to choose his reward, and he chose the casket of pearls lying on the trembling monarch's table, to store them up for his little Gracey. And the King gave them frankly, and regretted them a moment afterwards ; but nevertheless, before all was done, they found their way back again to the service of the Stuarts.

So Humphrey Bosville and Grace Allonby were as well-looking a couple as you shall see in a summer's day ; and we may be sure the young lady was satisfied with their joint appearance, and laughed and talked with a gaiety foreign to her usually reserved and quiet demeanour. The Cavalier, on the contrary, was absent and distracted ; glancing uneasily at the door, and looking about him with wandering eyes, as though he missed some accustomed face : by degrees the coldness of his manner threw a damp over the rest of the party. Grace began to feel chilled and disappointed, and withdrew into herself. Lord Vaux was distressed and unhappy at the news of the late action, and the price which a victory had cost. The three sat silent and moody ; and the afternoon, to which poor Grace had so looked forward during her toilet, and which had promised to be so bright and sunshiny, terminated, as such antici-pated hours too often terminate, in clouds and disappointment.

But it does not follow that because there are pique and vapours in the parlour, loud laugh and broad jest and noisy conversation should be wanting in the hall. There was no lack at Boughton of nut-brown ale brewed of the strongest, with which Lord Vaux's retainers had no objection to make merry whenever occasion offered. Such an opportunity as the present could not of course be suffered to pass over without an unusual amount of wassailing, a double health to the King, and many hearty pledges to worthy Master Dymocke, who, in his capacity of ambassador extraordinary from the army, and first accredited messenger with the news of victory, received all the compliments and congratulations poured upon him as no more than his due, and replied to the pledges of his admirers with a fervent cordiality that brought an unwonted colour to his cheek, and lustre to his eye. Not that Master Dymocke was ever known to succumb to the potent influence of John Barleycorn, or to lose the presence of mind and philosophical equanimity on which he prided himself: nothing of the kind; his was one of those phlegmatic temperaments derived from the Saxon element in our constitutions, which, partaking of the nature of a sponge, like that porous substance, become only the more dense and weighty the more liquid you pour into them. Dymocke had already pledged the steward in many a foaming horn, had emptied a beaker with the falconer in answer to that worthy's compliments and good wishes, had drunk to all the serving-men in turn, measure for measure and courtesy for courtesy, nor had shrunk from an extraordinary and overflowing bumper to the health of the king— and still his speech was unfaltering, and his head clear. Nay, more; although by general consent allowed to have all the conversation to himself—although he had told the story of the fight in all its different versions over and over again, each time long before the conclusion becoming the hero of his own tale, he had yet resisted the temptation of *talking* himself drunk; and it was with a steady foot and a deportment more solemn than ordinary, that he rose from the hall-board to betake himself to the stable, there, like a true soldier, to look after his own and his master's steeds.

As he fed and watered them, and littered them carefully down, and patted the good animals, of which none but a sportsman, or a soldier, or a highwayman, none but he whose life depends upon the merits of his horse, knows the real value, they seemed to be sleeker and fresher than usual, less wearied with their long journey, smoother in their coats, brighter in their eyes, and cooler in their legs, than was customary. Many healths conscientiously emptied are apt to have this effect of enhancing the good qualities of our possessions, and Dymocke, as he departed from the stable and proceeded towards the house, was in that frame of mind which sees everything in its brightest hues, and in which our weaknesses— if weaknesses we chance to have—are, as was once observed by an Irishman, at the strongest. Now, Dymocke, though an elderly man, or what he would himself have called in the prime of life, was, as we have already stated, still a bachelor, and like all other bachelors, of whatever age, an admirer of the fair. Marriage is somewhat apt to damp the woman-worship which sits so well upon the stronger sex, more's the pity ! but Hugh being still unmarried, was more susceptible to the fascinations of beauty than would have been supposed by those who only contemplated his lean austere-looking face, and were not aware that, like a rough and wrinkled walnut, he was kernel all through. It was therefore with a grim smile, and a sensation entirely pleasurable, that he met the pretty Puritan Faith in the outer court, and assisted that good-looking damsel to carry a certain ponderous clothes-basket from the washing-green into the house. Ladies'-maids were not above hard work in the seventeenth century, and had not as yet arrived at the pitch of refinement now so essential to the dignity of the *second table*; and so much in character with low evening dresses, white gloves, satin shoes, and short whist.

Faith, too, although a Puritan, had no objection to make the most of those personal charms with which she was blessed by nature. Though her hair was prudishly gathered beneath a little lace cap, it was sleek and glossy as the plumage of a bird. Her gown, though sad-coloured in hue, and coarse in texture, fitted her full shape with coquettish accuracy, and was pulled through the pocket-holes so as to display her bright stuff petticoat to the greatest advantage. Her trim ankles were covered by the tightest and best fitting of scarlet hose, and her high-heeled shoes protected a pair of neat little feet that many a well-born lady might have envied. She looked very nice, and Hugh Dymocke was thoroughly convinced of the fact, so it was no unpleasant reflection to remember that he was not immediately about to pursue his journey, and that the horses he had just been caring for would reap the full benefits of the comfortable stable in which they were housed. He was a grave man, and he said as much with a staid air, balancing the clothes-basket the while, and interposing his long person between the admiring damsel and her destination. Faith was nothing loth, too, for a chat; like all women, she was a hero-worshipper, and were not Bosville and his domestic heroes for the nonce ? but womanlike, she of course dissembled her gratification, and assumed the offensive.

'The sooner the better, Master Dymocke,' observed this seductive damsel, pertly, in allusion to the departure of her solemn admirer, which he informed her was to be postponed *sine die*. 'Soldiers only hinder work ; and I've got my young lady's things to attend to, and no time to stand here gossiping with you. Not but what you're a well-informed man, and a sober, Master Dymocke, and too good for your evil trade, which is only murder in disguise, and for your comrades, which is men of Belial, and miserable sinners, one worse than another.'

' By your leave, good Mistress Faith,' answered Dymocke, ' this is a subject I should be happy to explain to you, and one on which, with your good will, I shall enter during our journey— for you and I are to be fellow-travellers, as I understand—for our mutual improvement and advantage.'

' Journey, good lack ! ' exclaimed the waiting-maid, clasping her hands in well-feigned astonishment ; ' and where be you about to take me, Master Dymocke, and have you the King's authority to do what you will with us all ?   Forsooth, and I have a mind of my own, as you shall shortly find out ! '

' His gracious Majesty,' replied Dymocke, with the utmost gravity, ' when he thought fit to despatch myself and Captain Bosville on this important duty, confided to me, through an old friend of my own, now a yeoman in his guard, that I was to take charge of the ladies of this family, doubtless accompanied by their kinsman, Lord Vaux, to his right royal Court at Oxford, where I shall make it my duty to place ye in safety and good keeping till these troublous times be overpast.'

' And were *you* entrusted with the charge of my young lady as well as myself, Master Dymocke ? ' asked Faith with extreme *naïveté*, ' or was there no word of the captain, your master, in these marchings and countermarchings, of which you soldiers make so little account ? '

' My master's youth and inexperience in the ways of woman-kind would make him a bad guide without myself to counsel and assist him,' was the reply ; ' but take comfort, Mistress Faith, for your lady's sake, at least.   The lad is a good lad, and accompanies us to the Court.'

' And well pleased my lady will be ! ' burst out Faith, clapping her hands.   ' And a sweet pretty couple they make as does one's heart good to see.   A soldier and a soldier's daughter.   Well, it's a bad trade, but " like will to like," Master Dymocke.   Good lack ! it is all vanity.'

' Like will to like, as you observe, and it *is* vanity,' replied Dymocke, without moving a muscle of his countenance ; but the clothes-basket had got by this time set on end in the narrow passage they were just entering ; and there seemed to be some difficulty, and a good deal of shuffling of feet ere Faith could get past the obstacle.   When she did succeed, however, in effecting this manœuvre, she passed the back of her hand across her mouth, and set her cap to rights in a somewhat flurried manner, strongly in contrast with the staid demeanour from which Dymocke never wavered an instant. The latter was something of a herbalist, and it is probable that he had been practically impressing on her the botanical fact, ' that the gorse is in bloom the whole year round.'

CHAPTER XI.

MERTON COLLEGE.

OLD OXFORD never looked more picturesque and beautiful than late on an autumnal evening of the year of Grace 1643, when its spires and towers, its stately halls and splendid colleges, formed the court of an unfortunate king, and a refuge for the flower of England's aristocracy. The western sky, a-flame with the departing glories of a gorgeous sunset, tinged with a crimson glow the domes and pinnacles of those stately edifices looming gigantic in the dim haze of evening, already creeping on. Here and there a light twinkling through the gloom shone out starlike over the porch of some lodging where the noble of a hundred manors and a score of castles was content to take up his abode, or from some window where high-born dames, flowers and ornaments of the English court, now looked down like caged birds from their aviary over the busy street below. Groups of cavaliers, warlike retainers, peaceful citizens, grave and reverend churchmen, soldiers trained to war, and soldiers armed for the first time, from loyalty or necessity, filled the town to overflowing. Scarfs and feathers waved and fluttered, spurs jingled, brocades rustled, and steel clanked in the once peaceful resort of study and the arts. The clatter of troop-horses, the ring of the smithy, the joyous peal of the trumpet-call, and the ready chorus of reckless voices shouting some Cavalier ditty, mingled strangely with the solemn swell of an organ in a neighbouring chapel, with the toll of a death-bell from a distant cathedral tower. Stanch in her loyalty to the last, the old University town had willingly outraged all her own habits of discipline and decorum for the sake of her king, as she afterwards mortgaged her revenues and pawned her plate in the same failing cause. She was now filled to overflowing, for the Queen, accompanied by her own separate and special court, had lately joined her husband in the only refuge left to them, and still the

Cavaliers were pouring in to offer their homage and their swords to the devoted monarch.

A party on horseback have just arrived, and are alighting at the door of the lodging already provided for them. They are dusty and travel-stained, as though they had come a considerable distance, and the old man, clad in a dark sober dress, who rides at their head, seems weary and ill at ease. Lord Vaux would fain rest from his labours, and be allowed to stay quietly at home. Not so Grace Allonby, whom Bosville assists from her horse and places in her father's arms, for Sir Giles, safe and sound, smiling and unscathed, is waiting to receive his daughter, and thanks Humphrey for the care he has taken of her, and greets them all, including Faith and Dymocke, with his usual soldier-like cordiality. Grace is delighted with the bustle of her arrival as she has been pleased with the events of her journey. All is new to her, and there is a varnish over everything she sees just now, which brings it out in its brightest colours. She pats the sorrel with a grateful smile as she wishes its owner good-bye. He has performed his duty, and must take his leave for his own quarters, but whilst they inhabit the same town the chances are that they will often meet again. He shakes hands with her cordially, and looks straight into her face with his honest hazel eyes; but when in turn he lifts Mary Cave off her horse, who has been riding somewhat in the rear, those eyes are averted and downcast, his colour comes and goes, and though he lingers long over the pressure of that hand offered so frankly and would fain put it to his lips, he releases it abruptly, and walks away like a man in a dream.

Honest Dymocke, with a mysterious grin, whispers Faith; and the waiting-maid, who is convinced she has won a convert, bids him farewell with a warmth which nothing apparently but the publicity of the occasion tones down to the necessary degree of reserve and decorum. Our sedate friend has clearly made a conquest, but our business is at present with his master.

Humphrey Bosville strides absently up the street, and revolves in his own mind the events of the last few weeks, and the change that has come over him. He ruminates long and earnestly on one of the companions of his late journey. With the one-sided sharp-sightedness of love, he has totally ignored that which any other but himself must have detected, the interest he has created in the gentle heart of Grace Allonby; but he has keenly felt that in Mary Cave's thoughts there are depths which he has never sounded, aspirations in which he has no share, regrets which he is powerless to console. She has been charming and winning in her manner towards him, as it is her nature to charm and win all mankind ; she has vouchsafed both himself and the sorrel far more attention than he had any right to expect ; and yet there was a something with which he was discontented—a want somewhere unfulfilled, a longing unsatisfied. It worried him—it goaded him ; manlike, it made him think about her all the more.

As he strode moodily up the street a hand was laid upon his shoulder, and Effingham, paler and sterner than ever, stood before him : those wild eager eyes looked kindly as was their wont upon his comrade.

'Welcome, young one,' said George, in his deep stern tones ; ' welcome to the city of the plain ! If ten righteous men could have averted the doom from Sodom, it may be that one honest heart can save Oxford. I have looked for it here in vain, unless you, Humphrey, have bought it with you.'

Bosville returned his greeting warmly, and questioned him eagerly as to the numbers and prospects of the Cavaliers. Effingham's answers showed the desponding view which he at least entertained of the success of his party. ' It is a sinking ship, Humphrey,' said he, in a low melancholy voice, ' and the crew are drugging themselves into apathy before they are engulfed in the waves. With every wound of our bleeding country gaping afresh, nothing is thought of here but riot and wassailing, dicing and drinking, and masking and mumming, and the Frenchwomen dancing over the ruins of her husband's kingdom and the death of its bravest supporters, even as the daughter of Herodias danced to the destruction of John the Baptist. Oh, it is a sickening struggle, and we are fighting in a wrong cause ! Day by day the conviction grows stronger in my mind ; day by day I feel that I am acting against my conscience and to the loss of my own soul! Can such men as Goring and Wilmot and Lunsford be on the side of truth ? Will God prosper the cause of a faithless wife, with her bevy of minions, such as Holland and Jermyn and Digby ? Shall good men strive in the battle, and toil in the march, and leave home and duties and peril their lands and lives, nay, their very salvation, to be bought and sold by a painted traitress like Carlisle ? Must we have two Courts, forsooth, one opposed to the other ? and shall we serve both to be rewarded by neither, and give our all to a master who is himself subjected to the Jezebel of our day ? Verily, " a house divided against itself shall not stand," and I am sick and weary of it, and would fain that it was over. But judge for yourself, Humphrey, by what you will see to-night. The Queen holds her accustomed reception at Merton

College. You will attend, as in duty bound, to kiss her hand,
after so gallantly affording a convoy to these ladies who have
come to join her court. Judge for yourself, and may God give
you clearsightedness to choose the right path.' With these words
Effingham turned abruptly from his friend and strode rapidly
away.

But Humphrey was torn by none of these doubts and misgivings as to the side which he had adopted in the great struggle of
the day. He was a true Cavalier, and a characteristic type of the
party to which he belonged. All the enthusiasm of a chivalrous
nature was enlisted on behalf of the unfortunate monarch and of
his beautiful and fascinating Queen. All the veneration which
prevailed strongly in his disposition prompted him to reverence
the old sentiments of loyalty in which he had been brought up,
the *prestige* of a crown for which his ancestors had ever been ready
to suffer and to die. What mattered it to him that Goring was a
profligate and Lunsford a mercenary ? The reckless prodigality
of the one and the determined bravery of the other shed a halo
even over their worst deeds, and he could not in his heart entirely
repudiate the dashing courage so akin to his own, which checked
at no obstacle and hesitated for no results. If Jermyn was an
intriguer, and Holland, with his handsome face, a mass of duplicity, and Digby a most unworthy successor to the true and
generous Falkland, there was a charm in their polished kindly
manners, a dignity and chivalrous grace in their bearing, that
forbade his youthful admiration from judging them too harshly ;
and even if Henrietta had sacrificed her husband's interests to her
own caprices, had given him the most injudicious advice at the
worst possible time, and had proved at all junctures and under
all circumstances a clog round his neck and a difficulty in his
path, was it for him to judge one who united the charms of a
woman to the dignity of a Queen, who, with the ready tact of her
nature, had already won his heart at a review of Colepepper's
brigade by a judicious compliment to his own horsemanship and
the beauty of the sorrel he bestrode ? Above all, was not the idol
of his heart a stanch Cavalier—a partisan, ready and willing to
make any and every sacrifice for the royal cause ? Had not many
a sentiment of loyalty dropped from her in chance conversation
during their journey, and been garnered up in his heart as we
garner up alone the words of those we love. They sink deeply,
and we ponder on them long and earnestly. God help us ! we
forget them never in a lifetime.

So Mary Cave being a Cavalier, of course Humphrey Bosville

was a Cavalier too (there are reasons for political as well as for
other sentiments), and so it was but natural that he should don
his most magnificent attire, and present himself at Merton College
to pay his homage to his Queen. Sir Giles and Grace Allonby
would surely be there, and it was probable that Mary, notwithstanding the deep and bitter grief under which he could not but
see she was labouring, would accompany her kinsfolk to the
Court.

So his heart beat quicker than it had ever done in action, when
he found himself pacing through the double rank of guards,
furnished in rotation by the noblemen about the Court, who lined
the passages and entrance of Merton College, and we think that as
he entered the crowded reception-rooms it would have been almost
a relief not to have been aware, as he intuitively was, of the presence of his ladye-love.

It was indeed a gay and gorgeous assemblage, and could not
fail to strike even one so preoccupied as Bosville with interest and
admiration. Like a diamond set in a circle of precious stones,
Henrietta herself formed the centre of the sparkling throng, and
cast her brilliance on all around, as, with the wit for which she
was so remarkable, she scattered amongst her courtiers those
graceful nothings which cost so little, and yet buy so much.
Small in person, with fairy feet and beautifully formed hands and
arms, with radiant black eyes and delicate features, it was not
difficult to understand the fascination which she exercised over
the most loving and devoted husband that ever wore a crown ;
nor were the liveliness of her manners, and the toss of her small
well-shaped head, out of keeping with the *piquante* and somewhat
theatrical character of her beauty. Even as Bosville entered, she
had taken Lord Holland aside into a window, and by the well-
pleased expression which pervaded the handsome face of the
courtier, it was obvious that, not only was he flattered by the
attention, but that he was yielding most unreservedly to the request, whatever it might be, of his beautiful Sovereign.

Harry Jermyn stood by, apparently not too well pleased
Handsome Harry Jermyn, who would never have been distinguished by that epithet had he not been a Queen's minion, certainly did not at this moment show to advantage, a threatening
scowl contracting his features, and a paleness, more perhaps the
result of dissipation than ill-health, overspreading his somewhat
wasted face. A woman's tact saw the pain that a woman's pity
was too ready to alleviate, and a woman's wit was at no loss for
an excuse to break up the interview with Holland, and release

her favourite servant from his uneasiness. Beckoning him to her
side with a kind smile, of which she knew well the power, she
pointed to Bosville, who had just entered the presence-chamber,
and bid him inquire the name of the young Cavalier. 'I remember his face,' she said, fastening her black eyes on Jermyn,
'as I never forget a face that pleases me, and I will have him
brought up and presented to me. I will be personally acquainted
with all my comrades, for am not I too a soldier myself?' And
she pointed with her little hand, and laughed her sweet silvery
laugh, and Harry Jermyn looked as if the sun was shining once
again for him like the rest of the world.

So Humphrey was led up to the Queen, and kissed her hand,
and performed his obeisance, and Henrietta made a graceful
allusion to the conduct of his brigade at Newbury, and bantered
him on 'his new character,' as she was pleased to term it, of a
'Squire of Dames,' and beckoning to Mary Cave, bid her reward
her guardian for the care he had taken of her, by now placing
him *au fait* to all the gossip of the Court, 'in which no one is
better versed than thyself, *méchante Marie*,' added the Queen,
and so turned away to her own intrigues and her own devices,
having made at least one heart happy amongst her courtiers, and
bought its life-long devotion at the price of a little ready tact and
a few light words.

Mary could not but be sensible of the influence she was rapidly
obtaining over the young Cavalier captain. Women are usually
sufficiently quick-sighted in these matters, and she was no exception in this respect to the rest of her sex. Grieved and unhappy
as she now was, her every hope destroyed, and the light of her
life, as she felt, darkened for ever, there was yet something soothing and consolatory in the considerate and unselfish devotion of
this brave enthusiastic nature. She never considered that what
was 'sport to her' might be 'death to him;' that whilst she was
merely leaning on him, as it were, for a temporary support, lulled
and flattered by the romantic adoration which she felt she had
inspired, *he* might be twining round his heart a thousand links of
that golden chain which, when it is torn away, carries with it the
lacerated fragments of the treasure it enclosed, might be anchor-
ing all his trust and all his happiness on a dream, to wake from
which might be a life's misery, might even be madness or death.
'Children and fools,' saith the proverb, 'should not meddle with
edge-tools.' Are not all mankind more or less children, rather
more than less fools? Why will they persist in cutting their own
fingers; always ready to run the risk, however averse to paying

the penalty ? Mary thought but little of these things. If such a reflection did cross her mind, she saw in her victim a glorious instrument of the Cause—the Cause for which Falkland had died, the Cause to which she had vowed her life, her energies, her all ! In the intoxicating atmosphere of a Court, amongst all the glitter of rank, and fame, and beauty, it seemed so natural to be wooed and idolised, so pleasant to possess the charm that subjugates all mankind, so noble to use it for a patriotic cause. They were placed in the embrasure of a window, somewhat apart from the throng. She was seated with her head resting on one rounded arm, over which a ringlet of her nut-brown hair fell to the dimpled elbow ; he was standing by her side leaning over her, and trembling in every fibre to the notes of her silvery voice ; he, a stout swordsman, a gallant soldier, a young, strong, hearty man, and yet his cheek paled, and he withdrew his gaze every time she lifted her soft blue eyes to his face.

'We cannot fail,' she said, 'with such men as these on our side. See, Captain Bosville, look around you, the noblest names in England are gathered here to-night, and there is not one of them that will not risk his *all*, ay, and lose it too, contentedly, for the King. You men are strangely prejudiced,' she added, looking up at him with a smile, ' but you are very devoted to your prejudices ; if women are accused of being *wilful*, commend me at least to a man for *obstinacy* ! '

' And does not perseverance deserve to be rewarded ? ' asked he, with a somewhat faltering voice. ' If a man will devote himself body and soul, heart and energy, to the attainment of any one object, ought he not to prosper ? Does he not always succeed ? '

' Generally, if he is sufficiently obstinate,' answered Mary, with a laugh, at which her companion's face brightened into a pleasant smile. ' But self-devotion is indeed the noblest quality of a man. If there is one I admire more than all the rest of the world, it is he who can propose to himself a glorious end and aim in life, and who can strive for it through all obstacles, whatever be the danger, whatever the difficulty ; who never takes his eyes from off the goal, and who if he dies in the pursuit, at least dies stanch and unconquered to the last ! '

' And such a one,' exclaimed Bosville, with flashing eyes and quivering lip, ' such a one could command your admiration, could win your love ? '

' I said not that, Captain Bosville,' she replied, but her countenance never changed colour, and her eye never drooped, as it would once have done at words like these. He might have

G

known then that she did not love him, that hers was the master-mind of the two; but he was blind, as those are always blind, who see through the glasses of their own wilful affections. 'I said not that, but yet I may say that I never could care for one who lacked these qualities, and that if ever I could give my heart away, it would be to one such as I have described.' She sighed heavily while she spoke, and turned her head away. He did not hear the sigh, his blood was boiling, and his brain confused. He did not see the cold, rigid face of the dead at Newbury; the face that was haunting his fair companion day by day; he did not see another sweet pale face looking at him from her father's side in the very presence-chamber, singling him out from amongst the crowd of courtly gallants and beauteous dames, from the mass of silks and satins, and rustling brocade and flashing jewellery; a pale sweet face, with a mournful smile and a reproachful expression in its dark, fawn-like eyes. No, he had thoughts but for one, and the fingers that closed upon his sword-hilt were white with the pressure of his grasp, as he spoke almost in a whisper.

'And could such lifelong devotion win you, Mary, at the last? Will you accept life and fortune, and all, to give in return but one little word, one word of kindness, encouragement, and hope?'

She smiled sweetly up at him; how could she do otherwise? She must have been more or less than woman not to feel at least gratified by such admiration as his, and yet it was the smile of pity rather than affection, such a smile as wreathes the lips of those who have lived out their life of passion here.

'Hush,' she said, 'Captain Bosville. Loyalty before all; the King! the King!'

Even as she spoke a silence succeeded to the rustling of dresses and the hum of voices that had hitherto pervaded the presence-chamber, and a lane, formed by the bowing crowd, and extending from the large folding-doors up to the Queen herself, heralded the approach of royalty. A lane formed of the noblest and the best-born in England, of whom not one man or woman that bent the head in loyal reverence, but would have laid that head willingly to rest in the field, or forfeit it on the scaffold, for the sake of the unfortunate monarch who now paced up the hall, returning the obeisance of his subjects with the dignified and melancholy sweetness which never, even in his worst misfortunes, for an instant deserted him.

Bosville was not familiar with the person of his Sovereign; he had now an opportunity of studying the aspect of that man—a mere man like himself, after all, whose rank invested him with a magical interest that commanded the fortunes and the lives of his subjects. Charles bore on his whole exterior the impress of his character—nay, more—to a fanciful observer there was something in his countenance and manners that seemed to presage misfortune. Of no stately presence, he had yet a well-knit and graceful figure, hardened and trained into activity by those sports and exercises in which he had acquired no mean proficiency. Few of his subjects could vie with their monarch in his younger days at the games of balloon, rackets, or tennis; could handle the sword more skilfully, or ride ' the great horse ' with fairer grace and management; even at middle age, despite a trifling and scarcely perceptible malformation of the limbs, his pedestrian powers were such as to inconvenience to a great extent those dutiful courtiers who were compelled to keep pace with him in his walks, and although in his childhood of a weakly constitution, he had acquired before he grew up a firm and vigorous *physique* that was capable of sustaining, as he afterwards proved repeatedly in his unfortunate career, not only the extremes of bodily fatigue and hardship, but what is infinitely more hard to bear, the gnawing and destructive anxieties of daily failure and disappointment. But in Charles's face a physiognomist would too surely have discovered the signs of those mixed qualities which rendered him the most ill-fated of monarchs as he was the most amiable of men. There was ideality without comprehensiveness in the high narrow forehead, there was vacillation in the arched and elevated eyebrow, the full, well-cut eye was clear, and open, and beautiful, but its expression was dreamy and abstracted, the gaze of a sage, a philosopher, or a devotee, not the quick eager glance of a man of action and resource. His other features were well-formed and regular, but the upper lip was somewhat too curled and full for masculine beauty, whilst the jaw lacked that expression of power and firmness which is never absent 'from the face of a truly great man. His long, dark locks curling down upon his shoulders, his bushy moustache and pointed beard, added to the pleasing yet melancholy expression of his countenance, and with his rich attire, his magnificent lace collar, and jewelled ' George ' hanging about his neck, perfected the.ideal of a chivalrous high-minded monarch, who was worthy of the position he occupied and the devotion he commanded, who was no unfit centre around which grouped themselves the proudest, the bravest, the noblest, the most enthusiastic aristocracy that ever failed to save a sovereign.

They were thronging about him now. The chivalrous and princely Newcastle, who lavished fortunes for his monarch's entertainment as ungrudgingly as he poured forth his blood in his service; splendid in his apparel, stately in his person, magnificent in his bearing, a true specimen of the English nobleman ; a Paladin in the field, a *grand seigneur* in the drawing-room, kindly, and frank, and hearty in each ; wooing the Muses with no contemptible success during the intervals of his eventful career, and charging the Parliamentary troopers with a resolute energy that made the ' silken general,' as they were pleased to term him, the terror of all. Respected by the Prince of Wales, whose boyhood had been committed to his care, trusted by the Queen, who found in him all those noble sentiments she most admired and looked for in vain amongst her other favourites, and beloved by Charles himself, who recognised in him the more splendid qualities of Buckingham without Buckingham's selfishness, recklessness, and Protean vacillation of character. And we are best acquainted with Newcastle now as the author of a folio book upon horsemanship !

The scientific Leicester, skilled in classic lore, and a better mathematician than a soldier, as indeed the certainty of results exacted by the one is far removed from the haphazard readiness of resource indispensable to the other. Somewhat jealous, it may be, and displeased that his appointment to the Lieutenancy of Ireland had been cancelled, yet faithful in his heart to his Sovereign, and bearing next that heart a panacea for all bitterness and ill-feeling in a letter from his loving Countess, whose devoted attachment to the Earl was as proverbial in a Court more notorious for complicated intrigue than conjugal fidelity, as was that of the celebrated lady whose lord was alone qualified to drink out of the ' cup of gold ' which stood on King Arthur's round table, and which, if we are to believe the scandal of the old romances, spilt its contents over every beard save that of Caradoc, so rare in those days was the crown which virtuous women placed upon the brows of their husbands.

The courtly Wilmot, a professed wit, a finished gentleman, addicted to wine and debauchery, but a cool and scientific soldier, continually labouring under some imputation against his courage, which he was as continually wiping out by daring strategy and brilliant achievements. Looked upon with dislike by the Court, which yet feared him for the sting of his ready tongue, and mistrusted by the King, who nevertheless employed him on the most important duties, he seemed to rely solely on himself; and whilst his serene visage and equable demeanour totally repudiated all romance and enthusiasm, the repose and self-confidence of his bearing denoted the man who was all in all to his own require-

ments, *totus teres atque rotundus*, impassable as a Stoic and contented as an Epicurean.

Different indeed from his next neighbour, who was describing
to him, with a vast amount of action and energy, completely
thrown away upon Wilmot's unresponsive apathy, a new-fashioned
handle for that goodly weapon, the pike. Sir Jacob Astley was
no cool philosopher, no sneering cynic, but a warm-hearted,
warm-blooded, bold, hearty, and God-fearing man. A devoted
soldier, an active and judicious officer, a conscientious councillor;
whatever his hand found to do, that did he with all his heart and
all his soul. Threescore winters and more had shed their snows
upon his head, and wherever hard blows were going he had taken
fully his share, yet his eye was bright, his cheek was ruddy, and
his frame was still square and strong. A good conscience is a
wondrous specific for longevity; and who but a soldier with a
good conscience could have offered up Sir Jacob's famous prayer
at the head of his column before the Battle of Edgehill—'Oh
Lord! thou knowest how busy I must be this day; if I forget
thee do not thou forget me. March on, boys!'

Towering over Sir Jacob's grey head, his eagle eye wandering
far away into the distance, looking beyond that courtly web of
silk and satin, and his tall figure resting on his long straight sword,
stood Prince Rupert—the fiery Hotspur of his day, the cavalry
officer whose charge was always victorious, and whose victory
always terminated in defeat; of whom it has been said that he
never failed to win 'his share of the battle,' yet whose success, by
some fatality, invariably led to the discomfiture of his friends.
The active partisan, whose element seemed to be war, and who
had buckled on a sword and ridden side by side with distinguished
generals and fierce troopers at an age when most boys are flying
a kite or trundling a hoop; who, failing employment on land, was
fain to seek bloodshed and fighting at sea, embarking on the duties
of an admiral with the same bold recklessness that had equally
distinguished him at the head of a column of iron-clad cavalry,
or charging with a handful of Cavaliers in his shirt; and who,
when the sea refused to offer him opportunities of distinction, as
the land had long ago failed to give him scope for his ambition,
could sit down contentedly in a peaceful capital, and occupy himself with the gentle resources of chemistry and painting.

His high aquiline features, according so well with a stature
which, though light and sinewy, approached the gigantic, his
broad, clear, restless eye, and his wide, massive brow, shaded as
it was by a profusion of somewhat tangled hair, denoted the man
of courage and action, the gallant spirit that knew no calculation

of odds, the indomitable heart that acknowledged neither failure nor reverse. Sir Jacob had better have been talking to the Prince about his pike handles, for Rupert, like every real soldier, took a lively interest in them, as he had a thorough knowledge of details; but in his heart the old man thought the young one somewhat hot-headed and inexperienced, so he would rather not enter upon a discussion in which he would feel tempted to disagree with his Sovereign's nephew. He had seen him tried too, and he could not but acknowledge that 'the lad,' as he called him, was brave and active, a zealous captain and a shrewd tactician, but he had one fault which elderly men are apt to consider unpardonable in their juniors, although it is a fault which improves every day— he was *too young*.

So Prince Rupert stood musing all alone amongst that brilliant assemblage; gazing, in his mind's eye, on many a scene of rout and confusion, many a fancied skirmish and remembered victory; the broken enemy, the maddened troopers striking right and left with the savage recklessness of fiends; the compact columns of the reserve sweeping up like some strong wave to complete the destruction which has been commenced by its predecessors; the wild hurrah of victory rising loud and stirring above the ringing pistol-shots, and the tramp of squadrons, and the groans of the fallen; the loose chargers with streaming reins, galloping at random here and there; the plumes, and scarfs, and glittering steel of the Cavaliers waving and flashing through the smoke; all the fierce revelry and confusion of the battle he was picturing in his day-dream. Suddenly he started, and turned round to address one after his own heart, to greet him with the frank cordiality peculiar to men of the sword. Sir Ralph Hopton, maimed and disabled, scorched and scarred by the explosion of a powder-barrel at the Battle of Lansdowne, and only just capable of hobbling on crutches to pay his respects to the King, stood close to the Prince's elbow, and the dream of battle vanished, and the reality of warfare became more tangible as the two stanch, keen soldiers plunged into a deep and interesting discussion on the one absorbing interest of their lives.

And again Prince Rupert started, and the colour rose to his high broad forehead, and the eagle eye moved restlessly in its orbit. And to Sir Ralph's question upon the new cavalry formations lately introduced on the Continent, he returned an incoherent answer that hugely astonished the practical soldier; for the Queen, with her bevy of ladies, was moving through the hall; and as she approached the spot where her husband's nephew had stationed himself, one of the fair dames in attendance shot a glance at Prince Rupert that confused him far more than could have done a volley of small-arms; and the beautiful Duchess of Richmond passed on like some fairy vision, and Rupert was restless and uneasy for the rest of the night.

Yes; if the King was surrounded by a band of high-minded and sincere noblemen, ready to risk life and fortune in his cause, the Queen, too, on her side, had provided herself with a bodyguard of beauty, none the less stanch and uncompromising in the politics they espoused, that for push of pike and sweep of swordblade they used the more fatal weapons of grace and fascination with which they were familiar, dissolving alliances with the flutter of a fan, and scattering coalitions with the artillery of a glance. Merry Mrs. Kirke was there with her sparkling eyes and her dimpled smile, passing her jest, somewhat of the broadest, and laughing her laugh, somewhat of the loudest, with the daring freedom and conscious immunity of an acknowledged beauty. There, too, was lovely Lady Isabella Thynne, whose dignity and grace, and sweet romantic charms, were said by the voice of scandal to have made an impression even on the true uxorious heart of Charles himself. That Henrietta felt no jealousy of this dangerous lady, no mistrust in her hold over the affections of her doating husband, may be gathered from the confidence with which she encouraged her about her person, and the opportunities of unreserved intercourse she afforded her with the King. Was the lively Frenchwoman a stranger to this feminine feeling of jealousy ? or was she like Queen Guenever, who was willing to concede the liberty she exacted, and who, lenient

> To human frailty, construed mild,
> Looked upon Lancelot, and smiled?

And there too, in her weeds for her gallant young husband, moved the graceful form of Kate, Lady D'Aubigny, the young and interesting widow, who was weeping for the untimely fate of her chivalrous lord, yet whose witty sallies flashing occasionally through the gloom that overshadowed her, argued her not altogether inconsolable, and who was lending an ear already, with something more than a mere courteous interest, to Hawley's tender whispers and respectful adoration.

And fair 'Mistress Watt' stood by and seemed not to listen, and refrained, with congenial hypocrisy, from what she would have termed the offence of 'spoiling sport.' Pretty Mistress Watt, who had often herself been indebted to such consideration on the part of others, and whose charming face and lively manners and matchless impudence had conferred upon her a station at Court and an influence amongst courtiers to which neither her birth nor her attainments would have entitled her had she simply been demure and virtuous, instead of charming and good-for-nothing.

But of all intriguers of the gentle sex—of all traitresses in love, friendship, and politics—who could compare with the soft, quiet, innocent-looking woman who now stood next the Queen, and to whom Henrietta confided the inmost counsels of her husband, as she did the dearest secrets of her own heart? Lucy, Countess of Carlisle, with her dove-like eyes and her sweet angelic smile, was formed by nature to have deceived the very Serpent that tempted our mother Eve. How madly had ambitious Strafford loved that calm, fair face! how had the harassed statesman, the impeached and fallen minister, rested on the love she had professed for him, as a solace for all his sorrows, a refuge from all his dangers. For her he toiled, for her he was ambitious, for her he was long triumphant—and she betrayed him—first in love, then in politics; betrayed him into the hands of his enemy, and transferred her affections to his destroyer. Who shall say that the bitterest drop in his cup, deserted as he felt himself by his Sovereign, and deceived by his peers, was not poured into it by the hand of the woman he had adored?

Keen were his pangs, but keener far to feel
He nursed the pinion that impelled the steel;
And the same plumage that had warmed his nest,
Now drank the life-drops from his bleeding breast.

So she sacrificed him ruthlessly, and abandoned herself to the caresses of his enemy. And there was something about this woman that could subjugate even a busy voluptuary like Pym, one who combined in his own person the two most hardened of all characters—the professed politician and the confirmed sensualist. He was as devoted to her as his natural organization would allow of his being devoted to anything; and when she had thoroughly won him and subjugated him, and he trusted her, why, she deceived him too. And so she followed out her career of treachery, disloyal as a wife, heartless as a mistress, and false as a friend. Yet of all the ladies about the Court, the Countess of Carlisle had most influence with the Queen, was most conversant with her innermost thoughts, her secret intentions; was the busiest weaver of that web of intrigues and dissimulation in which Henrietta, to do her justice, took as much delight as any Arachne of her sex.

And all this glitter and pageantry, these beautiful women, these noble and distinguished men, passed before the eyes of Humphrey Bosville like a dream. Young as he was, scarcely a thrill of conscious pride shot through him to be recognised and kindly accosted by Prince Rupert as the daring soldier whose value was readily and generously acknowledged by the frank and outspoken Prince. Not an inch higher did he hold his head, to be conscious that amongst all these heroes and warriors he was of them as well as with them; that he, too, had a station and a name, and a chance of distinction that might raise him to a level with the proudest. Nay, when old Colepepper brought him up to the sacred circle of which Majesty itself formed the centre, and with a glow of good-natured gratification on his scarred visage recalled him to the monarch's memory, and Charles pleasantly reminded him of their last meeting at his simple bivouac, the day after Newbury, scarcely a flush of gratified vanity coloured the cheek of the young Cavalier. And no courtier of twenty years' standing could have sustained with a more unmoved air the favouring notice of the King, and the still more confusing glances from the bevy of beauties that surrounded the Queen, and on whom Humphrey's handsome exterior made no unpleasing impression.

'Who is he?' whispered Mr. Hyde to Lady Carlisle, bending his stiff and somewhat pompous figure to approach that dame with the air of a finished gallant—an air the lettered and accomplished historian much affected with indifferent success—an air that somehow is less easily caught by the brotherhood of the pen than those of the sword. 'Who is he, this imperturbable young gentleman, who seems as little affected by his Majesty's condescension as by the glances of your ladyship's dazzling and star-like eyes?'

Lady Carlisle laughed under the skin, but she was civil and conciliatory to all. It was part of her system never to throw a chance away; so she professed her ignorance with a gracious sentence and a sweet smile, and such a glance from the eyes he had praised as sent Mr. Hyde away delighted, and convinced that he had made a conquest. Truly, 'the wisest clerks are not the wisest men.'

And yet Humphrey had his dream too. Was he not young? and is it not the privilege of youth to lay up a store of disappointment for maturity? His dream was of distinction truly, and of laurels to be gathered, and honours to be gained; but it was not selfish distinction; and the honours and the laurels were but to be flung at the feet of another. And then the dream was to have a happy conclusion. Peace, and repose, and happiness he hardly dared to fancy, after he had done his duty and completed his task. A home of Love, and Beauty, and Content; a pair of blue eyes that would always smile kindly upon him—that would always make his heart leap, as it leaped to meet them now. A form that he adored entrusted to his guardianship, sleeping and waking to watch over and care for, and cherish to the end. After that, a purer and holier, a more lasting but not more ardent love, in another and a better world.

Dreams! dreams! Yet of all the dreamers that left Merton College that night—the scheming statesmen, the ambitious warriors, the intriguing courtiers—perhaps Humphrey was the one whose vision most elevated his moral being; whose awakening, unlike that of the others, bitter as it must be, would leave him, if a sadder, at least a wiser and a better man.

CHAPTER XII.

' NIGHT-HAWKS.'

FROM time immemorial—long ere poetry had sung of bright haired Endymion sleeping on the mountain bathed in the lustre of his Goddess-Love, or told how gentle Romeo sighed, and longing Juliet leaned and listened to his vows, the moon has been the planet especially consecrated to the worship of lovers and lunatics. ' *Arcades ambo*,' which is the greater insanity of the two ? To sit in a cell, a straw-crowned maniac, peopling the moonbeams as they stream in through the grated windows with visions of pomp and splendour and royalty, and all the picturesque pageantry of a madman's brain ? or to wander at large a harmless and pensive idiot, bareheaded, defiant of rheumatism, breathing sighs into the night-air, and identifying all the glories of the universe, the mellow beauty of earth, and the brilliant Infinite of heaven, with the image of a mere two-legged animal like himself, no whit loftier nor better than the rest of her kind, and exalted by the monomania of the worshipper alone into an idol, of which to his distempered fancy, the very stars of heaven do but glimmer in faint and envious rivalry ?

Humphrey Bosville paced thoughtfully along the quiet streets ; he marked not how the clear cold moonlight silvered the shafts and pinnacles of many a Gothic edifice, defining in bold relief the massive buttress and the stately tower, the deep embrasure of the

arched and pointed window, the delicate tracery of the elaborate
and florid scroll; shimmering over belfry and chancel, and quivering as it lost itself amongst the dark foliage of the lofty elms that
nodded and whispered over all; or if he did turn his face ever
and anon from the cold smooth pavement on which his eyes were
bent, and draw a full breath of the fresh night air, and feast his
sight upon the lustrous heaven, it was but to relieve a heart overcharged with its late happiness; to recall in the beauty of nature
the magic of that witching face which was fast becoming heaven
and earth, and all besides, to him.

He was in the mood for which solitude is an absolute necessity,
and yet which chance excitement or adventure can drive into the
wildest extremes—a mood in which the heart seems incapable of
supporting the weight of its own happiness, and seeks relief even
in tears from the intensity of its bliss. Does it not argue that
the child of man is born to sorrow rather than joy, thus to be
forced to acknowledge that there is suffering in an excess of the
latter—that poor weak human nature can but weep after all when
it is best pleased? But take comfort, such tears are not those
which we are too often called upon to shed; and he has not lived
in vain who has known what it is to weep for joy—ay, if it be but
once in a lifetime!

Nevertheless, as honest Iago says, or rather sings—

> A soldier's a man,
> A life's but a span,
> Why then let a soldier drink!

And the Cavaliers, if they were ' lads that loved the moon,' loved
her not so much for the peaceful and poetic thoughts that she inspired, as for the assistance afforded by her light to those home-
ward-bound wassailers who had been vindicating their loyalty by
drinking deeply to the King's health and to the detriment of their
own. Ere Humphrey was half way home to his lodging he was
arrested by the sounds of revelry and good fellowship issuing from
the portals of a venerable edifice, where dwelt a grave and portly
Churchman, now the courteous host of wild Lord Goring, and for
whom that reckless guest professed and entertained the pro-
foundest respect, because, to use his own words, ' the Doctor
could drink like a trooper and behave like a King, besides being
a thorough master of his own profession, of which,' quoth Goring,
' I do not pretend to be so good a judge.' His lordship was even
now at the height of his revelry, and was trilling forth in his rich
sweet voice, unimpaired by all his vices, a jingling Cavalier

melody, in the chorus of which the worthy Doctor's deep bass predominated, and to which, preoccupied as he was, Humphrey could not refrain from stopping to listen :—

Ho! fill me a flagon as deep as you please,
Ho! pledge me the health that we quaff on our knees;
And the knave who refuses to drink till he fall,
Why the hangman shall crop him—ears, love-locks, and all.
    Then a halter we'll string,
    And the rebel shall swing,
For the gallants of England are up for the King!

Ho! saddle my horses as quick as you may,
The sorrel, the black, and the white-footed bay;
The troop shall be mustered, the trumpets shall peal,
And the Roundheads shall taste of the Cavalier's steel.
    For the little birds sing,
    There are hawks on the wing
When the gallants of England are up for the King!

Ho! fling me my beaver, and toss me the glove
That but yesterday clung to the hand of my love,
To be bound on my crest—to be borne in the van,
And the rebel that reaps it must fight like a man!
    For the sabre shall swing,
    And the head-pieces ring,
When the gallants of England strike home for the King!

Ho! crush me a cup to the queen of my heart;
Ho! fill me a brimmer, the last ere we part;
A health to Prince Rupert! Success and renown!
To the dogs with the Commons! and up with the Crown.
    Then the stirrup-cup bring,
    Quaff it round in a ring!
To your horses! and ride to the death for the King!

As they shouted the concluding verses a party of five or six riotous Cavaliers emerged arm-in-arm from the deep archway of the gate opposite to where Humphrey stood. They were whooping, laughing, and jesting; and although they had left their worthy entertainer staid and sober as became a Churchman, were themselves more than half drunk. Goring had lighted a torch, and with mock gravity was brandishing it in the moonlight, as he said, to see 'what sort of night it was.' Wild Tom Lunsford, leaning on his long sheathed rapier, which bent and swayed beneath his weight, was ranting out some playhouse verses in praise of ' Cynthia's mellow light; ' and Black Will Scarthe, the fiercest of partisans and most savage of *condottieri*, was rocking himself to and fro against the wall, muttering fearful imprecations and vowing a deathless vengeance on some person or persons unknown, mingled with expressions of fervent admiration and undying regard for young Lord Francis Villiers, whom by some strange perversion of his drunken brain he persisted in addressing as Prince Rupert, and clothing in the attributes and endowments of that distinguished leader. Lord Francis laughed till his sides ached.

'Take him away, George,' said the young nobleman to Goring, 'or he will be the death of me. Why, Will!—Black Will!—dost not know thy friends from thy foes, man? Here be I, thy sworn comrade and companion for these three hours past, and thou canst mistake me for the Prince Palatine; he who would have tried thee at Edgehill for cowardice and hanged thee at Lansdowne for plunder. For shame, man, for shame!'

Black Will scowled fearfully, and his right hand closed involuntarily on the hilt of his rapier: but drunk as he was, he knew he must pay the penalty of associating with his betters, and submit if necessary to be their butt. So, although he winced and ground his teeth, he ventured on no open demonstrations of resentment, even when Goring aimed another shaft at him tipped with the venom of truth, and bid him remember the woman whose ear-rings he tore from her head in the Low Countries.

''Fore George, Will, thou hadst a narrow escape that time of the riding-school and the strappado! Had she gone with her complaint to Monk instead of me, thou hadst been sped—he would have hanged thee to the nearest tree; and had she been a likely wench, Will, even I must have seen justice done, and the halberds up. But she was a swarthy quean, black-browed and ill-favoured as Will himself, my lads! So we buckled to, and the Stadtholder's drunken chaplain married them; and she followed the army as Dame Scarthe, and Will had the ear-rings for a marriage portion, and he never got rid of her till we lost all our baggage at Breda; and she kicked Will out and took the command of the enemy's 'woman troop.' Egad, she was the veriest Tartar of them all! And thou wast not over sorry to be free once more, Will, for i'faith she was thy master!'

'At least, General, she was never thy mistress,' answered Will, with a sneer and a savage scowl; 'and that is more than can be boasted of many a daintier dame that rode a pillion in the rear of our troop. But enough said, my masters. Look you here—a sail, a sail!' And Black Will as he spoke staggered to his legs, and pointed to a white dress flitting rapidly away in the distance, accompanied by the tall dark figure of a man: and signing to his companions to follow him, proceeded rapidly in chase, though with wavering and uncertain steps.

'Let them go,' said Lord Francis, in whom, drunk or sober, the instincts of a gentleman predominated. '"Tis a lady from the Court or an honest citizen's wife at the least. If thou layest a hand on her, Will, I will cudgel the soul out of thee, by all the gods of love and war!'

'After midnight, my lord,' laughed out Tom Lunsford, recently returned from his imprisonment amongst the Puritans, and mad with delight to find himself once more surrounded by congenial spirits, wicked and reckless as his own, 'after midnight every sail's a prize! Black Will has not been on the Spanish Main for nothing, and he knows buccaneer's law better than his prayers. Down with the bunting! up with the hatches!—share and share alike, and no quarter!'

'Then here goes to be first aboard the prize!' exclaimed Goring, limping nimbly along despite his lameness, and waiving the rest on as he was used to waive his troopers forward in a charge, with shout and jeer, and strange, quaint, fearful oaths. The other Cavaliers whooped and laughed in the spirit of the jest, pushing and bantering each other as they hurried on in full pursuit of the rapidly retreating chase, making such way, notwithstanding reeling steps and singing brains, as promised soon to bring them alongside.

Meantime, pale and sick, her little heart beating fast against the arm of her protector, her knees knocking together, and her limbs failing at her need, the frightened woman, no other than our old acquaintance Faith, tripped rapidly on. She was returning from her nightly duties with her mistress to her own lodging in another street, and escorted by her faithful cavalier, the imperturbable Dymocke, had enjoyed and perhaps prolonged her moonlight walk to an unjustifiable extent. A moment ago she had been expatiating to her admirer on the beauties of Oxford, and the bewitching delights of a town; now she would have given all she possessed to be safe back at quiet Boughton, or anywhere else in the world out of hearing of those alarming footsteps! Like the hare closely pursued by the noisy pack, her heart sank within her, and her natural impulse was to sit down in despair and give in. The poor girl said as much as she clung closer and closer to the tall spare form against which she leaned.

Dymocke was staunch to the backbone. 'Don't ye leave go of my belt,' said he, grasping a goodly oak cudgel, the only weapon he had with him, in his brown bony hand, and preparing, with his usual grave demeanour, for a tough resistance. 'Keep you

behind me, my lass: and if it's wild Lord Goring himself, or the
devil, whose servant he is, I'll ring twelve o'clock on his pate if
he offers to lay a finger on you. Only don't ye leave go of my
belt.'

The words were scarcely out of his mouth when the foremost
of their pursuers came alongside.

'By your leave, kind madam,' said a soft sweet voice, in the
gentle accents of a courtier, while a white hand, adorned with a
rich lace ruffle, unceremoniously lifted the veil which covered
Faith's drooping head; and a perfumed moustache and good-
looking face, somewhat flushed with wine, approached closely to
her own, with the evident purpose of stealing a kiss. Dymocke's
cudgel was aloft in an instant, but ere it could come down, Goring's
quick eye had caught the movement, and his ready hand seized
the uplifted wrist, and grappling with Faith's defender, he sought
to trip him up with one of those tricks of wrestling which give
the initiated such advantage in a personal conflict. The nobleman
had, however, met with his match. Dymocke's tall, wiry person
was toughened by constant exercise into the consistency of steel;
and while his length of limb gave him every facility for performing
all feats of skill and agility, his extraordinary coolness of temper
enabled him to detect the slightest weakness on the part of his
adversary, and make ready use of it for his own benefit.

They had scarcely closed ere Goring measured his length upon
the pavement; and though he regained his feet in an instant, that
instant had sufficed to place Dymocke, with the uplifted cudgel,
once more upon his guard.

Goring's smile was not pleasant to look upon as his right hand
stole towards his sword. In another moment the wicked blade
was flashing in the moonlight, winding under the guard of honest
Dymocke's cudgel with quick glittering passes, all athirst for
blood; at the same time a blow from Tom Lunsford's sheathed
sword on the back of the serving-man's head somewhat stunned
him; while Black Will Scarthe, winding his arm round poor
Faith's waist, strove to detach her by main force from her protector, to whose person she clung with a tenacity that much impeded his efforts for their mutual defence. The other Cavaliers
stood around, laughing and shouting, and laying wagers on the
event of the skirmish.

'Fair play!' cried Lord Francis; 'two to one is no even match.
Give the knave a sword, some one; or do you, Goring, borrow
my riding-wand!'

'Hand us over the wench,' exclaimed another; 'she does but

hamper her man; and cold steel is an ugly neighbour for bodice and pinners.'

'Take her away from Black Will,' laughed a third. 'Look how she trembles, like a dove in the clutch of a night-hawk.'

'A rescue! a rescue!' shouted a fourth: 'here comes a heron for the hawk. 'Ware beak and talons, general, this is one of your high-flyers, and he'll soar his pitch before he has done with you, I'll warrant him!'

Even as he spoke, Humphrey Bosville, who in the outraged couple had recognised his own and Mistress Allonby's attendant, strode up, pale and breathless, his blood boiling with indignation, and all the soft feelings that had so lately pervaded his being turned to fierce and ungovernable wrath. Tearing away a good yard of Flanders lace as he seized him by the collar, with one turn of his wrist he put Black Will down on his back in the kennel as if he had been shot. Giving Lunsford at the same time the benefit of a push from his muscular shoulder that sent the tipsy, laughing Cavalier staggering into the middle of the street, he confronted Goring with scowling brows and flashing eyes, and bade him put up his sword for shame, drawn as it was against an unarmed man.

'I claim the quarrel for myself, my lord,' he exclaimed, 'whatever it may be. This man is my servant, this damsel belongs to the household of Sir Giles Allonby. Gentlemen, I take you all to witness! Lord Goring has put an affront on me that I am compelled to resent.'

With these words, he stepped quietly up to the astonished nobleman, who had now sheathed his rapier, and was listening to him with his usual air of amused *nonchalance*, and drawing his glove from his left hand, smote Goring gently with it across the cheek; then, erect and defiant, stood with his hand upon the guard of his sword, as if ready to draw and encounter the violence he had provoked.

'Gentlemen, dear gentlemen! for the love of Heaven!' pleaded poor Faith, now fairly frightened into tears. 'Oh, Captain Bosville, I entreat you, sir. The gentleman meant no harm. It was an accident; nothing but an accident from beginning to end!'

Faith was sufficiently a woman to feel very uncomfortable when fairly engaged in a broil, however ready she might be to enter upon its commencement; and although she little thought to what ulterior disturbances the admiration she had excited might lead, her intuitive tact told her that there was danger in the Captain's flushed brow, and mischief in Goring's pale, smiling face.

He kept his temper beautifully : he always kept his temper when he was *really* angry, that bold, bad man. Saving that his check was a shade paler, while the well-known smile deepened into furrows round his mouth, and that he caressed his sleek moustache with one white hand, even his old associate, Tom Lunsford, could not have told that aught had occurred to ruffle the general's equanimity, or that there was *murder* lurking beneath that passionless exterior.

'This is no case for chance medley, Captain Bosville!' he remarked, in quiet and studiedly polite tones; 'no offence that can be wiped out in a couple of passes, with a buff-coat on for defence, and perhaps a scratch of the arm for satisfaction. Are you aware that a file of musketeers and ten yards of sward is the punishment for mutiny in the Royal army ? Are you aware that you have struck your superior officer ?'

'I am aware that I have been insulted by a *gentleman*, and resented it as becomes a Cavalier,' was the bold and unhesitating reply. Such an answer was a conclusive argument in the days of which we write. Fairfax, Cromwell, Monk, some few of the Parliamentary generals, might have deemed their position excluded them from the duty of causelessly hazarding their lives on a point of honour ; but perhaps there was hardly an officer of the Royal army who would not have felt, like Goring, that in a case of private brawl it was incumbent on him to waive all considerations of relative rank and military discipline ; to take and give that irrational and after all inconclusive satisfaction which the ordeal by battle affords.

And yet there are many arguments to be urged by the advocates of duelling, which, in an imperfect state of society, it is difficult to refute. The practice has come down to us from the days of chivalry, when, in the absence of wholesome legal restraint, of an irresponsible tribunal to which to appeal, the God of battles was called upon to arbitrate between man and man, to vindicate the oppressed in the person of a champion, and to teach the oppressor, though backed by scores of warriors sheathed in steel, that his own good sword and his own right hand alone could avail him in his quarrel. The combat, *à l'outrance*, was in those days the representative of justice and the laws. It was never disputed that, upon the same principle by which nations were justified in going to war to protect their honour or their rights, private individuals might avenge their insults and redress their wrongs. Shriven by priest, and armed by squire, the champion rode into the lists, strong in his own rectitude and the justice of his cause. He had no morbid fear of bloodshed, no shrinking horror of death as the *worst* evil that can befal that compound of body and soul which we call man. If he had less reason than his descendant of the present day, he had more faith : which is the nobler quality of the two ? The former can scarcely compute time, the latter boldly grasps eternity. So he clasped his vizor down, and laid his lance in rest, and the marshal of the lists bid him good speed with the solemn adjuration, ' God defend the right.' But now we have the law to redress our wrongs, and public opinion to avenge our insults. Well, if it were really so. If there were not many a mortal stab aimed at the defenceless, of which no legal tribunal can take cognizance, many a deep and lasting injury inflicted, for which public opinion offers neither salve nor compensation, wounds dealt with a poisoned weapon, which spread and throb and fester, and of which the world and its laws take neither notice nor account. Where is the ordeal by battle, then ? ' Why,' we are tempted to exclaim in our agony, ' why can we not have it out, man to man, as Nature's first law, the law of self-defence, would seem to prompt ? ' Policy, expediency, a high state of civilization, the inadequacy of the redress, the chances of the conflict, all these are empty terms, signifying nothing ; they do not in the least affect the combative impulse inherent in man. There is but one good reason, and that a conclusive one. If God hath said, ' thou shalt not kill,' we must beware how we presume to interpret his command to suit our own views. The question becomes one, not of *morality*, but religion ; not of policy, but salvation. Hard is the struggle, bitter is the victory. God help him who has to encounter the one and win the other. And God *will* help him who makes His law the standard of his actions and the guide of his own rebellious heart.

' Well crowed ! ' remarked Goring aside to Lunsford, by no means displeased to find his antagonist thus disposed for combat, and involuntarily owning that respect for courage which is felt and acknowledged by every brave man, and that Goring was *brave* as his sword none will be found to deny. ' Well crowed, indeed,' he repeated. ' Captain Bosville, I should be sorry to baulk you : Sir Thomas Lunsford has the length of my weapon ; he lodges over against the tall old gates yonder. By the way, there is an absurd order about duelling, which will oblige us to go a mile or so outside the town. I told Crispe how it would be if he took the liberty of running Fred Aunion through the body within the precincts. 'Gad, the King would have shot him if we could have done without our useful " Nick." We must not fall into the same trap, Captain Bosville. Tom Lunsford shall inform your friend of the place, and for time, suppose we say to-morrow morning, or rather this morning at daybreak. Fair damsel, I kiss your hands' (to Faith, who was hovering white and trembling on the skirts of the conversation); ' Captain Bosville, my service to you. Tom, I shall run him through the brisket as sure as he wears boots' (aside to his friend); and with a courtly bow of his plumed hat, and a pleasant laugh, Goring strode off on the arm of Sir Thomas Lunsford, leaving Humphrey standing, as it were, transfixed at the extraordinary coolness and carelessness of his formidable antagonist.

Whilst they proceed to the lodgings alluded to, opposite the great gates, there to discuss their future measures over a posset of burnt sack and a pipe of true Virginian tobacco, we will accompany Bosville to the apartment of his comrade, Effingham, on whose assistance he seemed instinctively to rely, and to whose friendship in any matter of real danger or difficulty he had never trusted in vain. Late as was the hour, Effingham had not yet returned to his lodging, and it was with a feeling of impatience and annoyance which none but those who have been similarly situated can appreciate, that Humphrey sat him down on a hard high-backed chair to beguile the moments till his host's arrival with a dry discourse on cavalry tactics, the only literature the soldier's quarters afforded, and his own pleasant reflections on the scrape into which his chivalry had led him, and the dangerous enemy he had provoked, matter sufficient for grave cogitation, yet through it all there ran a golden thread of dreamy contentment, in the thought of Mary's approval and Mary's fair bewitching face.

CHAPTER XIII.

' FOR CONSCIENCE' SAKE.

AND where was George Effingham? The man of the sword, the upholder of tyranny, the confirmed malignant, an officer in the very army of Belial, a lost sheep, a brand deserving of the burning, a sinner in the last extremity of reprobation, for whom there was neither hope nor pity? Where had he spent his evening, that strange, dark, enthusiastic man? Let us follow his footsteps after he bade Humphrey farewell, when the latter was on his way to Merton College, and discover what startling scenes, what contrasts of life, and morals, and manners, and even men, loyal Oxford can afford.

With a stealthier step than usual, and many a backward glance,

strangely at variance with his wonted bold, frank bearing, Effingham strode swiftly along the most unfrequented streets and
narrowest lanes of the fair old town, nor did he slacken his pace
or stop to acknowledge the greeting of friend or comrade, till he
found himself in front of a low, dismal habitation, adorned with
a heavy frowning porch, and a door ominously clamped and
fastened with iron. Descending three very dirty steps, he pushed
open the door, which gave way at once, and entered a small dingy
apartment, to which a bare counter and a pair of rusty scales alone
seemed to affix the character of a shop. An ill-favoured woman
presided over the former, and to Effingham's mysterious inquiry,
' Are the children gathered?' returned the equally mysterious reply,
' Even so, thou sojourner by the way, and there is water even in
Zin for the children of the congregation!' This appeared a sufficient reason for the Cavalier officer to proceed, so passing through
the shop, he traversed another door of equal strength and thick-
ness, and descending a winding flight of steps, found himself in a
roomy vault or cellar, supported upon strong massive arches, and
lighted by the gloomy flicker of a few scattered torches, fixed at
intervals in the damp reeking walls.

The vault was full, nay, crowded to the very steps, down which
the Cavalier made his way; and though the contrast afforded by
his gay habiliments with the sombre garb of those around him was
sufficiently striking to excite remark, his arrival seemed to provoke no more attention than a momentary stir, and, as it were, a
buzz of approbation amongst the assemblage.

They were no weak enthusiasts, no empty fanatics, no vacillating casuists, those men of iron gathered together in that dark vault,
and now absorbed in prayer. 'Tis a strange compound, that Anglo-
Saxon constitution, of which a dogged tenacity, an unconquerable fixedness of purpose, constitutes so essential an element. In
all relations of life, in all climes, under all circumstances, in war,
trade, art, or mechanics, it wrests for itself the premium of success, and even religion, which softens the human character as it
exalts the intellectual and diviner part of man, which tempers the
wayward will and subdues the mutinous heart, fusing the moral
being into one harmonious whole, doth not totally eradicate that
unbending fixedness of purpose to which, under Providence, it
owes its present purity, and the veneration with which it is up-
held by our determined countrymen.

The flaring torches reddened many a bold and thoughtful brow
amongst those who now turned to scan Effingham, with an eager
yet satisfied gaze. As his foot reached the lowest step his hand

rested on the shoulder of one whose quiet smile, as he assisted the Cavalier's slight stumble, and whose Scriptural admonition to ' take heed lest he fall,' were characteristic of the confidence and self-dependence of his party, a confidence based upon things not of this world, a self-dependence peculiar to those who are persuaded that ' God is on their side.'

He was a low square-built man, with wide shoulders and deep chest, all the appearance of physical strength, without which solid foundation the finest moral structure is too apt to crumble to the ground. His wide forehead, prominent about the temples, from which the thin iron grey hair receded daily more and more, denoted that ideal organization which can derive from *belief* as full a satisfaction as coarser natures can from *knowledge*, whilst the broad cheek and firm wide jaw could only belong to one whose unconquerable resolution would prompt him to suffer for the Right, ay, even unto death, without yielding a hair's-breadth of his tenets, or giving way an inch in his argument. His deep-set eyes of light grey, shaded beneath a pair of bushy eyebrows, glittered in the torchlight with a ray of enthusiasm such as those alone experience who live more in the inner than the outer life, and his smile as he greeted Effingham was calm, and even melancholy, as that of one who had done with the empty vanities of the world, but paid his tribute to its courtesies, as one who rendered, though somewhat grudgingly, ' unto Cæsar the things which were Cæsar's.'

He was dressed in a suit of the darkest hues, and simplest cut, with high riding-boots drawn midway up the leg; his narrow band was of the plainest and coarsest linen, and he wore neither lace neckerchief nor ruffles, nor any such vanities, to relieve the sameness of his attire. A strong buff belt, however, about his waist contained a pair of serviceable pistols, and a long straight cut-and-thrust sword completed the equipment of one who was never unwilling to carry out the promptings of the spirit with the arm of the flesh. A black skull-cap sat close round his head, the closer that, in accordance with an inhuman decree of the Star Chamber, he had lost both his ears, and the contemptuous epithets applied to his party by the Cavaliers bore with him a cruelly-appropriate signification. It was an ignoble punishment, and yet who can withhold admiration from the Spartan constancy of the martyr? A shouting populace, ready as the ' many-headed monster thing ' ever is, to heap obloquy and insult on those delivered over to its tender mercies, are pelting with rotten eggs and dead cats, and other filthy missiles, the helpless sufferer who has been subjected to the pillory for his political opinions. Does it exact no resolution, no constancy, none of that British quality for which we have no other word than *pluck*, to sustain the jeers, the violence, the aggravated insults of a mob? Yet the victim never quails nor winces. Erect and defiant he faces them all, and faces them the more creditably that his position is, to say the least of it, ridiculous as well as painful. So the officers of justice release him from the pillory, to usher him up a flight of steps on to a wooden stage, where stands a brazier, a table with a volume lying thereon, and an ominous-looking figure in a mask, armed with a long knife. Here must he recant his heresies, burn with his own hands the book he has written to support them, or sustain the full amount of punishment awarded for his misdemeanour by the collective wisdom of Church and State. Again the light gleams from his eye, the inner light that in the infancy of faith, illumined the face of Stephen ' as it had been the face of an angel.' Again the head is reared erect, and a proud refusal hurled in the very teeth of judges and executioner. What though the quivering hand must be branded, and the cruel red-hot iron seethe and scorch into the hissing flesh? Not a groan escapes the martyr, and he raises the mutilated member as a testimony in the face of earth and heaven. But the penalty is not yet exacted—the sickening ceremony not yet over; merciless as the Red Man's tomahawk, the bright steel flashes round his head. The red blood flows free and fast, and a punishment degrading but for the offence of which it is the award, concludes, amidst the shudders and disgust of the spectators, moved from their previous brutality by the courage and constancy of the determined sufferer.

Such an ordeal had Effingham's neighbour but lately undergone. Who shall say that forgiveness for his enemies formed one of the petitions he seemed so fervently and abstractedly to offer up?

He was a specimen of the highest order of those enthusiasts who, under the progressive denominations of Independents, Brownists, and Fifth-Monarchy Men, deluged England with blood for conscience' sake, and eventually by their fanaticism effected the Restoration of that very dynasty which they deemed synonymous with Antichrist and sin.

All fanatics, however, were not necessarily martyrs, nor indeed by any means willing to become so. Another step as he shifted his position brought Effingham in contact with a worthy of a far different calibre, and one whose outward demeanour as it savoured of the extreme of sanctity, was but little in character, to use his own favourite expression, with the ' carnal self-seeking of the inner man.' He was a fat, unctuous-looking personage, with a broad flat face, to which the lank shining hair was plastered with grave precision, and on the surface of which a stereotyped expression of hypocritical gravity accorded ill with the humorous twinkle of the eye and the sensual curve of the thick full lip. Though his garments were of the darkest colour and the plainest workmanship, they fitted closely round a plump well-fed figure such as argued no mean appreciation of the good things of this world; and while, in accordance with the exigencies of the times, he wore a long straight sword in his belt, the weapon was dull and badly cleaned; and balanced on the other side by a huge clasped Bible, hung with no small amount of ostentation, and continually referred to on the most trivial occasions by the wearer.

Sanctimonious in his demeanour, wresting the words of Scripture to the meanest and most practical affairs of daily life, his religion was but a cloak of convenience and affectation, under which a course of self-indulgence could be carried on with the greater security and satisfaction. A man of peace by profession, his calling absolved him from the dangers of bearing arms in the civil war; a man of God, as he impiously termed himself, his assumed sanctity forbade suspicion and remark. One of the elect in his own estimation, he could indulge his sensual vices unchecked, and, as he strove to persuade himself, unpunished; and lastly, though but an atom in his own proper person, as a component part of that mighty body which was then shaking England to her very foundations, he enjoyed a sense of power and self-aggrandisement inexpressibly dear to the aspiring vanity of a selfish and ignoble nature.

Such were the extreme types of the Puritan party, and of every shade and grade between the two—from the high devoted martyr to the base and cowardly hypocrite—was that powerful faction constituted which overturned the dynasty of the Stuarts, which recruited Cromwell's Ironsides, and sent its dogged representatives to the Rump Parliament, which raised the son of a Lincolnshire grazier to the throne of Britain, and then, bursting asunder like a shell from its own internal violence, after fulfilling its deadly mission, and shedding rivers of the best and noblest blood in England, recalled the son of the very sovereign whose head it had taken on the block, and handed over the country whose liberties it had saved to the mal-administration of a good-natured profligate, who inherited not one of the high and generous qualities that had cost his misguided father life and crown.

Effingham's entrance, we have said, caused a momentary stir and excitement amongst the congregation, but it soon relapsed into the deep and mystical silence which had pervaded it before his arrival. To all appearance the members were absorbed in inward prayer, and an occasional sigh or broken interjection of more than common vehemence denoted the strength and fervency of their devotions. There were no women present, and the general aspect of the men was stern, preoccupied, and forbidding; yet the Cavalier officer could not but remark that a feeling of deep though unexpressed satisfaction pervaded every countenance when a loud sonorous cough and the rustling of a Bible's leaves heralded the principal event of the meeting—a discourse upon those topics of religion and politics which, when mingled together, afford such stimulating food to the appetites of those who hunger for excitement as for their daily bread. How strange it is, how suggestive of man's fallen state, how disheartening, how humiliating, to reflect that meek-eyed Religion—she whose 'ways are ways of pleasantness and all her paths are peace '—should so often have been perverted to excuse the worst and fiercest passions of our nature, should have been made the mask of vice and the cloak of cruelty, should have been so disguised as to lead her votaries to the commission of nearly every crime that can most degrade and brutalize a man! A few of the oldest and gravest of the assemblage now cleared a space around a high-backed chair which had hitherto stood unoccupied, and a pale thin man, on whose brow the sweat stood in large drops, and whose attenuated features seemed wasted with the inner workings of the spirit, whilst his glittering eye assumed a wild gleam not far removed from insanity, mounted this temporary pulpit and looked proudly around him with the commanding air of an orator who is sure of his own powers and the favourable attention of his audience. The light from a neighbouring torch gleamed upon Caryl's high pale forehead, and brought into bold relief the intellectual cast of his head and face, and the contour of his spare nervous figure, while the deep cavernous eyes flashed out from their recesses with a brilliancy that had in it something more than human. Careless, almost squalid in his attire, no weapon of fleshly warfare glittered by his side; but those white trembling fingers clasped the holy book with an energy and a grasp that seemed to say, 'this is my sword and my shield, my helmet and my breastplate, the weapon with which I can smite or heal, can destroy or save, can confound an army or hurl a sovereign from his throne;' and while he turned over its leaves with rapid and nervous eagerness, a deep ' hum ' of satisfaction and approval resounded from the grim, stern, defiant casuists that constituted his audience.

For a minute or so he stood erect, his eyes closed, his lips set tight, but the muscles of his face twitching and working with the strength of his emotions, as he wrapped his soul in the garment of silent and enthusiastic prayer; then swooping from his high-wrought pitch and pouncing as it were on a text from the holy volume which quivered in his hand, he plunged at once into such a discourse as suited his own excited and transcendental imagination no less than the fierce and dogmatic appetites of his con-gregation.

'My brethren,' he began in a low and tremulous voice, which gradually as he warmed with his subject rose into loud sonorous tones, clear and commanding as a trumpet-peal, 'my famished brethren, hungering and thirsting after the truth, whom the minister of the Word must nourish, as the pelican in the wilder-ness nourisheth her brood with the life-blood of her own devoted breast. My brethren, who look to me for bread as the children of Israel looked to Moses in the days of their wanderings, when manna fell from heaven plenteous as the night-dews and "man did eat angels' food," who cry to me with parched lips and faint-ing souls for water even as the people of God cried to their leader on the arid plains of Rephidim, and chid him to his face for that there was no water and they must die—what would ye here with me? Am I Moses, to stand between you and the Lord? Is this place Sin, between Elim and Sinai, that the dews from heaven should fall upon it as bread, white, like coriander seed, with a pleasant taste as that of wafers and wild honey? Is there here a rock like Horeb from whence should flow living waters that ye might drink and be satisfied, and depart rejoicing on your way? I trow not. Even as the defilement of Sodom, so is the defilement of Oxford; even as the punishment of Gomorrah, so shall be the fate of this accursed town! Peradventure there may be ten righteous men in the city, yet it may be that to-day the city shall not be saved for ten righteous men's sake. And now again, what would ye here with me? Silver and gold have I none, yet such as I have will I freely bestow upon you.' He paused, wiped his brow, opened the Bible as if at random, yet a close observer might have remarked there was a leaf turned back-ward to mark the page, and hurried on. ' "I will cut off the inhabitant from Ashdod, and him that holdeth the sceptre from Ashkelon, and I will turn mine hand against Ekron, and the remnant of the Philistines shall perish." It is not Caryl, my brethren, who speaks to you now—poor persecuted Caryl, scoffed at and reviled by Malignants, beaten with stripes, outraged by men of blood, and brought here into Oxford manacled and guarded, with his feet tied under a horse's belly. No; Caryl's voice is weak and small, his frame is feeble, and his spirit faint, but this is the voice of prophecy, loud as the shouts of an army, clear as the trumpet-peal in the day of battle—a prophecy that shall not fail the children at their need, a prophecy that is even now working out its own fulfilment, a prophecy that shall avenge us of our enemies and put to shame them that despitefully use us and persecute us. Who is the inhabitant of Ashdod—who is he that holdeth the sceptre in Ashkelon? Hath not Ekron deserved punishment, and shall the Philistines not perish like the very dogs by the wayside? Hearken unto me, and I will expound to you the interpretation thereof; ask your own hearts and they shall respond, even as the strings of a lute respond to the skilful fingers of the player. The inhabitant of Ashdod is he that cometh from afar to despoil the children of the congregation, to defile the holy places with his horses' hoofs, to work out his appointed portion of wickedness here, and receive his reward from the master whom he serves hereafter. Who is the bitterest enemy of the chosen people? Who is the merciless wolf that ravens round the sheepfolds in the wilderness to rend the lamb from the shepherd and lap the warm blood of the innocent? Who is he that rideth upon horses through the slaughter, and halteth to drink strong drink, and ravisheth the poor and the fatherless? whose flesh shall be torn by eagles in the day of battle, and his proud head laid low in the dust beneath the heel of his enemies? I wot ye know him well, the man of war from his youth upward, the spawn of her of Bohemia, whose words, like Jezebel's, are ever, " Take, take!—slay, slay!" and whose latter end shall be even as the latter end of Ahab's godless queen. Ye have seen him in his power and the pride of his might. Ye have fronted him, armed with the sword of the Lord and of Gideon; ye have turned him back, though he came on at the head of his men of war like the whirlwind that sweeps everything before it save the rampart whose foundations are in the living rock; and ye have seen the weapons of Satan shivered upon the panoply of Truth. But ye shall see mightier works than these; ye shall see vengeance for the anointed, and the inhabitant of Ashdod cut off, and the wicked Rupert stretched like Sisera upon the earth, and his horses and his horsemen scattered like chaff before the wind in the triumph of the children of the congregation.'

A deep hum of applause here greeted the preacher, whose *argumentum ad hominem* met with the usual success of such appeals in popular assemblies. Many an eye was turned with looks of mingled triumph and curiosity on Effingham, whose interest, although externally he appeared unmoved, was powerfully awakened, and whose whole attention was riveted on Caryl as he resumed his discourse.

'And what of him that holdeth the sceptre in Ashkelon? Shall he escape the vengeance of the pursuer, and yet abuse the trust that hath been confided to him by God and man? Shall he break the strong fence of the vineyard, and trample down the vines and the wild grapes, and shall not the thorns rend his garments and pierce his feet, and justice overtake him, and his inheritance pass from him and know him no more? Hath not London been visited by the pestilence that walketh at noonday? —and is not Oxford like the scorpion's nest, which nourisheth only evil, and calleth aloud to be purged and cleansed from its iniquity by the hand of the avenger of blood, who maketh no long tarrying? He who hath ruled over Ashkelon should have swayed a righteous sceptre, and done justice between man and man, leaving to Naboth his vineyard and to the poor his ewe lamb; but a hand hath held the scales, and the man Charles hath been found wanting. An eye hath meted out the measure, and hath seen that it is short, so the sceptre shall be taken away, and he that holdeth it shall be cut off, and Ashkelon shall acknowledge no human sovereign, for the fire that is sent upon Judah shall devour the palaces of Jerusalem, and a new kingdom shall be raised up—a structure not built with hands, imperishable and unfading, the true vineyard of which ye alone shall gather the vintage who are steadfast to the end—a Commonwealth of the Saints who shall inherit the earth, and have dominion here below, and own no lord and master save only the Lord of Hosts, whose servants and whose soldiers ye are. Will ye work in the heat of the noonday for wages such as these? Will ye run with the swift for so noble a prize, and do battle with the strong, ankle-deep in blood, to obtain so glorious a victory? I trow ye will; the voice within me calls ye to the fight, and ye shall smite and spare not; and he that attaineth to the end the same shall have his reward.'

Once more the preacher paused, once more there was a deep stir amongst his audience—a murmur of suppressed approbation, and then the solemn silence of profound attention. His eye was turned full upon Effingham now, and with the tact of a practised orator who intuitively recognises a convert, he seemed to address his discourse more particularly to the Cavalier.

' " I will turn mine hand against Ekron," and what is Ekron that it shall prevail against the hand of the Lord ? Hath Ekron a talisman that shall insure her from pestilence and famine, from the hunger that wasteth the cheek, and the dead-sickness that eateth the heart away? Are her walls loftier, her defences stronger than those of Jericho, which crumbled into dust at the trumpet-blast of the hosts of Israel ? Hath she men of war that shall stand against Joshua, or a Goliath in whom she trusteth for her champion against the soldiers of the truth ? Even now is the young David herding his flocks who shall overthrow the boast of the heathen, even now is the running water smoothing the pebble that shall sink into the forehead of the Philistine, and bring his gigantic frame, ringing in its armour, to the ground. Shall Ekron stand, though her garners be filled with provender and her arsenals stored with arms ? Though she be garrisoned by cruel Lunsford, who hath sold himself to Satan that he may work deeds of blood, slaughtering the faithful at their very prayers, and burning their churches to light him on his own journey to the bottomless pit, where his Master awaiteth him with his wages ; and reckless profligate Goring, who hath made a present of his soul to the devil, and refused for aught so valueless to accept any guerdon in exchange ; and hoary Colepepper, on whose forehead is set the mark of the beast, graven to the bone by the godly swordstroke of one of the troopers of the faithful ; and zealous Lucas, who serveth the darkness rather than the light, and who verily shall have his reward ; and Astley, the high priest of Baal, whose head is white with many winters, and who gnasheth with his teeth upon the prophets, and cutteth himself with knives, and calleth upon his gods to do him justice in the fore-front of the battle, as one who wearieth of his life, and who knoweth not of that which is to come ; and Rupert, with his magic and his witchcraft, his familiar spirit, and his spells of the black art—who eateth the substance of the faithful, and dasheth their children against the stones— shall his magic save him in the day of vengeance ? Shall the devil, in whom he trusteth, shield him from the outstretched arm and the consuming fire ? Though the evil spirit hath entered into the body of a white dog,* and in that shape watcheth over him,

---

* A well-known favourite that accompanied Rupert wherever he went, and was stated by the Puritans to be a wizard or familiar spirit, furnished by the prince of darkness, to whom he had sold himself, as an auxiliary in

as well ye know, in the battle and the leaguer, in the camp and
the council chamber, summer and winter, day and night, yet shall
the time come at length that it shall turn and rend him ; and the
latter end of the sorcerer shall be worse than the beginning. And
shall men of war such as these save Ekron from the fate that is
hanging over her? or shall councillors whose wisdom is vanity,
or priests who worship false gods, and at the best are but whited
sepulchres, be a bulwark to stem the wrath of the Avenger? I
trow not. Ekron shall fall with a crash that shall shake the land
to its extremities, and shall bury in her downfall the false prophets who have reared her, and the councillors who have counselled evil in her palaces, and the men of blood who have
defended her on her ramparts, and the daughters of Sin who
have made mirth and revelry in her halls, and the Sovereign
who hath forsaken his faith and abused his trust upon his throne.
On her ruins shall be erected a new Jerusalem, another kingdom,
of which no mortal head shall wear the crown; of which ye, the
faithful and the abiding, shall be the princes and the peers, the
priests and the senators, reigning upon earth in the radiant glory
of those whose garments have been cleansed in the washing of
blood, and purified by the ordeal of fire. Will ye triumph over
your enemies, and spurn beneath your feet him whose chariot-
wheels have passed over your necks and crushed your children
to the earth?—stand to your arms and believe ! Will ye win the
dominion here below, to the confusion of your enemies and the
saving of your own souls?—stand to your arms and believe !
Will ye work out the task that has been predestined for you in
the dark womb of Eternity, to be born in the fulness of time, and
attain its maturity in the glowing splendour of an everlasting
Future ? Will ye be princes and potentates on earth, and
glorified saints in heaven, again I say unto you, Stand to your
arms and believe !—so shall ye scatter your enemies, as the chaff
from the threshing-floor is scattered to the four winds of heaven,
and " the remnant of the Philistines shall perish." The Philistines ! the accursed Philistines ! whom ye have fought and resisted day by day ; whose squadrons ye have heard thundering on
the plain, and seen charging and forming, and charging again, to
shatter themselves and fall back from your goodly stand of pikes,

council and a defence in the field. Many years later a famous black charger
of John Grahame of Claverhouse, afterwards ' bonnie Dundee,' enjoyed the
same unenviable notoriety. The Prince's favourite died a soldier's death at
Marston Moor, where he was shot with many a nobler but not more faithful Cavalier.

even as the baffled breakers of the advancing tide from the bluff
face of the opposing rock. The Philistines ! who would fain make
ye their bond-slaves and their victims ; who would ravish from ye
your substance, and rob ye of your souls, yet whom ye shall despoil of their silver and gold, the needlework that they prize, and
the armour in which they trust; whose maidens ye shall make
captives to your bow and spear, and on the neck of whose great
ones ye, the soldiers of the congregation, shall set your foot.

'And who is he that would have his portion with the doomed
remnant? Who is he that would cast in his lot with the servants
of darkness, and serve in that troop whose captain is the Prince
of the Power of the Air ! Who would go up against the armies
of the Lord to the battle of Armageddon, in that great day when
the hosts of heaven shall join in conflict with the children of men ;
when a voice louder than thunder on the mountains shall peal
above the tramp of thousands, the clashing of arms, the rush of
many wings, the hosannas of the conquering righteous, and the
ghastly shrieks of the vanquished and the doomed, saying, " Who
is on my side?" When darkness shall cover the face of the
heavens at noonday, and the earth shall quake for very fear, and
amongst all her myriads the children of the congregation alone
shall be saved, who would have his portion on that day with the
remnant of the Philistines? Behold, there is yet an eleventh
hour. Behold, there is yet a ray of light in the utter darkness—
a chink left open in the narrow gate. Ye that are bidden to the
feast come hastily ere the door be shut. Ye that would save
yourselves and your households, bind your sandals on your feet,
lift up your burdens, rise and go on your way. Again, it is not
I, poor John Caryl, that speaketh to you. It is the Voice that
cannot lie. Believe not me ; believe the Voice. It prophesieth
to you ; it warneth you, it entreateth you, it commandeth you.
This is the way that leadeth to salvation; this is the way that
leadeth to righteousness; this is the way that leadeth to everlasting glory. Turn ye ! turn ye ! why *will* ye die ? '

The preacher concluded with almost a shriek of entreaty. His
face was deadly pale, and as he stretched his arms towards George
Effingham there was a wild appealing glance in those deep mournful eyes—a glance, as it were, of angelic pity and tenderness, that
went straight to the Cavalier's heart. He sank into the chair on
which he had been standing, apparently exhausted by his oratory.
A deep hum of applause, mingled with more open expressions of
approbation, greeted the conclusion of his sermon ; and the congregation, as they departed stealthily and silently, in twos and

threes, to their respective homes, congratulated each other in their
strange Scriptural parlance on the ' crumbs of comfort' they had
received, ' the draughts of living water' which had slaked their
thirst, and the ' crowning mercy of such a brand being snatched
from the burning' as the Cavalier officer who had joined in their
devotions, and whose conversion they deemed as good as completed
by the attention and interest with which he had listened to their
favourite preacher.

' The Brand' himself was one of the last to leave the vault.
The concluding words of the sermon he had just heard seemed to
ring on his ears; the wild, eager, imploring face to be still before
his eyes. ' Why *will* ye die ? ' The appeal seemed at once so
appropriate and so natural, the admonition so friendly, the warning so well-timed. It was the spark to the train of gunpowder,
the corner-stone to the edifice, the appeal to the feelings where the
Reason had long ago been satisfied. Effingham had been for
months a Puritan from conviction; he was now, as he was forced
to confess to himself, a Roundhead and a rebel at his heart.

As he ascended the steps leading from the vault into the shop,
an arm was thrust under his own, and looking round he discovered
that the only remaining individual of the congregation was about
to depart in his company, and signified his intention of so doing
in this somewhat unceremonious manner. It was the same person who had stood next him on his first entrance, and whose
mutilated head bore so fearful a witness to the sincerity of his professions. ' You may trust me,' said he abruptly, and without any
further apology or explanation ; ' I am a friend and brother. I
can read your soul, young man ; and you are *with* us, though not
of us. "The voice is Jacob's voice, though the hands are the
hands of Esau." I marked you when the shepherd invited you to
the flock ; and I cannot be deceived. Will you cast in your lot
with the children of the congregation ? '

Contrary to his wont, Effingham felt confused, and, so to speak,
taken by surprise at this sudden reading of his inmost feelings by
a thorough stranger. He could not but acknowledge that they
were interpreted aright; yet his bold, masculine mind shrank from
the avowal that his actual sentiments were so opposed to the profession he had adopted, nay, to the very clothes he wore. A
blush, half of eagerness, half of shame, clothed his bronzed features
as he replied, ' I would fain see a more righteous party at the
head of affairs. I would fain see a Godly Government, and a
people living in peace and morality, and the enjoyment of civil
as well as religious liberty. But I am a soldier of the Crown ; I

bear the King's commission ; what am I to do ?   And yet,' he
added abstractedly, and more as it were to himself than to his
companion, ' I have often thought ere this that Heaven is not on
our side.'

' Can you doubt it ?' eagerly urged the stranger, his features
lighting up with enthusiasm and excitement.   ' Can you doubt
that He whom we serve takes care of his own ?   Am not I myself
a living instance of his providence and his mercy ?   Have I not
survived the degradation of the pillory, despising the shame, and
endured the torment, regardless of the pain, in looking for the
martyr's crown—the crown that shall be doubly set with brilliants
because of this mutilated head ?   Listen to me, George Effingham.
I know you well, and I have watched you long.   It was to snatch
you like a brand from the burning that I ventured here into Oxford, into the very camp and stronghold of my enemies, and I will
save you from destruction—save you for that my heart yearneth
towards you as doth a mother's towards her first-born.   They
took me prisoner as I neared the godless city, and bound me on
one of their war-horses, and brought me into their guard-rooms;
and mocked me in the ribaldry of their mirth ; and I was dumb,
and spake not.   Then did one of their captains, a young and
well-favoured Malignant, whom the soldiers accosted with the
blasphemous title of Lord Francis, take pity on me, and bade his
men of war to scourge me, and let me go.   " Verily the tender
mercies of the wicked are cruel."   I was stripped and bound to
their accursed halberds; and two sons of Belial, tall and strong,
and stimulated with strong drink, were appointed for my execu-
tioners, when the young Malignant again interposed, and I was
suffered to depart, an object of derision and scorn, and cruel
mockery, which I pray may not be visited on my persecutors in
another world.   Then did I flee to the vault in which we met,
athirst for the living water, of which to-night we have both drunk
freely, and yet not athirst for myself alone.   It was borne in upon
me that he for whom I have prayed and wrestled would be there
too, and I found him for whom I looked seeking his portion with
the children of the congregation.   Verily, my prayers have been
answered.   Verily, the truth hath prevailed ; and now will not
you, George Effingham, cast in your lot with the elect for time
and for eternity ? '

They had already reached the street, and were pacing thoughtfully along in the moonlight.   One solitary figure walked slowly
on before them.   It was the preacher; his head bent down, his
whole being wrapped in meditation.   They neared him rapidly,

and were in the act of passing him when Effingham replied to the fervent appeal of his companion :—

' Could I do it with honour, I would shake to-morrow the very dust of the Court from off my feet. And yet what is earthly honour compared to eternal life? My friend!—if indeed you are my friend—I have never sought counsel yet from mortal man. I ask it now in my present strait, in the agony of my doubts. Are ye not too rash—too violent? Is there no possibility of saving our country, ay, and our religion, without bloodshed? Must we be all at each other's throats, in the name of peace and goodwill? Counsel me, I pray, for I am sorely distracted even to the very harrowing of my soul.'

The stranger looked at him with a satisfied air. ' The seed has fallen on good ground,' he muttered ; ' let it remain there and fructify.' Then added aloud, ' I will talk with you again on these matters. The night is now far advanced. To-morrow I will seek you at your own quarters. I know where you lie ; fear not, George Effingham, I will be with you in secret and unobserved.'

With these words he turned up a bye-street, and was soon out of sight, leaving Effingham a few paces in advance of the preacher, who now walked quietly up to him, laid his hand on the young man's shoulder, and looking into his face once more with the same wild, imploring, mournful glance, whispered in his ear, ' He that is not with me is against me. Turn ye, turn ye, why *will* ye die?' And he, too, disappeared like some unearthly vision that leaves behind it only a feeling of dread uncertainty and supernatural fear.

Effingham paced on, absorbed in meditation. With a strong sense of religion, that wanted but the stimulus of suffering and a consciousness of oppression to be fanned into the flame of fanaticism, he likewise entertained the feelings of a soldier on the point of honour and the sacred duty of remaining stanch to the banner under which he had once enlisted. It was a conflict that tore and vexed the strong man's mind to the verge of madness. Combining a wild and dreamy enthusiasm with keen reasoning powers, the imagination of a poet with the acute perspicuity of a logician, his was a nature above all others calculated to suffer from religious doubts, appreciating as it did, on the one hand, the importance of the subject, and on the other, the probability of error, where error was fatal and irremediable. He longed for the solitude of his own chamber, there to compose his powerful mind, and draw his own conclusions, uninterrupted and alone; and he

I

never greeted his friend Bosville with so inhospitable a welcome, as when he found him installed in that bare apartment which he had hoped was to afford him a refuge for the solitary meditation he required.

'What *have* you been doing?' exclaimed Humphrey, grasping his friend's hand with a cordiality which had in it something ominously suggestive of a desire for advice or assistance. 'Where *have* you been spending the livelong night? I trust you have employed it better than I have. I have been waiting here for hours to see you; and have read through the whole of that blundering tactician's work without understanding a word of it. George, I'm in a devil of a scrape, and I want you to see me through it!'

'A woman, of course,' answered Effingham, jumping, at once, like the rest of mankind, to the most charitable conclusion. 'Oh, Humphrey! I thought you knew better. I thought that even in Oxford you were too good to be lured like a kestrel by the flutter of a petticoat or the flirt of a fan. Young one, I'm ashamed of you!'

'Nay,' replied Humphrey, 'it's not so bad as that. Hear me. I've got into a quarrel, and we must fight it out according to the laws of the duello, and I want you to be one of my witnesses on the occasion. The worst of it is, it's with Goring, and you see he is the general of our division.'

Effingham drew a long breath, as if inexpressibly relieved. 'With Goring?' said he, 'and you know he's the best swordsman in the Royal army. Must you always fly at the highest game on the wing? Well, well, go thy ways, Humphrey; for a quiet amiable lad with far too much mother's milk still left in his constitution, thou certainly hast an inordinate liking for the whistle of hot lead, and the clink of cold steel. Nevertheless, if we *must* fight him, we *must*; and though it's contrary to my principles, and I had rather you had picked a quarrel with any one of them, except Lunsford, who has brought back a curious thrust in tierce from amongst the Puritans, that they boast no Royalist can parry, yet I cannot leave thee, lad, in the lurch. So open that cupboard, where you will find a flask of mine host's canary, and a couple of tall glasses; and let me know all about it. In the first place, hast got the length of his weapon?' Truly, the human mind, like the chameleon, takes its colouring from surrounding objects. A few minutes ago, and George Effingham was pondering deeply upon no less important a subject than his soul's salvation: behold him now, at the spell of a few words.

busily engaged in planning a *combat à l'outrance* between his
dearest friend and his superior officer. So the young men filled
their glasses and measured off the length of their weapons, and
sat till daybreak arranging the preliminaries of the duel.

CHAPTER XIV.

MAN TO MAN.

MORNING broke with a thick fog, highly favourable to those who
meditated such an undertaking as that of Bosville and his friend.
Notwithstanding the licence and immorality which pervaded the
Court, and which the so-called laws of honour scarce restrained
within the bounds of common decency, Charles, in a fit of con-
scientiousness, had issued a most stringent order against the
practice of duelling, and had threatened to inflict the punishment
of mutilation by the loss of the right hand on any who should
be found bold enough to transgress in this point—nay, under
aggravated circumstances the penalty of death was to be exacted
from the principals in the transaction. Such a state of things was
not calculated to inspire with confidence the anxious belligerent
who found himself thus hemmed in by a variety of evils, of which
it was scarcely possible for him to decide on choosing the least.
The alternative of being scouted for a coward, or run through an
empty stomach in the early morning, is sufficiently unpleasant
without the further aggravation of a gallows in perspective, should
superior 'cunning of fence' or strength of body enable the successful combatant to turn the tables on his adversary; and it is
no wonder that Bosville wrapped himself in his cloak with a chill
consciousness that the misty autumnal morning was more than
usually raw and lowering, and a sort of dismal foreboding that the
tufts of wet grass beneath his feet, saturated with the night dews,
might prove a very cold and uncomfortable resting-place after
some half a dozen passes with the keenest rapier in the Royal army.

Perhaps it may have been reflections such as these which
caused the young officer to hum a loyal air, expressive of great
devotion to his Majesty, a trifle louder than common, and to reply
to his companion's eager inquiries with a little more than his
usual gaiety and carelessness, though to do him justice every note
was in tune, and his manner, though excited, was as courteous
and kindly as ever. Mist or sunshine, up or down, in his stirrups

on the good sorrel, or on his back amongst the wet grass, there was no *white feather* about Humphrey Bosville.

He and Effingham were first upon the ground. It was a secluded spot at all times, and in a fog impervious at a hundred yards, offered every appearance of uninterrupted secrecy. A meadow some two acres-square, surrounded by a high blackthorn hedge not yet denuded of its leaves by the early frosts, and teeming with hips and haws and huge ripe blackberries, overshadowed moreover by a deep close copse of hazels, in which the nuts were ripening and the birds fluttering, and the quiet hares stealing about to crop the rank wet herbage, was no likely place for intruders at that early hour. A flat surface of thick, smooth turf afforded an excellent foothold for the combatants, and a distant farmhouse, from which, although its buildings were themselves unseen, the lowing of cows, the cackling of fowls, and other bucolic sounds were distinctly audible, promised shelter and assistance in the event of fatal consequences to the lawless *rencontre*. The two cavaliers looked about them, wrapped themselves closer in their cloaks, and walked to and fro, making foot tracks in the wet grass to keep themselves warm.

'I like a short blade best, after all,' quoth George Effingham, after a few minutes of deep cogitation, during which he had been perfectly silent, and his principal had hummed the same bars of his song over and over again. 'I like a short blade best against a delicate fighter. You must force Goring to close quarters, Humphrey, as soon as you can.'

'A short blade on foot, a long one on horseback,' answered his friend sententiously, and then relapsed into a profound silence. It was evident there was something on the minds of both foreign to the question of carte and tierce, and thrust and parry, and all the jargon of polite murder.

'Not here yet,' observed Effingham, once more peering through the fog on the look-out for the enemy. 'Zounds, Humphrey, I must speak out, lad! Thou and I are no two raw fledgelings to keep up an affectation of courage by pretending to ignore the presence of danger. Young as thou art I have seen thee tried, and I know thy mettle, man—ay, as well as I know my own sword. 'Twas but yesterday, so to speak, we held the old farm-house against Ireton's pikes, and we've had many a ride together after Waller before our last affair at Newbury. Look ye here, lad; Goring's a good blade. He's always in practice, and he's got a trick of turning his wrist down and coming in here just under your elbow that has put many a tall fellow on the grass.

You may get it in a queer place, Humphrey—mind, I don't say you will. Is there anything I can do for you, lad, any last word I can carry, if you should go back feet foremost into Oxford?'

Bosville's face brightened considerably. He pressed his friend's hand as he replied,

'I have been thinking of it all the morning, George, but it wasn't for me, you know, to begin on such a subject. I don't mind running my chance any more than my neighbours; and somehow, though my life has become dearer to me in the last twenty-four hours than it ever was before, yet I feel as if I could lose it contentedly and happily too. There is one favour you can do me, George, and that I would entrust to no man alive but yourself; one that I would only entrust to you at a moment like the present. George, I can depend upon you, I know. Give me your hand again.'

Effingham shook him cordially by the hand. 'Name it,' he said; 'if I'm alive I'll fulfil it for you.'

''Tis but a few words, a short message to deliver,' replied Bosville, with a smile that softened his whole face. 'If I fall, and *only* if I fall, seek out a lady in the court—you have never seen her, but you know her by name—it is—it is Mistress Mary Cave' (he blushed and hesitated when he mentioned her name); 'give her a glove you will find in my doublet, and tell her that I could not as a gentleman avoid this foolish quarrel, and that I regretted it chiefly because I had wished to devote my life wholly and exclusively to my Sovereign. Tell her I have not forgotten what she said to me; that I repeated with my last breath, "Loyalty before all!" And now, my dear Effingham, promise me that *you* will not fight if you can help it. It is a foolish custom, and leads to no good that the seconds should be involved in the quarrel of their principals. Do me this favour—promise me this, quick! —here they come.'

Even while he spoke two Cavaliers cloaked and wrapped up like Humphrey and Effingham, loomed through the fog as they surmounted the stile which gave them admittance at one angle of the orchard. They were talking and laughing loudly. It seemed they had neither regard for consequences nor fear of detection.

It was the fashion of the day to affect a haughty carelessness of bloodshed, and to look upon a duel as a pleasant opportunity for the interchange of lively sallies and jocose remarks.

Indeed, until the late Royal edict it had been the practice for each of the original combatants to appear upon the ground attended by two, three, sometimes even as many as four assistants,

chosen as a mark of the deepest respect amongst his own intimate
friends. As these gentlemen esteemed it a high point of honour
and an unspeakable privilege to engage their points with each
other on their own accounts, and totally irrespective of the quarrel
of their principals, it would sometimes happen that ten couples of
reasoning beings, hitherto constant associates and sworn friends,
would be doing battle to the death upon such weighty question of
dispute as the length of a lady's eyelashes or the colour of her
breast-knots. Now, however, the threats of death and mutilation issued from the Council, and which extended to all concerned in a duel, whether principals or witnesses, had somewhat
damped the ardour of the Royalists for this particular amusement,
and Goring had considered himself sufficiently befriended by the
single presence of his worthless associate, wicked Tom Lunsford,
on whose arm he leaned heavily as he approached the ground,
limping along with an affectation of more than his usual lameness,
probably with a view of enhancing his adversary's astonishment at
the activity which he would too surely display when stripped and
with steel in his hand.

He doffed his hat till its plume swept the grass, with a bow of
supreme courtesy to his antagonist, who returned the salute with
equally studied politeness; it being scrupulously exacted by the
laws of arms that the duellist should assume an attitude of the
most deferential humility towards the individual whose blood he
proposed to shed, whilst to all else on the ground it was considered
good taste to behave with a boisterous cordiality bordering upon
the jocose. Goring, too, was in the best of humours, for in addition to the natural gratification which he derived from all scenes
of this kind, he had passed the two or three previous hours much
to his own satisfaction in imbibing burnt canary, and as it was too
late to go to bed, in flinging a quiet main or two with his second,
which resulted, as usual, in his winning largely. True, Tom
Lunsford would never pay him; but still there was the prestige
of success, and he now proposed himself the pleasure of running
Bosville gracefully through the body, as an appropriate wind-up
to his night's amusement and preparation for his day's duties and
interview on business with the King.

'I fear we have kept you waiting, Captain Effingham,' he remarked, with a cordial greeting to that gentleman, for Goring
knew every officer in his division, and his private pursuits and
habits, better than those who only observed the surface of the
general's character would have supposed. 'My lameness must
be my excuse, though Tom and I have hurried hither as fast as

we could. Lunsford, let me present to you Captain George
Effingham, with whom, if you mean to try any of your cursed
Puritan tricks, you will meet with your match, for he has been
with the crop-ears later than yourself.'

Effingham started and coloured violently; his last night's visit
was then known—and to Goring! What if he should be de-
nounced, seized, examined as a traitor! perhaps lose his life without striking another blow on either side. For a moment he
forgot the duel and all about it. The image of Caryl and his
martyr-friend rose upon his mind. What would those good men
think of him now—what was he even now about to do? Nevertheless habit, as it always is, was too strong for conscience: he
manned himself with an effort, returned Goring's malicious leer
with a haughty though respectful stare, and saluted Sir Thomas
Lunsford with the punctilious politeness due to one whose sword-
point might probably that morning be at his throat. The latter,
with a facetious remark anent the coldness of the weather, and a
wish expressed with much unction, for a cup of burnt sack, produced a small piece of tape from beneath his cloak, and proceeded
to measure with it the swords of the combatants. ' Right to a
barleycorn,' remarked the Cavalier, returning to each the rapier
he had borrowed of him with a courteous bow. ' The morning
is too raw to waste your time in any further preliminaries, therefore, gentlemen, if you please, we will strip and get to work at
once.'

' Hold!' interrupted Effingham, as the duellists stripped to their
doublets and hose, first baring their breasts to show that no unfair
defences, no secret coat of mail or proof cuirass lurked beneath their
garments, took up their positions with watchful eager eyes and
bare quivering blades, and an ugly smile on each man's countenance, paler than his wont, though each was brave, and wearing
the peculiar set look that may be seen any day on the human face,
ay, even in a common street fight, when man is fairly pitted against
man. ' Hold, gentlemen! this duel is not to the death. Sir
Thomas Lunsford, by your leave we will draw and stand across
our men; at the first flesh-wound we can then strike their swords
up, and proclaim satisfaction given and received!' As he spoke
the two principals lowered their points, but etiquette forbade that
either should speak a word: strictly, they ought to have appeared
totally unconscious that any remark had been made, but although
their ground was taken they had not yet crossed swords, and the
duel had not begun.

Lunsford laughed loudly as he replied, ' Hardly, Captain Effing-

ham; and think what cold work it would be for you and me
standing to look on. Besides, sir,' he added, in a graver voice,
' consider the provocation, a blow struck and not returned!
Really, Captain, your notions of honour must have been somewhat
tarnished amongst your Puritan friends, when you can talk of bringing out four Cavaliers such a long walk on such a damp morning for
the mere child's-play you describe. No, sir, we decline anything
but the last satisfaction. Be good enough to waste no more time
about it, but place your man and begin!'

'Their blood be on their own head!' muttered Effingham, as
he advanced to Bosville once more, and, squeezing his hand, placed
him on the exact spot which the laws of the duello marked out for
him; then casting his cloak and plumed hat upon the ground,
drawing his trusty rapier and taking up his own position ' on
guard,' exactly six paces—the prescribed distance—on the right
of his friend, he called upon Lunsford to do likewise, reminding
him that ' when a duel is to be fought out to the death, it is incumbent on the seconds to mark their sense of the gravity of the
business by engaging themselves,' and adding, with peculiar courtesy, ' I hope Sir Thomas Lunsford will not disappoint me of a
lesson in fencing from the best blade now in Oxford.'

' At your service, sir,' replied Sir Thomas Lunsford, who could
scarcely refuse to accept so rational an invitation, but whose secret
inclinations for a ' pass or two ' were but little stimulated by
George's square muscular figure, easy attitude of practised swordsmanship and dark determined face, on which a remarkably dangerous look was gathering about the brows. As he spoke he also
drew, and placed himself in position, and the four men crossed
their thirsty blades at the same moment, with the same terrible
expression, the family likeness inherited from Cain coming out
fierce and ghastly on each forbidding face.

Humphrey Bosville was a young, active man, a complete swordsman, and of a bold determined nature, but he was no match for
his antagonist, who, to the confirmed strength of mature manhood,
added the ready facility of incessant practice, and the immovable
calmness peculiar to his own cold vigilant nature. Man of pleasure,
drunkard, debauchee as he was, Goring's passions, however strongly
they might be agitated, worked below the surface : nothing ever
seemed to shake his nerve or discompose his equanimity. Even
now, fighting to the death, an exasperated enemy in his front, and
a glittering small-sword thirsting for his blood within a few inches
of the laced bosom of his shirt, his eye was as steady, his colour
as unvarying, his whole demeanour as cool and insolent, as though

he had been standing in the presence-chamber or sitting at the council. In this he had a great advantage over his adversary, who, with all the exciteable feelings of youth, became less and less wary as he warmed to his work, and once or twice laid himself open to a thrust that might have put an end to the combat by inflicting on him a pretty smart flesh-wound, such as should incapacitate him from again holding a sword for a while. This, however, was not Goring's object. In a conversation with his second on their way to the ground, he had laid a bet of ten gold pieces that he would run his antagonist through the body without himself receiving a scratch, and he had made up his mind to do so by bringing into play a thrust in tierce for which he was celebrated, and which if unskilfully parried was a certainty. This deadly manœuvre, however, to be successfully carried out, demanded a very exact measurement of space, so, while Humphrey attacked fiercely again and again with all the impetuous ardour of his disposition, the more practised duellist lunged and parried and returned and traversed here and there, and drew his man inch by inch within the fatal distance.

In the mean time, Sir Thomas Lunsford and George Effingham, exchanging, to use the language of the day, ' a friendly pass or two,' to fill up the time, were sufficiently engaged with their own struggle to have but little observation to spare for their principals. The knight, however, weakened by his excesses, and of feebler frame than his antagonist, soon found himself a mere child in the hands of so powerful a fighter as the Cavalier captain. Twice he tried the *ruse* he had learned amongst the Puritans, and each time he found himself foiled by the iron arm and wrist opposed to him; twice he was driven from his ground, and only regained it by making in turn a furious attack, which left him each time more faint and breathless than before. Wicked Tom Lunsford thought his hour was come; and so it would have come indeed had Effingham been such another as himself; but George's heart, though he knew it not, was softened by his last night's company and conversation. Amidst the struggles of conscience had arisen a strange, awful sense of responsibility; and even in the heat and hurry of the assault, something seemed to whisper, ' Shall this man's blood too be on thy head ? ' So he contented himself with forcing his adversary to a disadvantage, and then rapidly disarming him by sheer superiority of strength.

As Lunsford's sword flew several paces from his hand, a heavy fall and a deep groan withdrew Effingham's attention from his own helpless enemy. Bosville was down at full length upon the wet grass, and Goring was wiping his bloody rapier carefully upon his glove ere he returned it to its sheath.

It was no time for punctilious courtesy. The accursed thrust had done its duty well. Humphrey's face was deadly pale; there were livid circles round his eyes, and the dark blood was welling up from his chest and saturating the white front of his delicate Flanders shirt. George's heart stopped beating as he knelt over his comrade to examine the wound. Even Goring was touched: and the man who had inflicted the injury—the man who but one short minute ago had hate burning in his eye and murder lurking in his heart—would have given his best horse, little as he valued human life, that he had left the deed undone.

' Take care of him, Tom,' said he, wrapping his cloak round him as he prepared to return to Oxford by another route, the only pre-caution he thought it necessary to take against discovery, ' and mind, you owe me ten gold pieces fairly won. D— it, I wish I hadn't, too,' he added, as he strode away; ' he was a fine bold lad, and the prettiest horseman I had in my whole division.'

Lunsford and Effingham, now fast friends, lifted poor Humphrey between them, and obtaining assistance at the farmhouse, bore him back with them to Oxford. As they entered the old city, morning service had but just concluded, and the bells were ushering in the day with a holy peaceful chime. And yet what a day's work had these men already finished! what a host of evil passions had they called up only to be allayed with blood! and now the blood was spilt, were the passions raging one whit less fiercely than before? Would not fresh provocation produce fresh crime, and so on, *ad infinitum*? Sin seems to be like hunger and thirst, repentance but the lassitude of repletion; anon we hunger and thirst again, and eat and drink our fill once more—only this once more—and then we are sorry for it, and promise faithfully this transgression shall be the last—till the next time—and so *audax omnia perpeti gens humana ruit*; and knowing this, we, who are never weary of re-quiring forgiveness, can refuse to forgive each other. Oh, man! man! created but a ' little lower than the angels,' how much higher wouldst thou be than the devils, if left to perish helpless by thyself?

CHAPTER XV.

CROSS PURPOSES.

SIR GILES ALLONBY, whistling cheerfully as he emerged from his lodgings to commence the military duties of his day, was no less horrified than astonished at the first sight that met his eyes in the street. A limp, helpless body, from which the life seemed to be ebbing rapidly away, covered with a dark cloak, was being borne upon a rude litter, formed hastily of a couple of hurdles, and a hedgestake or two, by four stout rustics, whom Sir Thomas Lunsford, with many oaths and entreaties, was adjuring to move as easily as possible to their burthen. Effingham, with a laced handkerchief in his hand, was wiping the froth from the lips of the sufferer, and the countenance of each Cavalier was darkened with an expression of ominous foreboding as to the result. Sir Giles, who expected to encounter nothing more alarming at that early hour than a tumbril of ammunition, a wagon-load of rations, or a drunken trooper deserving of the guard-room returning from his night's debauch, was fairly startled out of his self-command by the ghastly procession. 'Zounds, Tom,' said he, laying his hand upon Lunsford's arm, 'what mischief have you been at already since daybreak? This is some of your accursed tilting-work, I'll be sworn. Your staccatos and passados, and cursed Italian tricks of fence, that leave a good back-swordsman as helpless as a salmon on a gravel-walk. Who is it now that your quips and your punctilios, and your feints and your ins-and-outs, have placed heels uppermost, when the King sadly lacks soldiers, and every man's life is due to his sovereign? Who is it? Tell me, man, before I turn the guard out, and bring ye all up before the Council, who will take such order with ye that ye shall never so much as handle a riding-wand again!'

Lunsford, with all his impudence, was fairly brow-beaten by the old man's vehemence. 'Hold, Sir Giles,' he gasped out, quite humbly. 'The fight was a fair fight, and Captain Bosville brought it on himself. There is life in him still, Sir Giles, and leech-craft may bring him round yet. What, man, 'tis but a hole in his doublet, after all, and the fight was a fair fight, and fought with proper witnesses; ask Captain Effingham if 'twas not.'

'Bosville!' exclaimed old Sir Giles, the tears filling fast in his keen blue eyes, though with the instinctive repugnance of a good heart to a bad one, he turned from Lunsford, and dashed them away with the back of his hand. 'Bosville; the best lad in the whole Royal army. The bravest, the kindest, the cheeriest. Here the old man's voice faltered, and he was forced, as it were, to bully himself into composure again. 'Had it been ranting Will Scarthe, now, or fierce Nick Crispe, or thyself, Tom, who art never out of mischief save when the rest of us are fighting, I had said never a word. But Bosville,' he muttered under his breath, ' Bosville was worth a thousand of ye all. Within, there ! ' he cried, raising his voice, and turning back towards his own door. 'Grace! Mary! make ready the tapestry chamber. He lies nowhere but here. Steady there, men : bear him gently up the steps. Do you, sir,' to Effingham, ' run for a surgeon ; one practises at yonder shop, where you see the pole. Sound a gallop, sir, and hasten, for your life. My service to you, Sir Thomas Lunsford ; if this turns out badly, it will be a black day for some of ye when Prince Rupert comes to hear of it, or my name's not Giles Allonby.'

As he spoke, the old Cavalier officer busied himself in removing the cloak from Bosville's helpless form, and assisted in bearing him up the steps, and into his own house, where his servants relieved the rustics from their burthen. Those philosophers having been dismissed with a handsome gratuity, returned to their original obscurity, enlivened as long as the money lasted by a strenuous course of tippling, and many a revised version of the adventure in which they had been engaged : whilst Humphrey, now for the first time exhibiting signs of returning consciousness, was carefully conveyed to the tapestried chamber, and there laid under a magnificent canopy, adorned with ominously funereal feathers, on a huge state bed.

As they bore him upstairs, a pale scared face was seen looking over the banisters, belonging to no less important a person than Faith herself, the conscious cause of all this disturbance and bloodshed. Breathless and trembling, she rushed instinctively to Mary Cave's chamber, to bid her, as the bolder of the two, break the sad news to Grace Allonby ; but Mary had not returned from her early service about the person of the Queen, to whom she was again attached, and Faith, beside herself with mingled feelings of terror, pity, and remorse, was fain to seek her own pallet, and bury her face in the pillow in a fit of hysterical weeping, affording but little relief to her own agitation, and calculated to lead to no very decided result.

Thus it came to pass that Grace Allonby, leaving her chamber, neat, well dressed, and composed, to commence her daily duties.

was met in the passage by three or four servants bearing that which to all appearance was a corpse, and although Sir Giles considerately interposed his tall person between his daughter and the ghastly burthen, one glimpse which she caught was sufficient to assure her loving heart that it was Humphrey, and none but he, who lay stretched out there before her eyes.

Had Grace been a heroine of romance, she would have had two courses open to her. She might either have given vent to one piercing shriek, which should have rung in her listeners' ears till their dying day, and then, letting all her back hair down at once, have clasped both hands upon her heart, and fallen stone dead in the effort, but always with a tasteful regard to the disposition of her draperies, on the floor; or, with a lofty disdain for all feeling in such an emergency, but with a stony glare and a white statue-like face, she might have bled him herself on her own responsibility with her own bodkin, and so, seeing he had already bled nearly to the verge of the next world on his own account, have perfected the sacrifice of the man she loved, and exhibited at the same time her own presence of mind and mistaken notions of the healing art. But Grace Allonby was no heroine, only a loving, timid, trustful young woman, so her knees knocked together, and her lips grew quite white and twitched while she spoke, but she managed to clasp her hands upon Sir Giles's shoulder, and to ask him what she wanted.

'Oh, father, father! he's not quite—' she could not bring herself to say the word—'he's only wounded; only wounded, father!'

And as she could not *ask* if he was dead, so she could not bring herself to *think* him dead. 'Tis always so with the young, with those who have never known sorrow. There is an elasticity about the heart that has never been broken down, which bears up and protests as it were against the possibility of despair. Who knows how often she had brooded over her love, the love she scarcely confessed even to herself in the depths of her virgin heart; how many probabilities she had calculated, and possibilities she had fancied; how many chances had occurred to her that he might not perhaps care for *her*; that he might think her too plain, though her glass gave the lie to that; or too ignorant, or too humble and foolish and girlish for such a Paladin as she imagined him; how he might be separated from her by accident or duty, or her father's command, but by death—no, that had never entered her head; it could not be, she loved him so: it could *not* be. When George Effingham returned with the doctor, and the man of science, after shaking his own head and feeling his patient's pulse, and probing his wound, and otherwise putting him to no small pain and discomfort, declared that life was still hanging by a thread, a thread, moreover, that only required great care, and his own constant skill, to become once more the silver cord which Goring's rapier had so nearly severed, she felt scarcely grateful enough for the good news, she had been so persuaded of it all along. Die! she never thought he was going to die. He would get well, of course, quite well, and she would nurse him and wait upon him: there could be no harm in that, and it would take a long time to restore him, and when he was *quite* strong again, not before, he might leave them and go back to the army, to be wounded perhaps again. All this was consolatory, no doubt; nevertheless she went to her chamber, and prayed her heart out upon her knees, weeping plentifully, you may be sure, and such prayers never hurt a wounded man yet, to our thinking, nor a strong one either, for the matter of that. Happy he for whom such tears are shed, such orisons offered up.

She soon came back, with a pale steady face and red eyes, to take her place in the sick-chamber, where, according to the custom of the time, she quickly established herself as nurse and watcher, and general directress of the whole establishment. There was less mock-modesty in the days of which we write than in the present; less fancied evil, less of that strange prudish virtue which jumps at once to the most improper conclusions, and which, if there be any truth in the old adage, that ' to the pure all things are pure,' must have some dark mental spots of its own to justify its suspicions. Though the manners of the Court were sufficiently corrupt, the great bulk of the higher classes were to the full as correct and decorous in their demeanour as those of the present time; while for true purity and kindliness of heart, the charity that thinketh no evil, the generosity that forgiveth wrong, who shall say that the keen, high-minded Cavaliers, and their simple, straightforward dames, had not the best of it, as compared with the framework of our own cold, conventional, and somewhat cowardly state of society? with whose members the prime moral maxim is founded, not on what you *do*, but what people *say* of you; who wink conveniently enough at the infraction of every commandment in the Decalogue, provided you are scrupulous to keep the eleventh, which they have themselves added to it, and which says, 'thou shalt not be found out!'

George Effingham, returning from the doctor's house, he having accompanied that skilful practitioner home to his surgery, with lint, bandages, divers curiously coloured phials, and other munitions of the pharmacopœia, was somewhat startled to find an exceedingly fair and graceful young lady established in supreme command of the sick-room, and issuing her orders with the tact and decision of one to whom such a situation was neither new nor confusing. Indeed shrewd blows had been going now for some time between the Cavaliers and Roundheads, and Grace had already been often present at the healing of a broken-head, a sabre-cut, or the dangerous orifice of a musket-ball. Therefore George, as we have said, thrusting his grim face into the half-darkened chamber, started as though at the presence of an angel of light when his eyes encountered those of the young lady, and it was with a degree of bashfulness somewhat foreign to his nature that he assisted his new acquaintance in the disposition of the coverlets and pillows, and other arrangements for the ease of the sufferer, question and reply passing at the same time in subdued whispers, which promoted a far closer acquaintance in a short half-hour than would have sprung up under ordinary circumstances in a month.

Perhaps a woman never appears to such advantage as when tending the sick, moving gently through the room, or bending tenderly over the couch of the sufferer. George followed her about with his eyes, and wondered as he gazed. This was the sort of woman he had never seen before, or, if he had, only in the conventional circles of society, never as now in her own home, that home's prime ornament and chiefest blessing. Like many another, he had not arrived at manhood without experiencing certain partialities for those of the other sex,—here dazzled by a sparkling eye, there wooed by a saucy smile; but his experience had hitherto lain amongst women of a far different class and character from Grace Allonby. Phyllis was all he could wish, nay, more boisterous in her glee than accorded with George's melancholy temperament; but Phyllis must first of all have a purse of gold chucked into her lap—after that who so kind as Phyllis? Lalage, again, required constant devotion; but it must be offered at her shrine in public for all the world to see, or it was valueless, and he who would win her smiles must be content to take them as they came, share and share alike with fifty rivals. So George's higher feelings soon revolted from free, flaunting, flirting Lalage. He had got tired of women's society altogether, had devoted himself ardently to his profession, was plunged heart and soul in the whirlpool of controversy, engaged in a struggle of conscience against habit, prejudice, loyalty, and worldly honour; and now, just at the moment when of all times

in his career he had least leisure and least inclination to wear a
woman's chain, burst upon him the vision of what had been his
ideal all his life—a pure, high-bred, high-minded girl, simple
and sincere as the veriest wild flower in the woodland, yet cultivated and refined as the most fashionable lady about the Court.
Alas, poor George Effingham!   It was in short and broken
whispers that he explained to her the origin of the duel which
had terminated so seriously.   For once George found himself
quite eloquent as he defended his friend, and threw all the blame
of the affair on the aggressor.   'It was your maid, as I understand,
Mistress Grace, who was so shamefully insulted by Goring, and
Humphrey could not do otherwise, as a man of honour and a
gentleman, than interpose in her behalf.   Had it been any
other swordsman in the army we should have had the best of it;
but I knew from the first that trick in tierce of the General's
would be too much for the young one.   You see he feinted twice,
doubled, disengaged, and then came in under the arm—thus.
Pardon me, madam,' said George, interrupting himself as he
caught the bewildered expression of his listener's countenance,
and half laughing that his own clumsy enthusiasm should
have betrayed him into a disquisition on swordsmanship
with a young lady.   'Pardon me, you cannot be interested in
such details, but indeed it was no fault of Humphrey's that he was
led into this embroilment.   He was always a chivalrous lad, and
a gallant, and one who would face any odds to defend the weak
against the strong.'   And then he went on to tell her how the
young soldier now stretched out so pale and helpless on that bed,
had saved the child in a deadly cross fire at the attack of a small
redoubt in Flanders, and had held the back door of the farm-house
in Wiltshire so gallantly with his single rapier against half a score
of Ireton's pikes; and how he had given quarter to the tall
corporal that thrust at him from behind after he had taken him
prisoner at Kineton; and sundry other anecdotes illustrative of
Humphrey's chivalry and Humphrey's tender heart.

Grace listened with clasped hands and streaming eyes.   'I was
sure it could not be his fault,' she said; and equally *sure* she
would have been doubtless, had all the witnesses sworn and all
the juries in England found the reverse.   Will any amount of
proof destroy a woman's faith in the man she has once taken into
her heart?   On the contrary, it seems that the worse he behaves,
the closer she huddles him up and hides him there, and defies all
truth and reason to make her think ill of her nestling.   Verily
he who has a place in that *sanctum* should strive to bear himself

worthily of such unbounded faith and constancy. 'I was *sure* it could not be his fault,' she repeated, and removed the locks that had fallen across his brow, and propped the cushion under his shoulders with such a tender caressing hand that rough George Effingham turned his head away to hide his emotion; yet there was a strange feeling as of pain creeping about *his* heart too.

So they watched him silently a little longer, and presently he stirred and groaned and moved as if he would fain turn upon his couch, but the bandages prevented him, and the restraint seemed to arouse him, for he opened his eyes languidly, looked around as though in search of some one who was missing, and muttered a few indistinct words, of which his listeners only caught the sounds, 'Mary—loyalty—Mary,' and then groaned once more and his eyes closed, and poor Grace, becoming more and more painfully alive to his danger, thought for a moment that he was gone. It was not so, however. A potion had been left by the surgeon to be given the instant the patient should show signs of vitality, and the two strangely assorted nurses administered it to the best of their abilities, and again sat silently down in the darkened chamber to watch his slumbers and await his wakening, for on that wakening, so said the leech, would hang the issues of life and death. They might not speak now even in whispers, for such a slumber was on no account to be broken. Sir Giles, with a discretion that did him credit, had allowed no rumours of the *rencontre* to get about, dreading the disturbance visitors might occasion at his house. Mary, in fulfilment of her duties about the Queen, was ignorant that the man who had sworn fealty to her only the night before, whose devotion conjured up the vision of her dear face even on the confines of life and death, was lying within a few hundred paces, helpless, wounded, in the extremity of danger, and worked on in happy unconsciousness at her embroidery, receiving and returning the empty compliments of the flippant courtiers with her usual readiness and composure. Truth to tell, Mary had thought but little about him since the morning. So the house was quiet and the dark sick room silent as the grave, and the two watchers sat busied with their own thoughts. George Effingham scanning his fair companion with an ever-increasing interest, and she sitting with averted face and drooping head buried deep in thought or mayhap in prayer. Had she heard those few muttered words? could she interpret their meaning? had they caused that quiet look of suffering which contracted her gentle features? And yet to have had him safe she would have given him up willingly, nay thankfully, and her tears flowed afresh at the thought; so, womanlike, she waited and wept and watched. It was evening ere he woke, the crisis was past, and he was saved. Saved! she could scarcely demonstrate her gratitude sufficiently. With what a pleasant smile she gave George both her pretty hands, and shook his own large ones so kindly and cordially and thankfully. How she played about Sir Giles with childlike glee, and despatched the servants here and there in search of every comfort and luxury that could be wanted during the next month, and tripped up and down stairs in person after everything she had ordered, and finally flung herself into Mary Cave's arms, and burst out weeping yet again, ' vowing she was so happy—so happy ! she had never been so happy in her life before.' Deep and anxious thoughts had made their home too in the breast of that composed and dignified lady. From the moment of her return, when she had been informed of Humphrey's danger, she too had watched anxiously for the issues of life and death, had felt more than pity, more than interest, for the gallant warm-hearted youth who had given himself up to her with such devotion and self-abandonment. She had crept to the chamber-door, and listened to the heavy breathing of the sleeper, had trembled from head to foot for the result of his awakening, and when the moment of relief at length arrived, had sent back the tears that longed to burst forth with an effort of which she alone was capable. Stately and unmoved she came to look at him once where he lay: his eye brightened as it met hers, and, weak as he was, he strove to take her hand. He went to sleep again quite quietly after that, happy and peaceful like a child.

George Effingham, going back to his quarters loaded with the thanks and gratitude of the whole household, crossed the street to look up at a certain window, where a dim light seen through the curtain marked where his sick comrade lay, and a figure flitting across it ever and anon showed that the wounded man did not lie there uncared for. George must have been much attached to his brother officer, and much concerned for the care in which he left him, to judge by the deep sigh which he heaved, as after a good five minutes' watching he turned away and strode off to his own lodging.

A good constitution, unimpaired by too much claret, and over which not more than five-and-twenty summers have shed their roses and their thorns, soon recovers even from such an awkward injury as a thrust through the regions about the lungs, and the patient in such cases usually finds his relish and appetite for life enhanced in proportion to the narrow risk he has run of losing it.

A fortnight had scarcely elapsed from the period of Humphrey's duel, ere he was out of bed and able to enjoy to the utmost the many comforts and pleasures of convalescence. True, all violent exercise was forbidden for a time, and the sorrel was condemned to remain idle in the stable, whilst military duty of course was for the present not to be thought of; but there are certain circumstances which can make the sofa a very pleasant exchange for the saddle, and that soldier must indeed be devoted to his profession who would not sometimes wish to find his temporary bivouac in a fair lady's withdrawing-room.

A first-floor even in Oxford, with a solemn look-out upon the massive architecture of an old grey college, enlivened ever and anon by a squadron of cavalry marching by, their trumpets sounding, their bridles and stirrup-irons ringing, and their royal pennons flaunting on the breeze, or a party of plumed and brocaded courtiers sweeping haughtily up the street with the same air that became their stately persons and rich dresses so well in their own beloved Mall—an easy couch drawn to the window, and surrounded by all the little comforts that lady nurses alone know how to gather round the invalid—a few late autumnal flowers scattered tastefully about the room, a low wainscoted apartment, with carved and ornamented panels, elaborate cornices, Venetian mirrors, and strange quaint corners and cupboards, and fantastic ins and outs—two beautiful women pervading the whole, and shedding, as it were, an atmosphere of refined comfort around, the one worshipped and deified as a goddess, the other loving and devoted as a nymph—a tried and well-known comrade continually dropping in with the latest accounts from the army, the freshest news of the Court—and a merry, good-humoured host, never satisfied unless his wounded guest was supplied with the best of everything, and continually devising new indulgences and luxuries on his behalf—all this combined to make Humphrey's convalescence so delightful a process that we are fain to believe the only person who experienced a slight feeling of disappointment when he made his first journey round the room, with the aid of George Effingham's strong arm and a crutch, was the restored sufferer himself, so happy had he been in his illness, so loth was he to become once more independent of the care and kindness to which he had got accustomed.

Sir Giles was frequently absent on his military duties, so the two ladies and the two young Cavalier officers were thrown almost constantly together, for George Effingham esteemed it prudent to keep as quiet as possible after the duel, and Mary Cave easily obtained leave from her good-natured mistress to devote as much time as she pleased to the amusement of the wounded hero. Anything in the shape of sentiment found its way too surely to Henrietta's heart, and her lively imagination had already constructed a sufficiently interesting love tale out of the materials she was at no loss to gather from her gossiping courtiers. A beautiful woman, a pretty waiting-maid, a duel with Goring, and a handsome young soldier run through the body, constituted a framework on which to elaborate a romance voluminous as the *Grand Cyrus* itself. So the *quartette* sat and amused each other day by day, three of them rapidly and steadily imbibing that delicious poison which, like the fruit gathered from the tree of knowledge, gives the first insight into the inner life, and darkens the outer one for ever afterwards.

Mary alone seemed to boast immunity from the disease. She had had it, she thought, like the measles or the small-pox, and, except in a very modified form, scarce worth apprehension. She was safe from a fresh attack. How it had scarred and altered her is no matter. The visible face was still fresh, and rosy, and radiant, if her heart had grown prematurely old, and hard, and withered; the process of petrifaction had been painful, no doubt. Experience, however, had not blinded her, and she alone of the four companions saw clearly and judged rightly of what was going on. She said as much one afternoon over her embroidery, as they sat watching the early sunset gilding the opposite wall, plunged in a delicious day-dream, from which, even while she spoke, she felt it was cruelty to wake them. It was the very day on which Bosville had made his first tour round the room, having previously received a ceremonious visit of congratulation from his late antagonist; for Goring, as soon as he heard the wounded man was out of danger, had thought it, as he said, but common politeness to inquire after him, and had spent half an hour by his couch, during which he had made a thousand professions of regard and friendship, and rendered himself vastly agreeable to the two gentlemen. Of the ladies, Mary despised his character thoroughly, though she admired his talents; and as for Grace, if looks of scorn and hatred could kill, she would have run him through the body as he stood there upon the floor.

' 'Tis an idle winter,' quoth Mary, bending low over her sewing, and turning her head away, for she was not insensible to the pain her words would too surely inflict; 'and yet, from what Lord Goring tells us, there is still work to be done down in the west. What say you, Captain Effingham, a squadron of Cavaliers with Prince Rupert in Gloucestershire were merrier company than two quiet dames in an Oxford lodging-house?—a good horse and a *demi-pique* saddle a more health-restoring resting-place than yonder easy couch by the window?' Mary spoke quickly and uneasily, her colour went and came, and she could not forbear glancing towards Humphrey, whose pale cheek crimsoned immediately, and who turned on her a look of pain and reproach that well-nigh brought the tears to her eyes. Grace looked scared and confused. *She* did not think her patient was well enough yet for a *demi-pique* saddle. It was anything but an idle winter to *her.* She glanced fondly and gratefully at Effingham, and George felt his great strong heart thrill and bound with pleasure as he replied,

'We must not move him just yet, Mistress Mary. Such a wound as his might open again, and if it did, all the doctors in Oxford could not save him. When he gets better, he is to have a troop of "The Lambs," * so Hopton tells me, and then he will probably soon qualify himself for your nursing once more. As for me,' added Effingham, darkly, 'I doubt if I shall ever draw sword to the old war-cry again.'

'You, too, have been idle long enough,' replied Mary, with a piercing glance, under which George winced and lowered his eyes. 'The blade will get rusty that rests in the scabbard. There are other wounds to be taken than those dealt by a pair of dark eyes, Captain Effingham, and Oxford is a bad place for you, for more reasons than one. Listen.' She drew him aside into the window, and whispered so low as not to be overheard, though Humphrey's eyes wandered uneasily after her motions. 'You are too good to fight a losing battle all your days. You do not know what it is; better not learn the lesson. Take my advice, strike your tents, sound "boots and saddles!" Go back into active, stirring life, it is your element, and forget the dream you have been dreaming already too long.'

Effingham started, glanced uneasily at Grace, and replied at once,

'My sword may rust, and welcome, Mistress Mary. It has been drawn too often already in a bad cause. Must we all think there is no duty to fulfil in life but to tilt at each other's throats? Must

---

* So called from their wearing *white* doublets. Sir John Suckling had a troop in them called the 'coxcomb troop,' from the splendour of their appointments. Like 'the Duke's' dandies in the Peninsula, these coxcombs were not found to be the *last* in the fray.

we all be as hot-headed, and foolhardy, and inconsiderate as that romantic boy on the sofa yonder?'

'It is a pity you are not,' she replied quickly, with a glance of admiration, almost tenderness, at the wounded youth. 'Poor boy, he is one in a million! but it is of you, Captain Effingham, that I wish to speak. You are watched here in Oxford; your opinions are known. It was but last evening they talked of you in the Queen's apartments. They turned it all to jest, of course, as they do everything; but such jests are pointed and dangerous; it is better not to be the subject of them. Take my advice, leave Oxford, keep your heart unscathed and your head upon your shoulders; another day or two and it may be too late!'

Effingham bowed and sat down again. He seemed to be revolving her counsel thoughtfully in his mind: but he gazed at Grace the while, and Grace looked anxiously at Humphrey, whose eyes wandered after Mary as she moved about the room; and so the four played on their game at cross-purposes, and derived, doubtless, some incomprehensible satisfaction from the pastime. At length the fair disturber of their peace approached the sofa once more.

'I am going into waiting to-night,' she said to Bosville, with one of her sunny, winning looks. 'The Queen will ask me how you are; when shall I say you will be ready for your command?'

His eye sparkled: he seemed a new man.

'In a week at farthest,' said he boldly. The day after I can get into the saddle I will be with them. Thank you for the interest you take in me—thank you for all your kindness.' He seized her hand, and Grace walked away to arrange the flowers at the other end of the room. 'I *will* be worthy,' he whispered, the tears starting to his eyes, for he was still weak from loss of blood. ' "Loyalty before all !" '

' "Loyalty before all !" ' she repeated in her sweet, low voice, returning the pressure of his thin, wasted fingers; and from that moment the patient was a convalescent, and on the road to a rapid recovery.

So Mary went off to dress for her courtly duties, and Effingham, with a heavy heart, took leave of his kind friends, and left the well-known room, with its many attractions, for his lonely lodging —how dreary by the contrast! and Grace, who could not bear to-night of all nights to be left alone with the patient, betook herself to her chamber, whither, as we dislike to see young ladies in tears, we will not follow her; and Humphrey, left alone in the darkening twilight, sank into a refreshing sleep, gilded with dreams of a pair of loving eyes, and a fair fond face, and a soft voice that whispered ever, 'Loyalty before all!'

'I'm sure I don't know what's come to my young lady,' observed Faith to a staid and sober personage, who now seldom left her side. 'She's been and locked herself into her room again, and when I knock at the door, it's "Presently, Faith, presently," and I can't see through the keyhole, for she's gone and left the key in it, but by the sound of her voice I'll be sworn—that is,' amended the pretty Puritan, catching herself up—'I would venture to affirm, she's been crying; and what that's for, with all she can want in the house, and the Captain out of danger—bless his handsome face and bold spirit (though sinful)—is clean past me!'

'Women is mostly unaccountable,' replied the individual addressed, writhing his grim features into the semblance of a smile. 'Young ones 'specially, though I'm not sure that the middle-aged isn't the most tricksome. Perhaps they live and learn; live and learn, Mistress Faith, like their betters, but they can't be expected to be reasonable like and understanding for all that, poor things; it's a lower creation, there's no doubt it's a lower creation, and unaccountable accordingly.'

It may be remarked that our friend Dymocke's philosophy, for Dymocke, we need hardly inform the reader, it was who spoke, was of a somewhat vague and misty nature, inconsequent in its arguments and inconclusive in its results, and as such he doubtless considered it adapted for the softer sex, for Dymocke, though professing, and indeed demonstrating, a great regard and affection for that division of the species, still invariably assumed the attitude of superiority which he deemed becoming the dignity of the nobler variety, and was looked up to and reverenced by the women accordingly. He and Faith, since the midnight rencontre, and subsequent removal of Humphrey to Sir Giles Allonby's lodgings, had become inseparable, a sense of favour and protection on the one hand, accompanied by a strong partiality for a young and pretty face, and a consciousness of gratitude and inferiority, with a charitable desire for the conversion of a sinner on the other, cementing their friendship into an intimacy that every day assumed a more tender character. There is nothing makes a woman so keen as the chance of a proselyte. It stirs up in her the chief characteristics of her organization—her natural benevolence, her religious zeal, her unaccountable delight in upsetting all pre-existing arrangements, her little spice of contradiction, and her innate love of change. It is such a pleasing excitement, and she persuades herself she is doing so much good all the time, so she *converts* him, or *perverts* him, no matter which, and when she has turned him completely round to her own way of thinking, finds herself, after all, somewhat dissatisfied with the result.

Many an argument did Faith hold with her admirer upon all the vexed questions of the day, standing, as she did now, with her mistress's garments thrown over her arm, and a lighted candle in her hand, wherewith she illumined passages, staircases, entrance halls, and such out-of-the-way places as she selected for the theatre of her discourse. Faith's strongest point had hitherto been the unlawfulness of using weapons of fleshly warfare, even in self-defence, but she had been beaten somewhat from this by the events of the last fortnight, and the gallant stand made by her protector with his oaken cudgel in her defence. Now, however, this attack of her admirer on the sex roused her to make use of her old argument, and she replied with considerable volubility and a heightened colour, 'Lower creature or not, Master Hugh, and unaccountable, if *you* please, leastways we use the weapons of sense and reason in *our* behalf, not ranting like you men, with your weapons out at every wry word, and a stout cudgel ready to enforce your arguments, as you call them: pretty arguments, forsooth! And call yourselves reasoning creatures; get along with you, do!'

'An oak cudgel was the best argument t'other night, Mistress Faith,' replied Dymocke; 'd'ye think wild Goring and his troop of roaring fly-by-nights would have listened to any other? What would you have had me to do less when he lifted thy veil, the villain, and I tripped him up and laid him on his back on the pavement ere he could cry "hold?" What wouldst thou have done thyself, lass, answer me that, if I hadn't been too quick for him, general of horse though he be?'

'I should not have offered him the other cheek, for sure,' replied Faith, demurely; and Dymocke, taking the hint, put a period to the conversation by another of those practical rejoinders which the proverb informs us are only appropriate when the 'gorse is in bloom.'

CHAPTER XVI.

THE QUEEN'S APARTMENTS.

In three days Humphrey was sufficiently recovered to go abroad and taste the fresh air out of doors, a cordial best appreciated by the sufferer who has been long confined to a sick room. In three more he was sent for by the Queen, whose curiosity had been much roused by the history of the quarrel and the duel, whose interest, moreover, had been excited by Mary's account of the wounded man's chivalrous and romantic character, and who had seen with her own eyes that he was well-favoured, which with Henrietta added considerably to the chances of a courtier's advancement.

'You must bring your young *chevalier* to my private receptions, Marie,' said the goodnatured Queen, with her arch smile. 'Not on the great nights when his Majesty comes, and we are all as grave as councillors, and retire when the clock strikes ten, but to one of my own quiet evenings, when we will sup in the Round Room, and Lady Carlisle shall sing us a new "*roman*," and Kirke tell us her wickedest stories, and we will console the poor youth that he has got well so soon, and lost the pleasure of being nursed by pretty Marie. Are you very fond of him, *Mignonne?*'

'I have never said so, Madame,' answered Mary with quiet composure, but with a slight elevation of the head and neck that made her look far more like a queen than the thoughtless little lady who questioned her. 'It is not my custom to make confessions, and if it were, I have here nothing to confess.'

'But there is another,' interposed Henrietta, eagerly. 'Ah, now I see it all; Grace, that is her name. I know her, I have seen her; dark-haired and *gracieuse*, with a *petite mine*. You are jealous, Marie; jealous, and with good reason, the *gracieuse* is a dangerous rival, the wounded man cannot run away from her charms. She is always in the house, and my poor Marie has been obliged to be about *our* person here. She has lost him to the *gracieuse*, and she is jealous. My proud Marie jealous like any other woman, after all; it is too good a joke!' And Henrietta, who was not particular *why* she laughed, so long as she *did* laugh, broke out into a peal of hilarity, and clapped her hands like a merry, mischievous, light-hearted child.

Mary laughed too, a low, silvery, pleasant laugh. Had her mistress been a better judge of human nature she would have detected in that laugh no wounded feelings, no jealous apprehensions, nothing but a proud consciousness of power, an unshaken security in her own dominion, perhaps a touch of pity, perhaps a shadow of regret that she was not more engrossed with her conquest. Yet she had never liked Bosville so well as at that moment.

They were pleasant little meetings, those private receptions of the Queen at Merton College. That they conduced in any degree to the stability of the Royal party few will be found to assert, but none can deny that they furthered to a considerable extent the consumption of well-cooked dishes and sparkling wines, the expenditure of much compliment and small-talk, not to mention a large amount of flirtation and intrigue, political as well as private, and the occasional exchange of vows not sanctioned by the Church. The Puritans held these meetings in especial reprobation, and from Jezebel downwards, esteemed no reproachful name too abusive with which to vilify the royal lady who presided over them; whilst many a wise head amongst the old Cavalier party, and the more experienced advisers of the King, opined that neither Ireton's pikes nor Cromwell's Ironsides had inflicted half such deadly wounds on their Sovereign's cause as the empty, scheming, underhand circle of selfish gallants and flaunting dames that surrounded his misguided wife. Yet Charles could never be brought to believe it. With the touching obstinacy of a weak, yet conscientious and enthusiastic nature, he lavished on Henrietta a blind adoration that she seems thoroughly to have despised. He confided to her all his most secret schemes, even to the meditated treacheries that he seems to have persuaded himself were not only venial but meritorious; he laid bare for her his whole heart, with all its shortcomings and all its weaknesses; he reversed the order of the sexes in looking up to her for advice and assistance, and she despised him accordingly. It is a fatal mistake. Fond as women are of power, gladly as they see the man they love at their feet, thrilling as is the delicious consciousness that their lightest word can tame and turn the rougher nature to their will, yet, when the moment of danger and difficulty *really* comes, if he cannot act for himself, and for her too; if he cannot stand up and take the brunt of all, and shield her, so to speak, with his body; if he quails beneath the storm and leans upon her, the weaker reed, for support, he is never a *man* to her again.

Charles, in his council or his closet, writing in cipher to his generals, or armed in mail and plate at the head of his army, was never apart from his Queen in spirit. Every action of his life, every one of his letters, every turn he made out of the judicious path, proves beyond a doubt the romantic affection he cherished for that empty flirting little Frenchwoman. She was never out of his thoughts. Let us see how she returned the love of the ill-fated king.

Sitting on a low ottoman, sparkling with diamonds, a huge feathered fan in one hand, and setting down with the other an empty coffee-cup on a richly chased salver held by a black page-boy, Henrietta looked more brilliant than usual as she carried on a lively conversation with a plain, sallow gentleman, who appeared to occupy a high place in her Majesty's favour. Lord Jermyn knew his power well, and made unsparing use of it. With no very pleasing exterior, none of the physical advantages which are generally supposed to make such way in a lady's good graces, and to which she was quite as fully alive as the rest of her sex, he had obtained an ascendancy over the Queen which can only be ac-counted for by his extraordinary knowledge of character, his facility for adapting himself to the tastes and adopting the opinions of those whose favour he thought it worth his while to cultivate, and above all, his preeminent talent for, and unconquerable love of, that complicated system of intrigue which ruled the whole Court, and originating in the Queen's own private apartments, spread its meshes over the length and breadth of England, nullifying the deliberations of the wise, and paralysing the blows of the strong.

She was conversing with him in a low voice, mingling the most important political topics, the secret counsels of her husband, and the private intelligence from his generals, with the extravagant language of gallantry then in vogue, with the lightest jests, the silliest gossip, and the emptiest laughter that ever floated through a drawing-room. His manner was that of respectful admiration while he listened, yet there was at times an expression of authority in his eye, and tone of sarcasm in his voice, that argued his con-sciousness of his own power, and the value in which he was held by the voluble Queen. As he leaned over her reclining figure, and replied in corresponding tones to her whispered confidences, the pair had far more the appearance of a lover and his mistress than a subject and a sovereign.

Partly concealed by an old Japanese screen of grotesque carving and quaint ornament, but with ringing laugh and lively sally, declaring plainly their whereabout, Lord Bernard Stuart and Mrs. Kirke carried on an amicable warfare, according to their wont, half jest half earnest, sparkling with quips and innuendos and playful satire, and many a phrase implying far more than met the ear, with as much freedom from restraint as though they had been a hundred leagues from the presence of royalty. The young nobleman was attending on her Majesty in the execution of his duty; and a very pleasant duty it seemed to be, judging by the expression of his handsome countenance, enhanced by the uniform of the Life Guards, which he commanded. A breast-plate, back-piece, and cuisses of steel, set off his fine figure and chivalrous features to the best advantage, whilst the rich lace on his buff surcoat, the delicate embroidery of his collar, and gaudy folds of his crimson silk scarf, tempered with an air of courtly splendour these warlike accessories of costume. Long fair curls, soft and perfumed like a woman's, floated over his shoulders; as Mrs. Kirke looked up in his face from the low couch on which she had placed herself, she could not withhold from that handsome smiling countenance a part of the admiration which she believed in her heart to be alone due to a certain pair of arch blue eyes and a certain mischievous dimpled smile that met her in the glass every day. Like many another carpet knight, Lord Bernard was no contemptible adversary to encounter when blows were falling thick and fast on a stricken field. On more than one occasion he had petitioned in his own name, and that of the brother coxcombs whom he commanded, for leave to abandon their peculiar duty of guarding the King's person, and to charge in the van with Prince Rupert and his desperadoes. The stanch stern Ironsides, the grim Presbyterian pikemen, found these curled Malignants very fiends in fighting; and though they compared them energetically to Absalom and other good-looking reprobates, and cursed them with fervent piety, yet did they go down before them like barley in harvest-time notwithstanding.

Now, however, Lord Bernard was on guard, and his own sense of responsibility not permitting him to retire to rest, whilst the Queen's partiality for handsome faces afforded him a certain welcome in her private apartments, he was combining duty with pleasure by flirting furiously with Mrs. Kirke—a lady for whom he openly avowed an ardent attachment, which she as openly returned, and which was not likely to do either of them the slightest harm.

Some men might have been in danger, too, for the Syren was a fearfully well-favoured Syren, and sat upon her rock in the most bewitching of attitudes, and sang her seducing song in the most enchanting of tones. Besides she had spent her whole life in the luring of mariners; had stranded them by scores on different shoals and quicksands; had frightened them, and teased them, and ducked them and drowned them, and never wet her own feet, so she boasted, in the process.

If Lord Bernard had only admired blue eyes and golden locks, and smiles and dimples, and white skins and dazzling teeth, he had been in danger too; but the Life-Guardsman's heart was of capacious proportions—constructed, so to speak, in compartments, of which he could empty a drawer at any time to make room for fresher contents; or if need were, shut it up and desist from using it altogether. So the pair were but fencing with buttons on their foils, after all.

Their engagement was at its height: she was shaking her curls like a shower of gold all over her saucy face and white shapely neck and shoulders; he was picking up the fan she had purposely dropped, and pressing it enthusiastically to his lips, when the Queen called him suddenly to her side; and Lord Bernard, at once changing his manner for one of the most reserved and stately decorum, returned the fan with a profound bow, and stalked across the room to wait her Majesty's command with another solemn and reverential obeisance.

She was determined to punish Jermyn for something he had said; womanlike, she had no difficulty in finding an opportunity. Handsome Lord Bernard had been always rather a favourite, so she beckoned him across to her, and the Life-Guardsman obeyed accordingly.

'Lady Carlisle tells me you have a vacancy in the troop, my lord!' she said, pushing away the little black boy to make room for the young nobleman—an action not lost upon Jermyn, and the observation of which did not improve the expression of his sallow face; 'if so, I have already disposed of it.'

'If your Majesty condescends to review us again, we shall have nothing but vacancies left,' was the reply; 'we cannot sustain the bright glances of yourself and your ladies; they pierce our breast-plates, and wither us up like roses in the noon-day sun. With regard to a vacancy, there was none in the force when I inspected it this evening at curfew. Lady Carlisle, however, was later than usual in the presence—she may have made one since then.'

Lord Bernard was a courtier, but he was a commanding officer as well, and the instincts of the latter will always predominate over every other consideration. He did not approve of this interference with his prerogative, and he did not care if the Queen and Lady Carlisle both knew it.

Henrietta laughed. 'What say you, Lucy?' she called out to

her favourite, who was working quietly with Mary Cave at the far end of the room, 'have you been tampering with Lord Bernard's command since nightfall? If not, we want a vacancy, and you have our commands to go and kill us a Life-Guardsman before supper time.'

Lady Carlisle looked up with her calm innocent smile.

'Shall I begin with Lord Bernard himself, Madame?' she asked; 'he seems half dead already; unless you, Mrs. Kirke, will finish what you have nearly accomplished so well.'

Mrs. Kirke did not like Lady Carlisle; she was no match for her, and she knew it; the peeress, in addition to an immovable countenance, possessing the immense advantage of hesitating at *nothing*. But she never refused an appeal to arms even when sure of being worsted, so she laughed merrily and answered—

'I only kill *my foes*, and that when I am angry. Now, Lord Bernard and I have hardly quarrelled once the whole night. I am not like Lady Carlisle: my ship is but a poor little privateer, with letters of marque against the enemy—not a pirate, that destroys both sides alike, and knows no distinction when she has hoisted the black flag!'

'You are quite right not to sail under false colours,' answered Lady Carlisle, with such a clear, guileless look full into Mrs. Kirke's *rouge*—which indeed was put on a little too thick, and somewhat nearer the cheekbones than Nature plants her own roses —that the discomfited little woman was fain to hide her face behind her fan, and retire into one of her explosions of laughter to cover her confusion. The Queen, however, was amused and delighted at this little passage of arms, and reverted to the subject.

'Our proud *Marie*,' she observed, 'has a *protégé* that we should wish to have about our person. He is young, gallant, and good-looking,' with a glance at Jermyn, who either winced or pretended to do so—'Marie and I would like him to be near us. What say you, my dear, shall I make Lord Bernard appoint him to the Life-Guards? One word from either of us, and it is done?'

'Your Majesty is most kind,' answered Mary, 'but I entreat you do nothing of the sort. He is pledged already to another service. His honour demands that he should be in the field the instant he is well. He wishes to leave for the West immediately. Your Majesty cannot confer on him a greater kindness than by bidding him depart.'

Mary spoke eagerly, though she retained her self-command. 'Never' (she thought in her own heart), 'never shall he become selfish and intriguing, even if he be a courtier, like all of these.'

Alas! she would fain have made him a second Falkland; and if she had succeeded what would it have profited? Was he not far too good for her even now?

The Queen laughed at her determination, and rallied her according to her wont. 'You dare not trust him with Lucy and Mrs. Kirke,' she exclaimed; 'you want to detach him from the *gracieuse.* You are jealous, *Marie,* jealous!—and that is the best fun of all. Hush! here he comes.'

A stately yeoman here attended Bosville into the anteroom, through which he was conducted by a decorous gentleman usher in black, armed with a white wand, as far as the door of the presence chamber, where he was handed over to the care of Lord Jermyn, who in right of his office led him up to the Queen herself. Henrietta looked graciously upon the young soldier, and gave him her hand to kiss.

The ladies about a Court are no exception to the general rule of their sex. They prize a novelty as much as do the cherriest-cheeked maidens that take butter to the fair. When the novelty, too, is handsome, graceful, richly dressed, and imbued with a certain air of becoming softness and langour which recent illness leaves upon the young, they are apt to give vent to their curiosity and interest with an ardour that borders upon admiration. This, by the way, is another quality which renders woman-worship so satisfactory and profitable a service.

Mrs. Kirke's fan was down in an instant. 'Who is he?' she whispered to Lord Bernard, who was again by her side; 'very handsome for a brown man (Lord Bernard was fair and fresh-coloured); 'but what makes him so pale? and why does he move as if he had stays on? Bandaged, is he, and nearly killed by Goring? How wicked of Goring!—who is charming, too. By the way, why is he not here to-night?' So Mrs. Kirke ran on, keeping her admirer by her side to answer her questions, and ogling the new arrival the while with all the artillery of her mischief-loving eyes.

Lady Carlisle, too, in her quiet modest way—that soft, gentle demeanour, that she flattered herself no mortal man could resist, that left all her noisy, laughing, chattering rivals miles and miles behind—vouchsafed to bestow no small share of attention upon Humphrey Bosville. He was the lion of the evening, and provoked his share of observation accordingly. It so happened that the duel took place at a period when the Court was unusually devoid of incident, and this in times when every week brought news of a battle fought or a town lost or won. Such a state of stagnation as three days without an event of some sort was unbearable; and Bosville's *rencontre* with Goring at so dead a time was a perfect windfall to the weary gossiping courtiers. Even the Queen vouchsafed to inquire particularly after his wounds: and when supper was announced, and the little party adjourned to discuss that merry meal in the Round Room, her Majesty condescended to pour him out a glass of Hippocras with her own white hand, and desired him to quaff it, with a complimentary jeer at his blanched cheeks that brought the colour back to his face.

He sat between Lady Carlisle and Mary Cave. With the former he bore his share bravely enough in that fictitious species of dialogue which then as now constituted the language of fashionable life, but which was essentially distasteful to the romantic temperament of the simple soldier. To the latter he scarcely spoke three words, but his voice was quite altered; and Lady Carlisle, an experienced practitioner, found him out immediately.

Therefore she could not of course let him alone. Too confident in her own charms, and too essentially heartless to be *jealous* of any woman on earth, she was yet *rapacious* of admiration. If nineteen men out of a score were paying her their homage, she could not rest till she had brought the twentieth also to her feet. Humphrey was young, graceful, and good-looking; but had he been old, misshapen, and ugly, he possessed an infallible charm in Lady Carlisle's eyes—he was evidently the property of another, and must be trespassed on accordingly.

She had been too often at the game not to know exactly how to lay her snares. She waited till the Queen had done with him, and Mrs. Kirke had laughed him out of countenance, and then turned to him with her soft voice and her deep eyes, and talked to him of flowers and music, and such topics as she thought most congenial to his temperament, sighing gently between whiles, as giving him to understand that she too was out of her element in that gay circle, and that he was the only man capable of understanding her, if he would but give himself the trouble to try.

Had Bosville been ten years older, he would at once have flung himself into the spirit of the contest. He would have known that with a disposition like that of Mary Cave, to awaken her jealousy was the nearest road to her heart—that blind submission would never conquer the proud spirit which bends alone to a prouder than itself.

But he was too loyal, too true-hearted to enter into such calculations. There was but one woman in the world for him; so he was stanch to his faith, here in a Queen's drawing-room as he would have been in his lonely bivouac under the winter sky, or down amongst the horses' feet in a charge, with the life-blood ebbing fast, and everything but his great unconquerable love passing dreamily away. It was his nature to be tyrannized over, as it is the nature of many of the bravest, and gentlest, and noblest of God's creatures. The highest couraged horse winces the most readily from the spurs. Do not drive them in too pitilessly, lest you rouse him once too often. He may fail at last, and fall with you some day to rise no more.

The Queen clapped her hands as the repast concluded, and the black page handed round the grace-cup of spiced wine in a huge antique goblet.

'One of your sweetest songs, Lucy,' said her Majesty to Lady Carlisle, 'and then a fair good night to all.'

As she spoke she signed to the little page to bring a guitar which rested in a corner for the Syren, and withdrawing somewhat apart with Mary Cave, lent a listening ear to the conversation of that lady, who by her animated gestures and eager face appeared to engross her mistress's attention with some subject of more than common importance.

'The Queen hates music,' said Lady Carlisle, bending languidly over the guitar, and looking softly into Bosville's eyes; 'but I will sing to *you*. What do you like? something about love and war, I am sure. Will you promise to observe the moral if I take the trouble to sing you the song?'

Humphrey answered not much to the purpose. His eyes and thoughts were at the other end of the room, and he had not yet acquired the knack, so useful at Court, of attending to two people at once.

Lady Carlisle swept her hand across the strings; the gesture became her admirably, and with many a covert glance of sly allusion, sang in a low, sweet voice the not inappropriate ballad of

The Proud Ladye.

''Tis a cheerless morn for a gallant to swim,
  And the moat shines cold and clear;
Sir knight! I was never yet baulked of my whim,
And I long for the lilies that float on the brim:
  Go bring me those blossoms here!'
Then I offered them low on my bended knee;
'They are faded and wet,' said the proud Ladye

L.

A jay screamed out from the topmost pine
   That waved by the castle wall,
And she vowed if I loved her I'd never decline
To harry his nest for this mistress of mine,
   Though I broke my own neck in the fall.
So I brought her the eggs, and she flouted me;
' You would climb too high,' quoth the proud Ladye.

The lists were dressed, and the lances in rest,
   And our knightly band arrayed;
'Twas stout Sir Hubert who bore him the best,
With a Queen's white glove carried high on his crest,
   Till I shore it away with my blade.
But I reeled as I laid it before her.—' See!
It is soiled with your blood,' said the proud Ladye.

' You have sweet red lips and an ivory brow,
   But your heart is hard as a stone;
Though I loved you so long and so dearly, now
I have broken my fetters, and cancelled my vow,—
   You may sigh at your lattice alone.
There are women as fair, who are kinder to me;
Go look for another, my proud Ladye.'

Her tears fell fast—she began to rue
   When she counted the cost of her pride;
Till she played, and lost it, she never knew
The worth of a heart both kindly and true,
   And she beckoned me back to her side;
While softly she whispered, 'I love but thee!'
So I won her at last, my proud Ladye.

She fixed her eyes on Bosville as she concluded; but his whole attention was taken up by Mary, who, from the corner in which she was established with the Queen, had been looking at him with more than usual observation—he even flattered himself more than usual interest. As Henrietta rose to retire, and distributed a general bow amongst her courtiers in token of dismissal, Mary crossed the room to where he stood, and taking him by the hand, spoke to him in a low agitated voice that thrilled every nerve in his body, weakened as he was by illness, and excited by the scene, the music, the Royal circle, and above all, the presence of her he loved.

'The Queen has promised me your majority,' she said, and her voice trembled a little : ' but you must join the army immediately. Perhaps we may not meet again, even to say, "Farewell !" We shall often think of you. Good-bye, Captain Bosville '—she hesitated, as though about to say something more, but only repeated, ' Good-bye,' and vanished after the Queen and her retreating ladies.

So this was all ! The guerdon of how many thoughts, how much devotion, how deep a tenderness ! He was giving gold for silver, he felt it now. Well, he did not grudge it ; but he declined Lord Bernard's invitation to drink spiced canary with him in the guard room, and returned to his own quarters at Sir Giles Allonby's with a slow step and a saddened mien. Was he thinking of his choice—his peerless, proud Ladye ? Come what might he would never change it now.

CHAPTER XVII.

' THE PROSELYTE.'

THERE are martyrs in every faith, ascetics of every denomination. 'Tis not by the sincerity of its worshippers that we must argue the infallibility of any creed. The macerated monk, flagellating his bleeding person in his cell, is not more in earnest than the Indian faqueer, erect under a burning sun, his arm stretched out motionless, till the flesh withers from the bone, his hand clenched till the nails grow through the palm. The howling Dervish bids his Moslem monastery echo to his cries at intervals as regular as matins, and complines, and vespers, and all the periods of melodious worship enjoined by the Catholic Church. The bonze of Tartary, the priest of Brahma, meditate for weeks on the Ineffable ; whilst the disciple of Juggernaut immolates himself unhesitatingly beneath the wheels of his monstrous idol. Even our own true Faith is not without its fanatics. The tortures of the Inquisition, the massacre of St. Bartholomew, the fires of Smithfield, were strange sacrifices with which to glorify the religion of Love. Laud presiding over the Council and signing the inhuman decree by which the culprit was sentenced to lose his ears, doubtless believed he was serving the cause of truth and morality, as fervently as did Leighton himself when he published that abusive pamphlet against the Queen which drew down upon him the hideous vengeance of the Star Chamber. His sentence, in addition to mutilation, had been imprisonment for life ; but a large sum of money furnished in high quarters had bought his escape from his gaolers, and he was even now in Oxford, under the feigned name of Simeon—by which we must in future call him—snatching proselytes out of the lion's mouth; or as he himself termed it, 'labouring in the vineyard through the burden and heat of the day.'

He had promised to meet Effingham again when last they parted at the door of the conventicle, and he had not forgotten his promise. Night after night had he visited the Cavalier officer at his quarters, argued with him, prayed with him, implored him, till, notwithstanding all his previous associations—notwithstanding the first real ardent passion he had ever cherished in his life—Effingham gave way, yielding to his new friend's persuasions and his own convictions; and resolving to become not almost but altogether an adherent of the Puritan party, and a supporter of those zealots who had determined to go the farthest and fastest to the destruction of all government that was not based upon their own wild notions of a direct Theocracy.

Truly, it needed a strong hand and a cool head to rule these stormy elements; to reconcile the conflicting ideas of the speculative, the selfish, and the sincere; to guide the turbulent enthusiast and urge the wavering time-servers, and thus to rear at last a goodly edifice out of such various and chaotic materials; but when the time comes it is generally found that the Man is also ready, and the Man was even now drilling his Ironsides at Gloucester whose destiny it was to ride rough-shod to power on the blind faith of those who deemed him as fanatical and short-sighted as themselves.

Gaunt and thin, his fine frame square and angular from deficiency of covering, his features sharpened, and his dark eyes shining out more fiercely than usual from under their projecting brows, George Effingham sat alone in his dreary, comfortless room, wrapped in profound meditation, musing darkly on his recent doubts, his present resolution, and the sacrifice he had determined to make of those hopes which were to him as the very light of his eyes—the very breath of his nostrils.

Conflicting passions, the struggles of conscience, the 'worm that dieth not' gnawing at his heart, had wrought upon him in a few weeks the work of years. He looked a middle-aged man already, as the light from the lamp above his head brought out his sunken features in high relief, and deepened the lines upon his forehead and about his mouth. His beard, too, was flecked with here and there a silvery streak; his dress was careless and disordered; his whole bearing dejected, weary, and worn. With compressed lip and dilated nostril, as of one who suffers inwardly, but is too proud to yield, though none be there to witness, he seemed to watch and wait, though the clenched hand and the foot beating at regular intervals against the floor, denoted that his vigil was one of impatience and anxiety, almost too irritating to be borne.

At length a step was heard upon the stairs, and with a deep sigh of relief, Effingham opened the door and admitted his new friend Simeon, armed, as usual, to the teeth, and bearing on his countenance its wonted expression of fervent zeal and rapt enthusiasm.

'At last,' said George, as his guest seated himself, and disposed his arms in the most convenient position to be snatched up at a moment's notice; 'at last! I have wearied for you as the sick man wearies for the visit of the Leech; I have expected you since twilight. It is done—my brother, it is done at last. What it has cost me, neither you nor any other man can imagine. But it is done. I am a disgraced and branded man, and "the place that hath known me shall know me no more."'

Simeon took him affectionately by the hand. 'No cross, no crown, my brother!' he replied. 'Would you buy the incalculable treasure with that which costs you nothing? See! I have been in the hospitals, and beheld the wounded, maimed and writhing upon their stretchers. I have seen the strong man's limb shattered by gun-shot, and the surgeon's knife, merciful in that it spared not, lop off the agonised member, and save the patient from destruction. What though he shiver and faint when the operation is completed? He is a living man instead of a senseless corpse; so is it with the moral gangrene. If thou wouldst preserve thy soul, cut it out. Are we not told that it is better to sacrifice an eye or a limb than to risk the destruction of soul and body? and shall we grudge to offer up the dearest treasures of our lives, the pride that was as the breath of our nostrils, the earthly honour that was as our daily bread: nay, the fonder, softer feelings that had become as the very life-blood of our hearts, when they are required of us by Him who gives and who takes away? The gift we lay upon the altar, can it cost too much? Suffer, brother—so shalt thou qualify for happiness. Weep and gnash with thy teeth *here* rather than hereafter?'

It was a high stern doctrine, and as such qualified to make a due impression on the nature to which it was addressed. Effingham reared his head proudly, and the resolute lip compressed itself tighter than before as he detailed to his friend the doings of that day—doings which even now to his soldier nature could not but teem pregnant with physical degradation.

'I took my commission back to Colepepper,' said he, 'and the old general laughed in my face. I have seen him laugh so, Simeon, when your musqueteers were making a target of his body. He accepted it, however, and then he spoke such words—such bitter words! He dared not have used them to Captain Effingham of his own brigade. General or no general, I had paraded him at point of fox, with a yard and a half of green turf between us; and to give him his due, I think he would fain have provoked me to it even to-day. But I suppose every loyal Cavalier has a right to insult me now!'

He spoke in bitter scorn, scarcely in accordance with the character he was fain to profess.

'But you will meet him yet again in the field,' urged the warlike religionist; 'you will meet him where you can draw the sword with a good conscience, and strike fair downright blows for the cause of Israel. You will meet him again, though he be hemmed in by his Amalekites; and I, Simeon the persecuted, say unto you, "Smite and spare not!"'

Apparently somewhat comforted by this reflection, Effingham, who had been indignantly pacing the narrow room, sat down again, and proceeded with his narrative.

'When I left him I passed through the guard-room, and I thought the very troopers—my own troopers, some of them fellows that I have seen ere now flinch from following where I led—looked askance at me, as though I was traitor and coward both. Coward!—psha! the dogs know better than that. But I bore it and passed on. Nay, the very citizens in the street—the knaves that have never handled weapon in their lives weightier than an ell-wand or a yard of satin velvet, seemed to take the wall of the disgraced officer, to shoulder the renegade Cavalier into the kennel—and I kept my riding-rod quiet in my hand and passed on. Then I met Sir Giles Allonby—good old Sir Giles, her father, Simeon—and he stopped and asked me if it was true? He spoke so kindly, so sorrowfully. " I grieve for it, lad!" said he, and he meant what he said, I know; " I grieve for it, as if I had lost my falcon Diamond or the best horse in my stable. Zounds, man! art not ashamed? Some would be angry with thee, and roundly too, but I grieve for it, lad—by St. George, I do! We all liked thee so well—Grace and Mary, and all—and now we shall see thee no more. Fare thee well, lad; I would give thee my blessing, were't not clean against my conscience. Fare thee well!" And now I shall see them no more. Simeon!' (and he seized his friend's arm fiercely as he looked him in the face) 'if

my sacrifice be not accepted it had been better for me that I had
never been born !'

The enthusiast led him to the window, and pointed out into the
cold clear night, brilliant with a million stars. 'Shall He who
hath the treasures of the universe in the hollow of His hand not
reward thee ? oh, man of little faith ! Thou hast put thy hand
to the plough, see that thou look not back. To-morrow we will
shake the dust of Oxford from off our feet, and journey hence,
even as Lot journeyed into the desert from the accursed city of
the plain !'

With these words, Simeon shook the proselyte warmly by the
hand, and taking up his arms, departed stealthily as he had come.
Fanatic as he was, Leighton had been in earnest all his life. He
had never flinched yet from that narrow and rugged path which
he considered it his duty to follow, and his nerve was as unshaken,
his confidence in the protection of Heaven as unbounded, here in
Oxford, in the very stronghold of his enemies, as it had been when
exposed to the jeers of the mob in the pillory at Newgate, or on
the scaffold at Tower-hill under the knife of the executioner.
With Leighton, as with many others who come from the northern
side of the Tweed, the characteristic caution of his countrymen
was completely overborne and nullified by that religious enthusiasm which takes such a powerful hold of the Scottish character ;
and although in trifling matters, such as the preparations for his
own and Effingham's journey, about which he proceeded to busy
himself, it produced a degree of forethought highly advantageous
to a proscribed fugitive, it never checked him for an instant in the
prosecution of any enterprise, however desperate, on which he
thought his religion bade him embark.

With the sword in one hand and the Bible in the other, he, and
thousands such as he, were indeed invincible. So he hurried off
to the stables, and saw to the feeding of his own and Effingham's
steeds, and looked carefully to the arms of fleshly warfare which
were too likely to be needed ; nor did he neglect those creature
comforts, without which saint and sinner must equally faint by the
way on a long journey, doing everything in a spirit of trustful
confidence, that all the dangers and sufferings he had already
passed through were powerless to shake.

And Effingham watched the stars die out one by one in the sky.
The deep-toned clocks of the different colleges striking the morning
hours each after each, smote with a dull, unmeaning sound upon
his ear. His preparations for the journey were completed, and
his apartment, never luxuriously furnished, was indeed cheerless

and uncomfortable.   His eye wandered round its bare walls and
took no heed.   A few withered flowers, fresh and fragrant a week
ago—stay, could it be only a *week* ago?—stood in a drinking-cup
on the chimney-piece.   He had begged them of Grace at her
father's house ; and indeed she had given them somewhat unwillingly.   They caught his attention now—they looked so faded
and unhappy.   He started like a man who wakes up from a dream.
Then he saw it all before him, as though he was standing by, a
careless spectator : the wounded youth on the sofa, the graceful
womanly forms, gliding about the room, his own stately figure
erect by the low window, and the soft sweet face, with star-like
eyes—the face that stood between his soul and its salvation—the
face without which, Satan whispered in his ear, eternal glory
itself would be no heaven to him.

He seized his hat and cloak, girded on his rapier, and rushed
forth into the street.   A chill, moist wind, moaning through the
leafless trees, and round the pinnacles of the cathedral towers, blew
refreshingly in his face.   The first streaks of dawn were already
lightening the sky.   A new day was breaking, with its stores of
sorrows and anxieties and troubles, and its leavening of hope.   He
drew a long, full breath of the fresh air, he walked faster now, and
the colour mounted to his cheek.   He would stand under Grace's
windows once again, and though he would not see her face, yet his
spirit would bid her farewell.   He was a strong, practical man
once, ay, not many weeks ago ; and now he could find relief, like
any pitiful, sighing swain, in pacing a muddy street, and staring
at a closed shutter.   Something of his former self rose within him
as he smiled in scorn, but the smile was too near akin to tears not
to soften him ; and soon he thought that, however contemptible
such abject devotion might be in other cases, Grace was worth it
all ; so he would watch here for a while, and this should be his
leave-taking.

Again the proud spirit rose—the master-will that would not
be denied.   Speculating vaguely on the future, a long vista
seemed to open before him of fame and patriotism ; and the
triumph of religious freedom wrought out by the efforts of himself
and such as he.   Her party would fail ; it *must* yield to the voice
of the country—the strong power of right.   George Effingham,
one of the pillars of the State, one of the Councillors of England,
might aspire to the broken-down Cavalier's daughter.   *Aspire*,
forsooth ! it would be condescension, then.   Still, she would always
be a queen to him.   Prejudice and party-feeling would vanish
before the light of Truth.   Sir Giles would respect the stout,

successful soldier, though an enemy and a conqueror ; the sage, conscientious statesman, though a rebel to the Crown. *She* could not say him nay, after years of absence and constancy, after fame had been won to do her honour, and victory achieved for her sake. Then the bright day would dawn at last; the dream that is dreamed by all,—to be realized by how many ?—the magic presence, the golden sunshine, and the happy home. If he could but see her just once again ! One more draught to slake that thirst which, like the longing of the dram-drinker, grows the fiercer for indulgence, which unsatisfied, leaves but a dreary and shattered existence for the slave of its moral intoxication. If he could only take away with him for his long, long absence one more look, he would ask for nothing besides, not so much as a kind word : it would be enough to see her, and so depart upon his cheerless way.

He started, and turned pale. It was already nearly light. The shutter was unclosed, and a hand from within the chamber drew aside the blind.

At the same instant, the tramp of horses was heard clattering up the street. Effingham, who had good reasons of his own for not wishing to be recognised, shrunk aside to take shelter in the deep archway of a college-gate. He was invisible to the two horse-men as they rode by. Cloaked and booted, it was no easy task to recognise the form or features of either of those cavaliers. Quick and sharp as is the glance of jealousy, it is far behind the intuitive perception of love. A pair of dark eyes that had not slept all night, were peering out from behind those curtains into the chill, dull morning; they recognised in the leading horseman the person of Humphrey Bosville, long ere George, under his archway, had de-cided in his own mind that the strong shapely sorrel, with his light true action, was none other than his comrade's well-known charger. A thrill of mingled feelings shot through him as they passed. Something within told him that the hand he had seen at the win-dow belonged to Grace. It was a galling and a bitter thought that the woman he loved should have thus kept her vigil to obtain a farewell glimpse of another : but there was comfort in the re-flection that the other was even now, like himself, bound on a long and dangerous journey, from which perhaps he might never return ; and though he could not conceal from himself the attach-ment, which his own observation had told him was springing up in Grace's heart for his young and handsome brother officer, he took comfort in reflecting on all those sage aphorisms so rife amongst the male sex, which turn upon the fickle disposition of

woman, and her insatiable love of change—aphorisms which,
whether just or unjust, are as gall and wormwood to the successful
lover.

Insensibly, a kindly feeling sprang up in him towards his open-
hearted, unconscious rival.   He would fain have shaken hands with
him, and bidden him farewell; but even as the impulse arose, the
white hand was withdrawn, the curtain fell once more, and the
two horsemen turned the corner of the street, and disappeared.

With one longing look at the casement, with a prayer upon his
lips, and his strong heart aching with a strange, dull pain, George
Effingham took his silent, solitary farewell of the only thing he
cared for upon earth, and went his way drearily into the desert.

Weep on! pretty Grace; turning your pale cheek down towards
your pillow, and shedding the hot tears thick and fast, that you
need not be ashamed of now, for you are alone.   Weep on, and
so calm and soothe your wounded spirit, and hush it off to sleep,
and teach it that for it, as for any other babe, 'care comes with
waking as light comes with day.'   Good Sir Giles, snoring healthily
on the floor beneath you, little dreams that his bonnie Grace,
whom he remembers a year or two ago a prattling child, whom
he still persists in considering a mere girl, is broad awake within
a few yards of him, waging the fierce battle that is to teach her
the veritable lesson how to struggle and endure.   A woman's
passions and a woman's pride are making wild work in yonder
quiet chamber with the prostrate sufferer.   The light streams in
broader and broader, deepening into day, and every minute of daylight takes him farther and farther on his journey.

Weep on! it will do you good.   And be thankful that you *can*
weep.   Pray that the time may never come for you when the fire
that wastes blood and brain alike, leaves the eyes dry.   Weep on!
nor believe that you are the only sufferer.   He, too, has left his
heart behind him, but not with you, pretty Grace—not with you.

Bosville, too, had looked back at the house which contained all
he loved, ere he turned the corner of the street.   By this time, he
knew his mistress so well that he did not expect so much as the
wave of a handkerchief to cheer him on his journey, and yet he
was disappointed too that she made no sign.

Mary Cave had prayed for him long and earnestly ere she slept.
When he passed beneath her window she was dreaming of the
roses that had faded away last autumn; and Falkland stood with
her on the terrace at Boughton once more.

It was sad to awake to cold reality from such a dream.

CHAPTER XVIII.

'SAUVE QUI PEUT.'

THE sorrel was fresh and lively after his long rest; he snorted and shook his head, ringing his bridle playfully in the clear frosty air, as though he too enjoyed the music that he made. Dymocke, albeit he had much improved his opportunities during his interval of repose at Oxford, was yet a man of ambition in a quiet way, fond of adventure, as is often the case with these dry, immovable natures, and as he set by no means too low a value on his own worth, he was not unwilling to impose upon pretty Faith a little more anxiety, a little more uncertainty, ere he yielded his grim person altogether a captive to her charms. 'A young man,' quoth Dymocke 'must not think of settling too early in life.' It was a clear bright morning, the white hoar frost of early winter was rapidly evaporating in the sunshine; a few straggling leaves, withered up by the nipping air, still clung to tree and coppice; the lowing of cattle, the bleating of sheep, all the sounds of a rural and cultivated district, came shrill and sharp through the rarefied atmosphere upon the ear; the partridge whirred away from her sedgy, grass-grown covert by the wayside; the horses' hoofs rang cheerily on the road. Humphrey's spirits rose as he trotted along; health and strength seemed to enter at every pore, as he breathed the pure cold air: the future looked bright and promising before him now. The sorrel moved lightly and nimbly along as he sat well down in his demi-pique saddle, swaying easily to every motion of his favourite: it seemed that with his sword in his hand and his good horse under him, there was no task he would shrink to undertake, no prize he did not feel man enough to win.

Honest Dymocke, too, was in his highest spirits and his best of humours. When in such a happy frame of mind his discourse, like that of a provident soldier, was apt to turn upon the victualling department, and to this topic he reverted again and again, dropping behind at intervals to pursue his own reflections undisturbed, and anon riding up alongside of his master to pour the result of his cogitations in his ear.

'The Pied Bull at the next hamlet is an excellent hostelry both for man and beast,' quoth Dymocke, who prided himself on his knowledge of such matters, much as a 'courier' of the present day would deem it incumbent on him to point out the most fashionable hotel. 'Their oats weigh over two score the bushel;

the hay is won off the uplands just above the hamlet, clean and
dry and sweet as a nut; there's a turkey and chine, I'll warrant
me, against Christmas in the larder; and as for the ale, why ever
since the war times they've brewed it with a double strike of malt
to the hogshead, on purpose, as they say, for the Cavaliers!   I
know it, master, for the hostess is a kinswoman of my own, though
for the matter of that "the Puritans like it stiffish as well," quoth
Nance; "and I'd rather keep a regiment of Cavaliers for a month,"
says she, "than a troop of Waller's knaves for a fortnight!"   Ah,
she's honest, is Nance, and a buxom lass, too, or *was*,' added
Dymocke, with a grim retrospective leer, ' afore she was buckled
to old Giles Leatherhead.'

'It will make our journey to-day over short,' replied Humphrey
absently, for his heart was at that moment many a mile away
from good Dame Leatherhead. 'No, Hugh, there is no time to
be lost; we must push on while daylight lasts,' and he tightened
his rein as he spoke, and urged the sorrel forward at a rapid trot.
He was already in imagination at Goring's head-quarters, assuming
the command to which his lately attained rank would entitle him,
and furthering to the best of his abilities the great work which
he connected in his own mind with the ever-recurring motto,
' Loyalty before all.'

This pushing on, however, is a process of much difficulty and
some disappointment when the traveller is provided with no relays
of horses, and it is necessary to keep his own beast fresh and strong
for future services.   Roads get deep and muddy as the day wanes
and the frost melts, miles seem to lengthen themselves out, and
hill and dale unexpectedly diversify the surface of a country that
the wayfarer has hitherto believed to be a dead flat.   The steed
that never before would trot less than nine miles an hour without
pressing, sinks shamelessly to seven, and clinks his feet against
each other in a manner most distressing to the nerves of his rider
and jarring to his ear.   Just as darkness falls a shoe is nearly
certain to come off, and as surely the blacksmith in the next village
turns out to be drunk or absent, perhaps both.   Then at a place
where two ways meet, if there be any doubt it is odds that the
traveller takes the wrong direction, and though he soon discovers
his error and turns back grumbling if not swearing, the distance
has been lost and the daylight too.   Bosville's journey was no
exception to the general rule.   Notwithstanding his impatience,
he was forced to listen to the counsels of his servant, which,
though delivered in that person's quaint and oracular style, were
not without sense and forethought.

'The country hereabouts is "honest,"' observed Dymocke,
'so we may travel slowly and run no risk. If we stay all night
at the Pied Bull, we can refresh ourselves and rest our horses
well after their first day's journey. To-morrow we shall be ready
for whatever turns up; and to-morrow, master, before we can
reach Goring, we must pass under the very noses of Waller's
outposts. There are hawks abroad all over Gloucestershire, and
we may have to fight, ay, and perhaps ride, for our lives before
the sun sets. I like a fresh horse better than a tired one either
way, and my kinswoman is a decent dame and a comely, and
yonder swings the Bull, and the sun will be down in an hour—
think better of it, master, and stop while you can.'

A dark threatening cloud, heavy with a whole lapful of winter's
rain, seconded Dymocke's arguments so forcibly that his master
yielded to his entreaties and put up for the night at the friendly
hostelry, where, it is but justice to the Pied Bull to record, he
was regaled on the best of fare, and won golden opinions from his
buxom hostess, whose interest in her own kinsman, his grim
serving-man, was largely shared by the handsome Cavalier major.

An hour after daybreak Bosville was in the saddle once more,
his reckoning was paid, Dymocke was bringing his own horse
from the stable, everything was prepared for departure, when
Dame Leatherhead, looking very handsome in her Sunday bodice
and striped stuff petticoat, with her silver holiday ear-rings large
and weighty in her ears, made her appearance with the stirrup-
cup in her hand, which she mounted on the horse-block to
administer in due form. As Humphrey received it with a kindly
smile of thanks and put it to his lips, the fair hostess whispered
in his ear, 'Waller lies within six miles of us, at "The Ashes."
Bold Prince Rupert beat up their quarters, and took seventeen of
their horses o' Monday last. The rebels are up and stirring like
a wasp's nest. Ride with your beard over your shoulder, and
make for the river at Little Fordham-bridge. If you can cross
there you're safe, for Goring's "hell-babes" have got a post on
the opposite bank, and whenever you come this way again don't
ye forget the Pied Bull and old Giles Leatherhead and his dame,
and so good speed ye, and fare ye well.' The young Major
thanked her heartily for her counsel and spurred on, while Dame
Leatherhead jumped down from the horse-block with rather a
disappointed look on her comely features, and watched the retreating horsemen out of sight. Far be it from us to attribute motives
to any of that inexplicable sex for which we profess so deep a
reverence, or to speculate on the whims concealed beneath a

bodice, the flights of fancy that originate under maiden's snood
or matron's cap. We would only venture to hint that a time-
honoured custom in the seventeenth century permitted without
scandal the process of osculation to take place in all such ceremonies as welcomes, leave-takings, and the administering of stirrup-
cups; and to remark, not without reproval, that Humphrey's
inadvertence neglected to take advantage of this liberality, notwithstanding the convenient proximity of a willing hostess on a
horse-block to a departing Cavalier in the saddle. That such a
salute was expected we do not presume to infer, but merely remark
as an additional instance of the uncertainty of the female temper,
that Dame Leatherhead was shorter with old Giles and sharper
with her maids than usual during the whole subsequent fore-
noon.

With their flints carefully examined, their swords loose in the
scabbard, and their horses well in hand, the two Cavaliers rode on
in silent vigilance, keenly scanning every copse and hedgerow,
and peering anxiously over every rising ground as they approached
it. The way was somewhat difficult to find, crossed as it was by
several narrow lanes in the low country, and occasionally merging
into half a dozen separate tracks on the down. The river, however, lay visible at a considerable distance below them, and they
were descending the last hill into the vale which it fertilized, and
congratulating themselves on having so satisfactorily performed
the greater part of their march, when a ball singing over their
heads, followed by the report of a musquetoon, and the sudden
appearance of half a dozen bright head-pieces flashing above a
rising ground on their flank, startled them from their security,
and made them disagreeably aware that their safety was more
likely to depend on the speed of their horses and the erring aim
of their adversaries than on their own good swords, out-numbered
as they saw themselves three or four to one.

Like that of his master, Dymocke's first impulse, to do him
justice, was always for fighting, right or wrong. He counted the
enemy in a twinkling: 'Six—seven—eight, and a corporal. Shall
we turn and show our teeth, Major, or set spurs and show them
our heels?' said honest Hugh, his long lean countenance unmoved
as usual, and a gleam of grim humour in his eye. 'No use,
Hugh,' answered his master. 'Four to one! Sound a gallop
and make for the bridge. Keep close to me; we can always fight
if we have to turn.' As he spoke he struck spurs into the sorrel,
and sped away down the hill at a good hand gallop, closely followed
by his servant, and pursued with a loud cheer by the party of

Parliamentary cavalry, of whom ever and anon some godly warrior would halt and dismount, taking a long shot with his musquetoon at the diminishing forms of the fugitives, over the heads of his own comrades, to whom indeed the angry missile was far more dangerous than to the Malignants it was intended to reach.

'Hold up!' exclaimed Humphrey, as the sorrel cleared a high wall, with a drop into a sandy lane which promised to shelter them somewhat from the fire of their pursuers. 'Hold up!' echoed Hugh as the bay landed gallantly behind his stable companion. 'Trapped at last!' he added. 'Look yonder, master,' and Bosville, following the direction of his glance, beheld to his dismay at the bottom of the hill a whole troop of Waller's well-armed cavalry, commanded by an officer whose gaudy-coloured garments, flashing breast-plate, and orange scarf, were plainly discernible, and who was even then employed in sending out 'flankers' on each side of the lane to stop the fugitives should they attempt to emerge over its deep embankment. This, however, was impracticable. To get in was a fair leap for a good horse; to get out would have required the agility of a deer. There was but one chance left, and Bosville's practised eye saw it in an instant.

'We must go slap through those fellows, Dymocke,' he said, setting his teeth a little, and settling himself in the saddle as a horseman does when about to encounter a large fence. 'Take fast hold of your horse's head, and when we get within twenty yards, send him at it as hard as you can lay legs to the ground!'

So speaking he drew his sword, waved it round his head, and shouting 'God and the King!' galloped pell-mell into the leading files of the enemy, knocking over the first trooper he encountered with the very impetus of his charge, delivering so vicious a thrust at a second as sent him down amongst the horses' legs with six inches of steel through his midriff, and dealing a swinging sabre-cut at a third as he passed him that would have laid his back open from shoulder to loin had he been provided with no other defences than his stout buff coat and his faith in the righteousness of his cause. It was well for 'Ebenezer the Gideonite'* that he carried his short horseman's musquetoon slung across his back. The iron barrel of the weapon turned the edge of the sabre as it fell, and though Humphrey's blow was delivered with such good will as to knock the Parliamentarian on to his horse's neck, he sustained no

* Like Indian 'braves,' these sanctified warriors boasted each his 'nom de guerre.'

further damage from the encounter, and passed on unscathed, to
turn rein once more, and assume the offensive.

Humphrey shot through the first division of his enemy as a
sportsman of modern times crashes through a Northamptonshire
bull-finch, but he had to do with an adversary skilled in all the
wiles of war; and Harrison, for it was no less a person that commanded the opposing party, had calculated on this characteristic
rush of the impetuous Cavalier, and taken his measures accordingly. So with his horse blown, the momentum of his charge
expended, and his servant separated from him in the *mêlée*, Humphrey found himself surrounded by a fresh dozen of troopers, with
swords drawn, pistols cocked, and calm defiant looks of conscious
strength that seemed to say escape was hopeless and resistance
impossible.

In a twinkling his sword was beaten down, his bridle seized.
his arms pinioned, a stalwart trooper on either hand threatening
instant death if he attempted further violence, which was indeed
physically impossible; and thus, breathless, exhausted, and a
prisoner, he was brought before the officer in command of the
party who had taken him.

Harrison was more of the soldier than the saint. Of a goodly
presence, commanding figure, and honest expression of countenance, his appearance formed a pleasing contrast to that of many
who drew the sword by his side. He was not above the vanities
of dress, and with a short velvet *montero* floating over his new buff
coat, an orange scarf richly fringed about his waist, and a burnished helmet adorned with a drooping feather upon his head, his
exterior presented an air of military coxcombry by no means
common amongst the ranks of the Presbyterians. He affected, too,
the *bon camarade* in his manners, and greeted his prisoner with
an off-hand soldierlike cordiality that seemed to make no account
of the prejudices of party and the chances of war.

'Take a pull at my flask, young sir,' he said, heartily and good-
humouredly, offering at the same time a horn measure of excellent
brandy, which he drew from one of his holsters, and which
balanced an ominous-looking horse-pistol in the other. 'Get your
breath, give up your despatches, tell me your name and rank, and
we'll make you as comfortable as we can under the circumstances.'

Humphrey answered courteously, and looking anxiously round
for Dymocke, begged to know whether his servant had been slain
in the affray. Harrison laughed outright. 'The knave has got
clear off, Major Bosville,' said he; 'not one of my bunglers here
could either catch him for speed, or drop him at a long shot.

' 'Tis a pity, too,' he added reflectively; 'I should like to have had that bay horse. Fairfax would have given me any price I chose to ask for him. And now, sir, your despatches, if you please. Unbind the gentleman, you knaves! My fellows are rough valets, Major; but you will excuse the fortune of war.'

Humphrey was obliged to submit with a good grace. He had one consolation in his disasters. Dymocke possessed a duplicate set of these despatches; and Dymocke, he had every reason to hope, was safe, so he bore his misfortunes with an outward air of cheerful indifference, and won golden opinions of Harrison accordingly.

'You have been lately wounded, you say,' observed the latter as he rode alongside of his prisoner, whom he had ordered his men to unbind, and for whose security the practised soldier relied on his own quick eye and ready hand, which never strayed far from the sorrel's head. 'Faith, you look pale and weak, and sit your horse as though you had had nearly enough. That was a gallant dash too of yours. If I hadn't expected it you might have got clear off. Ay, you're all alike, you officers of Prince Rupert. Undeniable at a dash, but you don't rally well after your first charge. There are but three cavalry officers in England : Cromwell's one, old Leslie's another, and I'll leave you to guess the third. My service to you, Major Bosville. Take another pull at the flask.'

Humphrey declined the proffered courtesy, and his captor drank to him with an air of much satisfaction. He wiped his beard and moustaches on a delicate laced handkerchief after his draught, and resumed his discourse.

'You have a short ride before you to-day; but if you are too weak to proceed I will order half an hour's halt for rest and refreshment. No? Well, you'll have plenty of time to rest yourself now for a while. Bah! what is it after all?—a month or two, and then an exchange of prisoners, and you are free. You and I may meet again in the field before long; and I promise you I wont forget the charge down the lane, and the swinging blow you lent "Ebenezer" yonder, though 'twas but the flat of the sword. See, the knave rides with his back up even now. It stings him, I'll be sworn. Meantime, another hour will bring us in sight of Gloucester; and to Gloucester, Major Bosville, it is my duty to conduct you as a prisoner. When we near the town, I shall be unwillingly compelled to leave you bound once more.'

In effect, a couple of hours' ride diversified by such light soldier's talk as the above, chequered in Humphrey's mind with

M

many a sad and bitter reflection, brought them to the gates of the godly town. Here the commander called a halt for the purpose of again pinioning his prisoner (an operation which he good-naturedly insisted should be done as lightly as possible), and getting his men into order for their entrance. The sanctified inhabitants of Gloucester being rigid disciplinarians in all military matters, and moreover somewhat sore at present from the recent visits of Prince Rupert almost to the walls of the town, any laxity of discipline or appearance of indulgence towards a prisoner would have called down upon Harrison the strictures of the townsmen and the reproofs of his superior officers.

As they rode up the principal street, the population seemed to have turned out for the express purpose of sharing in the triumph of the Parliamentarian's capture. Angry brows were bent, and bitter texts of Scripture levelled at the captive 'Malignant.' Grim, sour-faced elders, clad in sombre colours, pointed the finger, and gibed at him as he passed, launching into far-fetched anathemas drawn from the Old Testament, and comparing the young Cavalier major, in a somewhat ludicrous and disrespectful manner, to every reprobate mentioned in holy writ. Little children came out and spat at him with precocious virulence; and rancorous old dames sharpened their shrill tongues, and kept them, so to speak, edged and pointed for domestic use upon this fortuitous whetstone. Only some of the younger and fairer daughters of Eve demonstrated feelings of natural interest in the captive. His pale, handsome face, graceful figure, and long dark curls, were meet objects for compassion; and 'Malignant' as he was, glances were cast upon him as he rode by from the blackest and brownest and bluest eyes in Gloucester, of mingled pity and admiration, not always undimmed by tears.

A low stone archway, flanked by a long dismal building that had all the appearance of a guard-room, and watched by two grim and warlike sentinels, received the prisoner. Satisfied that he will be well cared for, and not suffered to escape, we must here take leave of Major Bosville, and cast a retrospective glance at the fortunes of his faithful servant, the redoubtable Dymocke.

Mounted on a high-couraged and excellent horse, that experienced warrior had no difficulty in keeping pace with his master in the headlong charge which well nigh carried them both right through the Parliamentary party.

Riding on the major's bridle-hand, he took his share of the buffets that were flying about somewhat at a disadvantage, yet with his usual coolness and philosophy. His head-piece was fortunately thick and strong, the skull it defended by no means of soft materials, and the arm which should cover both, practised in every feint and trick of consummate swordsmanship. The cudgel-play of Old England was no bad training for the use of the sabre, and many a broken sconce had Dymocke inflicted on his rustic adversaries in more peaceful times. It was only when he saw his master surrounded and helpless, that the idea of escape and the responsibility of his own duplicate despatches flashed across his mind.

Quick as thought, he espied a gap in the wall which flanked the deep narrow lane wherein the skirmish had taken place, and forcing his horse vigorously up the bank, he gained once more the open fields, and put his head straight for the bridge, now but a few hundred yards distant. With shout and cheer and the thunder of horses' hoofs ringing behind him, diversified by an occasional random shot whistling over his head, he sped down to the river, gaining at every stride upon his pursuers—for not a trooper in Waller's division could hold his own for speed with the gallant bay—and so reached the bridge with a fair start, and at least half a dozen of the enemy pretty close upon his heels.

'Confusion! they've broke it down,' muttered the fugitive to himself, as he neared the dismantled masonry, and saw that a huge gap had been left in the middle arch which spanned the stream; 'this is Goring's work, I'll be bound! Ay, he never throws a chance away. Well, it's "over shoes over boots now," and sink or swim, I won't give in for the fear of a ducking!'

Thus muttering, and taking his despatches from his breast to place them in his head-piece, he slid cautiously down the bank, and leaning his weight forward upon his horse's neck, forced the good animal into the stream. That which he had thought would prove his destruction turned out to be his salvation. The Puritans, who had made sure of their prey when he reached the broken bridge, shrunk from following him into the deep and treacherous river. With an angry shout they pulled up and fired a parting volley at him from the brink.

With characteristic coolness Dymocke halted on the opposite shore to dismount and wring the wet from his dripping garments; then, waving his disappointed enemies an ironical farewell, he trotted leisurely on in the direction of General Goring's head-quarters.

Here as elsewhere in the ranks of the Cavaliers, laxity of discipline, and, to use a military term which carries with it its own signification, a general *slackness*, seemed to pervade all alike, from

the chief to the trumpeter, neutralizing the courage and abilities
which were so conspicuous in the Royal army, and giving to their
stricter and better-trained foes an incalculable advantage. When
Dymocke drew rein at the door of the General's quarters, the very
sentry on duty seemed flustered with his noonday draught, and
lounged about his post with an air of roystering joviality scarcely
in accordance with Hugh's ideas of military etiquette, although
he lent a ready ear to the new arrival's request to see Lord Goring
forthwith, and even proffered an invitation to stroll away with
him to the guard-room for something to drink, and so avoid the
enormity of delivering his message dry-lipped. In the general's
ante-room a couple of young Cavaliers were fulfilling their duties
as 'aides-de-camp' by shaking a dice-box with alarming energy,
applying themselves meanwhile to a tankard that stood between
them with impartial zeal. Goring himself, sitting in a luxurious
apartment—for he had as usual taken the best house in the village,
the property of a Puritan lawyer, for his own residence—was
unbraced and slippered, surrounded by piles of papers, writing
nevertheless with all his natural facility, yet quaffing ever and
anon deep draughts from a large silver measure at his elbow,
seeking, as it seemed in vain, to quench the feverish thirst left by
his last night's debauch.

'Ha! my late antagonist's servant,' exclaimed the General, who
never forgot a face, as he never remembered a debt; 'I may say
my late antagonist himself. 'Slife, man, I have never paid thee
the cudgelling I owe thee; some of my knaves, doubtless, will
take it off my hands! But what dost here?—dripping, too, like
a water-dog. Keep thy distance, man, and deliver up thy papers.
Sure 'tis not another cartel from the young feather-brain!'

Dymocke knew his place right well, and feared neither man
nor devil, or he had hesitated ere he presented himself to a general
of division in his own quarters, whom he had struck so shrewdly
with an oaken cudgel some few weeks before. He delivered his
papers, taking them out of his head-piece, where they had
remained perfectly dry (a piece of caution not unremarked by
Goring, whom nothing escaped), in severe and soldierlike silence,
and stood gaunt and dripping at 'attention' till the latter had
concluded their perusal. Twice he read them over with careful
avidity, impressing them as it were indelibly on his memory, and
then looked up and laughed outright at the solemn figure before
him.

'And what brought thee here, knave?' he inquired; 'is thy
master killed, or wounded, or taken prisoner? Hath he learned

to parry that thrust in tierce yet, or hath he been practising his swordsmanship anew amongst the Roundheads? What brought thee here, and how came these letters in thy hands?'

Still erect and rigid, Dymocke detailed to him in a few words the events of the skirmish, and his own escape from Waller's pursuing cavalry. Goring listened with an expression of interest and approval on his face.

'Thou hast done well!' he said, at the conclusion of Dymocke's narrative; 'I will forgive thee the debt I owe thee in consideration of thy ready service. 'Tis not every trooper would have thought of keeping his papers dry, with Waller's saints singing "glory" behind him. Let me see thee here again to-morrow at noon. Thy master shall be looked to. 'Tis a cockerel of the game, and will fly a fair pitch when his pin-feathers are grown. Zounds! I had better spared many a better man, than that mettled lad with his smooth face. Ho! without there—D'Arcy, Langdale! —bid them take this knave to the guard-room, ration his horse, and give himself a drench of brandy, to dry him within and without. Order up Master Quillet's housekeeper with another measure of burnt sack, and let no one else disturb me till supper time.

So Goring went back to his correspondence; and Dymocke, nothing loth, found himself before a huge measure of brandy and a roaring fire in the guard-room, surrounded by a circle of admiring comrades, listening open-mouthed to his exploits, and to whom he fully indemnified himself for the brevity of his narrative as reported to their busy General.

CHAPTER XIX.

' THE NEWS THAT FLIES APACE.'

DEEPER and deeper still, Mary Cave found herself engulphed in the whirlpool of political intrigue. Almost the only courtier f the Queen's party who united activity of brain to uncompromising resolution, who was capable of strong effort and sound reflection, unwarped and unfettered by the promptings of self-interest, she had insensibly become the principal link that connected the policy of Merton College with the wiser counsels of the King's honest advisers. It was no womanly office she thus found herself compelled to undertake. False as is the position of a mediator between parties neither of whom are essentially quite sincere, it becomes doubly so, when that mediator is one of the softer sex. She must guide the helm with so skilful a hand, she must trim the boat with so careful an eye; she must seize her opportunities so deftly, or make them so skilfully; and through it all she must exercise so jealous a vigilance over her own weaknesses, and even her own reputation, distinguishing so nicely between public duty and private feeling—doing such constant violence to her own affections and her own prejudices—that it is not too much to say nothing *but* a woman is capable of reconciling all these conflicting necessities into one harmonious whole. Yet it is not womanly to encourage admirers up to a certain point, in order to obtain their secrets, and then make use of them for a political purpose; it is not womanly to promote likings and dislikings between individuals of opposite sexes, or otherwise, for the furtherance of a State intrigue; it is not womanly to be in correspondence with half a dozen ambitious and unprincipled men, some of them profligates whose very names in connection with a lady were sufficient to blast her fair fame for ever; and it is not womanly to have but one object in life, to which duty, inclination, happiness must be sacrificed, and that object a political one.

Mary sat reading her letters on the very sofa that Bosville had occupied during his convalescence in Sir Giles Allonby's house at Oxford. It was a day off duty with the Queen, and she had come to spend it with her kind old kinsman and his daughter. The two ladies were alone; and contrary to their wont, an unbroken silence, varied only by the pattering of a dismal winter rain against the window, was preserved between them. Grace sat musing over her work, and seemed buried in thought. She looked paler and thinner than usual, and her eye had lost the merry sparkle that used so to gladden Sir Giles. It was less like her mother's now, so thought the old knight; and his heart bounded after all those years to reflect how that mother had never known sorrow, and had told him on her death-bed that ' she was sure she was only taken away because her lot in this world had been too happy.' Ay! you may well laugh on, Sir Giles, and troll out your loyal old songs, and drink and ride and strike for the King! Roystering, careless, war-worn veteran as you seem to be, there are depths in that stout old heart of yours that few have sounded; and when ' little Gracy' is settled and provided for, you care not how soon you go to join that gentle, loving lady, whom you still see many and many a night in your dreams, walking in her white dress in the golden summer evenings under

the lime-trees at home : whom your simple faith persuades you
you shall look on again with the same angel-face, to part from
never more.   And where is the Sadducee that shall say you nay ?
   Meantime, Sir Giles is drilling a newly-raised levy of cavalry
on Bullingdon Common, notwithstanding the wet ; and Grace sits
pensive over her work ; and Mary reads her letters with a flushed
cheek and a contracted brow, and a restless unquiet look in her
deep blue eye that has got there very often of late, and that de-
notes anything but repose of mind.   Suddenly she starts and turns
pale as she peruses one elaborately-written missive, scented and
silk-bound, and inscribed ' These for Mistress Mary Cave.   Ride,
ride, ride !' according to the polite manner of the time.   A look
of consummate scorn passes over her features as she reads it through
once more, but her face is still white, and she drops it from her
hand upon the carpet, unmarked by her pre-occupied companion.
Here it is :—

' These for Mistress Mary Cave.

   ' GENTLE MISTRESS MARY—
   ' Deign to accept the heartfelt good wishes, none the less sincere
for that the heart hath been pierced and mangled by the glances
of your bright eyes, of the humblest of your slaves ; and scorn
not at the same time to vouchsafe your favour and interest to one
who, languishing to be parted from so much beauty as he hath
left at Oxford, and specially at Merton College, where Mistress
Mary reigns second to none, still endeavoureth to fulfil his duty
religiously to the King, and to her Majesty, as Mistress Mary
esteems to be the devoir of a knight who hath placed himself
under her very feet.   The good cause in which it is my pride that
we are fellow-labourers, languisheth somewhat here in Gloucestershire, more from want of unity in counsel than from any lack of
men and munitions of war in the field.   Would his blessed
Majesty but vouchsafe to confer upon your knight and slave a
separate and independent command, it is not too much to say that
it would be in my power to make short work and a speedy account
of Waller, who lieth with a goodly force of cavalry within ten
miles of me.   It was but last Monday that a small body of my
" lambs," taking their orders directly from myself, beat up his
quarters within a mile of Gloucester, and drove off seventeen of
his horses, besides considerable spoil, of which I thought the less
as compared with that which might be done but for the impracticable nature of the Commander-in-Chief.   Gentle Mistress Mary !
it would not be unbecoming in you to implore our gracious and

passionately-adored Queen to hint to his blessed Majesty that I do indeed but desire to receive my orders under his own hand, as I should in this wise have more authority to guide the council of the army thereby to obedience ; and as my requests are mostly denied out-of-hand by Prince Rupert, at whose disposal nevertheless I remain for life and death, as his Majesty's nephew and loving kinsman, I would humbly beg a positive order from his Majesty for my undertakings, to dispose the officers more cheerfully to conduct them, and to assure his Majesty that the least intimation of his pleasure is sufficient to make me run through all manner of difficulties and hazard to perform my duty, and to prove myself entirely and faithfully devoted to his sacred service. As Mistress Mary hath the key to the heart of her beauteous and beloved Sovereign, whose will must ever be law with all who come within the sphere of her enchantments, methinks that a word spoken in season under the roof of Merton College will more than fulfil all my most ardent desires, and leave me nothing to grieve for save that which must ever cause me to languish in hopeless sorrow—the adoration which it is alike my pride and grief to entertain for the fairest and proudest dame that adorns our English Court.

' From intelligence I receive at sure and friendly hands, I learn that Wilmot is wavering ; and some speech is even abroad of a treasonable correspondence with Essex, and an intercepted letter from Fairfax, which is to be laid before the Council.

' Such treachery would merit a summary dismissal from his office, and clemency in this case could scarcely be extended to an officer of so high a rank.

' Digby, too, is far from being unsuspected ; and should these two commands become vacant, it would be a fertile opportunity for the uniting of his Majesty's whole body of horse under one independent head, acting conjointly with Prince Rupert, who would still remain Commander-in-Chief, but deriving his authority direct from the hand of his blessed Majesty himself.

' Should events work in this direction, I can safely confide in your discretion to select a proper time at which to whisper in the Queen's ear the humble name of, sweet Mistress Mary,

> ' Your most passionately-devoted
> 'and faithful knight and humble slave,
> ' GEORGE GORING.

' *Post scriptum.*—The despatches alluded to in 106 Cipher have arrived. They are duplicate, and were delivered to me yesterday by an honest serving-man, who narrowly escaped with his life and his letters from a party of Waller's horse.

'His master, it seems, was sorely wounded, and led off prisoner into Gloucester. This is of less account as his despatches are in cipher, and the duplicates are safe. He is one Master Bosville, with whom I am personally well acquainted, and whom Mistress Mary may deign to remember when lying wounded by the weapon of her own true knight and slave.

'He is a good officer, and a mettlesome lad too. I would fain have him back with us, but have nothing to exchange against him but a couple of scriveners and a canting Puritan divine; the latter I shall probably hang. Once more—Fare thee well!'

It was the *post scriptum*, written in her correspondent's own natural off-hand style, and very different from the stilted and exaggerated form of compliment and inuendo contained in the body of the letter, which drove the blood from Mary's cheek, and caused her bosom to heave so restlessly beneath her bodice, her slender foot to beat so impatiently upon the floor. Wounded and a prisoner !—and this so soon after his illness, when weak and scarcely recovered from the consequences of his duel. And it was her doing—hers !—whom he loved so madly, the foolish boy !— who counted his life as nothing at the mere wave of her hand. Why was she so eager to get him this majority, for which she had so implored her unwilling and bantering mistress ? Why had she sent him off in such a hurry, before he was half recovered, and hardly strong enough to sit upon his horse ? And then of course he had fought—so like him ! when his servant wisely ran away. And the stern Puritans had struck his weakened frame to the earth ! Ah ! he was a strong bold horseman when he was well, and a match for the best of them ; but now his arm was powerless, though his courage was as high as ever. And perhaps they had slashed his handsome face—how handsome it was ! and what kind eyes those were that used to meet hers so timidly and gently —and he was a prisoner—wounded, perhaps dying. And she shut her eyes and fancied she saw him, pale and faint, in his cell—alone, too, all alone. No, that should never be ! She picked the letter up, and once more she read it through from beginning to end, scarcely noting the fulsome compliments, the strain of selfish intrigue, and only dwelling on the ill-omened and distressing *post scriptum* which Goring had written so lightly ; but in which, to do him justice, the reckless General showed more feeling than he generally did ; and even as she read she would fain have given utterance to her grief, and wrung her hands and wept aloud.

Self-command, however, we need not now observe, was a salient point in Mary Cave's character. Whatever she may have known, or whatever she may have suspected, she looked at Grace's pale face and dejected attitude and held her tongue. There was a sisterly feeling between these two far stronger than was warranted by their actual relationship. Ever since their late intimacy, which had grown closer and closer in the quiet shades of Boughton, Mary had seemed to take care of her gentle friend, Grace in return looking up to her protectress with confiding attachment; and yet there was a secret between them—a secret at which neither ventured to hint, yet with which each could not but suspect the other was acquainted. But they never came to an explanation, notwithstanding. We believe women never do. We believe that, however unreservedly they may confide in a brother, a lover, or a husband, they never lay their hearts completely bare before one of their own sex. Perhaps they are right; perhaps they know each other too well.

There was yet another difficulty in Mary's path, for to succour Bosville at all hazards we need hardly say she had resolved, even on her first perusal of the letter. In whom was she to confide? to whom could she entrust the secret of his failure and capture without letting the bad news reach Grace's ears? Sir Giles?— the stout old Cavalier never could keep a secret in his life; his child would worm it all out of him the first time she sat on his knee for two minutes after supper. The Queen?—that volatile lady would not only put the very worst construction upon her motives, but would detail the whole of the confidence reposed in her to each of her household separately, under strict promises of secrecy, no doubt, which would be tantamount to a general proclamation by the herald king-at-arms.

Of the courtiers she could scarcely bethink herself of one who was not so busily engaged in some personal and selfish intrigue as to have no room for any other consideration whatsoever, who would not scruple to sacrifice honour and mercy and good feeling merely to score up, so to speak, another point in the game. What to do for Bosville and how to do it—this was the problem Mary had to solve; and resolute as she generally was, full of expedients and fertile in resources, she was now obliged to confess herself fairly at her wit's end.

It so fell out, however, that the blind deity whom men call chance and gods Destiny, who never helps us till we are at the very utmost extremity, befriended Mary through the medium of the very last person about the Court in whom she would have dreamt of confiding — an individual who perhaps was more selfish, intriguing, and reckless than all the rest of the royal circle put together, but who, being a woman, and consequently *born* an angel, had still retained a scarce perceptible leavening of the celestial nature from which she had fallen.

As Mary sat that evening, pensive and graver than her wont, in the Queen's withdrawing-room, Lady Carlisle crossed the apartment with her calm brow and decorous step, and placed herself by her side. She liked Mary Cave, as far as it was in her nature to like one of her own sex. Perhaps she recognised in Mary somewhat of her own positive character—the uncompromising force of will that, for good or for evil, marches directly on towards its purpose steadfast and unwavering, not to be moved from the path by any consideration of danger or of pity, and like the volume of a mighty river forcing its way through every obstacle with silent energy.

She sat quietly down by Mary's side and heaved a deep sigh, with a sympathising and plaintive expression of countenance, like a consummate actress as she was.

'It is bad news I have to break to you, Mistress Cave,' she whispered, bending her graceful head over the other's work, 'if indeed you know it not already. That handsome Captain Bosville who was stabbed by Goring has fallen into the hands of the rebels! Jermyn only heard it this evening; I think he is telling the Queen now. They have got him in prison at Gloucester, as far as we can learn. He must be saved by some means. Heaven forfend he should be sacrificed by those villains!'

Mary's heart was full: she could only falter out the word 'exchanged.'

'*Exchanged*!' repeated Lady Carlisle, now thoroughly in earnest. Do you not know—have you not heard? Since they hanged our Irish officers in the north the Council has ordered reprisals. Fairfax, Ireton, Cromwell—all of them are furious. They will hang every Royalist prisoner they take now! It was but last week Prince Rupert strung thirteen Roundheads upon one oak tree; they must have heard of it by this time. Poor Bosville is in the utmost danger. We talked of it but now in the presence-chamber. Even Jermyn is in despair. Alas! 'tis a sad business.'

Mary turned sick and white! Was it even so? The room seemed to spin round with her, and Lady Carlisle's voice was as the rush of many waters in her ear.

'It is hopeless to talk of exchanges,' proceeded her ladyship in a tone of real pity for the too obvious distress of her listener. She had once had a soft place in that corrupted heart, ay, long before she was dazzled with Strafford's fame, or lured by Pym's political influence; before she had sold her lovely womanhood for a coronet, and bartered the peace she could never know again for empty splendour. 'Interest must be made with the Parliament. Some of the rising rebels must be cajoled. Essex is in disgrace with them now, and Essex is of no use, or I had brought the prisoner safe off with my own hand in a week from this day. But they are all alike, my dear, Courtiers and Puritans, generals and statesmen, Cavaliers and Roundheads, all are *men*, weak and vain, all are alike fools, and all are alike to be won. An effort must be made, and we can save him.'

'What would you do?' gasped poor Mary, her self-command now completely deserting her.

'Do!' repeated her ladyship, with her soft lisping voice and dimpled smile; 'I would beg him a free pardon if I dragged Cromwell round the room on my bare knees for it, or die with him,' she added beneath her breath, 'if I really cared one snap of the fingers about the man!'

She was no coward, my Lady Carlisle, and there was more of the tigress about her than the mere beauty of her skin.

<hr />

CHAPTER XX.

THE MAN OF DESTINY.

In an open space, long since built over by an increasing population, but forming at the time of which we write alternately a play and drill-ground for the godly inhabitants of Gloucester, is drawn up a regiment of heavy cavalry, singularly well appointed as to all the details of harness and horseflesh which constitute the efficiency of dragoons. The troopers exhibit strength, symmetry, and action, bone to carry the stalwart weight of their riders, and blood to execute the forced marches and rapid evolutions which are the very essence of cavalry tactics. The men themselves are worthy of a close inspection. Picked from the flower of England's yeomanry, from the middle class of farmers and petty squires of the northern and eastern counties, their fine stature and broad shoulders denote that physical strength which independent agricultural labour so surely produces, whilst their stern brows, grave faces, and manly upright bearing, distinguish them from such of their fellows as have not yet experienced the inspiration derived from military confidence mingled with religious zeal. These are the men who are firmly persuaded that on their weapons depends the government of earth and heaven; that they are predestined to win dominion here and glory hereafter with their own strong arms; that their paradise, like that of the Moslem enthusiast, is to be won sword-in-hand, and that a violent death is the surest passport to eternal life. Fanatics are they, and of the wildest class, but they are also stern disciplinarians. Enthusiasm is a glorious quality, no doubt, but it has seldom turned the tide of a general action when unsupported by discipline: it is the combination of the two that is *invincible.* Thus did the swarms of the Great Arab Impostor overrun the fairest portion of Europe, and the chivalrous knights of the Cross charge home with their lances in rest at Jerusalem. Thus in later times were the high-couraged Royalists broken and scattered at Marston Moor, and the tide of victory at Naseby turned to a shameful and irrevocable defeat. Deep as is the influence of religious zeal, doubly as is that man armed who fights under the banner of righteousness, it is over life and not death that it exercises its peculiar sway. A high sense of honour, a reckless spirit of ambition, the romantic enthusiasm of glory, will face shot and steel as fearlessly as the devout confidence of faith; and the drinking, swaggering, unprincipled troopers of Goring, Lunsford, and such as they, for a long time proved a match, and more than a match, for the godly soldiers of the Parliament. It was the 'Threes Right!'—the steady confidence inspired by drill, that turned the scale at last: that confidence and that drill the grim Puritan dragoons are now acquiring on the parade-ground at Gloucester.

They sit their horses as only Englishmen can, the only seat, moreover, that is at all adapted to the propulsive powers of an English horse, a very different animal from that of any other country. They are armed with long straight cut-and-thrust swords, two-edged and basket-hilted, glittering and sharp as razors, with large horse-pistols of the best locks and workmanship, with the short handy musquetoon, deadly for outpost duty, and hanging readily at the hip. Breastplates and backpieces of steel enhance the confidence inspired by faith, and the men ride to and fro in their armour with the very look and air of invincibles. Yes, these are the Ironsides—the famous Ironsides that turned the destinies of England.

They are drawn up in open column, waiting for the word of command. Their squadrons are dressed with mathematical precision; their distances correct to an inch—woe be to the culprit, officer or soldier, who fails in the most trifling of such *minutiæ*. The eye of the commander would discover him in a twinkling—that commander sitting there so square and erect on his good horse. Like all great men, he is not above detail: he would detect a button awry as readily as the rout of a division.

He scans his favourite regiment with a quick, bold, satisfied glance—the glance of a practised workman at his tools. There is no peculiarity in his dress or appointments to distinguish him from a simple trooper; his horse is perhaps the most powerful and the speediest on the ground, and he sits in the saddle with a rare combination of strength and ease; in every other respect his exterior is simple and unremarkable. He even seems to affect a plainness of attire not far removed from sloth, and in regard to cleanliness of linen and brightness of accoutrements presents a striking contrast to Fairfax, Harrison, and other of the Parliamentary officers, who vie with their Cavalier antagonists in the splendour of their apparel.

It is the man's voice which arrests immediate attention. Harsh and deep, there is yet something so confident and impressive in its tones, that the listener feels at once its natural element is command, ay, command, too, when the emergency is imminent, the storm at its greatest violence. It forces him to scan the features and person of the speaker, and he beholds a square, powerful man of middle stature, loosely and awkwardly made, but in the liberal mould that promises great physical strength, with coarse hands and feet, such as the patrician pretends are never seen in his own race, and with a depth of chest which readily accounts for the powerful tones of that authoritative voice. This vigorous frame is surmounted by a countenance that, without the slightest pretensions to comeliness, cannot but make a deep impression on the beholder. The scoffing Cavaliers may jeer at ' red-nosed Noll,' but Cromwell's face is the face of a great man. The sanguine temperament, which expresses, if we may so speak, the *material* strength of the mind, is denoted by the deep ruddy colouring of the skin. The strong broad jaw belongs to the decided and immovable will of the man of action, capable of carrying out the thoughts that are matured beneath those prominent temples, from which the thin hair is already worn away; and although the nose is somewhat large and full, the mouth somewhat coarse and wide, these distinguishing characteristics seem less the brand of indulgence and sensuality than the adjuncts of a ripe, manly nature almost always the accompaniment of great physical power. Though the eyes are small and deep-set, they glow like coals of fire; when excited or angered (for the General's temper is none of the sweetest, and he has more difficulty in commanding it than in enforcing the obedience of an army), they seem to flash out sparks from beneath his heavy head-piece. A winning smile is on his countenance now. The Ironsides have executed an 'advance in line' that brings them up even and regular as a wall of steel to his very horse's head, and the reflection steals pleasantly across his mind, that the tools are fit for service at last, that the tedious process of discipline will ere long bring him to the glorious moment of gratified ambition.

A new officer has this moment been appointed to the regiment. He seems thoroughly acquainted with his duty, and manœuvres his squadron with the ready skill of a veteran. Already George Effingham has caught the Puritan look and tone. Already he has made no little progress in Cromwell's good graces. That keen observing eye has discovered a tool calculated to do good service in extremity. A desperate man, bankrupt in earthly hopes, and whose piety is far exceeded by his fanaticism, is no contemptible recruit for the ranks of the Ironsides, when he brings with him a frame of adamant, a heart of steel, and a thorough knowledge of the duties of a cavalry officer. Pale, gaunt, and worn, looking ten years older than when he last saw these same troopers at Newbury, Effingham still works with the eager, restless zeal of a man who would fain stifle remembrance and drive reflection from his mind.

The line breaks into column once more—the squadrons wheel rapidly, the rays of a winter's sun flashing from their steel head-pieces and breastplates—the horses snort and ring their bridles cheerily—the word of command flies sonorous from line to line— the General gallops to and fro, pleased with the progress of the mimic war—the drill is going on most satisfactorily, when a small escort of cavalry is seen to approach the parade-ground, and remains at a cautious distance from the manœuvres. An officer flaunting in scarf and feathers singles himself out, gallops up to the General, and salutes with his drawn sword as he makes his report. Cromwell thunders out a 'Halt!' that brings every charger upon his haunches. The men are permitted to dismount; the officers gather round their chief, and Harrison— for it is Harrison—who has just arrived, sits immovable upon his horse, with his sword-point lowered, waiting to learn the

General's pleasure as to the disposal of his prisoner, whose sex makes it a somewhat puzzling matter to decide.

' They have made reprisals upon *us*,' said Cromwell, in his deep, harsh tones, patting and making much of the good horse under him. ' Man or woman, let the prisoner be placed in secure ward. Verily, we are more merciful than just in that we spare the weaker sex. The Malignants deal more harshly with the saints. Their blood be on their own head ! ' he added solemnly.

Harrison turned his horse's head to depart. Little cared he, that reckless soldier, how they disposed of the lady he had taken prisoner ; he was thinking how he should billet the men and horses he had brought in, not of the fate of his unhappy captive.

' Stay,' said Cromwell, ' dismiss the soldiers, and bring the Malignant woman hither. I will myself question her ere she be placed in ward.'

As he spoke he dismounted, and entered a large stone building converted into a barrack, attended by a few of his officers, amongst whom was Effingham, and followed by the prisoner under escort of two stalwart troopers, who ' advanced ' their musquetoons with a ludicrous disinclination thus to guard an enemy of the softer sex.

The prisoner was a fair, handsome woman in the prime of her beauty. She was dressed in a lady's riding-gear of her time, which, notwithstanding its masculine character, was powerless to diminish her feminine attractions ; and looked thoroughly exhausted and worn out by physical fatigue. Yet was there a haughty turn about her head, an impatient gesture of her gloved hand, that denoted the spirit within was dauntless and indomitable as ever.

The instant that the short cloak she wore was removed, and the beaver hitherto slouched over her face taken off by Cromwell's orders, an operation which allowed a profusion of rich brown hair to fall nearly to her waist, Effingham started as if he had been shot. He would have spoken, but an imperious glance from the prisoner seemed to freeze the words upon his lips. He held his peace, and stood there, deadly pale, and trembling like a child.

Harrison's report was soon made, and amounted to this :—

That in his duty of patrolling the open country lying nearest to Goring's outposts, and visiting his videttes, he had espied a lady, mounted on a good horse, who had ridden boldly into the centre of his escort, and demanded to be conducted at once to Gloucester, and brought before Cromwell—that she avowed she belonged to the Royalist party, but had abandoned their cause, and was the bearer of important papers, which were to be laid before Cromwell

alone—that on his proposition that she should be searched for
these papers, and a corporal's attempting to do so, she had snapped
a pistol in the sub-officer's face, which providentially flashing in
the pan, only singed his beard and eyebrows—that out of respect
to Cromwell he had brought her on without further violence,
' though that she has not some evil intentions I never can believe,'
concluded Harrison, ' for she is the very first woman I ever came
across yet that could ride nearly a dozen miles and never open
her lips to speak a word, good or bad.'

The General scanned his prisoner carefully. His usual tact
and discernment were here at fault. ' Woman ! ' he said, rudely
and sternly, ' what want you here—whence came you—and why
venture you thus amongst the people of the Lord ? '

' I would see Cromwell alone,' replied Mary Cave (for Mary
Cave it was, as Effingham too surely knew), and she no longer
looked exhausted and fatigued, but the blood came back to her
cheek, the haughty turn to her head and neck, the indomitable
curve to her lip, as she felt the crisis had come, and her spirit
mounted with the occasion. ' I have ridden far and fast to see
you, General,' she added, with a certain tone of irony in her voice ;
' you will not refuse to grant an interview when a lady asks it.'

Effingham felt a strange thrill to hear her voice. How it took
him back to that which seemed now some other stage of existence,
albeit so short a time ago. How associated she was in his mind
with that *other* one. To him, though ' she was not the Rose, she
had been near the Rose,' and he would willingly at that moment
have given a year of his life to ask tidings of her whose name was
still nestling at his heart.

Cromwell hesitated. Bold schemer, undaunted soldier as he
was, he entertained a morbid dread of assassination, a dread that
in later days, when in the full flush of his prosperity, and seated
on the throne, caused him to wear proof-armour on all public
occasions under his clothes.

He had read, too, of women who would not scruple to sacrifice
their lives in a political cause ; his own enterprising spirit told
him how readily it was possible to encounter certain death for a
great object ; and this lady did not look as if she was likely to
shrink from any desperate deed because of its danger. And yet
to fear a woman ! Pshaw ! it seemed absurd. He would grant
her the interview she desired ; though, according to Harrison's
report, she had been so ready with her pistol, she was now obviously disarmed ; besides, he was well guarded, surrounded by
his troopers and his friends. He looked upon his officers, for the

N

most part trustworthy, fearless veterans, whose courage and fidelity he had already tried on many a well-fought field. Effingham alone was a new acquaintance, and his quick eye caught the expression of George's countenance watching the prisoner's face.

'Do you know anything of the lady?' said he, in short, imperious tones, and turning sharply round upon his new officer, with a frown of displeasure gathering on his thick brows.

'You may speak the truth, Captain Effingham!' said Mary, with a look of quiet contempt.

Thus adjured, Effingham hesitated no longer to acknowledge his acquaintance with the beautiful 'Malignant.'

'Mistress Mary Cave is too well known at the Court not to have won the respect and confidence of all who have ever breathed that polluted atmosphere. I will answer for her faith and honesty with my head. If she fail you, my life shall be for the life of her.'

Mary thanked him with a grateful glance.

'I have a boon to ask of you, General; a bargain to drive if you will. Grant me the interview I require, and bid me go in peace.'

Cromwell signed to her to follow him into a smaller apartment, in which a fire was burning, and which contained a chair, a writing-table, and a few articles of rough comfort.

'Captain Effingham,' he said, in his short, stern tones, 'place two sentries at the door. Remain yourself within call. Madam, I am now at your service. Speak on; we are alone.'

He doffed his heavy head-piece, placed it on the writing-table, and was about to throw himself into the chair. The General was no polished courtier—above all, no woman-worshipper—but there was that in Mary Cave's bearing which checked his first impulse, and bade him stand up respectfully before his prisoner.

Never in all her life before had Mary such need to call up the presence of mind and resolution that formed so important a part of her character. Here she stood, a gentle, soft-nurtured lady, brought up in all the exaggerated refinement of a court, before her bitterest enemy, the most uncompromising as he was the most powerful champion of her adversaries' party. Completely in his power, dependent on his generosity for immunity, from exposure, insult—nay, death itself (for, alas! the exasperated feelings aroused by the cruelties practised on both sides were not always restrained by consideration for age or sex); and, save for her accidental meeting with Effingham, whom she had little expected to see here, utterly friendless in the rebel camp. This was the interview that she had been looking forward to for days, that she had so prayed and hoped might be accomplished; that, seeming tolerably easy when seen from a distance, had been the goal to which all her schemes and wishes tended; and now that she was actually face to face with Cromwell, she shook from head to foot as she had never trembled in her life before—but once.

His manner, though reserved, became less stern than at first. Show us the man of any profession, soldier, statesman, Puritan, or archbishop, from eighteen to eighty (a fair margin), on whom beauty, real womanly beauty, makes no impression, and we will show you the eighth wonder of the world.

'Reassure yourself, madam,' said Cromwell, with a tone of kindness in his harsh voice; 'I do not to-day hear the name of Mistress Mary Cave for the first time. I can safely affirm I would long ago have given much to obtain possession of the lady who thus voluntarily surrenders herself as a prisoner. I have yet to learn what brings her into the very stronghold of the enemy. Had she been a man, there had been a price on her head.'

These words were alarming; but the smile that stole over the General's face was softer and kindlier than his wont.

Mary began her answer with a degree of composure far too obvious not to be affected.

'I am come,' said she, 'to negotiate the exchange of a prisoner. A messenger might have lingered, letters been intercepted, even a white flag outraged, so, General—so—I came myself. Major Bosville is languishing, perhaps dying, in Gloucester gaol. May he not be ransomed, can he not be exchanged? Any sum of money, any number of prisoners—ay, ten for one.'

Cromwell's brow grew dark. You ask too much, madam,' he replied, shaking his head sternly. ' That officer lies even now under sentence of death. He has refused to give any information concerning the strength or movements of the enemy. A confirmed Malignant, he shall die the death! Hath not Rupert slain in cold blood thirteen godly warriors taken with arms in their hands? The blood of the Lord's anointed cries aloud for vengeance! God do so to me, and more also, if I smite not root and branch, till the Amalekite is destroyed out of the land!'

He was chafing now—angry and restless, like some noble beast of prey.

Mary fitted the last arrow to her bowstring. 'You know me, General,' she said, with something of her old proud air. 'You know my power, my influence, my information. Listen; I will buy Bosville's life of you. You shall make your own terms.'

Cromwell smiled. Perhaps he had his private opinion of these lady politicians, these fair intriguers with the Queen at their head, who hampered the counsels of their friends far more effectually than they anticipated the designs of their enemies. He was perfectly courteous, but somewhat ironical in his reply.

'You cannot bribe me, madam,' said he, 'valuable as I doubt not is the price you offer. Your information may or may not be far superior to my own—your talent for intrigue doubtless many degrees finer. I am a simple soldier; my duty lies plain before me. I will have blood for blood, and I have the warrant of Scripture for my determination.'

Poor Mary! she broke down altogether now. The bold warrior-spirit, the craft of statesmanship, the artificial pride of rank and station, all gave way before the overwhelming flood of womanly pity and womanly fear. She seized the General's rough coarse hand in both her own, so white and soft by the contrast. Ere he could prevent her she pressed it to her lips: she bent over it, and clung to it, and folded it to her bosom. Down on her knees she implored him, she besought him, she *prayed* to him, with tears and sobs, to spare the prisoner's life. Her pride was fallen altogether now, her humiliation complete. It was no longer the stately Mary Cave, the Queen's minion, the adviser of statesmen, the ornament of a Court, but a broken-hearted woman pleading for life and death.

'Save him, General,' she gasped, gazing wildly up in his face, 'save him, for mercy's sake, as you hope to be saved yourself at the last day! What is it to you, a life the more or less? What is your authority worth if you can hesitate to exercise it for so trifling a matter? Is Cromwell so completely under the orders of Fairfax, so subservient to Ireton, such a sworn slave of the Parliament, that in his own camp he cannot extend mercy to whom he will?'

Her woman's instinct told her through all her distress and all her confusion where lay the weak point in the fortress she assailed; bid her attack him through his pride, his self-respect, his jealousy of command; and dimmed as were her eyes with tears, she saw she had shot her arrow home.

Cromwell flushed a deeper red up to his very temples, the scowl upon his bent brows, and the conspicuous wart over his right eye, lending an ominous and sinister expression to his whole countenance. He spoke not, but the hand she grasped was rudely withdrawn, and the high-born, gently-nurtured lady was fain to clasp him round the knees, cased in those wide, solid riding-boots, with their heavy spurs, that rang and jingled as he stamped twice in his passion against the floor.

'Save him, General!' she repeated. 'Is there no consideration you will listen to, no appeal you will respect? Hear me. I sent him on his errand. I got him his appointment. I bade him go forth wounded and helpless into the very jaws of your troopers, and now if he is to die his blood is on *my* head. Oh! think of your own mother! think of your own child! think of any one that you have ever loved! Would you see her kneeling as I do now? would you see her, lonely, helpless amongst strangers and enemies, pleading for dear life, and bear to know that she was refused? Think better of it, for the love of mercy, General, think better of it. Grant me this one boon, and I will pray for you, enemy though you be, night and morning, on my bended knees, till my dying day.'

His voice sounded hoarser than usual, and he loosened the plain linen band around his throat as he muttered the word— 'Reprisals!'

She sprang fiercely from her knees, flung his hand, which she had again taken, away from her in scorn, and flashed at him such a glance as made even Cromwell quail.

'Reprisals!' she repeated. 'It is the Puritan's English for murder. You have refused me—refused Mary Cave on her bended knees, who never knelt before to mortal man—beware of my revenge! Oh! I meant it not—forgive me!' she added, her whole manner changing once more to one of the softest, the most imploring entreaty, as the impotence and impolicy of her anger struck chill and sickening to her heart: 'forgive my hasty words, my pride that has never yet learned to stoop. You talk of reprisals, General; one life is worth another—take mine instead of his. Lead me out now—this minute—I am ready, and let *him* go free.'

She had touched the keystone now; the sympathy for courage and devotion which every brave man feels. He turned his face away that she might not see his emotion, for there were tears in Cromwell's eyes. She took the gesture for one of refusal, and it was in sad plaintive tones she proffered her last despairing request.

'At least grant me the one last boon I have ridden so far to ask. It is not a little thing that will tempt a woman to the step I have taken. You cannot refuse me this—if I cannot save him, at least I can die with him. Shot, steel, or hempen noose, whatever penalty is exacted from Humphrey Bosville shall be shared by

her who sent him here to die. I ask you no more favours—I
claim it as a right—he shall not suffer for my sake alone. Do not
think I shall flinch at the last moment. See! there is not a
trooper of all your Ironsides that fears death less than Mary
Cave!'

She had conquered triumphantly at last. The brave spirit
could not but recognise its kindred nature. He had made up his
mind now, and not a hair of Humphrey's head should have fallen
had the whole Parliament of England voted his death to a man.
Kindly, courteously, nay, almost tenderly, the rough Puritan
soldier raised the kneeling lady to her feet. With a consideration she little expected, he placed her carefully in the chair, sent
an orderly trooper for food and wine, and even bestirred himself
to ascertain where she might be most safely lodged till her departure with a safe conduct under his own hand.

'I grant your request, Mistress Mary Cave, and I attach to my
concession but two conditions. The one, it is needless to state,
is that Major Bosville passes his *parole* never again to bear arms
against the Parliament, and the other '—his glance softened more
and more as he proceeded—' that you will not quite forget plain
Oliver Cromwell, and that hereafter when you hear his harshness
censured, and his rustic breeding derided, you will not be
ashamed to say you have known him to show the courtesy of a
gentleman and the feeling of a man!'

With an obeisance, the respectful deference of which could not
have been outdone by any plumed hat that ever swept the floors
of Whitehall, Cromwell took his leave of his fair suppliant, con-
signing her to the care of George Effingham for the present, and
promising her a written pardon in his own hand, and safe conduct through his outposts for herself and Humphrey Bosville, by
the morrow's dawn.

Her spirit had kept her up hitherto, but fatigue, watching, and
anxiety were too much for her woman's strength; and as Cromwell's massive figure disappeared through the doorway, she laid
her head upon the coarse deal table and gave way to a passion of
tears.

CHAPTER XXI.

' UNDER SENTENCE.'

CONDEMNED TO DIE ! Reader, have you ever realised to yourself all that is contained in those three words? Have you ever considered how large a share of your daily life is comprised in what we may term the immediate future, in the cares, so to speak, of ' what you shall eat, and what you shall drink, and wherewithal you shall be clothed?' Have you ever reflected how your own petty schemes and intrigues—equally petty when viewed at the supreme moment, whether you be a politician on the cross benches, or a grocer behind your counter—fill up the measure of your hopes and wishes? how your own financial budget, whether it affect the revenues of a kingdom or the contents of a till, is the subject that occupies most of your thoughts? and how, when sagacity and foresight upon such matters become superfluous, there is a blank in your whole being, which you feel, perhaps for the first time, ought to have been filled up long ago with something that would not have deserted you at your need, that would have accompanied you into that *terra incognita* which the most material of us feel at some moments is really our home?

And yet at the crisis, it seems as though the spirit-wings were weaker than ever, and instead of soaring aloft into the blue heaven, can but flap heavily and wearily along the surface of earth, as though the mind were incapable of projecting itself into the Future, and must needs dwell mistily and inconclusively on the Past ; and there is no proverb truer than that ' the ruling passion is strong in death,' as all will readily admit whose lot it has ever been to look the King of Terrors in the face.

Humphrey Bosville lay condemned to death in Gloucester gaol. His examination, after a short imprisonment, had been conducted by Cromwell himself, with the few rude formalities extended to the trial of a prisoner-of-war. He had been questioned as to the strength of the King's army, and the deliberation of his councillors; like a soldier and a man of honour, he had steadfastly declined to divulge even the little he knew. The court that tried him was composed simply enough, consisting, besides Cromwell, of Harrison and another. The former of these two vainly endeavoured to persuade his prisoner, for whom he had taken a great liking, to turn traitor, and save his own life. Humphrey, however, was immovable, and Harrison liked him all the better. The proceedings were short, and not at all complicated. 'You refuse, then, to answer the questions put to you by the court?' said Cromwell, folding a sheet of paper in his hands with an ominous frown.

'I do, distinctly,' replied the prisoner, regardless of a meaning look from Harrison, and a strenuous nudge from that stout soldier's elbow.

'Sentence of death recorded. His blood be on his own head!' commented Cromwell; adding, with a look that lent a fearful interest to the simple words, 'to-morrow morning, at gun-fire.'

'God and the King!' exclaimed Humphrey, in a loud, fearless voice, placing his plumed hat jauntily on his head, and marching off between his gaolers, humming cheerfully the Royalist air of 'Cuckolds, come, dig!'

So the court broke up. Cromwell went to drill his Ironsides; Harrison to visit his outposts, with what result we have already learned; and another Cavalier was to die.

They placed food and wine in his cell; the grim troopers who guarded him looked on him no longer as an enemy. Already he was invested with the fearful interest of the departing traveller: he who ere twenty-four hours have elapsed will be in that land of which all of us have thought, and which none of us have seen. They were soldiers, too, and they liked his *pluck*, his gallant bearing, his cheerful good humour, his considerate courtesy even to his escort; for Humphrey was a gentleman at heart, and one essential peculiarity of the breed is, that it never shows its purity so much as when *in extremis*. Not a rough dragoon in the guard-room, including Ebenezer the Gideonite, who was still black and blue from shoulder to hip, but would have shared his ration willingly, 'Malignant' though he was, with the Cavalier officer.

He ate his portion of food with a good appetite, and drank off his wine to the King's health. The winter sun streamed in at the grating of his cell, the heavy tramp of the sentry at his door rung through the silence of the long stone corridor. It was all over now. It was come at last, and Humphrey sat him down to think.

Yes, he had looked upon Death as a near neighbour for years; he had fronted him pretty often in Flanders before this unhappy civil war, and had improved his acquaintance with him since at Edge-Hill, Roundway-Down, Newbury, and elsewhere; nay, he had felt the grasp of his icy hand but very lately, when he failed to parry that delicate thrust of Goring's. What an awkward thrust it was! and should he not have met it in carte, rather than tierce, and so gone round his adversary's blade? Pshaw! how his mind wandered. And what was the use of thinking of such matters now ?—now that he had not twenty-four hours to live—now that he should fix his thoughts on the next world, and pray ardently for the welfare of his soul? Ay, 'twas well that he had not neglected this duty, and put it off till to-day ; do what he would he could not control his mind, and bid it obey his will. Thoughts after thoughts came surging in like ocean waves, and bore him on and swamped him, so to speak, in their resistless tide. Might he but have chosen, he would not have died quite like this. No ! he had hoped to go down in some victorious onset, stirrup to stirrup with hot Prince Rupert, the best blood in England, charging madly behind him to the old war-cry that made his blood boil even now—the stirring battle-word of 'God and the King ! ' —sword in hand, and the sorrel pulling hard !—the poor sorrel. Harrison had promised his prisoner to take care of the good horse ; there was some comfort in that, and Harrison was a soldier, though a Roundhead. Ay, that had been a glorious death ; or, better still, to have dragged his wounded frame to Mary's feet and laid his head upon her knee, and died there so peaceful, so happy, like a child hushing off to its sleep. Mary would think of him—mourn him, surely—and never forget him now. How would she look when they told her of it in the Queen's chamber? He tried to fancy her, pale and wobegone, bending to hide her face over the embroidery he knew so well—the embroidery he had told her playfully was to be finished ere he came back again. He would never come back to her now ; and the large tears that his own fate had failed to draw from him, gathered in his eyes as he thought of that glorious lady's desolation, and fell unheeded on his clasped hands. Well, he had promised her, if need were, to give his life ungrudgingly for the Cause—and he had redeemed his word. Perhaps in another world he might meet her again, and be proud to show her the stainless purity of his shield. He thought over his past life—he was no casuist, no theologian ; his simple faith, like that of his knightly ancestors, was comprised in a few words—'*Für Gott und für ihr,*' might have been engraved on his blade, as it was emblazoned on the banner of the chivalrous Lord Craven—he whose romantic attachment to the Queen of Bohemia was never outdone in the imagination of a Troubadour, who worshipped his royal ladye-love as purely and unselfishly as he risked life and fortune ungrudgingly in her cause. So was it with Humphrey—' For God and for her ' was the sentiment that had ruled his every action of late—that consoled him and bore him up now, when he was about to die. It was not wisdom, it

was not philosophy, it was not perhaps true religion ; but it served
him well enough—it stood him in the stead of all these—it carried
him forward into the spirit-life where, it may be, that some things
we wot not of in our worldly forethought, are the true reality, and
others that we have worshipped here faithfully and to our own
benefit—such as prudential considerations, external respectability,
and 'good common-sense'—are found to be the myths and the
delusions, the bubbles that the cold air of death has dispelled
for evermore.

At least, Humphrey knew he had but another night to live,
and when he had prayed, hopefully and resignedly, with but one
small grain of discontent, one faint repining that he might not see
her just *once* again, he drew his pallet from the corner of his cell,
and with folded arms and calm placid brow, laid him down peacefully to sleep.

So sound were his slumbers, that they were not disturbed by
the armed tread of the captain of the ward, a fierce old Puritan,
who ushered up the corridor the cloaked and hooded figure of a
woman, accompanied by an officer of the Ironsides, who had shown
him an order signed by Cromwell's own hand, which he dared
not disobey. The grim warder, however, influenced by the prisoner's gallant and gentle demeanour, would fain have dissuaded
the visitors from disturbing his repose.

'If you be friends of the Major's,' said he, in the gruff tones
peculiar to all such custodians, 'you would act more kindly to
let him be; they mostly gets their little snooze about this time
of night; and if he's not roused, he'll sleep right on till to-morrow
morning; and the nearer he wakes to gun-fire, the better for him.
You'll excuse my making so free, madam; the Major's got to be
shot at daybreak. But if you're come to examine of him, or to
get anything more out of him than what he told the Court, I tell
ye it's no use, and a burning shame into the bargain. I can't
keep ye out, seeing it's the General's order—and Cromwell's a
man who *will* be obeyed; but I can't bear to see the Major put
upon neither, and he such a nice, well-spoken gentleman, and the
last night as he's to be with us and all.' So grumbling, the old
gaoler, who was not without a sort of rough coarse kindness of his
own, opened the cell door, and admitting the visitors, set his lamp
down on the floor for their service ; after which civility he returned
to cough and grumble by himself in the passage.

Mary looked on the face of the sleeper, and for the first time
since she had known him realised the unassuming courage of that
honest heart. Could this be the man who, ere twelve hours should

elapse, was doomed to die? this calm and placid sleeper, breathing so heavily and regularly, with a smile on his lips, and his fair brow smooth and unruffled as a child's? She turned proudly to Effingham. 'Is he not worthy of the Cause?' was all she said; and Effingham, looking there upon his comrade and his rival, wiped the dew from his forehead, for the conflict of his feelings was more than he could bear.

Mary bent over him till her long hair swept across his face. 'Humphrey,' she whispered, in the sweetest of her soft caressing tones, 'Humphrey, wake up; do you not know me?—wake up.'

The sleeper stirred and turned. The well-known voice must have called up some association of ideas in his mind; perhaps he was dreaming of her even then and there. He muttered something. In the deep silence of the cell both his listeners caught it at once. Mary blushed crimson for very shame; and Effingham felt his heart leap as it had never leapt before.

The sleeper had but whispered three words—'Mary, Loyalty, Mary,' was all he said; and then he woke, and stared wildly upon his visitors.

In another instant he had seized Mary's hand, and was folding it to his heart in a transport of affection and delight. He knew not that his life had been spared—he still thought he was to die; but he believed his prayers had been answered—that, whether in the body or out of the body, he was permitted to look on her once again—and that was enough for him.

Effingham did as he would be done by, and left the cell. If 'he jests at scars who never felt a wound,' on the other hand he is wondrously quick-witted and sympathizing who has himself gone through the *peine.forte et dure* of real affection.

And Effingham, too, felt a weight taken off his heart. He could rejoice now without a single drawback at his comrade's pardon. To do him justice, he would have given all he had in the world to save him yesterday; but now he felt that though henceforth they would never again fight side by side, Bosville was his friend and brother once more. He felt, too, that there was something to live for still, that Hope was not dead within him, and his arm would henceforth be nerved for the struggle by a nobler motive than despair. His future existed once more. Yesterday his life was a blank; to-day, simply because a sleeping captive had muttered a proper name, that blank was filled again with colours bright and rosy as the tints of the morning sky. Such are the ups and downs of poor mortality; such is the weakness of what we are pleased to term the godlike mind that rules our mass of clay.

We will follow Effingham's example; we will not rob Humphrey of his *tête-à-tête* with his mistress, nor intrude upon his transports when he learned that the hand he loved so dearly was the one that had saved him from death. It was too delightful—it was almost maddening to reflect on all she had undergone for his sake: how she had pleaded with Cromwell for his pardon, and having obtained it, had taken possession of him, as it were, at once, and passed her word for his *parole* as if he belonged to her, body and soul; and so he *did* belong to her, and so he would. Oh, if she would but accept his devotion! he longed to pour out his very heart's blood at her feet. Poor Humphrey! he was young, you see, and of a bold honest nature, so he knew no better.

The three left the prison together, with a cordial farewell from the kind old governor, and walked through the dark night to the hostelry in the town. Mary was very silent. Did she regret what she had done? did she grudge her efforts for the prisoner? Far from it! She was thinking of all he deserved at her hands, of how she never could repay him for all his fondness and devotion, of the debtor and creditor account between them, and how she wished he could be a little, ever so little, less infatuated about her.

Again we say, poor Humphrey!

CHAPTER XXII.

'FATHER AND CHILD.'

GRACE ALLONBY is very sad and lonely now. Anxiety and distress have told upon her health and spirits, and the girl, once so fresh and elastic, goes about her household duties with a pale cheek and a listless step that worry her father to his heart's core. Sir Giles has but little time for speculation on private affairs, his duty to his sovereign keeps him constantly employed, and it requires no astute politician to discover that, whatever apprehensions he may have to spare, are due to that sovereign's critical position. The Royal Parliament has been convened at Oxford, and has voted anything and everything except *supplies*. Its sister assemblage at Westminster, bitter in successful rivalry, has refused to treat for peace; Hopton has sustained a conclusive defeat from Waller at Alresford. Oxford is no longer a secure haven; and the King, deprived of the society and counsels of his wife, feels himself more than usually perplexed and disheartened. Sir Giles has enough

to do with his own regimental duties, for, come what may, he
never neglects for an instant that task of organization and discipline on which the old soldier feels that life and honour must
depend. His advice, too, is constantly required, and as constantly
neglected by the King; but bitter and unpalatable as it may be,
it is always proffered with the same frank honesty and singleness
of purpose. He has succeeded in raising and arming no contemptible force of cavalry. With his own stout heart at their head,
he thinks they can ride through and through a stand of pikes
with a dash that shall win Prince Rupert's grim approval on a
stricken field. He cannot foresee that, ere long, they will prove
the speed of their horses, rather than the temper of their blades,
on the wide expanse of fatal Marston-Moor. In the meantime
they are equipped and ready to march.

An escort is provided to guard 'Gracey' back to her kinswoman's house at Boughton, where she will remain in bodily
safety, no doubt, and will fulfil her destiny as a woman, by wasting
her own heart in anxiety for the fate of others. Oxford will be
emptied soon of all but its loyal professors and stanch war-worn
garrison. Grace does not seem to regret her departure, nor to
look forward to her journey with any anticipations of delight, nor
to care much whether she goes or stays. Her father's return to
active service seems to alarm and depress her, and she wanders
about the house with her eyes full of tears; but he has often left
her to go campaigning before, and never seen her 'take on,' as he
expresses it, like this. What can have come over the girl?

'If she had but a mother now,' thinks Sir Giles, with a half
bitter pang to feel that his own honest affection should be insuf-
ficient for his daughter. He could almost reproach himself that
he has not married a second time; but no, Gracey! not even for
you could he consent to sacrifice that dream of the past, which is
all the old man has left to him on earth. Why do we persist in
cherishing the *little* we have, so much the more the *less* it is?
Why is the widow's mite, being her all, so much *more* than the rich
man's stores of silver and gold, being *his all* too? Perhaps it is
that we must suffer before we can enjoy, must pine in poverty
before we can revel in possession; and therefore Lazarus devours
his crust with famished eagerness, whilst Dives pushes his plate
disdainfully away, and curses fretfully cook and butler, who
cannot make him hungry or thirsty, albeit his viands are served
on silver, and his wine bubbles in a cup of gold. Sir Giles loves
a memory fifteen years old better than all the rest of the world,
and Gracey into the bargain.

He sits after supper with a huge goblet of claret untasted at his elbow. Leaning his head on his hand he watches his daughter unobserved. All day she has been busied about little matters for his comfort. He marches to-morrow at dawn, and she too leaves Oxford for Northamptonshire. She was more cheerful, he thinks, this afternoon, and the interest and bustle had brought a colour again to her cheek: but how pale and tired she looks now, bending over that strip of work. The delicate fingers, too, though they fly nimbly as ever in and out, are thinner than they used to be— and she always turns her face away from the lamp. A father's eyes, Grace, are sharper than you think for; he is watching you narrowly from under his shaded brows, and he sees the tears raining down thick upon your work and your wasted hands. In the whole of her married life your mother never wept like that.

He can stand it no longer.

'Gracey,' says he, in his deep kind tones; 'Gracey! little woman! what's the matter?'

He took her on his knee, as he used to do when she was a little curly-headed thing, and she hid her face on his shoulder, her long dark hair mingling with the old man's white locks and beard.

She clung to him and sobbed wearily, and told him, 'it was nothing—she was tired, and anxious, and nervous, but well— quite well—and, it was nothing.'

He had long lost his place in his daughter's heart, though he knew it not.

He strove to cheer her up gently and warily, with a womanly tact and tenderness you could hardly have expected from the war-worn soldier, leading her insensibly from domestic details to the hopes and proceedings of the Royalists, and she struggled to be calm, and appeared to lend an anxious ear to all his details.

'We shall have a large army in the North, Grace,' said the old Cavalier; 'and when Prince Rupert has relieved York—and relieve it he will, my lass, for hot as he is, there is not a better officer in the three kingdoms, when his hands are loose—he will effect a junction with the King, and we shall then be able to show the Roundheads a front that will keep their ragged Parliament in check once more. What, girl, we have still Langdale and Lisle and the Shrewsbury Foot, and gallant Northampton with all his merry men at his back, not to mention my own knaves, whose rear-guard you saw march out this morning. I have taken some trouble with them, you know, and they're the best brigade I've commanded yet by a good deal. Why, what said young Bosville when he lay in this very room?—ay, on the sofa where you always sit at your stitching—and saw them file past the windows before they were half-drilled. " Sir Giles," said he, " they're the only cavalry we have that can *ride*." And there's no better judge and no better soldier for a young man than Humphrey, whom I love as my own son. They'll win your old father his peerage yet before I've done with 'em. Fill me out the claret, my darling, and we'll drink a health to Lady Grace ! '

She did as she was desired, and he could not have accused her of paleness now. Was it the anticipation of her exalted rank that thus brought the blood in a rush to Grace's cheeks ?

' Ay ! if worst comes to worst,' proceeded the old knight, after a hearty pull at the claret, ' the rebels will be glad to come to terms. I am an old man now, sweetheart, and I want to live at peace with my neighbours. When I've had these new levies in a good rousing fire once and again, and seen the knaves hold their own with Cromwell and his men in iron, I shall be satisfied for my part. Besides, we fight unencumbered now ; the Queen's safe enough down in the West. I heard from Mary this morning by Jermyn, who travelled here post with despatches ; and the Queen——'

' From Mary ! ' interrupted Grace, her eyes sparkling and her face flushing once more ; ' what says she ? Does she talk about herself ?—does she give you any news ? '

She spoke in a sharp quick tone ; and the slender fingers that rested on her father's glass clasped it tight round the stem.

' She writes mostly of the Cause, as is her wont,' replied Sir Giles, not noticing his daughter's eagerness. ' They have hopes of more men and horses down in the West. Ay, there is talk too of foreign assistance ; but for my part I put little faith in that. The Queen's household is much diminished,—that's a good job at least. I read my Bible, Grace, I hope, like a good Christian, and I believe every word in it, but I have never yet *seen* that " in the multitude of counsellors there is safety." Howsoever, there is but little pomp now in the Queen's court at Exeter. Mary only mentions herself and Mrs. Kirke, and Lady Carlisle, whom I never could abide ; and Dormer and Bosville as gentlemen of the chamber ; and that is all.'

Grace's breath came quick and short. She was still on her father's knee, but in such a posture that he could not see her face. She would have given much to be able to ask one simple question, but she dared not—no, she *dared* not. She held her peace, feeling as if she was stifled.

' The Queen were best on the Continent,' pursued Sir Giles,

'and Mary seems to think she will go ere long, taking her house-hold with her. God be with them! England is well rid of the half of them.'

Grace laughed—such a faint, forced, miserable laugh. Poor Grace! the blow had been long coming, and it had fallen at last. Of course he would accompany his Royal mistress abroad; of course, she would never, never see him again; of course he was nothing to her, and amidst all his duties and occupations she could have no place in his thoughts. The pertinacity with which she dwelt upon this consolatory reflection was sufficiently edify-ing; and of course she ought to have foreseen it all long ago, and it was far better that she should know the worst, and accustom herself to it at once. Oh, far better! A positive relief! And the poor face that she put up to kiss her father when he wished her 'Good night,' looked whiter and more drawn than ever; the footfall that he listened to so wistfully going up the stairs dwelt wearily and heavily at every step. Sir Giles shook his head, finished his claret at a draught, and betook himself too to his couch; but the old Cavalier was restless and uneasy, his sleep little less unbroken than his daughter's.

Alas, Gracey!—she was his own child no more. He re-membered her so well in her white frock, tottering across the room with her merry laugh, and holding his finger tight in the clasp of that warm little hand; he remembered her a slender slip of girlhood, galloping on her pony with a certain graceful timidity peculiarly her own, her long dark ringlets floating in the breeze, her bright eyes sparkling with the exercise, and always, fright-ened or confident, trusting and appealing to 'Father' alone. He remembered her, scores and scores of times, sitting on his knee as she had done this evening, nestling her head upon his shoulder, and vowing in her pretty positive way—positive always and only with *him*—that she would never marry and leave him, never trust her old father to any hands but her own; she was sure he couldn't do without her, and if *he* wasn't sure he ought to be!

And now somebody had come and taken away all this affection from him that he considered his by right; and she was no longer his child—his very own—and never would be again. Sir Giles could not have put his thoughts explicitly into words, but he had a dim consciousness of the fact, and it saddened while it almost angered him. Though he slept but little he was up and astir long before daybreak; and the 'God bless thee, Gracey,' which was always his last words at parting with his daughter, was de-livered more hoarsely and solemnly than his wont. The pale face with its red eyelids haunted him as he rode; and except once to give a beggar an alms, and once to swear testily at his best horse for a stumble, Sir Giles never uttered a syllable for the first ten miles of his journey.

And Grace, too, in the train of her kinsman, Lord Vaux, travelled wearily back to his house at Boughton, which she considered her home. Faith, riding alongside of her, to cheer her mistress's spirits, forgot her own griefs—for Faith too had lost a lover—in sympathy for the lady's meek uncomplaining sadness.

'It's all along of the Captain!' thought Faith, whose own affairs had not dimmed the natural sharpness of her sight; 'it's all along of the Captain, and he ought to be ashamed of himself, so he ought!'

Faith, like the rest of her class, was not particular as to the amount of blame she laid upon the absent; and with the happy impartiality of her sex, invariably considered and proclaimed *the man* to be in the wrong. In this instance she condemned Humphrey without the slightest hesitation. It was clear he had left her young mistress without distinctly promising marriage, and when she contrasted such lukewarm negligence with the ardent passages of leave-taking that had been reciprocated by Dymocke and herself, she could scarcely contain her indignation. 'If Hugh had used *me* so,' thought Faith, and the colour rose to her cheeks as she dwelt on the possible injustice, 'as sure as I've two hands I'd have scratched his eyes out!'

CHAPTER XXIII.

'THE TRUE DESPOTISM.'

'NEVER to bear arms against the Parliament!—never to be a soldier again!—scarcely to have a right to draw a sword! Ah, Mary! life would be dear at such a price, were it not that *you* had offered it; were it not that *your* will, your lightest word, is omnipotent with me. But oh! how I long to hear the trumpets sounding a charge again, and to see the sorrel in headstall and holsters shaking his bit as he used to do. He's too good for anything but a charger. Oh, if I could but ride him alongside of Prince Rupert once more!'

Half ashamed of his enthusiasm, the speaker's colour rose, and he laughed as he glanced almost timidly at the lady he addressed. She was tending some roses that drooped over the garden bench on which he sat. There was this attraction about Mary Cave that perhaps endeared her to the imagination more than all her wit and all her beauty—she was constantly occupied in some graceful womanly task, and fulfilled it in such a graceful womanly way. Were she writing a letter, or threading a needle, or engaged in any other trifling occupation, her figure seemed to take insensibly the most becoming attitude, her rich brown hair to throw off the light at the exact angle you would have selected for a picture, the roseate bloom to deepen into the very tint that accorded best with her soft winning eyes. It was not her intellect, though that was of no inferior class; nor her form and features, though both were dangerously attractive: it was *her ways* that captivated and enslaved, that constituted the deadliest weapon in the whole armoury of which, womanlike, she knew so well the advantage and the use.

As she pruned the roses and trained them downwards from their stems, shaking a shower of the delicate pink petals into the sun, she looked like a rose herself—a sweet, blooming moss-rose, shedding its fragrance on all that came within its sphere; the type of pure loveliness and rich, bright, womanly beauty.

He thought so as he looked up at her, and his heart thrilled to the tones of her melodious voice. It was all over with him now—

Inch thick, knee-deep, o'er head and ears,—a forked one.

She knew her power, too, and made no sparing use of it. They must be either slaves or tyrants, these women; and, like fire, they make good servants but bad mistresses.

'You are better here than wasting your life in Gloucester gaol,' answered Mary, 'and you can serve the King as well with your head as with your hands. Any man with the heart of a man can be a soldier; there is not one in a million that will make a states-man. Do you think I would have taken such care of you if I had thought you fit for nothing better than the front-rank of one of Prince Rupert's foolhardy attacks?'

She asked the question with an inexpressibly mischievous and provoking air. She could not resist the temptation of teasing and irritating him on occasion; she loved to strike the keys, so to speak, and evoke its every sound, at whatever cost of wear and tear to the instrument itself. He winced, and his countenance fell at once, so she was satisfied, and went on.

'If you cannot serve the King on the sorrel's back, do you think you are of no use to the Queen at her need here in Exeter? That poor lady, with her infant daughter, has but few friends and protectors now. A loyal and chivalrous gentleman always finds his post of honour in defending the weak. If you seek for danger you will find enough, and more than enough, in doing your duty by your Royal mistress—in fulfilling the orders, Major Bosville, that I shall have the honour of conveying to you.'

She laughed merrily and made him a grand courtesy as she spoke, spreading out her white robes with a mock and playful dignity. Mary did not often thus unbend, and he could not but confess to himself that she was inexpressibly charming so ; yet would he have been better pleased had she been in a more serious mood too.

He rose from the garden-bench and stood by her, bending down over the roses, and speaking in a low grave tone—

'I am ready, as you know, none better, to sacrifice life and all for the King's cause. Do me the justice to allow that I have never yet flinched a hair's-breadth from difficulty or danger. I desire no better fate than to shed my blood for his Majesty and the Queen. If I may not draw my sword with my old comrades, I may yet show them how to die like a Cavalier. My life is of little value to any one,' he added in a somewhat bitter tone, 'least of all to myself; and why should I be regretted when so many that were nobler and wiser and better are forgotten ?'

It was a random shaft, but it quivered in the bull's-eye. She shot a sharp quick glance at him. Did he mean it? Was he too thinking, then, of Falkland? No! that pained, sorrowing countenance forbade the suspicion of any *arrière pensée*. Her heart smote her as she scanned it. She looked kindly and fondly at him.

'Are you nothing to *me*?' she said. 'Should not I miss you and mourn you—and oh ! do you think *I* could do without you at all? Hush ! here comes Lady Carlisle.'

In effect that lady's graceful figure, with its courtly gait and rustling draperies, was seen advancing up the gravel path to put an end to the *tête-à-tête*. Such interruptions are the peculiar lot of those who have anything *very* particular to communicate ; but we do not take upon ourselves to affirm that Mary's quick ear had not caught the sound of a door opening from Lady Carlisle's apartments ere she permitted herself to bestow on Humphrey such words of encouragement as made the June sunshine and the June roses brighter and sweeter than roses and sunshine had ever seemed before.

With his loyal heart bounding happily beneath his doublet, and a light on his handsome face that Lady Carlisle—no mean judge

of masculine attractions—regarded with critical approval, he
followed the two ladies into the antechamber of his Royal mistress, now seeking with her new-born baby an asylum in the still
faithful town of Exeter, one of the few strongholds in the kingdom
left to the Royal cause; and yet, alas! but a short distance removed from the contamination of rebellion, for Essex was already
establishing his head-quarters at Chard, and but two-and-twenty
miles of the loveliest hill and dale in Britain intervened between
the stern Parliamentary General and the now vacillating and in-
timidated Queen.

It was a strange contrast to the magnificence of Whitehall, even
to the more chastened splendours of Merton College, that quiet
residence of majesty in the beautiful old town—the town that can
afford to challenge all England to rival it in the loveliness of its
outskirts and the beauty of its women. Exeter has always particularly plumed itself on the latter qualification; and many a
dragoon of the present day, whose heart is no harder under its
covering of scarlet and gold than was that of the chivalrous
Cavalier in buff and steel breastplate, has to rue his death-wound
from a shaft that penetrated all his defences, when shot deftly
home by a pair of wicked Devonshire eyes. Of the pic-nics in its
vicinity, of the drives home by moonlight—of the strolls to hear 'our
band play,' and the tender cloakings and shawlings, and puttings
on of goloshes afterwards (for in that happy land our natural
enemies likewise enjoy the incalculable advantage of an uncertain
climate and occasional showers), are not the results chronicled in
every parish register in England?—and do not the beadle at St.
George's, Hanover Square, and other hymeneal authorities, know
'the reason why?'

The Queen occupied a large quiet house, that had formerly been
a convent, on the outskirts of the town. Its roomy apartments
and somewhat secluded situation made it a fitting residence for
Royalty, particularly for Royalty seeking privacy and repose;
while the large garden adjoining, in which the holy sisters had
been wont to stroll and ponder, yearning, it may be, for the
worldly sunshine they had left *without* the walls, formed a pleasant
haunt for the Queen's diminished household, and a resort on the
fine June mornings of which Mary and Humphrey, who were both
early risers, did not fail to make constant use.

Their duties about the Queen's person had of late been unusually light. The birth, under circumstances of difficulty and
danger, of a daughter, whose arrival on the worldly stage seemed
to augur the misfortunes that, beautiful and gifted as she was,

dogged her to her grave, had confined Henrietta to her chamber, and precluded her from her usual interference in affairs of State. The instincts of maternity were in the ascendant, and what were crowns and kingdoms in comparison with that little pink morsel of humanity lying so helplessly in her bosom? Well is it for us that we cannot foresee the destinies of our children; merciful the blindness that shuts out from us the long perspective of the future —the coming struggles we should none of us have courage to confront. Could Henrietta have foretold that daughter's fate, bound in her beauty and freshness for a weary lifetime to the worst of the evil dukes who bore the title d'Orleans, would she have hung over the tiny treasure with such quiet happiness? Would she have neglected all besides in the world at the very faintest cry of the little new-born Princess?

We must return to Humphrey Bosville and Mary Cave, and the terms of close friendship, to call it by no softer name, on which they now found themselves. Since his rescue from imminent death by her exertions, his devotion to her had assumed, if possible, a more reverential character than before. To owe his life to a woman for whom he had felt a slight attachment, would have been an obligation rather galling and inconvenient than otherwise; but to owe his life to *the* woman whom alone of all on earth he had loved with the deep absorbing fervour of which such a nature was capable, brought with it a sensation of delight which was truly intoxicating. It was such an additional link to bind him to her for ever; it made him seem to belong to her now so thoroughly; it was such a good excuse for giving way to her most trifling caprices, and obeying her lightest whim. Come what might, he felt that they could never now be entirely independent of each other; so he entered the Queen's service immediately on his return to Oxford, giving up his commission in the Royal army, and resigning his right to wear a sword, as indeed the terms of his *parole* enjoined, with as little hesitation as he would have displayed in jumping with his hands tied into the Isis, had Mary only told him to do the one instead of the other.

It was no small inducement either to serve his Royal mistress assiduously, that his situation in her household brought him into close and daily contact with his ladye-love. Probably at no period of his life before had Humphrey been so happy as during the few golden weeks of Henrietta's confinement at Exeter. To meet Mary day by day in the performance of his duty; to see her in every phase of courtly life, from the strict observance of etiquette to the joyous moments of relaxation, over which, nevertheless, the atmosphere

of Royalty shed a certain refinement and reserve; to admire her
ready tact and winning bearing in all the different relations of
a courtier's life; and above all, to walk with her morning after
morning in those happy gardens, feeling that she too enjoyed
and counted on their half-hour of uninterrupted conversation, and
was little less punctual at the trysting-place than himself; all this
constituted an existence for which it was very seldom he repined
that he had bartered his life's ambition, his visions of military
distinction and renown. Mary, too, whose knowledge of human
nature was far deeper than that of the generality of her sex, whose
organisation forced her to be calculating, so to speak, and provident even in her affections, Mary felt herself day by day losing
much of the hard, stern, practical force of character that had en-
crusted and petrified her woman's heart. She was often surprised
in her moments of reflection (for Mary was a rigid and severe self-
examiner) to find how little interested she was comparatively in
the progress of the Royal Cause—how satisfied she could be to
remain idle week after week at Exeter—how happily she could
bask away her time in the summer sunshine, wandering, but not
alone, through those shady gardens. She was ashamed—yes,
ashamed—to confess to herself how often the image of a certain
kindly, handsome face, with its long love-locks and dark drooping
moustaches, rose between her mental vision and all considerations
of duty, loyalty, and interest—ay, even between her deep sorrow
and the memory of the dead. Yet the shame had in it a burning,
thrilling happiness too; and though she threw up her haughty
head, and a scornful smile curled her full lips as she pondered,
she would not have had it otherwise if she could.

But she ruled him, nevertheless, with an iron hand. It is unnecessary to admit that the prominent and chief fault in this lady's
character was that destructive quality which, forming, as it does,
a principal ingredient in the noblest spirits, is yet perhaps the
cause of more sorrow and suffering than all the cardinal vices (if
such there be) put together—Pride, the bane of that resplendent
being whom the angels themselves called 'the Son of the Morning;'
the awful and eternal curse of him who made his election 'rather
to rule in Hell than serve in Heaven.' Pride was with Mary Cave
as the very air she breathed. It prompted her to conceal and
stifle, nay, even to mock at, the better feelings of her nature; to
grudge the man that loved her the full and free confession, to
which, if he deserved anything at all, he was fully entitled, and
which would have made him the happiest Cavalier in England;
to check and warp even his kind feelings, overflowing as they did

with a fond and chivalrous devotion, that would have made a humbler woman's heaven, that she herself would have felt it a weary blank to be without; to embitter for him many a moment that but for this would have been tinged with golden hues; and to goad and madden him for no fault of his own when most he needed soothing and repose.

He too had his share of pride, which she never seemed to acknowledge; but in his singleness of heart he sacrificed it to hers, as he did everything else he had. She never knew, and he would never tell her, the long hours and days of grief that she had cost him. If he was sad, he suffered uncomplaining by himself. The kind look was always there to greet her; she never read reproach in the fond, frank eyes. She was his first love and his last, that was enough for him. It was a brave, confiding nature, this young gentleman's; simple and honest, and one that it had been a pity to see delivered over to bitter disappointment, reckless guilt, and wild remorse.

He did not understand women, poor boy! God forbid he ever should!

A council had been assembled, and the increasing hopelessness of the Royal Cause had called up a rueful expression of dismay on the faces of the Queen's advisers as they stared blankly at each other. Jermyn had returned with but little encouragement from the King. Charles was hardly the man to see the shortest way out of a difficulty, and had been so accustomed to rely upon his Queen for advice and assistance, that when he found himself in turn applied to by his wife, he was more than usually helpless and undecided. The Queen's own advisers consisted but of the refuse of her party. Jermyn and a few subordinate courtiers were scarcely a crew to weather the storm when the ship was so crazy and the navigation so intricate. Goring's pregnant brain and reckless hand might have been useful now; but Goring was far away, drinking and countermarching in the West Riding of Yorkshire. Ashburnham had retired from Weymouth before 'the Coming Man,' whose Ironsides had ere this perfected their drill on many a stricken field. Prince Maurice had lost so many men in the siege of Lynn, he could show no front to the dreaded and determined Essex. The enemy was near, ay, even at the very gates, and what was to be done?

At this crisis, weakened in body and disheartened in mind, Henrietta's royal spirit gave way. The determination was arrived at to sue the Parliamentary General for mercy, and on the most plausible grounds of common courtesy and chivalrous forbearance towards a woman, to entreat Essex to tamper with his duty towards the Parliament, and to forfeit his own character by conniving at the Queen's escape. Like many another measure of policy, this step originated, not in the council, but in the bedchamber.

Supported by a few of her weeping ladies, the Queen came to the resolution of thus humbling herself before the Parliamentary General; and of those frightened and despairing women, among whom even Lady Carlisle had lost heart and courage, there was but one dissentient voice to this humiliating proposition. Need we say it was Mary Cave's?

'I would rather take my child in my arms,' said she, when called on by her Majesty to give her unbiassed opinion, 'and placing myself at the head of our garrison here, march at once upon Essex's head-quarters. I would cut my way through them, or leave my body on the field. If we succeeded, we should make a junction with the King in the north, and maybe restore the *prestige* of the Royal arms; if we failed, 'tis but an honourable death after all, and one right worthy of a Queen.'

The old Bourbon blood rose for an instant to Henrietta's cheek, and she almost wavered in her purpose; but it ebbed back again chill about her heart as she thought of her helpless condition and her little crying child.

'It could not be,' she said: 'there was a limit to all things, even the courage of a Queen. No; she would send a flag of truce to Essex, and a message he could not refuse to consider. But whom to send? Which of her courtiers would undertake the task? Savage reprisals were now the daily custom of the war: the white flag did not always secure the life of its bearer. Who would risk himself in the lion's den?'

'Perhaps Mrs. Mary will go herself?' suggested Lady Carlisle in her soft, smooth tones. 'She fears nothing, so she says, but dishonour. She would be safe enough, methinks, with Essex.'

Mary smiled proudly. 'I have been in the rebel camp ere this,' she said, 'and it was your ladyship's self that bade me go; for that counsel I shall always feel grateful. Your Majesty has one servant at least that will be proud to execute your will.'

She glanced as she spoke to where Bosville, with another gentleman of the chamber, stood in attendance in the next room. The Queen smiled faintly and stretched her thin hand towards Mary with a gesture of caress.

'He is a *preux chevalier*, *mâmie*,' she said, 'and would go to the death, I believe, for you or me; though I think I know which is the queen that owns all *his* loyalty. I have watched him often,

Marie, and I *know.*' She nodded her head with something of her old playful **air**, but she sighed after she spoke, and relapsed into the melancholy silence that was becoming habitual to her.

Was she thinking that, Princess and Sovereign though she were, in the bloom of her beauty and the hey-day of her prosperity, she had never enjoyed such an unqualified dominion as was possessed by her undemonstrative waiting-woman, proud Mary Cave?

CHAPTER XXIV.

' FAREWELL.'

EFFINGHAM had ere this made considerable progress in the favour of the party he had espoused. His knowledge of his profession, coupled with a certain reckless daring of temperament, had won him the good opinion of Cromwell, whilst his readiness of resource, deep reflection, and powerful intellect rendered him indispensable to Essex, Fairfax, and such of the Parliamentary Generals as cherished liberal views of policy and an unselfish desire for the liberation of their countrymen. He had fought his way in a short space of time to the colonelcy of a regiment of pikes, and was now advancing with Essex on Exeter at the head of some five hundred stout hearts, such as have made British soldiers from time immemorial the best infantry in the world. Proud of his command, conscious of doing his duty, rising rapidly in his profession and in the opinion of those who were in the fair road to guide the destinies of England, there was yet in Effingham's bearing a restlessness and a reserve that denoted a mind ill at ease with itself—an unquiet sadness that spoke of some deep anxiety—some bitter disappointment. His friendship with Simeon had grown to a close intimacy, and he seemed to derive much consolation and refreshment from the conversation of that stern enthusiast.

They were walking up and down in front of Essex's headquarters at Chard—a square brick house in the centre of the village, from which the proprietor had been ejected with as little ceremony by the Puritan General as he could have been by any one of his noisy Cavalier opponents. They formed a strange contrast, that pair, as they paced to and fro, buried in deep discourse—the stalwart iron-looking soldier, with his tall figure and warlike **air** and dress, thus listening with such respectful deference to the soberly-clad divine, whose eager gestures and speaking countenance betrayed the flame of enthusiasm that consumed him, body and soul.

The guard was being relieved, with the customary noise and pomp of all military proceedings, not to be dispensed with even by the staid and sober Puritans; but the pair heeded not the clash of arms nor the clang of trumpets, and pursued their walk and their conversation regardless of aught but the topic which seemed to engross their whole attention.

'There is yet a black drop in thy heart, my brother,' said Simeon, in his deep impressive tones; 'there is yet one jewel left that thou hast grudged to cast into the treasury—and if thou givest not thine all, of what avail is thy silver and gold, thy flocks and herds, thy raiment of needle-work and thy worldly possessions? The daughter of the Canaanite is a fair damsel and a comely, but the children of the congregation have no dealings with the heathen, and she must henceforth be to thee as the forbidden food, and the plague-spot of leprosy—unclean! unclean!'

'It is hard,' answered Effingham, and his voice betrayed how bitterly hard it was—'it *is* hard to give up my only dream of earthly happiness—the one bright ray that has lightened my existence all these weary months—that has cheered me in the bivouac, and encouraged me in the field. I am not like you, Simeon; would that I were! I cannot hold to the future alone, and resign this world and all it contains without a pang. I fear I am of the doomed—predestined to guilt—predestined to punishment. Lost! lost!'

He shuddered as he spoke, and yet something of the old Titan instinct, the daring of despair that bade the sons of Earth confront the power of Heaven, in those old days when good and evil bore gigantic fruit here below—made him rear his head more proudly, tower above his comrade more erect and bold, as he seemed in his rebellious imagination to 'stand the shot.'

'Whom He loveth He chasteneth,' was Simeon's answer. 'I tell thee, brother, once and again, it is not so. Thy fight is a stern and severe conflict, but it has been borne in upon me that thou shalt be victorious; and to him that prevaileth is given the crown of glory. I have wrestled for thee long and earnestly, and I shall not fail. Thou art as the drowning man, whose struggles serve but to drag down into the depths the friend that would save him from perdition. I tell thee, watch and pray!'

'I can watch,' answered Effingham, bitterly; 'none better. Sleep seldom visits my eyelids, and my waking is sad and painful indeed; but I can *not* pray!'

It was even so. The stubborn human will might be bent and warped from that which was, after all, a holy and God-given instinct, though fanaticism and superstition might vote it folly and sin; but the poor aching human heart could not force itself to supplicate at the throne of Mercy for that forgetfulness which it felt would be a more bitter curse than all the pain it was now becoming inured to bear. Fallible sons of men! Simeon *felt* he was right; Effingham thought himself to be wrong. Both were arguing foolishly and presumptuously from strong human passions interpreted by fanaticism into revelations from on high.

George had struggled on wearily for months. In occupation and danger he had been striving hard to forget. He thought he was making sufficient progress in the lesson, when the sight of his old friend Bosville riding into Essex's camp under a flag of truce re-awakened all those feelings which he had fondly hoped were stifled, if not eradicated, and made him too painfully conscious that time and distance were not quite such effective auxiliaries as he had hoped.

The General had called in some of his principal officers to aid him in his deliberations; nor could he, according to his custom, come to any decision without the assistance of one or two Puritan divines. Caryl had already been sent for; and ere long a grim orderly trooper, who had been expounding to his comrades a knotty text of scripture with interpretations peculiarly his own, was despatched to summon Simeon to the Council, and Effingham was left to pursue his walk and his meditations alone.

He did not remain uninterrupted for long. A bustle at the door of Essex's quarters, the clash of arms as the sentries saluted their departing officers, and the roll of a drum mustering a regiment of foot for inspection, announced that the Council was over; and Bosville, who, contrary to his expectation, had found himself treated with all the respect and consideration due to the bearer of a flag of truce, advanced toward his old comrade with his hand extended, and a frank air of greeting upon his face.

He looked somewhat flushed and disconcerted too—a thought angry, perhaps, and a little discontented besides, as he cast a soldier's eye up and down the ranks of an efficient battalion of pikemen, and thought he must never measure swords with the Roundheads again; but he was glad to see Effingham, nevertheless; and the latter's heart leapt within him, for many reasons, to grasp a 'Malignant' by the hand once more.

'I thought not we should ever have come to this, George,' observed Bosville, half bitterly, half laughingly, after their first greeting was over. 'When thou and I rode through Ramsay's pikes at Edge-hill side by side, and drove them pell-mell right through their reserve and off the field, I little thought I should live to see myself a messenger of peace fit to be clad only in boddice and pinners—for 'ifaith 'tis but a woman's work, after all —and thee, George, a rank rebel, openly in arms against the King. And yet, 'slife, man, were't not for thy company, I could find it in my heart to envy thee, too. They behave well these pikemen —hey, George? Dost remember how close the knaves stood upon the slope at Newbury?'

Effingham smiled absently. He was chafing to ask a hundred questions of his old comrade; and yet, bold stout soldier as he was, his heart failed him like a girl's.

Bosville, too, was indignant at the ill-success of his embassy; in the presence of Essex he had had the good taste and prudence to dissemble his generous wrath, but it required a vent, and blazed up afresh as he took the Parliamentary Colonel by the arm, and they strolled out of ear-shot of the listening escort, already under arms to conduct the embassy back to his own lines.

'There is no chivalry amongst thy new friends, George,' he proceeded, the blood rising to his handsome face. 'You can fight, to do you justice, but there's nothing more of the lion about you than his courage. And as for your ministers! men of peace are they? More like croaking ravens and filthy birds of prey. Don't be offended, George: I am like a woman, you know, now, and the only weapon I have to use is my tongue. 'Faith, my blood boils when I think of the last hour's work. Essex is a gentleman, I grant you—I always thought so. We have both of us seen him walk his horse coolly along his line under a raking fire from our culverins; and he received my message with all the courtesy due to the emissary of a queen. It was not much we required. A safe conduct for herself and child to Bath, or maybe Bristol, for her health's sake. She has suffered much, poor lady, and looks so thin and weak—so unlike what she was when we saw her at Merton, George, whilst thou wert *honest*. Well, he seemed to entertain the proposal at first! and one of his Generals, a stout bluff-faced man—Ireton, was it? —voted point-blank in her favour, with some remarks, I am bound to admit, not flattering to the stability of our party, or the efficiency of her Majesty's defenders. Had my position allowed it, I had taken leave to differ with him on that point, but I thought the bowl seemed to trundle with the bias, so I held my peace. Then his lordship turned to a spare pale man in a Geneva

band and black cassock, and asked him what he thought of the
matter. Was that Caryl? So, I wouldn't be in *his* cassock,
when the charity that covereth a multitude of sins is wanted to
ward off punishment from *him*! My hands were bound, so to
speak, or no man living, minister or layman, should have applied
such terms to my royal mistress. Jezebel was the best name he
called her; and if blasphemy and indecency be religion, my service to Dr. Caryl! Goring hasn't a match for him among his
" hell-babes " for piety! They seemed to believe in him devoutly, though, for all that; and I saw Essex waver as I can see
thee, George, wince. Well, one ecclesiastic I suppose wasn't
enough, for there came in another knave, without his ears too;
would the hangman had done his work yeomanly when he was
about it, and cut his tongue out as well. They asked his advice,
man (grant me patience), as he had been a bishop! And what
said the Crop-ear in reply? " Go see now this cursed woman,"
quoth he, " and bury her, for she is a king's daughter." And
again—" What peace so long as the witchcrafts of Jezebel are so
many?" The devil can quote holy writ, we all know; but it
was well they turned me out, to deliberate with closed doors, for
I was almost beside myself with passion.'

The Cavalier paused to take breath. His listener gazed at him
wistfully, with a sort of pitiful interest.

'And what was the result of their deliberations?' he inquired.
' I see they came to a speedy conclusion, for the escort is waiting
even now to take you back.'

'When I returned,' answered Bosville, ' the General looked
grave and stern, I thought a little pained and grieved too. " Tell
those that sent you, Major Bosville," he said, in a slow, deliberate
voice, " that if her Majesty pleases, I will not only give her a
safe conduct, but wait upon her myself to London, where she
may have the best advice and means for the recovery of her
health; but as for either of the other places, I cannot obey her
Majesty's desires without directions from the Parliament. We
will not blindfold you," he added, courteously. " You are welcome to take note, and report to their Majesties on the men and
munitions of war that you find in my camp." So he dismissed
me civilly enough. George, my mind misgives me, that I have
come on a sleeveless errand.'

' It is even so,' answered Effingham, solemnly. The Truth is
great, and it shall prevail. But tell me, Humphrey, of those you
have left behind. We have but few minutes to spare, and perhaps we may never meet again, unless it be on a stricken field.

What of those who were once my friends who ministered to me in the house of bondage? What of Mistress Cave—of Sir Giles Allonby—of—of—his daughter?'

For reasons of his own Effingham hesitated as he put the question, the latter part of which alone, for reasons of *his* own, Bosville thought worthy of a reply.

'Sir Giles is hearty and busy as usual,' he answered. 'He has raised a large force of cavalry, and is with the King. Mistress Grace is anxious and ill at ease. As far as I can learn, they say she grows pale and thin, and has lost her bright looks and joyous ways. God forbid she should be really ailing, for if aught should befal her, it would go nigh to break old Sir Giles's heart!'

He spoke without the slightest change of voice or colour, and looked frank and straight into his companion's eyes, which never-theless refused to meet his glance. It was hard to say whether grief, or joy, or anxious fear was uppermost in Effingham's being at that moment.

'If you should chance to see her, Humphrey,' he said, with a quivering, broken voice, 'or to write to her mayhap, tell her that I sought tidings of her welfare, and Sir Giles, you know; and that—that—though I am a rebel, and a Roundhead, and all, I have not for that forgotten them; and if ever the time comes that I can serve them, I will. Fare thee well! fare thee well!' he added, grasping Humphrey warmly by the hand as the latter mounted to depart. 'Would that thou, too, couldst be brought to see the truth; but God bless thee, lad! Forget not George Effingham altogether, whatever comes uppermost.'

He gazed wistfully after the horseman's retreating figure as the escort closed round their charge and disappeared. It was his last link with the old life that shone back in such glowing hues. A tear glittered on his shaggy eyelashes as he strode off towards his quarters.

'Weak! weak!' he muttered. 'Unworthy, unprofitable servant. And yet perhaps even now she is not lost entirely and for ever?'

Bosville was destined to bring with him sad dismay into the mimic court at Exeter. Like all weak minds in extremity, Henrietta had fully persuaded herself that the last card she played must win her the game; that this extreme measure of entreaty and humiliation could not but produce the result she so much desired. When it failed, she was indeed at the utmost of her need. Indignation, too, mingled with alarm; and like some bitter tonic, helped to brace her mind into a sufficiently vigorous frame to come to some definite resolution. Impeached as she was of treason by both Houses of Parliament, this proposal of Essex thus to carry her into the very jaws of her enemies was almost tantamount to an insult; and the queenly spirit, not yet thoroughly broken, felt and resented it accordingly. The foe, too, was in far too close proximity to be pleasant. Exeter was no longer a secure refuge, and she must depart. But whither? To join the King without bringing him supplies of men or money, was but to clog the sinking monarch's efforts at extrication, and to drag him deeper and deeper into the slough of his difficulties.

No part of England was safe from the dreaded Parliamentary army, numbering as it now did amongst its formidable soldiery such tacticians as Fairfax, and such strategists as Cromwell. There was but one haven left, and that was her native country. We may imagine the struggle in the mind of that proud though vain and frivolous nature, ere she could bring herself to return as a homeless suppliant to the land she had left in her maidenhood a prosperous and queenly bride. She was altered, too, in her very person, and this to a woman added no inconsiderable ingredient to the bitterness of her cup. Sorrow and anxiety had hollowed the fair cheeks and clouded the brilliant complexion that in girlhood with fine eyes and delicate features had constituted such an attractive countenance; and the fresh bloom of her spring time had withered sadly and prematurely ere 'twas May. It was with galling self-consciousness that she used to avow no woman could have any pretensions to beauty after two-and-twenty.

So the daughter of Henry of Navarre, and the wife of England's King, must fly for her very life to the sea-board of her adopted country, must embark from Falmouth in a Dutch man-of-war, attended by sundry lighter craft, to the speediest of which it might prove necessary to entrust the destinies of a queen; must sustain the insult of being fired on by her own navy—for Warwick's squadron, stationed in Tor-bay, actually gave chase to the Royal lady—and must land in poor and desperate plight on the shores of her brother's kingdom, to seek the repose and safety denied her in her own.

All these events, however, are matters of history; and except in so far as they affect the proceedings of those subordinate dolls whose strings in our puppet-show we have undertaken to pull, they will bear neither relation nor comment at the humble hands of the mere story-teller, who can only flutter to and fro *tenui penná* through the shaded gardens of fiction, but dare not trust his feeble pinions to soar aloft into the dazzling sunshine of Fact.

Mary Cave followed her Royal mistress to the very shallop in which she left the British shore. It was but a small household she carried with her from England ; and though Mary would fain have accompanied her, it was agreed that her talents could be more usefully employed at home, and that living quietly in retirement here she might still aid the Royal cause with all the energies of her astute and far-seeing intellect, whilst she could keep a watchful eye on the state of public opinion, and communicate constantly and unreservedly by means of their own cipher with Henrietta in France.

To one of the household, this arrangement was the only consolation for a parting which he felt far more painfully than even *he* had expected. By Mary's wish he had consented to follow the fortunes of his Royal mistress, who was nothing loth to retain the services of one who had already proved himself so willing and devoted ; but it was with a heavy heart, and a foreboding of evil by no means natural to his temperament, that Humphrey took leave of his ladye-love on the morning of the embarkation at Falmouth.

He was saddened, too, to think that for the last few days her manner to him had been colder and more reserved than it usually was. She had studiously avoided every chance of a private interview, had apparently wantonly and unfeelingly neglected every hint and allusion that he had ventured to make as to his wish of seeing her alone once more to bid her ' farewell ; ' and had shown, to his thinking, an amount of heartlessness and carelessness of his feelings which grieved him as it would have angered another.

Humphrey, though a young man, was no inexperienced soldier. He had assisted ere this at the scaling of many a rampart, the assault of many a beleaguered town ; yet it never occurred to him that the last efforts of the besieged are desperate in proportion to their extremity—the resistance never so obstinate as on the eve of surrender. The weak are sometimes cruel, and a stern front is often but the mask that hides a failing heart.

He was leaving the Queen's apartments to make preparations for her Majesty to go abroad. He walked moodily and sadly, for he thought he should not see Mary again, and he was wondering in his simple faith how he could have offended her, and why she should thus think it worth while to grieve him, when perhaps they might never meet again. Like a child unjustly punished, he was less irritated than spirit-broken. Alas ! like many a brave and gallant man, he was a sad coward, if only attacked in the right place.

A door opened in the gallery of the hostelry honoured by the presence of royalty. Mary advanced towards him, holding out her hand.

'I am come to wish you good-bye,' she said in her kind, frank tones. 'I looked for you an hour ago in the gallery. Humphrey,' she added, her voice trembling as she marked his whole countenance flush and soften, 'I have used you ill. Forgive me. I did not mean it—at least I did not mean to make you so unhappy,' and she gave him ever so slight a pressure of that warm soft hand —that hand which only to touch he would at any time have given a year of his life.

He was a sad coward in some things we have already said. He bent over the white hand without speaking a word, but she felt the hot tears dropping on it as he lifted his head and tried to smile unconcernedly in her face.

They were both silent. Had any eavesdropper been watching them in that long gallery, he would have thought the gentleman a strangely uncourteous gallant—the lady a dame of wondrously stiff and reserved demeanour.

Humphrey spoke at length, scarcely above a whisper.

'It is no use,' he said. I am a bad dissembler. Mary, you know all. Only give me one word, one kind word of hope, before I go. I will treasure it for years!'

Again that faint, scarcely perceptible pressure of the hand he had never relinquished.

'The task must be accomplished first,' she murmured. '"Loyalty before all."'

He raised her hand to his lips, and imprinted on it one long passionate kiss. Either by accident or design a bow of pink ribbon which she wore on her sleeve had become detached. Somehow it remained in his grasp when she was gone.

The wind blew fresh off-shore, and the Dutchman made gallant way, whilst Humphrey stood on deck, and watched the dim headlands of his home with a strange wistful glance that was yet mingled with triumph and joy.

Had he not won his decoration? And was not his heart beating against the ribbon of his order?

CHAPTER XXV.

NASEBY FIELD.

The undulating prairie of rich grazing ground which stretches far and wide round Market Harborough was blooming a brighter green in the declining rays of a hot June sun, sinking gradually to tip the wooded crests of Marston Hills with gold. Beeves of huge proportion and promising fatness, all unconscious of the dangerous proximity of two hostile armies, grazed contentedly in the sunlight or ruminated philosophically in the shade. Swarms of insects quivered in the still warm air ; the note of thrush and blackbird, hushed during the blaze of noon, was awakening once more from tangled hedgerow, leafy coppice, and deep woodland dell, dense and darkling in the rank growth of midsummer luxuriance. Anon the quest's soft, plaintive lullaby stole drowsily on the ear, from her forest home amid the oaks of Kelmarsh, or the tall elm-grove nodding on Dingley's distant hill. It was a scene of peace, prosperity, and repose. What had they to do there, those burnished headpieces and steel breast-plates, flashing back the slanting sunbeams, and glittering like gold in all the pomp and panoply of war ?

It was a goodly sight to see them, too, as they wound slowly along the plain, those stalwart troopers on their tall chargers, with their dancing plumes and their royal guidons waving above the track of yellow dust that floated on their line of march. To mark their military air, their practised discipline, their bold bronzed faces, and the stately form of their commander, with his white moustache and his keen blue eye. 'Tis the vanguard of the royal army, now, in consequence of the King's counter-march from Daventry forming its rear. These are the flower of Prince Rupert's cavalry, the survivors of the route of Marston Moor—the remnant of Sir Giles Allonby's brigade—the swordsmen that will follow that daring old man, as long ago he trusted they would at Oxford, ' through and through a stand of pikes once and again on a stricken field.' They had fought, and bled, and conquered, and retreated since then. Sir Giles looks a thought older and more worn about the face, the beard is whiter, and the locks thinner, but the spare form, the gallant seat on horseback, lithe and erect as ever.

See ! a noble-looking Cavalier, followed by a toiling aide-de-camp, who has tired two horses to-day in attending the hasty movements of his chief, dashes up at a gallop from the rear. Sir Giles salutes him with military precision and an air of frank admiration he is at no pains to conceal. With all his recklessness, there is but one cavalry officer in the world, so thinks Sir Giles, and that is Rupert.

The Prince's words are short, peremptory, and to the point.

'Throw forward an outpost on Naseby village, Sir Giles. The scout-master reports no enemy within sight, but Fairfax cannot be far off—best to make sure. Send young Dalyson in command. I owe him a chance for Marston Moor;—bid him double his picket and mind his videttes! Good even to you!'

The Prince had already turned his horse's head to depart. Sir Giles hesitated; Dalyson was but a boy—bold as a lion, but wild as a hawk; his nineteen summers had hardly given him experience for so critical a duty, and though at Marston Moor, his maiden field, he had behaved like a hero, Sir Giles mistrusted the 'young one' might be out-manœuvred by some of those Parliamentary veterans ere he was aware.

'Lieutenant Dalyson is a very inexperienced officer,' hazarded Sir Giles; but the Prince, turning a deaf ear, was already on the gallop, and the old soldier knew his duty too well not to obey orders, at whatever cost to his own private apprehensions. With no slight misgivings, he gave the delighted young officer his instructions, lavishing on him all the stores of caution and experience he had to bestow. He called out, moreover, a grim, ancient-looking personage from his own especial escort, and accosting him by the name of Sergeant Dymocke, bade him accompany the party, adding in a low tone, 'I think I can trust *you* not to be surprised.'

It needed but the grim smile with which the compliment was accepted to identify our old acquaintance, who, having left the service of Major Bosville, temporarily, and under protest, during the latter's absence in France, was now doing a turn of soldiering to keep his hand in. He was yet too young, as he told the expectant Faith, to settle permanently in life.

Sir Giles, pursuant to his orders, held on with the main body for Market Harborough, whilst the party he had detached, striking into a sharp trot, made the best of their way for Naseby village.

The dews of evening were falling heavily, and the twilight darkened into night ere they reached their destination. For the last mile or two, under the sergeant's influence, great caution had been observed, flankers thrown out, and an advanced and rear-guard detached from the little party, till, as Dalyson laughingly observed, 'there was nothing left to form the main body but himself and his trumpeter.'

Still there seemed to be no vestige of the enemy; the few
peasants that could be questioned at that late hour were either
too ignorant or too stupid to give any intelligence, and on arriving
at the village, the young officer's first care was rather to refresh
his men and horses, than to pry about in the darkness, looking
for that which did not seem to exist.

In the Royalist army so many born gentlemen rode in the ranks
as simple privates, that there was but a narrow line of demarcation
drawn between officers and men.   It was therefore no breach of
etiquette, though it argued culpable negligence, for the officer to
dismount his party in the small hostelry at Naseby, calling for the
best, after the fashion of Royalists, and making his men welcome
as they dropped in after seeing their horses fed, and drew round
the old oak table, which bears to this day the marks of many a
wild carousal dinted on its surface.   He would have unsaddled,
had it not been for the expostulation of the sergeant, who with
difficulty persuaded three or four of the troopers to forego their
suppers and accompany him on his look-out.

The rest of the party were drinking 'The King,' or 'The
Ladies,' or some such customary toast, when a couple of shots
ringing through the still night air, within two hundred paces, and
the warning of the trumpeter pealing out the alarum of 'boots
and saddles,' startled them from their carouse.   Alas! too late.
Ireton's troopers were upon them.   Dymocke and his scouts
galloping in upon their comrades, would certainly have been
shot by mistake had the Cavaliers been a little more on the alert.
It was the sergeant's pistols that had given the alarm.

The Royalists, half of them dismounted, and all unformed, were
ridden down like sheep by the disciplined Parliamentarians.   Such
as accepted quarter were taken prisoners, but Dalyson paid for
his negligence with his blood.   He had doffed his steel morion
and his breastplate.   Alone, with his head bare and his buff coat
open, he sustained the shock of the leading files and the points of
some half-dozen thirsty blades.   He was dead ere he fell from the
saddle, and of all his followers not one escaped save the wily
sergeant, who with his usual imperturbability, when he saw all
was lost, turned his bridle and rode for his life.   The darkness
of the night and his own familiarity with the country (for in
happier times he and his old master had hunted and hawked over
all that wide champaign, till they knew it every inch) favoured
his escape, and he set his horse's head straight for the old hall at
Lubenham, where Charles lay sleeping in fancied security.

That locality is celebrated for its exhaustive properties on the

equine race. We question, nevertheless, if it ever witnessed a
steed more thoroughly jaded and overdone, than the panting animal
that shook its reeking sides at Lubenham gate, as Hugh banged
and shouted at the fastened door to arouse the sleeping inmates of
the Hall.

Though we dwell not habitually in kings' houses, we take the
privilege of the story-teller's ubiquity to peep at Charles Stuart
in his humble sleeping-room at old Lubenham Hall.

The face on which the night-lamp throws its shaded rays looks
careworn and anxious even in slumber. The doomed expression
which he has borne all his life comes out more strongly now on
the haggard brow and the features sharpened by suspense and toil.
Yet, sleeping or waking, there is a certain trustful confidence on
that face still, the inner light of a pure unspotted nature breaking
through the clouds of vacillation and incompetency. That breast
on which in its deep-breathing heaves a golden locket containing
his Queen's hair, his Queen, who has forgotten him already, whom
he has not seen for more than a year, whom he shall never see on
earth again—that breast may and does ache with sorrow, but it
knows not the sting of remorse. Not even now, though the
perspiration starts upon his forehead, and his white hands clench
themselves rigidly in the agony of his dream. And this was
Charles's dream the night before Naseby field :—

He stood with Strafford in the condemned cell. The cell in his
own royal Tower of London, which he had never seen, and yet it
seemed strangely familiar in its hideous arrangements and its
gloomy security. The minister sat in his splendid dress of state,
yet there were handcuffs on the slender wrists under his lace
ruffles, and the jewelled garter at his knee contrasted with the
heavy clanking fetters of the condemned nobleman. He knelt
before his sovereign, but it was not to plead for pardon or reprieve.
Those entreaties were not to save Strafford, but the King. He
implored his master not to trust to arms, at least, not now.

'To-morrow,' said he, ' I die on Tower-hill. I beseech your
Majesty to accept the sacrifice. I give back your Majesty's
generous promise of interference. I die willingly for the Crown ;
but I can foresee the course of destiny at this my last hour, and
I implore your Majesty that mine may be the only blood spilt
under to-morrow's sun !'

The royal impulse was stronger in the sleeping monarch at
Lubenham, than it had been in his waking earnest in the day of
power at Whitehall, and he seemed to strive with the futile efforts
of a dreamer to unclasp the fetters of his councillor and his friend.

'I will save you,' quoth Charles, in his vision. 'Are these not my walls, my gaolers? Is not this my own royal Tower of London?'

And he beat with bruised hands and noisy blows against the iron door of the doomed man's cell. In the struggle he awoke, and the awe-stricken monarch, sitting up in bed to listen, with a pale, wet face, was aware that the noise of his dream was not entirely the work of fancy, but that an express with important information was even then battering for admittance at the door.

We pass over Dymocke's cool and concise report, as unmoved in the presence of royalty as when galloping for his life from Ireton's deadly troopers. The King, dressing himself hastily, and accompanied only by two or three startled gentlemen of his household, was in the saddle ere his informant had answered half his questions, and rode at a gallop into Harborough, to his nephew's quarters, where he summoned a hasty council of war to assemble on the spot. The early summer morning of the 14th of June was already breaking, when Rupert, Digby, Ashburnham, Sir Marmaduke Langdale, and a few others met to decide the fate of the Royal cause. The hot Prince, for all his haste and bold impetuous bearing in a charge, was no mean strategist, and contrary to his wont, counselled retreat. Digby and Ashburnham, reckless at the wrong time, opposed him strongly, and urged an immediate engagement. The King, flushed with the late news of Montrose's victory a month before at Auldearne, and prompted by his unaccountable instinct always to choose the most injudicious course, decided on battle. The gallant Rupert, perhaps for the first time in his life, made ready to go into action with an unwilling heart.

Leaving the Royal column marching in the cool prime of the bright June morning over the hills towards Naseby, eager and anxious to meet the enemy, whose movements they have been dodging and watching so many weary days, we must take a glimpse at the Parliamentary army, now a compact, well-disciplined, and numerous force, taking up the strong position which they held stubbornly during the day; and from the selection of which, and his consequent victory, he who led their right wing found himself, ere another lustre had elapsed, the occupant of a throne.

Cromwell had effected his junction with Fairfax the evening before, bringing to that commander the efficient aid of his own cool resolution and his formidable well-trained Ironsides, by this time the best cavalry in Europe. When Ireton's advanced guard had driven in the Cavalier outpost on the previous evening, they had discovered that the plain in front of Naseby village was still unoccupied. With grim satisfaction and practised skill, the Parliamentary General took up the strongest position that the ground admitted of—Fairfax throwing forward his left, and lining the thick boundary hedge which divides the manors of Sulby and Naseby with dismounted dragoons, thus doubly protecting his baggage (drawn up in battle order behind his left), his communications and line of retreat if necessary and his rear, occupied the centre in person, where he had placed the bulk of his heavy guns on a commanding slope to the north of the village, whence they could play upon any attacking column advancing up the hill, and open an enfilading fire on any flank movement of the enemy, should he show himself above the crest of the opposite eminence. Cromwell, as Lieutenant-General of the Parliamentary Horse, commanded the right wing, composed chiefly of his own invincible Ironsides, supported, as was the practice in those days, by a stout and trusty *tertia* * or two of foot. His extreme right, again, rested on an abrupt declivity and a succession of broken ground, which must effectually discomfort any attempt at turning his flank, whilst the downward slope in front of him, and the open nature of the plain, offered a tempting opportunity for one of those irresistible charges with which, when once *the pace is in them*, cavalry sweep all before them. Skill and experience had done their utmost to make the best of that position on the celebrated arena where the decisive struggle was fought out between the King and his Parliament.

To return to the humble actors in our drama. Effingham, commanding his trusty regiment of Pikes, was placed in support of Ireton's Horse on the left wing—a duty which his previous experience rendered peculiarly suitable to the old officer of Royalist cavalry. With a critical eye he reconnoitred the ground upon his flanks and front, taking advantage of a few wet ditches and a marshy surface to render his position less assailable by cavalry, and retiring somewhat to afford greater protection to Bartlett's waggon-train in his rear. He had scarcely made his arrangements, and was in the act of emptying his havresack of his frugal breakfast, when a horseman rode rapidly up, and grasping him warmly by the hand, pointed to the dark columns of the Parliamentarians deploying slowly into line along the crest of the acclivity on his right, and preparing to pour their masses with every advantage of ground into the plain.

---

* Equivalent to a battalion.

'Brother,' exclaimed the horseman, 'the armies are gathering to the slaughter. Lo! the eagles are already hovering over the plain of Armageddon. Verily it is the day of the Lord.'

Effingham looked up astonished. The voice was that of Simeon, but the armed figure in buff and breastplate and morion, sitting so soldierlike upon his horse, was a strange contrast to the preacher in his black gown and Geneva band, to whose exhortations he had himself listened patiently on the eve of battle the day before.

The divine marked his surprise with a grim smile. 'The harvest indeed is ripe,' said he, 'but the reapers are few, therefore have I, Simeon the persecuted, entreated permission of the man of destiny, even Cromwell, that I might this day cast in my lot with his men of war, and charge, brother, through and through the Amalekites in the front rank of his Ironsides! Horse and armour have been provided for me even as the ravens provided Elijah with food, yet lack I still a sword. I put not my trust in the arm of the flesh; but methinks, with a long straight basket-hilted blade of keen temper I could do somewhat to further the good work. Hast thou such an one by thee, to lend for an hour or so?'

Effingham could not help smiling as he sent a sergeant to the rear, where, amongst his baggage, such a weapon was indeed to be found. Pending its arrival the soldier-divine and the commandant of pikes, sharing their frugal meal, watched the movements of the enemy with an increasing interest.

Already the King's baggage and rear-guard had taken up their position, just beyond the opposite eminence of Broadmoor, whence, though not a mile distant, the gradual rise of the ground prevented their discerning more than an occasional standard or the fluttering pennon of a lance. The plain between was still unoccupied; but gradually troop after troop of horse wound slowly into sight, extending themselves towards their proper right, where those green impervious hedges concealed the deadly musketeers, and supported by dark masses of infantry, above whose serried forest of shafts the steel pike-heads flashed dazzling in the morning sun.

'I can make out no guns,' observed Effingham, straining his eyes till they watered. 'And by the standard, I judge Charles himself occupies the centre. What a force of cavalry he must have! I can see them swarming by the young plantation on his far left. This will be a heavy day for England, Simeon!'

'Rather say a day of wrath and retribution for the ungodly,' replied the fanatic, poising and examining with a critical eye the heavy blade which had just been put in his hands. '"For this day shall the wine-press be trodden out, and blood shall come out

of the wine-press, even to the horse bridles." Fare thee well, my
brother! Lo! I gird my sword upon my thigh, and go my ways
even into the forefront of the battle!'

As he spoke he set spurs to his charger, and galloping along
the rear made the best of his way to where Cromwell was marshalling his cavalry on the extreme right. Effingham, gazing
after his retreating figure, marvelled to note the warlike air and
consummate horsemanship of the formidable divine.

He had little leisure to observe him, though, for a dropping fire
flashing from the masking blackthorn hedge announced that the
Royalist right was advancing, whilst the heavy 'boom' of Fairfax's
ordnance proclaimed that ere long the action would be general
along the whole line.

A few detached skirmishers dotting the plain, and reckless of
the withering fire they sustained, dashed boldly out to clear the
boundary hedge of its dangerous occupants, and succeeded so far
as to drive the dismounted musketeers back upon their supports.
Ireton, fearing a panic which might endanger his whole left,
ordered a brigade of cavalry to their assistance; and Rupert's
eagle eye spying the flank movement at a glance, the Prince
seized the opportunity, and advancing his whole wing at a gallop,
gave the word to 'Charge!'

The Royalist trumpets ring out merrily as the best blood of
man and horse in England comes sweeping down the slope. There
is Rupert, with his short red cloak floating on the breeze, three
horses' lengths in front of Britain's proudest chivalry, waving his
sword above his head, and shouting 'God and Queen Mary;'
'For the King! for the King!' There is his brother Maurice,
with calm, indomitable energy and stern knitted brows; ever and
anon glancing warily behind him at the line of which, even at the
moment of contact, he hopes to preserve the even regularity.
There is gentle Northampton, like a Paladin of romance, with a
hero's arm, a lion's heart, and a woman's smile upon his face.
There is fierce Sir William Vaughan, grim and unmoved in the
onset of battle as in the manœuvres of parade; and old Sir Giles,
swaying so easily to the long regular stride of that good sorrel
horse, the property of one who would fain have been on him now
—his eyes sparkling with delight and a cheerful smile curling his
moustaches as he thinks of his pet brigade behind him, and
chuckles to reflect how he will have the knaves through a stand
of pikes yet; for he sees the grim steel-headed forest dark and
lowering between the squadrons of the enemy. Every man has
his favourite theory, and Sir Giles holds that cavalry properly led

ought to break any infantry in the world.   He is spurring to its
demonstration even now.

Ireton is too good an officer not to rectify his mistake.   He
forms line like lightning, and advances to meet them; but the
Royalists are irresistible, and although the hill is somewhat against
them, those gallant horses fail not in their pace, and they ride
down the wavering Roundheads with the very impetus of their
charge.

In vain Ireton shouts and gesticulates and curses, Puritan
though he be, both loud and deep.   A pistol shot disables his
bridle arm, and a sabre-cut slashes his brave stern face.   ' God
with us!' gasps the General—for the rebels, too, have their
battle-word—and he cleaves the last assailant to the brisket: but
he is faint and exhausted, and his share of the battle is well nigh
lost.   Through and through the Roundhead horse ride the maddened Cavaliers, shouting, striking, spurring wildly on, every
heart afire to follow to the death where the short red cloak flashes
like a tongue of flame through the dust and smoke of the encounter.
But the torrent is checked—the tide is turned at last.   Sir Giles
Allonby, catching sight of Effingham's regiment, calm and immovable like a rock amongst the breakers, shouts to his men to
follow him, and makes a furious dash at the enemy.   Another
voice, clear and full as a trumpet-blast, rings above the confusion
of the *mêlée*.

' Steady, men!—form four deep!   Advance your pikes!—
stand to your pikes!' are the Colonel's confident orders; and
the resolute veterans he commands know only too well that, if
once broken, they have nothing to hope for.   They have met
Prince Rupert before: so they set their teeth and stand shoulder
to shoulder, fierce and grim, like the old ' Die-hards' they are.
The wet ditches and yielding nature of the ground, sapped by
springs of running water, destroy the impetus of Sir Giles's
charge, and the fiery old soldier can but reach his enemy at a
trot.   Nevertheless, so good is the sorrel, so resolute his rider,
and so well backed up by a few of his gallant followers, that the
old knight, striking madly right and left, forces his way completely
through the front rank of the pikemen, and only finds himself
unhorsed and bleeding in the very midst of the enemy, when it
is too late to do aught but meet the death he has so long tempted,
fearless and unshrinking, like a man.

A dozen pike-heads are flashing round the prostrate Cavalier;
a dozen faces with the awful expression, not of anger, but of
stern, pitiless hatred, are bending their brows and setting their

teeth for the death-thrust, when Effingham's arm strikes up the weapons, and Effingham's voice interposes to the rescue.

'Quarter, my lads,' exclaims the Colonel. 'For shame, men! —spare his grey head. He is my father!'

If ever falsehood counted to the credit side of man's account, surely this one did; and it speaks well for Effingham's control over his men and their affection to his person, that even at such an appeal they could spare a foe red-handed.

'Sir Giles,' whispered the Colonel, 'with me you are safe. Your wounds shall be looked to. You are my prisoner, but I will answer for your life with my own. We shall stand our ground here, I *think*;' then added in a louder tone to a sergeant, 'Catch that sorrel horse! 'Tis the best charger in England, and I would not aught should befal him for Humphrey's dear old sake!'

Sir Giles sat ruefully on the ground, and uttered not a word, for he was pondering deeply. He was wounded in two places, and the blood streamed down his white locks and beard, but of this he seemed utterly unconscious. At last he spoke, in the thoughtful tone of a man who balances the *pros* and *cons* of some knotty argument:—

'It was those wet ditches that did it,' quoth the old Cavalier, with a sigh. 'They broke our stride and so disordered us; otherwise, if we'd come in at a gallop, I still maintain we should have gone through!'

The check sustained by Sir Giles's brigade had meantime somewhat damped the success of the Royalist wing. Half the horses were blown, and from the very nature of cavalry it is impossible to sustain the efficiency of a charge for any lengthened period. Some horses tire sooner than others; men get excited and maddened; some go too far—others have had enough;—all separate. And that which, half a mile back, was an irresistible and well-ordered onset, becomes a mere aimless and undisciplined rush, like a scatter of beads when the string breaks.

Ere Rupert had reached the baggage under Naseby village, he found himself accompanied by scarce half his force. The baggage guard, entrenched behind their waggons, met him with a dropping fire. They presented a resolute and formidable front; the example of their comrades encouraged them to resistance, and their defences and position rendered them a dangerous enemy for blown and disordered cavalry to attack. The Prince summoned them to surrender.

From the centre of his fortress rose the grim reply, in Bartlett's loud fearless tones—

'God with us!   Make ready, men, and fire a volley!'

A few Cavalier saddles were emptied.   The Prince knew well
that he had gone too far.   With voice and gesture he strove to
rally his followers, who had now got completely 'out of his
hand;' and wheeling the small body that he could retain in his
command rapidly along the eminence, he turned to see how fared
the battle in the plain below.

Rupert was a thorough soldier.   It needed no second glance to
satisfy him that the day was indeed lost; and that all he could do
now was to hasten back with his division on the centre, where
the King himself commanded in person, and endeavour to cover
that retreat which was fast degenerating into a rout.

The same courage, the same dash and metal of man and horse,
that had demoralized Prince Rupert's division, had, when tempered by discipline, crowned the Ironsides with victory.   The
future Protector, advancing his cavalry by alternate brigades,
and retaining a strong reserve to turn the tide in the event of any
unforeseen catastrophe, moved steadily upon the left wing of the
enemy almost at the same moment that the corresponding onset
of the Royalists sustained its first check from the grim resistance
of Elfingham's pikemen.   Cromwell's thorough familiarity with
cavalry manœuvres enabled him to take every advantage of the
ground, and his leading squadrons came down upon Sir Marmaduke Langdale's division with the force and velocity of a torrent.
Regardless of a withering volley from Carey's musketeers, placed
in support of the Royalist cavalry, he drove the latter from their
position, and their further movements being impeded and disordered by the nature of the ground into which he had forced
them—a treacherous rabbit warren and a young plantation—they
fell back in confusion upon their supports, consisting of two regiments of North-country horse, whom they carried with them
to the rear, despite of the efforts and entreaties of the gallant Sir
Marmaduke and the Yorkshire officers.   Cromwell saw his
advantage, but was not to be led away by the brilliancy of his
success into a departure from those tactics which he had studied
so long and so effectually.   Despatching a less formidable brigade
in pursuit, he kept the Ironsides well in hand; and perceiving an
advance of the King's centre, already checked and disordered by
the heavy fire of Fairfax's ordnance, let them loose upon the flank
of the Royalists at the happy moment when their cavalry were
wavering and their infantry deploying into line.

Now came the fiercest of the carnage.   The famous 'Blue
Regiments,' forming with Lord Bernard Stuart's Life Guards the

flower of the King's cavalry, sustained the charge of the rebels with their usual devoted courage and gallantry. Half the noblest names in England were striking for their lives—ay, and more than that, their honour and their order, and their King! The gentle Norman blood was flowing free and fast, as it has ever flowed when deeds of chivalry and daring have been required; but the stubborn Saxon element was boiling too in the veins of many a stalwart freeman ; and those iron-clad warriors, in their faith and their enthusiasm, and the flush of their success, were *not* to be denied. Hand to hand and steel to steel, it was the death-grapple of the war ; and he who played his bold stake to win a kingdom on that ghastly board spared not his own person in the encounter. Wherever blows were going thickest, there was Cromwell's square form and waving arm ; there was the eagle eye, the loud confident voice, the cool head, unmoved and resolute on the field as in the Council ; while not a lance's length behind him, smiting like a blacksmith on the anvil, and pouring with every blow a prophet's malediction on the enemy he struck to earth, Simeon the persecuted took ample vengeance on the Royalists for the inhumanity of their Star Chamber and his own cruel mutilation.

Like all non-combatants, when his blood was really up he fought as madly as a Berserkar; and many a goodly warrior, many a practised swordsman, went down to rise no more before the sweeping arm and the deadly thrust of him who represented a teacher of that religion which has long-suffering for its foundation, and mercy for its crown.

And now the Ironsides are almost upon the King's centre, where, pale, yet firm, the monarch rides in person, longing, for all his stately demeanour and enforced reserve, to strike in amongst the fray. With the one exception of his father, not a Stuart of the line ever shrank from personal danger; and had Charles's moral courage been equal to his physical, the grazier's son had not been now within a hundred paces, stretching with bloody grasp at his crown.

A desperate rally is made by the Cavaliers, and Colonel St. George, recognising Cromwell, deals him such a sabre stroke on the helmet as knocks the morion from his head and leaves him bare and defenceless, but cool and courageous as ever. The effect upon his Ironsides is encouraging rather than the reverse ; they believe him to be under the especial protection of Heaven, as they believe themselves to be the veritable saints that shall inherit the earth. A reversion they seem well content to fight for to the death ; the enthusiastic Simeon perceives his plight, and bringing his horse alongside of him, unfastens his own helmet and forces it on his chief. In the hurry Cromwell places it reversed on his head, and thus armed, fights on more fiercely than before. Does no secret sympathy tell him he is battling over his very grave? —not to-day, bold unswerving man ; not till thou hast fulfilled thy destiny, and, to use thine own language, hast 'purged the threshing-floor and trodden out the wine-press,' shalt thou lie down on Naseby field to take thy rest !

In the dead of night, in secrecy and apprehension, shall he be brought here again who was once more than a king ; and the man who ruled for years the destinies of England shall be buried in shame and sorrow, like some obscure malefactor, on the spot where the grass grows thick and tangled, because of the crimson rain that fell so heavily on the field of his greatest victory.

And Simeon, bare-headed and maddened, fights fiercely on. His devotion costs him dear. The goodly head-piece would have saved him from that swinging sabre-stroke that lays open cheek and temple, and deluges neck and shoulder with the hot red stream. His arm flies aimlessly up, and the sword drops from his grasp. The battle swims before his eyes ere they seem to darken and fill with blood; he reels in his saddle; he is down amongst the wounded and the dying, and his horse gallops masterless out of the *mêlée*.

And now Charles sees with his own eyes that all is lost. His right is scattered and disordered. Rupert is returning with but the shattered remnants of his glorious force. His left is swept from the field and flying in hopeless confusion nearly to Leicester. His centre is broken and dismayed; his very baggage unprotected and at the mercy of the enemy. The blood of a king rises for the effort; he will put himself at the head of his reserve and make one desperate struggle for his crown, or die like a Stuart in his harness. He has drawn his royal sword, and waves his last devoted remnant on.

'Od's heart, sire !' exclaims the Scottish Earl of Carnewath; 'will ye go upon your death in an instant?' and turns the King's bridle out of the press. Degenerate earl ! it was not thus thy steel-clad ancestor backed his father's great-grandsire at Flodden ! But the deed is done ! the King turns round ; the rout becomes a flight, and, save the wounded and the dead, the helpless women and the dogged prisoners, not a Royalist is left upon the field.

Effingham's regiment of Pikes has ere this moved to the very centre of the plain. When Fairfax saw and seized the opportunity to advance his whole line, the Colonel moved with the rest of the infantry in support of a large cavalry reserve, and thus reached the spot the King had so recently quitted, where the fight had been deadliest and the carnage most severe. Marching in close column, and still keeping Sir Giles and the sorrel in the centre of his Pikes, Effingham took up a position where the dead lay thick in heaps, and at the spot from whence the track of the distant flight might be marked by the rising dust and the occasional shots fired by the pursuers, he placed Sir Giles once more upon his horse, and bade him escape in the confusion.

The old Cavalier grasped him heartily by the hand. 'I wouldn't have believed it of thee, lad,' said Sir Giles. 'I never thought much of thee after thou changed sides; but faith! thou'rt a good lad still, I see, though thou be'st on the winning side, and a murrain to it! Well, well, I've lived long enough when I've seen the coil of to-day. I wouldn't care to be there with many an honest fellow,' pointing to a heap of corpses, 'were't not for Grace's sake.'

'It is for Grace's sake,' answered Effingham, and, squeezing him by the hand, bade him ride for his life.

Sir Giles turned his horse's head, but checked him for one last word. 'I think I could have broken in, too, lad, if I'd come up at a gallop,' said he, argumentatively.

In another minute he was striding away amongst pursuers and pursued over the plain.

A deep groan caused Effingham to start as he looked down. Simeon lay dying at his feet. 'Too late, my brother,' gasped the enthusiast, as the Colonel propped him on his knee, and strove to stanch the gaping death-wounds. 'Fare thee well, my brother: we meet no more on earth.' Then faintly pushing away the flask George pressed to his lips, and pointing to a dying Cavalier, murmured, 'If thine enemy thirst, give him drink;' and so, his features setting and darkening, his lips muttering faint words and texts of Scripture, in which George caught the accents of self-reproach and regret, and the awful emphasis of fear on the words, 'Whoso smiteth with the sword shall perish by the sword;' and 'Blessed are the merciful, for they shall obtain mercy,' the soul of the enthusiast passed to its account. George stood and gazed upon the ghastly harvest gathered in on Naseby field, and not for the first time a shudder of horror seemed to chill his very soul as the thought swept across it, 'Can this be true religion, after all?— the religion of peace on earth and good-will amongst men?'

CHAPTER XXVI.

'THE WHEEL GOES ROUND.'

THE cultivated enclosures round Naseby village have been reaped and sown once and again. The grass on the wide expanse of Naseby field, so poached and trodden down scarce two short years ago, has yielded one heavy crop, and promises again to enrich the peasant with its luxurious produce. In certain spots the sheep refused to feed, so rank and coarse grows the herbage where the earth has been fattened with the blood of her children. The shepherd tending his flocks, or the herd watching his drowsy cattle, scarce stoops to notice sword or helmet, pike-head or musket-barrel, stained with rust, and protruding from the surface of the moor, so thickly are they strewn, these implements of slaughter that flashed bravely in the summer sun when he shone on the great battle only the year before last. Nay, there are ghastlier tokens than these of man's goodly handiwork and the devil's high festival. Bones of horse and rider still lie bleaching on the slopes, and skulls of the half-buried combatants grin at the labourer as he passes, whistling cheerfully, to his work. He heeds them not. Why should he? What though yon mouldering sphere of bone, with its broad white teeth and vacant sockets, was once the type of manly beauty and divine intellect, was once so fair and gallant, with its love-locks flaunting under its burnished head-piece, was once tended so carefully, and prized so highly, and kissed so fondly by lips that are even now perhaps writhing in their misery at the thought of the loved one lying where he fell on Naseby field—why should the labourer care? He has his daily toil to urge, his daily pittance to receive, his daily wants to provide for. He turns the skull over with coarse raillery and a kick from his heavy boot. A peasant's jest is the epitaph of him who died with his blood aflame for victory and renown, his heart beating high with the noblest impulses of chivalry and romance. What matter? Were he any better lapped in lead, under a marble monument, side by side with his knightly ancestors in the old church at home, than lying here under the wide changing sky, to rot, a nameless skeleton on Naseby field?

Time takes no note of human life and worldly changes. The old mower works steadily on, stroke by stroke, and furrow by furrow; when he reaches the end of the ridge he pauses not to wipe the toil-drops from his brow, but turns and applies him to his task unchecked and unwearied, sparing the shrinking wild flower no more than the tall rank weed, and sweeping down all indiscriminately, level with the short close sward.

And yet, Destroyer though he be, he is the great Restorer too —at least in the natural world. Where the storm of civil war has passed over merry England, sullying many a fair scene and blighting many a happy homestead, the lull of even one short twelvemonth has done much to bring back fertility to the meadow and comfort to the hearth. Spring has thrown her fair green mantle over the horrors of many a battle-field; and the daily recurring hopes and fears of Life have choked the pangs of sorrow, and dried the tears of many a weeping mourner. All but the few desolate ones that refuse to be comforted by Time, trusting, not unwisely, in the sure consolation of Eternity. The months that have passed over since the battle of Naseby have indeed been pregnant with great events; but ever since that fatal struggle the Royal Cause has been hastening step by step to its final downfall. The flame has flickered up in the north and west with a fitful and delusive flash, but in middle England a sombre and melancholy apathy seems to brood over the land. It is peace where there is no peace—a fusion of opposite interests into a hollow truce, a stifling under the strong hand of discontent that rankles now, and will burst into hatred hereafter.

Still the Northamptonshire peasant goes to his work unstartled by the tramp of squadrons or the clash of steel—undisturbed by the apprehension that his best team-horse may be taken from him to drag a gun, or himself snatched rudely away from wife and supper to act as a trembling guide, strapped behind some godless trooper, and stimulated to the better exercise of his local faculties by the cold circle of a pistol-barrel pressed ominously against his temple. The traders of Northampton's goodly town can ride abroad in security with their comely dames mounted on pillions or reclining in litters, without fear of exposure to scurrilous jests or rude insolence from Rupert's troopers and Goring's ' hell-babes.' Although the knaves mourn the decrease of the unnatural stimulus given to trade by the war, and the consequent waning of their own profits, they cannot but congratulate themselves on the combination of advantages offered to their town by the protection of a strong Parliamentary government, and the return of their own lawful Sovereign to their neighbourhood at his Royal Palace of Holmby.

Yes, the old oak at Holmby spreads its gaunt arms again over the plumed heads and rich dresses of courtly gallants, and puts forth its fresh green leaves to rest the aching eyes of a weary monarch who will see but one more earthly spring.

Charles is holding mimic state in his own fair palace; and, although he is to all intents and purposes a prisoner, the outward semblances of royalty are faithfully preserved, and the pleasant fiction still adhered to, that even in acts of coercion and opposition on the part of the Commons, it is his Majesty's Parliament which, under the authority of his Majesty, makes arrangements for the security of his Majesty's person; nay, actually denounces under pains of treason those who should harbour or conceal that sacred property, and, in truth, sets a price on his Majesty's head.

The game is indeed lost now. After the flight from Naseby, when camp-followers and baggage and all fell into the hands of the conquerors, even Charles's private cabinet did not escape. His letters were made public by the Parliament, and the sacred motives of a bigoted though conscientious nature, warped by the influence of an injudicious wife, and constantly acted on by the opinions of selfish and intriguing statesmen, were submitted to the judgment of the English people—perhaps of all people in the world the least disposed to make allowances for motives, and the most prone to decide entirely from results. It may be questioned whether such a defeat, even as that of Naseby, inflicted so deadly a blow on the Royal Cause as the publication of these papers. It never again held up its head till the atonement had been made in a king's blood. Meantime, disaster after disaster marked its decline and fall. Bridgewater surrendered to Fairfax without a blow. Even Rupert counselled peace; and, as though the very counsel had unmanned him, lost Bristol at the first assault. At Rowton Heath, the King narrowly escaped with his life, and saw his favourite cousin, the gallant Earl of Lichfield, struck down by his very side. Then came misunderstandings and heartburnings; even faithful Rupert made terms for himself to abandon the sinking ship, though he returned in compunction to throw himself at the royal feet and demand forgiveness for his dereliction. Monmouth and Hereford, Wales and all the north-country, were lost; Chester, Newark, and Belvoir besieged; Glamorgan's treaty with the Irish Catholics discovered, and that faithful scapegoat bearing his imprisonment and attainder on the charge of high treason with loyal resignation. Gallant old Astley, the last remaining prop, was beaten and taken prisoner at Stow-in-the-Wold, and Charles was compelled to make preparations to deliver himself up to the victorious Parliament.

Then came the negotiations with the Scottish people, conducted through the intervention of the French agent, Montreuil; the consequent escape of the King and Lord Ashburnham from Oxford, and their arrival at the quarters of the Scottish army— an army that, to their eternal disgrace, fairly and literally sold the person of their Sovereign for the amount of arrears of pay due to them. Four hundred thousand pounds was thus established to be the market value of an English monarch's head. Some of the grim old northern Covenanters hugged themselves over their bargain, whilst the Independent party south of the Border doubtless esteemed Charles Stuart very dear at the money. Nevertheless the sale was concluded, and the King, accompanied by certain Parliamentary Commissioners, journeyed in royal state, though *de facto* a prisoner, to take up his temporary residence in Holmby House.

With politic clemency the Parliament had granted the most liberal terms of amnesty and forgiveness to the vanquished Royalists. Lives were spared, estates rarely sequestered, and but few fines imposed on the 'Malignants,' who indeed had by this time little ready money left. The adherents of Charles Edward suffered far more severely from the tender mercies of the House of Hanover than did the Cavaliers of the most unfortunate of his unfortunate line at the hands of the stern Parliamentarians whom they had encountered on so many battle-fields. The adviser of the ruling-party was as subtle a politician as he was a skilful soldier, and Cromwell possessed not only the daring intellect that can seize a Crown, but the consistent wisdom which keeps it firm on the head.

Far and near the inhabitants of Northamptonshire flocked to Holmby to pay their respects to their Sovereign. Peasants cheered him as he walked or rode in the neighbourhood of his Palace. Honest yeomen and sturdy farmers, who had ridden not so long ago in 'buff and bandeliers' to the sound of his trumpets, sent in their humble offerings of rural produce to his household; and the gentry, flaunting in as much state as their reduced circumstances would allow, crowded in their coaches and on horseback to pay their last tribute of loyalty to a monarch in whose cause many of them had sacrificed all they loved best on earth.

What was the charm about these Stuarts that men would thus pour out before them their treasure as readily as their blood, would offer up to them their liberties as ungrudgingly as their lives? Is it a peculiarity in their race that has thus served them? or is it simply the fact of their misfortunes? simply that they have been the only family who have found it necessary to draw upon the loyalty of the English people, whose drafts that people have never suffered to be dishonoured? Let the materialist scoff as he will, this same loyalty, like many another abstract sentiment, is a glorious quality, and has originated some of the noblest deeds which human nature can boast.

'I never thought to see him again,' soliloquized Sir Giles Allonby, as he reined in the well-broke sorrel, and looked back at a huge swinging vehicle, splashing and lumbering through Brampton ford. 'Never again! at least in courtly state like this. How pleased those foolish wenches will be too. Oh, if it be only not too good to last!'

Sir Giles sits in the saddle gallantly enough still, but the defeat on Naseby field, to say nothing of the accompanying hard knocks and subsequent reverses, has aged the bold Cavalier sadly. The blue eye is dim now, the furrows deep and numerous on his sunken face, and the hand on which Diamond is still encouraged to perch trembles till her bells and jesses ring and jingle again. Nevertheless he loves a hawk, a hound, and a horse as dearly as of old:—nor was Humphrey's sorrel ever better taken care of than in the stable at Boughton, where he is fed and littered by his former attendant, Hugh Dymocke, and regaled with many a choice morsel by two indulgent ladies, each of whom pays her visit to his stable at an hour when her friend is otherwise engaged.

They have not forgotten his master, though they rarely speak of him now. He has been long absent in France and elsewhere; no tidings have reached them for many a weary month. He has done his duty nobly by the Queen, that is all they know, and that is surely enough. Grace is satisfied, and so ought the loyal Mary to be, and so she affirms with unnecessary energy she is; yet her cheek looks a shade paler, her manner is a thought less stately and more restless than her wont.

The two ladies are decked out in the utmost splendour of Court dress, and roomy as is the interior of the old coach, they occupy the whole of it. Notwithstanding its four horses driven in hand, with a postillion and pair in front of these, they make but a slow five miles an hour, for the roads even in summer are rough and treacherous; while divers sturdy serving-men, armed to the teeth —of whom our friend Hugh is not the least prominent—cling to the outside of the vehicle. They are about to pay a visit of state to their sovereign, and should be overloaded accordingly.

Two handsomer specimens of English beauty were hard to be met with than the fair inmates of the coach. Grace, rejoicing in the elasticity of youth, has recovered her health and spirits. She has got her father safe back from the wars, and this is a wonderful cordial to poor Gracey. Moreover, she is at that period of life when every year adds fresh charms to the development of womanhood; and the long months that with their attendant anxieties have tarnished ever so little the freshness of her companion's beauty, have but rounded the lines of Grace's bewitching form, deepened the colour on her cheek, and brightened the lustre of her eye.

The dress she wears, much like the Court costume of the present day, is peculiarly adapted to her charms. For a description of this voluminous fabric of lace, brocade, tulle, transparency, and other dangerous materials, we must refer our reader to the columns of that daily organ of fashionable life which describes in glowing colours and accurate detail the costly armour decorating our enslavers at any of her gracious Majesty's drawing-rooms. If a gentleman, let him peruse the inventory therein set forth of the articles of clothing worn on such high festival by the prettiest woman of his acquaintance; if a lady, by the rival for whom she entertains the most cordial aversion (probably it may be the same individual in both cases), and let each profit accordingly.

Mary contemplates her friend, and wonders in her own heart how any man can resist the attractions of that beautiful young face. To do her justice, the element of jealousy lies deep below the surface in Mistress Cave's character. Like many a woman of strong intellect, high courage, and a somewhat masculine turn of thought and ideas (an organization that is apt to be accompanied by the utmost womanly gentleness of bearing and refinement of manner), she is above the petty feelings and little weaknesses that disfigure the generality of her sex. She can and does admire beauty in another without envy or detraction. She does not at first sight set down to the worst of motives every word and action of an attractive sister; nay, she can even pardon that sister freely for winning the admiration of the opposite sex. Conscious of her own worth, and proud it may be in her secret heart to know of a certain shrine or so where that worth is worshipped as it deserves, she can afford to see another win her share of incense without grudging or discontent. In the abstract she is not of a jealous disposition. Individually, as she is never likely to have cause, God forbid she should ever become so! Such a passion in such a nature would work a wreck over which devils might smile in triumph, and angels weep for very shame.

Despite the jolting of the coach, it would be unnatural to suppose that an unbroken silence is preserved between the two. Far from it. They talk incessantly, and laugh merrily enough at intervals. Whatever may be the subject lying deepest at their hearts, whatever hopes or fears, secrets or intrigues, private or political, may be nestling in those sanctuaries, we are bound to confess that their dialogue is frivolous as the veriest woman-hating philosopher could imagine. It turns upon dress, ribbons, courtly forms, and such trivial topics. Even now, as they jingle down into the ford, though each is thinking of a certain return from hawking that took place at this very spot some few years ago, and the consequent introduction of a young Cavalier officer, who has since occupied a large share of each lady's thoughts, neither reverts by word or sign to the reminiscence; and, to judge by their conversation and demeanour, it would be supposed that neither of those fair heads contained an anxiety or an idea beyond the preservation of their curls and dresses from that untidy state which is termed 'rumpled' in the expressive language of the female vocabulary.

'I wish they would mend the bridge,' observed Grace, as a tremendous jolt over a stone under water brought a ludicrous expression of dismay to her pretty features; 'father says it's not safe for a coach since the parapet tumbled down; but they will surely repair it now the King's come.'

'I wish they would, indeed!' assented Mary; 'it's hardly fit for horse-folk now, and Bayard and I have many a quarrel about going so near the edge. It's wide enough for a coach too,' she added, 'and I dread the water coming in every time we go through this treacherous ford. Of all days in my life, I wouldn't have a fold out of place to-day, Grace. I should like to make my courtesy to him in his reverses with more ceremony than I ever did at White——'

The word was never finished. Another jolt, accompanied by much splashing, struggling, and a volley of expletives from Sir Giles, who had turned his horse back into the water, and was swearing lustily by the carriage window, interrupted the speaker, and announced that some catastrophe had taken place.

It was even so. A spring had given way in the ford, and on arriving at the further bank it was moreover discovered that an axle was injured so much as to necessitate a halt for the repair of damages. Sir Giles dismounted, the ladies alighted; and Dymocke, who was provided with the necessary tools—without which indeed none ever dreamed of travelling—commenced his operations; the party, congratulating themselves on the fine summer's day which, notwithstanding their Court dresses, made

half an hour's lounge in the pleasant meadows not even an inconvenience. In the seventeenth century such trifling mishaps
were the daily concomitants of a morning's drive.

'Woa, my man!' said Sir Giles, who was holding the sorrel by
the bridle, whilst Mary patted and smoothed his glossy neck,
and Grace gathered a posy of wildflowers by the river's brim.
The horse erected his ears, snorted and neighed loudly, fidgeting,
moreover, despite of Mary's caresses and Sir Giles's impatient
jerks, and describing circles round the pair, as if he would fain
break from his restraint and gallop off.

'The devil's in the beast!' quoth Sir Giles, testily, as a
shabbily-dressed man with a rod and line, apparently intent upon
his angling, moved slowly down the river bank to where they
stood, and the horse whinnied and pawed, and became more uneasy every moment.

The fisherman was clad in a worn-out suit of coarse brown
stuff, his hat was slouched completely over his eyes; the upper
part of his face—all that could be seen, however—was deadly
pale; and the unsteadiness of his hand imparted a tremulous
motion to his angle, which seemed either the result of inward
agitation or the triumph of manual art.

Sir Giles was a brother of the craft—as indeed in what department of field-sports had the old Cavalier not taken his degree?
Of course he entered into conversation with the angler despite
the restlessness of his charge.

'What sport, master?' quoth Sir Giles in his cheery, boisterous
tones; 'methinks the sun is somewhat too bright for your fishing
to-day, and indeed the weight of your basket will scarce trouble
you much if you have not better luck after your morning's
draught. Zounds, man! have you caught never a fish since
daybreak?'

The basket, as Sir Giles could see, was indeed open and—
empty!

Thus adjured, the fisherman halted within ten paces of the
knight, but apparently he was so intent on his occupation that
he could not spare breath for a reply. He spoke never a word,
and the sorrel was more troublesome than ever.

Sir Giles's wrath began to rise.

'The insolent Roundhead knave!' muttered the old Cavalier;
'shall he not answer when a gentleman accosts him thus civilly?
Let me alone, Mistress Mary; I will cudgel the soul out of him,
and fling him into the river afterwards, sweetheart, as sure as
he stands there!'

Mary suggested that the poor man might perhaps be really deaf, and succeeded in pacifying her companion ; whilst the angler, slouching his hat more than ever over his face, fished on, apparently quite unconscious of their presence.

Sir Giles and the sorrel—the latter most unwillingly—strolled off towards the coach, and Mary remained watching the fisherman's movements with a sort of dreamy satisfaction ; she had become subject to these idle absent fits of late, and something about this man's coarsely-clad figure seemed to embark her thoughts upon a tide of pleasing associations that carried her far, far back into the past.

P'shaw ! this dreaming is a pernicious habit, and must be broken through. She would accost the fisherman, and ascertain if he remained as deaf to a lady's voice as he had been to that of old Sir Giles. Just then, however, Grace called to her to say the carriage was ready, and Mary with a heavy sigh turned slowly to depart.

The fisherman's line trembled as though a hundred perches were tugging at it from the depths of the sluggish *Nene*. He watched her retreating figure, but never moved from his position She reached her party, and they mounted once more into the coach, compressing as much as possible their spreading dresses to make room for Sir Giles, who was easily fatigued now, and who handed over the still refractory sorrel to the care of Dymocke, and proceeded to perform the rest of the journey on wheels.

As the coach lumbered heavily away, it passed the very spot where the angler still stood intent on his fishing. Both ladies glanced at his ill-dressed form as they drove by, and watched long afterwards from opposite windows the unusual proceedings of the sorrel, who, instead of suffering Dymocke to mount him quietly as was his wont, broke completely away from that attendant, and after a frolic round the meadow trotted quietly up to the stranger, and proceeded to rub his head against the brown jerkin with a violence that threatened to push its wearer bodily into the water.

The last the ladies saw as they ascended the hill towards the small hamlet of Chapel-Brampton was their serving-man in close conversation with the angler whom they had erroneously inferred to be deaf. Though it must have struck each of them as a strange circumstance, it is remarkable that neither expressed an opinion on the subject, and a silence broken only by the snores of Sir Giles, who always went to sleep in a carriage, reigned between them for at least two miles. At the termination of that distance, however, Grace, rousing herself from a fit of abstraction, addressed her no less absent companion : 'Did you notice that fisherman's dress, Mary?' was her innocent and appropriate observation. ' Shabby as it was, he had got a knot of faded pink ribbon under his doublet. I saw it quite plain when he lifted his arm to throw his line. Wasn't it strange ? '

Mary grew as white as the laced handkerchief in her hand, and in proportion as the blood forsook her cheeks her companion flushed to the very temples. Each turned to her own window and her own thoughts once more. Despite the jolting, Sir Giles slept on. Dymocke, too, overtook the carriage ; but it would have been indeed hopeless to question that functionary, whose gravity and reserve became deeper day by day, and who, since his interview with the King the night before Naseby, was never known to unbend even under the influence of the strongest potations.

Sir Giles snored comfortably on, and thus, without another word being exchanged, the Royalists arrived to pay their respects to their unhappy sovereign under the sheltering roof of Holmby House.

CHAPTER XXVII.

' HOLMBY HOUSE.'

ON the fairest site perhaps in the whole fair country of North-ampton stand to this day the outward walls, the lofty gates, and an inconsiderable remnant of what was once the goodly edifice of Holmby House. The slope of the ground which declines from it on all sides, offers a succession of the richest and most pastoral views which this rich and pastoral country can afford. Like the rolling prairie of the Far West, valley after valley of sunny meadows, dotted with oak and elm and other noble trees, un-dulates in ceaseless variety far as the eye can reach ; but unlike the boundless prairie, deep dark copses and thick luxuriant hedgerows, bright and fragrant with wild flowers and astir with the glad song of birds, diversify the foreground and blend the distance into a mass of woodland beauty that gladdens alike the fastidious eye of the artist and the stolid gaze of the clown. In June it is a dream of Fairyland to wander along that crested emi-nence, and turn from the ruins of those tall old gateways cutting their segments of blue out of the deep summer sky, or from the flickering masses of still tender leaves upon the lofty oaks, yellowing in the floods of golden light that stream through the

network of their tangled branches, every tree to the up-gazing
eye a study of forest scenery in itself, and so to glance earthward
at the fair expanse of homely beauty stretching away from one's
very feet. Down in the nearest valley, massed like a solid square
of Titan warriors, and scattered like advanced champions from the
gigantic array profusely up the opposite slope, the huge old oaks
of Althorpe quiver in the summer haze, backed by the thickly-
wooded hills that melt in softened outlines into the southern
sky. The fresh light green of the distant larches blooming on
far Harlestone Heath, is relieved by the dark belt of firs that
draws a thin black line against the horizon. A light cloud of
smoke floats above the spot where lies fair Northampton town,
but the intervening trees and hedgerows are so clothed in foliage
that scarce a building can be discerned, though the tall sharp
spire of Kingsthorpe pierces upward into the sky. To the west,
a confusion of wooded knolls and distant copses are bathed in the
vapoury haze of the declining sun, and you rest your dazzled
eyes, swimming with so much beauty, and stoop to gather the
wild flower at your feet. Ah, 'tis a pleasant season, that same
merry month of June! Then in December—who doth not know
and appreciate the merits of December at such a spot as Holmby?
Of all climates upon earth, it is well known that none can produce
the equal of a soft mild English winter's day, and such a day at
Holmby is worth living for through the gales of blustering
October and the fogs of sad November, with its depressing atmosphere and continuous drizzle. Ay, these are rare pastures to
breathe a goodly steed, and there are fences too hereabouts that
will prove his courage and your own! But enough of this. Is
not Northamptonshire the very homestead of horse and hound,
and Pytchley but a synonym of Paradise for all who delight
therein?

Lord Chancellor Hatton—he whose skilful performances in the
dance so charmed our Royal Elizabeth, and whose ' shoestrings
green,' ' whose bushy beard and satin doublet '

> Moved the stout heart of England's Queen,
> Though Pope and Spaniard could not trouble it—

seems to have been a nobleman of undoubted taste in architecture as well as a thorough master of the Terpsichorean art. At a
sufficiently mature age he built the fair palace which was destined
hereafter for the residence of a king, to be, as he coxcombically
expressed it, ' the last and greatest monument of his youth.' Its
exterior was accordingly decorated with all the quaint ins and

outs, mullioned windows, superfluity of chimneys, and elaborate ornaments which distinguish the 'earlier and lesser monuments' of the agile Lord Keeper. A huge stone gateway, with the Hatton arms carved on a shield above their heads, admitted our coach and its occupants into a large court-yard, around two sides of which extended the state and reception-rooms of the palace. This court itself was now filled with officers of the King's household and other personal retainers of a peaceful character; there were even a few goodly beef-eaters, but no clash of swords nor waving of standards; none of the gallant troop of Life Guards that seemed so appropriate to the vicinity of a sovereign. Alas! how many of them were sleeping where they fell, a couple of leagues away yonder, where the flat skyline of Naseby field bounds the horizon to the north. Not even a blast of trumpets or a roll of kettledrums aroused Sir Giles from his slumbers, and Grace was forced to wake him with a merry jest anent his drowsiness as they lumbered in beneath the archway, and sent their names on from one official to another, waiting patiently for their turn to alight, inasmuch as the forms and ceremonies of a court were the more scrupulously observed the more the fortunes of the monarch were on the wane, and an old family coach of another country grandee was immediately before them. The disembarkation of these honest courtiers was a matter of time and trouble. Loyalty and valour had deprived them of their coach-horses, six of which had failed to save one of the King's guns in the flight from Naseby, and four huge unwieldy animals from the plough had been substituted for the team of Flanders mares with their long plaited tails and their slow but showy action. One of these agricultural animals, a colt, who seemed to feel that neither by birth nor appearance was he entitled to the position he now occupied, could in no wise be induced to face the glories of the royal serving-men who crowded round the door of reception. In vain the coachman flogged, the grooms and running-footmen kicked and jerked at the bridle, the ladies inside screamed, and the Cavalier in charge of them swore a volley of the deepest Royalist oaths; the colt was very refractory, and pending his reduction, Sir Giles had ample time to look around him at the walls he knew so well, and reflect how unaltered they were when everything else was so changed.

Many a cup had he emptied here with gentle King Jamie, who to his natural inefficiency and stupidity added the disgusting tendencies of a sot. Many a jest had he exchanged with Archie Armstrong, the King's fool—like others of his profession, not half such a fool as his master. Many a rousing night had he passed in yonder turret, where was the little round chamber termed the King's Closet, and many a fair morn had he ridden out through this very gateway to hunt the stag on the moorlands by Haddon, or the wild hills of Ashby, far away with hound and horn to Fawsley's sheltering coverts, or the deep woodland of distant Castle-Dykes. Ay, 'twas the very morrow of the day when Grace's mother had made him a certain confession and a certain promise, that he saw the finest run it was ever his lot to enjoy with an outlying deer that had escaped from this very park, and though he killed his best horse in the chase, it was the happiest day in his life. He looked at Gracey, and the old man's eyes filled with tears. Sir Giles was getting a good deal broke now, so his neighbours said.

The country grandees are disembarked at last. The succeeding coach lumbers heavily up to the palace-door, and as their names are passed from official to official, Sir Giles and his two ladies stand once more under the roof of their sovereign, who, despite all his reverses, still holds royal state and semblance in his own court. They like to think so, and to deceive themselves and him, if only for an hour.

As far as actual luxury or pleasure was concerned, Charles's daily habits, wherever he was, partook of a sufficiently self-denying and ascetic character to make his enforced residence at Holmby no more secluded than had been his life in the full flush of his early prosperity at Whitehall. The King was always, even in his youthful days, of a remarkably studious turn of mind, regular in his habits, and punctilious of all such small observances on the part of his household as preserved that regularity in its most unbroken course. The hours of devotion, of study, of state, of exercise, and of eating, were strictly portioned out to the very minute, and this arrangement of his time enabled the monarch, even in the midst of his busiest and most pressing avocations, to devote his leisure to those classical studies of which he was so fond. From his warlike ancestors—who indeed had been used to keep their crown with the strong hand, and who, thanks to Armstrongs and Elliotts on the border, not to mention a refractory Douglas or two nearer home, never left off their mail and plate, or forgot to close steel gauntlet on ashen spear for many months together—he had inherited a certain muscular energy of body and vigour of constitution which he strove to retain by the regular observance of daily exercise. 'It is well worth our observation,' says his faithful chronicler, worthy

Sir Thomas Herbert, 'that in all the time of his Majesty's restraint and solitude he was never sick, nor took anything to prevent sickness, nor had need of a physician, which, under God, is attributed to his quiet disposition and unparalleled patience, to his exercise (when at home walking in the gallery and privy garden, and other recreations when abroad), to his abstemiousness at meat, eating but of few dishes, and, as he used to say, agreeable to his exercise, drinking but twice every dinner and supper, once of beer, and once of wine and water mixed, only after fish a glass of *French* wine ; the beverage he himself mixed at the cupboard, so he would have it. He very seldom ate and drank before dinner, nor between meals.'

Thus did the captive monarch keep himself, so to speak, in training, both of body and mind, for whatever exercises either of effort or endurance might be required of him ; and thus perhaps rendered more tolerable that period of restraint and *surveillance* which is so calculated to enervate the physical as well as the intellectual powers, and to resist the effects of which requires perhaps a combination of nobler qualities than to conquer armies and subjugate empires with the strong hand.

But the Stuart, though in reality worsted, conquered, and in ward, was permitted to enjoy all the outward semblance of royalty ; was served with all the strict observances and ceremonious etiquette due to a sovereign. He had a household, too, and a Court, though neither were of his own choosing ; and Court and household vied with each other in respectful deference to their charge. The Parliamentary Commission, stated, in the document which gave them their authority, to be his Majesty's *loyal* subjects, was composed, partially at least, of noblemen and gentlemen who were not personally obnoxious to their Sovereign, and who had for long supported him in his claims, till their better judgment convinced them those claims were unconstitutional and subversive of real liberty. The Earls of Pembroke, of Denbigh, and Lord Montague, were no violent Roundheads ; whilst of the inferior members who represented the Lower House, Major-General Browne was an especial favourite with the King ; and Sir James Harrington came of a family on whose loyalty the slightest imputation had never hitherto been cast.

It rested with the discretion of this Committee to nominate the principal officers of his Majesty's household ; and the list of their selection, including as it does the name of Herbert, afterwards Sir Thomas, who filled the post of Groom of the Chambers to the King, and attended him, an attached and faithful servant to the

last, betrays at least a respect for Charles's prejudices, and a consideration for his comfort. Dr. Wilson was retained as the Royal
physician; and the accustomed staff of cup-bearers, carvers, cooks,
and barbers, were continued in their offices, with the single proviso, that such alone should be dismissed as had borne arms against
the Parliament. The duties of roasting, boiling, filling, serving,
and shaving, being of no warlike tendency, it is not to be supposed
that this exception would weed the household of more than a very
few familiar faces; and Charles found himself at Holmby surrounded by much the same number and class of domestics that
would have been eating his Royal substance at Whitehall.

With a liberality that does credit to the rebellious Parliament,
we find in their records a sumptuous provision for the maintenance
of the King's table, and the payment of his attendance here. The
roll of officials indispensable to a Court, comprises a variety of
subordinates charitably presumed to be necessary to the daily
wants of royalty; and the 'clerks of green cloth, clerks of the
assignment, of the bakehouse, pantrie, cellar, butterie, spicerie,
confectionary, chaundrie, ewrie, laudrie, and kitchen,' must have
had but little to do, and plenty of time to do it, in the rural retirement of this Northamptonshire residence. Cooks—head and
subordinate—'turn-brouches, porters and scowrers, with knaves
of the boiling-house, larder, poultrie, scaulding-house, accaterie,
pastrie, wood-yard, and sculcrie,' help to swell the hungry
phalanx; nor must the 'gate-ward' be forgotten, and another
functionary termed the 'harbinger,' who, like the 'odd man' of
modern times in large establishments, was probably the deliverer
of messages, and did more work than all the rest put together.

'It is conceived that there be a number of the guard proposed
to carry upp the King's meat,' quoth the record; and for this
purpose was daily told off a goodly detachment, consisting of two
yeomen-ushers, two yeomen-hangers, and twenty yeomen of the
guard; when to this numerous force was added the swarm of ' pages
of the bedchamber and back-stairs, gentlemen-ushers, gentlemen of
the privy-chamber, cup-bearer, carver, server, and esquire of the
body, grooms of the robes and privy-chamber, daily wayters, and
quarter wayters, pages of the presence, and the removing wardrobe,
grooms of the chamber, messengers of the chamber, physician,
apothecary barber, chirurgeon, and laundresse,' the King's household in his captivity will, we submit, bear comparison with that of
any of his Royal brethren in the full enjoyment of their power.

Thirty pounds sterling a day for his Majesty's ' diet of twenty-
eight dishes,' was the very handsome allowance accorded by the

Parliament; and the amount of expenses incurred by the Royal household at Holmby for the twenty days commencing on the 13th February, and ending on the 4th of March, reaches the large sum of 2990*l*., between 50,000*l*. and 60,000*l*. a year.

There being a deficiency, too, of plate for the Royal table, that article of festive state having been long ago converted into steel, horseflesh, gunpowder, and such munitions of war, it was suggested by the inventive genius of the Committee, that the communion-plate formerly set on the altar of his Majesty's chapel of Whitehall —consisting of ' one gilt shyppe, two gilt vases, two gilt euyres, a square bason and fountain, and a silver rod '—should be melted down to make plate for the King's use at Holmby, there being none remaining in the jewel-office fit for service ; and this some-what startling, not to say sacrilegious, proposal seems to have been entertained, and acted on accordingly.

For the bodily wants of the Sovereign no demand seems to have been considered too exorbitant, but for his spiritual needs the Parliament would not hear of any but their own nominees, and instead of the Bishops of London, Salisbury, or Peterborough, or such other divines as his Majesty desired to consult, they substi-tuted the bigoted Marshall and the enthusiastic Caryl to be the keepers of the King's conscience, and trustees for the welfare of his soul. Perhaps this arrangement was of all the most galling to Charles's feelings, and the most distasteful to the very strong tendency which he had always shown for casuistry and contro-versial religion. Though these chaplains preached alternately, in the chapel attached to the palace, every Sunday morning and afternoon to the Commissioners and the Royal household, the King, while he permitted such of his retinue to attend as were so disposed, preferred to perform his own devotions in private, rather than sanction with his presence the Presbyterian form of worship to which he was so opposed ; and even at his meals the conscien-tious Monarch invariably said ' grace ' himself rather than accept the services of either chaplain, both of whom were nevertheless always in close attendance upon his Majesty.

The King's daily life at Holmby seems to have been studious and regular to a degree. An early riser, he devoted the first hours of the morning to his religious exercises, praying with great fervour in his closet, and there studying and reading such works of controversial divinity as most delighted his somewhat narrow intellect and formal turn of mind. At the same hour every morning a poached egg was brought him, and a glass of fair water ; after which, accompanied either by the Earl of Pembroke or

General Browne, he took his regular exercise by walking to and fro for an allotted time, in fair weather, up and down the green terraces which lay smooth and level to the south of the palace, and in wet, through the long corridors and spacious chambers which adorned its eastern wing. At the expiration of the exact period, the King again retired to his own private apartments, where such public business as he still conceived himself empowered to undertake, the study of the classics, and the prosecution of a correspondence which indeed seldom reached its destination, occupied him till the hour of dinner, in those days punctually at noon. This meal, we need hardly say, was served with great state and ceremony. Ewer-bearers with napkin and golden bason, ushers with their white wands, preceded the entrance and presided over the conclusion of the banquet. No form was omitted which could enhance the stately nature of the ceremony; and the King dined on a raised dais six inches above the level floor of the dining-hall. After dinner a quarter of an hour exactly was devoted to conversation of a light and frivolous character, the only period in the day, be it observed, that such conversation was encouraged, or even tolerated, by the grave Charles; but anything approaching to levity, not to say indecency, was severely rebuked by that decorous Monarch, who could not endure that a high officer of his household should once boast in his presence of his proficiency in hard drinking, but inflicted on him a caustic and admonitory reprimand for his indiscretion. What a contrast to his successor!

A game at chess, played with the due attention and silence which befit that pastime, succeeded to this short space of relaxation; and we can imagine the reflections that must have obtruded themselves on the Monarch's mind when the ivory king was reduced to his last straits, cooped up to the three or four squares which formed his only battle-ground—his queen gone, his bishops, knights, and castles all in the hands of the adversary—now checking him at every turn, and the issue of the contest too painfully like that catastrophe in real life, which he *must* have seen advancing to meet him with giant strides.

At the conclusion of this suggestive pursuit, it was his Majesty's custom, when the weather permitted, to ride out on horseback, accompanied by one or more of the Commissioners, and attended by an armed escort, which might more properly be termed a guard. The King's rides usually took the direction of the Earl of Sunderland's house at Althorpe, or that of Lord Vaux at Boughton, at either of which places he could enjoy his favourite diversion of 'bowls;' for the green at Holmby, though level and spacious enough, did not run sufficiently true to please the critical eye and hand of so eminent a performer at this game as was Charles I.

The evening passed off in the like formal and somewhat tedious routine. An hour of meditation succeeded the ride, and supper was served with the same observances as the noonday meal. Grave discourse, turning chiefly upon the Latin classical authors, and studiously avoiding all allusion to those political topics which probably formed the staple of conversation in every other household in the kingdom, furbished up the schoolboy lore of the Commissioners, and gave the Royal pedant an opportunity of exhibiting his superiority to his keepers in this department of literature. The King's devotions then occupied him for a considerable period in his closet, and he retired to rest at an early hour, with a degree of languid composure surprising to witness in one so circumstanced, and which never seems to have deserted him even in the last extremity.

Such was the daily life of the vanquished King, varied only by such a public reception as the present, when his earlier glories seemed to flicker up once more in an illusive flash ere they were quenched in darkness for ever.

We have left Sir Giles and his fair charges in an inner-hall, which led directly to the presence of Royalty.

This chamber, lined with beautifully carved oak, and adorned with escutcheons and other heraldic devices, presented a quaint and pleasing appearance, not out of keeping with the rustling dames and plumed gallants that crowded its polished floor. In its centre stood three carved pyramids, of which the middle overtopped its two supporters by several feet; and around this shrine of heraldry were emblazoned the different coats of arms of the nobility and gentry of the surrounding districts.

At the further extremity of the hall stood a high wooden screen, such as in cathedrals portions off the altar from the nave, wrought into elaborate and fantastic ornaments, in which the grotesque nature of the imagery was only equalled by the excellence of the carving; and as the recess behind this framework communicated directly with the Presence Chamber, Maxwell, the Usher of the Black Rod, was here stationed to announce the names of those loyal gentlefolks who came to pay their respects to his Majesty.

' It reminds one of Whitehall,' whispered Mary to Sir Giles, as the latter delivered their names in the subdued and reverential whisper becoming the atmosphere of a Court, ' only there are some ludicrous figures amongst the ladies' dresses,' she added, woman-like, with a downward glance of satisfaction at her own well-chosen costume, and another of admiration at her companion's beautiful figure.

Sir Giles did not answer. He was thinking of the many Royal receptions he had attended during the troubles, and how each after each seemed thinner of the old familiar faces, the hearty friends and good blades that had hedged their Sovereign round with the wall of steel in vain; whose bones were strewed far and wide over the surface of merry England; whose estates were gone, their families scattered, their hearths desolate. How few were left now! and those few, like himself, rusty, worn-out, dis-used, yet retaining the keen temper of the true steel to the last.

'Welcome, Sir Giles,' whispered Maxwell, a courtier of forty years' standing, who had spent many a merry hour with the old knight under this very roof in days of yore, and who, albeit a man of peace from his youth upward, showed the marks of Time as plainly on his wrinkled face and snowy locks as did his more adventurous comrade, without however attaining the dignified and stately bearing of the veteran warrior. 'Welcome! The King spoke of you but yesterday. His Majesty will be indeed glad to see you. Fair ladies, you may enter at once. The dragon that watched over the gardens of the Hesperides neglected his post under the dazzling rays of beauty, whilst he was but Jupiter's Usher of the Black Rod!'

Maxwell esteemed himself only second to his royal master in classical lore, and piqued himself on two things in the world—the whiteness of his laced ruffles and the laborious pedantry of his compliments.

Grace smiled. 'What a formidable dragon!' she whispered, with an arch glance at the ancient courtier, that penetrated through brocade and embroidery—ay, and a flannel bulwark against rheumatism—to his susceptible old heart. Such shafts were never aimed at him in vain, but invariably reached their mark. Need we add that Maxwell was a confirmed bachelor of many years' standing?

Grace pursed up her pretty mouth into an expression of the gravest decorum, for she had now entered the magic circle, of which the centre was the King.

It was indeed a sad contrast to the assembly she remembered so well at Merton College. Where were the Newcastles, the Winchesters, and the Worcesters?—the brilliant aristocracy that had once formed the brightest jewels of the Crown? Where was

Ormond's sagacious courage and Rupert's ready gallantry? Lich-field's goodly person and Sir Jacob Astley's fine old war-worn face? Where were the nobility and the chivalry of England? Alas! not here in Holmby, rallying round their King; and there-fore dead, scattered, and swept away from the face of the earth.

Constrained and gloomy countenances surround him now, instead of those frank haughty fronts that quailed not before a Sovereign's eye, but ever greeted him with manly looks of loyalty and friendship—faces in which he could confide, and before which it was no shame even for a monarch to unbend. His manner, always stately, has now become gloomy and reserved to the extreme of coldness. He cannot but be aware that every word of his lips, every glance of his eye, is watched with the utmost vigilance, noted down, and in all probability reported for the behoof of his bitterest enemies; yet must he never betray his consciousness of *surveillance*—must never for an instant lose his judgment and self-command.

'Twas but this very morning that, taking his accustomed exercise abroad, accompanied by Major-General Browne and the devout Caryl, whose zeal to convert his Sovereign never suffered him to be absent a moment from his side, a poor squalid woman, carrying a child in her arms, marked and scarred with that scrofulous disease which, though its superstitious remedy has been long ago discarded, bears to this day the name of 'king's evil,' approached the person of her Sovereign, and begged him, in tones of piteous appeal, only to touch her child, that it might be healed. Poor woman! she had watched, and waited, and dodged the park-keepers, and stilled her own panting heart many a weary hour, ere she could penetrate to the King's presence; and she pleaded earnestly now, for she had implicit faith in the remedy.

Charles, ever merciful, ever kindly, and, like all his family, ever *good-natured*, listened patiently to the poor woman's tale; and whilst he bestowed on her a broad piece or two, borrowed from the General for the occasion, stretched forth his own royal hand to heal the whining infant of its malady.

'Hold, woman!' exclaimed Caryl, indignantly interposing his person between the royal physician and the little sufferer. 'Wouldst thou blaspheme before the very face of a minister of the Word? Who can heal save He alone, whose servants we are? And thou, sire!' he added, turning roughly upon the King, 'what art thou that thou shouldest arrogate to thyself the issues of life and death? Thou—a man! a worm!—a mere insect crawling on the face of the earth! Away with thee, Charles Stuart! in shame and penitence, lest a worse thing befal thee! Have we not read the Scriptures?—do they not enjoin us to "fear God?"'

'And "honour the king,"' added Charles, very quietly, and passing his hand gently over the child's forehead. Caryl sank back abashed, and the Major-General gave vent to his indignation in a volley of stifled oaths, which, Parliamentarian though he was, his military education called up at this instance of what he was pleased to term in his mutterings, 'a conceited parson's insubordination, worthy of the strappado!'

The King's gloomy countenance, however, broke into a melancholy smile when he recognised the honest face of Sir Giles Allonby advancing into the presence. He made a step forward, and extending both hands as the old Cavalier sank upon his knee, raised him to his feet, and led him a little aside from the surrounding throng, as though anxious to distinguish him by some especial mark of his royal favour. The devoted Royalist's whole face brightened at this instance of his Sovereign's condescension, and Sir Giles looked ten years younger for the moment as he basked in the rays of this declining sun of royalty.

'Express to good Lord Vaux our sympathy and sorrow for his malady, which confines him thus to his chamber. He must indeed be ill at ease when he fails to attend our Court, as well we know. Tell him that we will ourselves visit him ere long at his own good house at Boughton. Hark ye, Sir Giles! I have heard much of the excellence of your bowling-green yonder; we will play a set once more for a broad piece, as we did long ago, in days that were somewhat merrier than these are now.'

He sighed as he spoke; and Sir Giles professed himself, as indeed he was, overpowered at the condescension of his Sovereign.

The King warmed to the subject. He could interest himself in trifles still.

'The green below these windows,' said he, 'is so badly levelled that the bowl runs constantly against the bias. Even my Lord Pembroke can make nothing of it, and you and I can remember him, Sir Giles, many a point better than either of us. 'Tis a game I love well,' added Charles, abstractedly; 'and yet methinks 'tis but a type of the life of men—and kings. How many are started fair upon their object with the surest aim and the best intentions; how few ever reach the goal. How the bias turns this one aside, and the want of force lets another die out in mid career, and an inch more would make a third the winner, but that it fails at the last hair's-breadth. That is the truest bowl that can best sustain the rubs of the green. 'Tis the noblest heart that scorns to escape from its crosses, but can *endure* as well as face the ills of life—

> Rebus in adversis facile est contemnere vitam,
> Fortiter ille facit qui miser esse potest.'

'Very true, your Majesty—quite correct,' observed the delighted Sir Giles, whose Latin had been long effaced by far more important pursuits. 'Everything shall be ready for your Majesty and in order. We cannot thank your Majesty enough.'

The old Cavalier was quite overcome by his emotion.

'And this is your daughter,' pursued Charles, gravely and courteously saluting the young lady, who followed close upon her father's steps; 'a fair flower from a stanch old stem ; and Mistress Mary Cave too, whom I rejoice once more to welcome to my Court.' But a cloud passed across the King's brow as he spoke, and the deep melancholy expression darkened his large eyes as Mary's face recalled to him the light of happier days and the image of his absent Queen. He turned from them with a sigh, and they passed on, whilst a fresh arrival and a fresh presentation took their place. His great-grandfather or his son would have detained somewhat longer in conversation the two fairest ladies that adorned the Court; but Charles I. was as insensible to female beauty as James V. and Charles II. were too dangerously susceptible of its attractions.

The party from Boughton sauntered through the lofty apartments of the palace, and entered into conversation with such of their friends and acquaintance as had passed through the Presence Chamber. Then the heavy coach once more lumbered through the courtyard, and they returned the way they came.

Sir Giles was in high spirits at the anticipation of his Majesty's visit, and talked of nothing else the whole way home. Mary, contrary to her wont, looked pale and tired, whilst Grace seemed somewhat abstracted and occupied with her own thoughts.

As they traversed Brampton ford they both looked for the strange fisherman, but he was nowhere to be seen. The river stole on quiet and undisturbed, its surface burnished into gold by the hot afternoon sun, and rippled only by the kiss of the stooping swallow, or the light track of the passing water-fly.

CHAPTER XXVIII.

KEEPING SECRETS.

HARD held in the sinewy grasp of honest Dymocke, whose features expanded into grim smiles with the excitement of a rousing gallop, the sorrel's regular stride swept round the park at Boughton, despite the heat of the afternoon sun and the hardness of the ground. Such a proceeding was indeed a flagrant departure from the rules of stable discipline, which would have enjoined the serving-man to bring his charge quietly home, and bed him up incontinently for the night. To judge, however, by Hugh's countenance, he had good reasons for this unusual measure, and after half-an-hour's walk through the cool shade of the avenues, he jumped from the saddle in the stable-yard, and contemplated the still reeking sides of his favourite with an expression of grave and critical approval.

' Ay,' said he, as the sorrel, after snorting once or twice, raised his excited head, as if ready and willing for another gallop, ' you could make some of them look pretty foolish even now. Regular work and good food has not done you any harm since you left off your soldierin' ; and after this bit of a breather to-night, if you *should* be wanted to-morrow, why—whew ! '

The prolonged whistle which concluded this soliloquy denoted an idea of such rapidity as words were totally inadequate to convey ; and Dymocke proceeded to wash his charge's feet, and rub down his bright glossy sides in the cool air of the spacious stable-yard, with a demeanour of mysterious importance which argued the most alarming results.

Now by a curious coincidence it so happened that Faith, despising the allurements of the buttery, in which the other servants were partaking of one of their many repasts, tripped softly through the yard on her way to the laundry, one of those domestic offices the vicinity of which to the stables offers the men and maids of an establishment many opportunities of innocent gaiety and improving conversation. It was not surprising that Faith should loiter for a few minutes to enjoy the society of an individual with whom she avowedly ' kept company,' or that hereditary curiosity should prompt her to demand the cause of the horse's heated appearance, and the unusual care bestowed on him by his rider.

' You do frighten one so, Sergeant,' said Faith, addressing her swain by his title of brevet rank, with a coy look and one of her sweetest smiles—such a look and smile as argued ulterior intentions. ' It gave me quite a turn to see you as I did from Mistress Grace's window coming round the Cedars at such a break-neck rate. Is anything the matter, Hugh ? ' she added, anxiously. ' You're not going to leave us again for sure ? '

Dymocke was splashing and hissing for hard life. He paused, winked ominously in his questioner's face, and shifting the bucket of water to the off side, set to work again more vigorously than before.

She had not ' kept company ' with him all these months without knowing exactly how to manage him. She pulled a bunch of green leaves for the sorrel, caressed him admiringly, and looking askance at Dymocke's stooping figure, addressed her conversation to the horse.

' Poor fellow ! ' she said, smoothing his glossy neck, ' how you must miss your master. He wouldn't have rode you so unmercifully such a baking day as this. I wonder where he is now, poor young man. Far enough away, I'll be bound, or *you* wouldn't be put upon as you have been this blessed afternoon.'

The taunt rankled. Hugh looked up from his operations.

' There's reason for it, Mistress Faith; take my word, there's reason for it, though you can't expect to be told the whys and the wherefores every time as one of our horses gets a gallop.'

There *was* a mystery, then. To a woman such an admission was in itself a challenge. Faith vowed to know all about it ere she slept that night.

A sprig of green remained in her hand. She pulled it asunder pensively, leaf by leaf, and heaved one or two deep sighs. She knew her man thoroughly ; despite his vinegar face his heart was as soft as butter to the sex.

' Ah, Hugh,' she said, ' it's an anxious time for us poor women, that sits and cries our eyes out, when you men you've nothing to brood over. I was in hopes the troubles was all done now. Whatever should I do to lose you again, dear ? Tell me, Hugh, leastways, it's nothing up about yourself, is it ? '

Faith's eyes were very soft and pretty, and she used them at this juncture with considerable skill.

Dymocke looked up, undoubtedly mollified.

' Well, it's nothing about myself—there ! ' he grunted out, in a rough voice.

A step was gained ; he had made an admission. She would wheedle it all out of him now before the supper-bell rang.

'Nor yet the Captain,' exclaimed Faith, clasping her hands in
an agony of affected alarm. 'Say it's not the Captain, Hugh, for
any sake. Oh, my poor young mistress! Say it's not the
Captain, or Major, or whatever he be; only say the word, Hugh,
that he's safe.'

'Well, he's safe enough as yet, for the matter of that,' answered
Hugh, saying the word, however, with considerable unwillingness. In such a 'pumping' process as the present the struggles
of the victim are the more painful from his total inability to
escape.

'As yet, Hugh?' repeated the operator: 'as yet? Then you
know something about him? you know where he is? you've
heard of him? he's alive and well? He's come back from
abroad? he's in England? perhaps he's in Northamptonshire
even now?'

Dymocke's whole attention seemed bent on his currycomb and
accompanying sibilations.

Faith set her lips tight.

'Sergeant Dymocke,' she said, with an air of solemn warning,
'you and me has kept company now for many a long day, and
none can say as I've so much as looked over my shoulder at ever
a young man but yourself. There's Master Snood, the mercer in
Northampton, and long Will Bucksfoot, the wild forester at
Rockingham, as has been down scores and scores of times on their
bended knees to me to say the word, and I never said the word,
and I never wouldn't. I won't say what I've thought, and I
won't say what I've hoped; but if things is to end as they've
begun between you and me, I wouldn't answer for the consequences!'

With this mysterious and comprehensive threat, Faith burst
into a passion of tears, and burying her face in her apron, wept
aloud, refusing to be comforted.

Another point gained. She had dexterously shifted her ground,
and put him in the position of the suppliant.

He was forced to abandon his horse and console her to the best
of his abilities, with awkward caresses and blunt assurances of
affection. By degrees the sobs became less frequent; certain
vague hints, tending to hymeneal results, produced, as usual, a
sedative effect. Peace was established, and Faith returned to
the attack much invigorated by the tears that had so relieved her
feelings.

'Of course you'd trust a *wife* with everything you knew,'
observed Faith, in answer to an observation of Dymocke's, which

we are bound to admit was not marked by his usual caution. 'And the Major *is* come back?' she added, in her most coaxing accents and with her sunniest smile.

'Yes, he's back,' said Hugh, laconically.

'And you've seen him?' added Faith, who felt she was winning easy.

Hugh nodded.

'This afternoon?'

Another nod, implying a cautious affirmative.

'Where?'

'Close by, at Brampton. The horse knowed him at once, for all his disguise. It was beautiful to see the dumb creature's affection,' urged Hugh, emphatically.

'Disguised, was he?' echoed Faith, delighted with the result of her perseverance. 'Where had he come from? where was he going to? what was he doing? You may as well tell me all about it now, Hugh. Come, out with it; there's a dear.'

Out it all came, indeed, as a secret generally does, much to the relief of the proprietor and the satisfaction of the curious. Like a goat-skin of Spanish wine in which the point of a mountaineer's knife has been dexterously inserted, there is a little frothing and bubbling at first, then a few precious drops ooze through the orifice, and anon a fine generous stream comes flowing out continuously till the skin is emptied.

So Faith learned that the shabby fisherman at Brampton ford was none other than Major Bosville; that he was waiting there with a political object, which it would be more than his life's worth to disclose; that he had been fishing there for two whole days, and had not achieved the object for which he had come; that the ladies and Sir Giles had been within ten yards of him, and never recognised him; and lastly, that the sorrel's attachment to his master was not to be obliterated by time, nor to be deceived by appearances.

'It *was* a sight to do your eyes good, my dear,' said Hugh, stroking the horse's nose, 'to see him break away from me and gallop all round the miller's close, as if he'd never be caught nor tamed again, and then trotting up to Major Humphrey as if he'd been a dog, and neighing for joy, and rubbing his head against his master, and the Major looking a'most as pleased as the horse. They've more sense and more affection too than many human beings,' added Hugh, impressively; 'and now you needn't to be told, my dear, why I gave him this bit of a turn to keep his pipes clear in case of accidents. He might be wanted to-morrow, or he might *not*; but if so be that he were, it shall never be said that he came out of *this* stable and wasn't fit to save a man's life. They're like the female sex, my dear, in many particulars, but in none so much as this. It's ruling them well and working of them easy that makes them *good*; but it's ruling them strict and working of them hard that makes them *better*.'

With this philosophical axiom, the result, doubtless, of much attentive observation, Dymocke clothed up the sorrel, and led him into the stable, whilst Faith, with an expression of deeper anxiety than often troubled her pretty face, tripped away to her mistress's room, and to the best of our belief never visited the laundry after all.

Grace had to be dressed for supper. In those simple days people supped by daylight in the summer, and revised their toilets carefully for the meal, much as they dress for dinner now; and in those days, as in the present, a lady's 'back hair' was a source of much manual labour to her maid, and much mental anxiety to herself.

Though Faith worked away at the ebon masses with an unmerciful number of jerks and twitches and an unusually hard brush, she did not succeed in exciting the attention of the sufferer, who sat patient and motionless in her hands—not even looking at herself in the glass.

Faith heaved one or two surprisingly deep sighs, and even ventured upon a catching of the breath, such as with ladies of her profession is the usual precursor to a flood of tears, but without the slightest effect. Grace never lifted her eyes from the point of her foot, which peeped out beneath her robe.

At length the waiting-maid pressed her hand against her side, with an audible expression of pain.

'What's the matter, Faith?' said her mistress, turning round, with a wondering abstracted gaze, which brightened into one of curiosity, as she marked the excited expression of her attendant's countenance.

'Nothing, ma'am,' replied Faith, with another catching of the breath, real enough this time; 'leastways nothing's the matter at present, though what's to come of it, goodness only knows. Oh, Mistress Grace! Mistress Grace!' she added, letting all the 'back hair' down *en masse*, and clasping her two hands upon her bosom, 'who d'ye think's come back again? who d'ye think's within a mile of this house at this blessed minute? who d'ye think's been disguised and fishing by Brampton mill this very day? and the sorrel knew him though nobody else didn't, and all the troubles that was clean gone and over is to begin again; and who d'ye think it is, Mistress Grace, that might be walking up the stairs and into this very room even now?'

Startling as was the possibility, Grace seemed to contemplate it with wondrous calmness. Though she was blushing deeply, she exhibited no signs of surprise or alarm as she asked very quietly, 'Who?'

'Why, who but Major Humphrey?' replied Faith, triumphantly. 'Now, don't ye take on, Mistress Grace, my sweet young lady, don't you go for to frighten yourself, there's a dear! It's Dymocke that saw him; and the sergeant's a discreet man, you know, and as true as steel. And he says, the Major looked so worn and thin, and as pale as a ghost. But the horse he knew him, bless his sorrel skin; and the sergeant says he wouldn't have discovered the Major himself, if it hadn't been for the dumb animal. It's as much as his life's worth to be here, Mistress Grace, so the sergeant says; and the Roundheads—that's the rebels, as we was used to call them—the Parliamentarians (wise and godly men, too, some of them) would shoot him to death as soon as ever they set eyes on him; but don't you worrit and fret yourself, Mistress Grace, don't ye now!'

Grace received the intelligence with surprising composure. 'He *was* looking dreadfully altered,' she muttered to herself; but she only told Faith that if this very improbable story were really true, it was incumbent on the possessor of so deadly a secret to bridle her tongue, and not allow the slightest hint to escape that might be the means of throwing Bosville into the hands of his enemies; and she went down to supper with an unfaltering step and an air of outward composure that astonished, and even somewhat displeased, her susceptible handmaiden.

'She can't care for him one morsel,' said Faith, as she folded up her lady's things, and put them carefully away. The girl had no idea of the power possessed by some natures to 'suffer and be still.' In a parallel case she would have cried her own eyes out, she thought, and it would have done her good. She did not know, and would not have appreciated, the 'enduring faculty' that seems most fully developed in the two extreme races of the patrician and the savage, and esteemed herself doubtless happier without the pride that dries our tears, 'tis true, but dries them much in the same way that the red-hot searing-iron scorches up and stanches the stream from a gaping wound. Grace possessed her share of this well-born quality, for all her gentle manner and her quiet voice; nor did she ever draw more largely upon her stores of

self-command than while she sat opposite Sir Giles at supper that
evening, and filled out his 'dish of claret' again and again with
her own pretty hands. She thought the meal never would be
over. This stanch old Cavalier was in unusual spirits with the
prospect of his Majesty's visit, and laughed and joked with his
thoughtful 'Gracey' so perseveringly as almost to drive her wild.
She absolutely *thirsted* for solitude, and the enjoyment, if such
it could be called, of her own thoughts. But supper was over at
last. Sir Giles, leaning back in his high carved chair, sank to his
usual slumber, and Grace was free to come and go unnoticed, for
Lord Vaux was still on a sick bed, and Mary Cave, pleading
fatigue and indisposition, had remained in her own chamber.

Now, it is a singular fact, that although neither of the ladies
who occupied Lord Vaux's roomy old coach had immediately
recognised the disguised fisherman at Brampton mill, a certain
instinctive consciousness of his identity had come upon each of
them at the same instant; and it is no less singular that neither
of them should have offered the slightest hint of her suspicions to
her companion ; and that although the manner of each was more
affectionate than usual, by a sort of tacit understanding they
should have avoided one another's society for the rest of the day.

Thus it came to pass that Mary, who never used to be tired,
went to her own room immediately she returned from Holmby,
and begged she might not be disturbed even by the 'burnt posset,' which was our ancestors' jolly substitute for a 'cup of tea.'

It may seem strange that Mistress Cave should have been so
ignorant of Bosville's movements, and that she of all women
should have been so startled by his unexpected appearance in
Northamptonshire ; but truth to tell, Mary had long ceased to
know his intentions, or to be consulted as of old about his every
action. Though he had written to her frequently, all correspondence from the Queen's Court was so carefully watched, that his
letters never reached their destination ; and the same cause had
intercepted an epistle which, after a long interval of suspense,
proud Mary Cave had brought herself to write to the man whose
absence she was astonished to find she bore so impatiently. It
was galling, doubtless, but it was none the less true. When she
parted from him at Exeter, there was indeed every probability
that in those troublous times they might never meet again on
earth ; and this separation she could not but feel was a most unpleasant contingency. Nay, it was actually painful, and many a
secret tear it cost her. This it was which had made her so cold
and haughty till he actually bid her farewell ; and how often since

had she wished, till her heart ached, that she could live those few days over again! As month after month passed on without further tidings, she seemed to feel her loss more and more. Self-reproach, curiosity, and pique combined to make her think and ponder on the absent one, whose merits, both of mind and body, seemed to come out so vividly now that it was possible they belonged to *her* no longer. Mary was no dull observer of human nature, and she knew well that if she really cared to retain his affections, she had been playing a somewhat dangerous game. Had he been employed in the alarms and excitement of warfare, subjected day by day to the ennobling influence of danger, his higher and better feelings kept awake by the inspiring stimulus of military glory, and the deepest, truest affections of his heart, enhanced as they always are by the daily habit of looking death in the face, she felt she would have reigned in that heart more imperiously than ever; but the case was quite different now. He was living in the atmosphere of a pleasure-loving and profligate Court. He was subjected to just so much excitement and dissipation as would serve to distract his thoughts, just so much interesting employment as would forbid his mind from dwelling continuously upon any single topic. From his position he was sure to be courted by the great, and with his person to be welcomed by the fair. To do him justice, he had ever shown himself sufficiently callous to the latter temptation, and yet—— Mary remembered the wit and the attractions of those French ladies amongst whom she had spent her youth; she even caught herself recalling his admiration of one or two of her own accomplishments derived from that source. He might find others fairer than she was now—kinder than she had ever been; some gentle heart would be sure to love him dearly, and the very intensity of its affection would win his in return; and then indeed he would be lost to her altogether; *she would rather he was lying dead and buried yonder on Naseby field!* And yet, no! no!—anything were better than that. Mary was startled at the bitterness and the strength of her own passions. It was frightful! it was humiliating! it was unwomanly! to feel like this. Was she weaker as she grew older, that she could thus confess to herself so deep an interest in one who might perhaps already have forgotten her? She had not loved Falkland so—that was a pure, lofty, and ennobling sentiment—there was much more of the earthly element in this strange, wild fascination. Perhaps it was none the less dear, none the less dangerous on that account.

So she resolved that whatever cause had brought him back at

last (for too surely she felt the disguised fisherman was no other than Bosville), *she* at least would appear to be ignorant and careless of his movements. Till his long silence was explained, of course he could be nothing to her; and even then, if people could forget for two whole years, *other* people could forget altogether. Yes, it would be far better so. He must be changed indeed not to have spoken to her that very day by the water side. Then she remembered what Grace had said about the knot of pink ribbon; and womanlike, after judging him so harshly, her heart smote her for her unkindness, and she wept.

The sun was sinking below the horizon when Grace stepped out upon the terrace at Boughton, and wrapping a scarf around her shoulders, paced slowly away for a stroll in the cool atmosphere and refreshing breezes of the park. It was delicious to get into the pure evening air after the hot drive and the crowded court, and Sir Giles's interminable supper; to be alone once more under God's heaven, and able to think undisturbed. The deer were already couching for the night amongst the fern, the rooks had gone home hours ago, but a solitary and belated heron, high up in the calm sky, was winging his soft, silent way towards the flush of sunset which crimsoned all the west. It was the hour of peace and repose, when nature subsides to a dreamy stillness ere she sinks to her majestic sleep, when the ox lies down in his pasture, and the wild bird is hushed on the bough, when all is at rest on earth save only the restless human heart, which will never know peace but in the grave.

Grace threaded the stems of the tall old trees, her foot falling lightly upon the mossy sward, her white figure glancing ghostlike in and out the dusky avenues, her fair brow, from which she put back the masses of hair with both hands, cooling in the evening breeze.

What did she here? She scarce knew herself why she had sought this woodland solitude—why she had been so restless, so impatient, so dissatisfied with everything and everybody, so longing to be alone. Deeply she pondered on Faith's narrative, though indeed she had guessed the truth long before her handmaiden's confidences. Much she wondered what *he* was doing here—whence had he come?—when was he going away?—what was this political mystery in which foolish Faith believed so implicitly? Why was he in Northamptonshire at all? Was there a chance of his wandering here to-night to visit his old haunts?—and if he should, what was that to her? The girl's cheek flushed, though she was alone, with mingled pain and pride as she reflected that she had given her heart unasked. No! not quite given it, but suffered it to wander sadly out of her own control; and that though she was better now, there *had* been a time when she cared for him a great deal more than was good for her. Well, it was over, and yet she *should* like to see him once again, she confessed, if it were only to wish him 'good-bye.' Were there fairies still on earth? Could it be possible her wish was granted? There he was!

Grace's heart beat violently, and her breath came and went very quick as the dark figure of a man emerged from the shade of an old oak under which he had been standing, not ten paces from her. She almost repented of her wish, that seemed to have been accorded so readily. Poor Grace! there was no occasion for penitence; ere he had made three strides towards her she had recognised him; and it was with a voice in which disappointment struggled with unfeigned surprise, that she exclaimed, ' Captain Effingham ! '

He doffed his hat, and begged her, with the old manly courtesy she remembered so well, not to be alarmed. ' His duty,' he said, ' had brought him into the neighbourhood, and he could not resist the temptation of visiting the haunts of those who had once been so kind to him before these unhappy troubles had turned his best friends to strangers, if not to enemies.' His voice shook as he spoke, and Grace could not forbear extending her hand to him; as she touched his it was like ice, and he trembled, that iron soldier, as if he was cold.

Darkness was coming on apace, yet even in the fading light Grace could not but see how hardly Time had dealt with her old admirer—an admirer of whom, although undeclared, her womanly instinct had been long ago conscious as a very devoted and a very worthy one.

George's whole countenance had deepened into the marked lines and grave expression of middle age. The hair and beard, once so raven black, were now grizzled; and although the tall strong form was square and erect as ever, its gestures had lost the buoyant elasticity of youth, and had acquired the slow and somewhat listless air of those who have outlived their prime.

He seemed to have got something to communicate, yet he walked by her side without uttering another syllable. Grace looked down at the ground, and could not mark the sidelong gaze of deep, melancholy tenderness with which he regarded her beautiful profile and shapely form. The silence became very embarrassing; after the second turn she began to get quite frightened.

He spoke at last as it seemed with a mighty effort, and in a. low, choking voice.

'You are surprised to see me, Mistress Grace, and with reason; perhaps I am guilty of presumption in even entering your kins-man's domain. Well, it is for the last time. Forgive me if I have startled you, or intruded on your solitude. May I speak to you for five minutes? I will not detain you long. Believe me, I never expected to see *you* here to-night.'

'Then why on earth did you come?' was Grace's very natural reflection, but she only bowed and faltered out a few words expressive of her willingness to hear all he had got to say.

'I only arrived to-day at Northampton,' he proceeded, calming as he went on; 'I have been appointed to the command of a division of the army, to watch this district, and preserve the peace of his Majesty and his Parliament. We have reason to believe that a conspiracy is being organized to plunge this country once more in civil war. Suspicious persons are about.'

Grace glanced sharply at him.

'My troopers are even now scouring the country to arrest a messenger from France, of whom I have received information. It is sad work; my duty will compel me to hang him to the nearest tree.'

It was fortunate that the failing light prevented his seeing how pale she had turned.

'Believe me, Mistress Grace, it is hopeless for the " Malignants " to stir up civil war again. His Majesty's Parliament will act for the safety of his Majesty's person, and it will be my duty, with the large force I command, to escort him in security to the neigh-bourhood of London.'

Grace listened attentively—the little Royalist was half fright-ened, and half indignant at the calm tone of conscious power in which the successful soldier of the Parliament announced his intentions.

Ellingham paused, as if to gather courage, then proceeded, speaking very rapidly, and looking studiously away from the person he addressed.

'You have never known, Mistress Grace—God forbid you ever should know—such suffering and such anxiety as I have expe-rienced now for many long months. I did not come here to-night to tell you this. I did not come here expecting to see you at all. It was weak, I grant you, and unmanly; but I could not resist the temptation of wandering near your home once again, of watching the house in which you were, and perhaps looking on the light that shone from your window. I am no love-sick swain, Mistress Grace,' he added smiling bitterly, 'with my rough soldier's manners and my gray hair; but I plead guilty to this one infatuation, and you may despise me for it if you will. Well! as I have met you to-night I will tell you all—listen. Ever since I have known you, I have loved you—God help me!—better than my own soul. You will never know, Grace, you *shall* never know, how truly, how dearly, how worse than madly—I feel it is hopeless—I feel it is no use—that I can never be more to you than the successful rebel, the enemy that is only *not* hated because you are too gentle and kind to hate any human being. Many a weary day have I longed to tell you this, and so to bid you farewell, and see you never more. It is over now, and I am happier for the confession. God bless you, Grace! If you *could* have cared for me I should have been worthy of you—it cannot be—I shall never forget you—farewell!'

He raised her hand, pressed it once to his lips, and ere she had recovered from her astonishment he was gone.

Grace looked wildly around her, as one who wakes from a dream. It seemed like a dream indeed, but she still heard the tramp of his step as he walked away in the calm night, and listening for a few minutes after he was gone, distinguished the clatter of a horse's hoofs on the hard road leading to Northampton. Grace was utterly bewildered and confused. There was something not unpleasant in the sensation too. Long ago, though she was a good deal afraid of it, she had hugely admired that stern enthusiastic nature, but the image of another had prevented the impression ripening into any feeling deeper than interest and esteem. And now to discover for a certainty that she had subjugated that strong, brave heart, that the rebel warrior had been worshipping her in secret all those long months, in the midst of his dangers and his victories, that her influence had softened his rigour to many a Royalist, and that he had saved her own dear old father at Naseby for *her* sake,—all this was anything but disagreeable to that innate love of dominion which exists in the gentlest of her sex, and such a conquest as that of the famous Parliamentary general (for to that rank George had speedily risen) was one that any woman might be proud of, and was indeed a soothing salve to her heart, wounded and mortified by the neglect of another. But then the danger to that other smote her with a chill and sickening apprehension. It could be none but Bosville that had been seen and suspected by the keen-eyed Parliamentarians. He might be a prisoner even now, and she shuddered as she reflected on that

S

ghastly observation of Effingham's about the nearest tree. ·Word by word she recalled his conversation, and the design upon the King's liberty, which she had somewhat overlooked in the contemplation of more personal topics, assumed a frightful importance as she remembered that she was the depositary of this important intelligence. What ought she to do? Though Effingham had trusted her, he had extorted no promise of secresy, and as she had always been taught besides that her first duty was towards her Sovereign, there was no time for consideration. What was to be done? The King was in danger—Bosville was in danger—and she alone had the knowledge, though without the power of prevention. What was she to do? What *could* she do? She was completely at her wits' end!

In this predicament Grace's proceedings were characteristic, if not conclusive; she first of all began to cry, and then resolved upon consulting Mary, and making a 'clean breast of it,' which she felt would be an inexpressible relief. With this object, she returned at once to the house, and hurried without delay to her friend's chamber.

That lady's indisposition had apparently not been severe enough to cause her to go to bed. On the contrary, she was sitting up, still completely dressed, and with a wakeful, not to say harassed, expression on her countenance, which precluded all idea of sleep for many hours to come. She welcomed Grace with some little astonishment, 'her headache was better, and it was kind of dear Gracey to come and inquire after her—she was just going to bed—she had been sitting up writing,' she said.

There was a sheet of paper on the table, only it was blank.

Grace flung herself into her arms, and had 'the cry' fairly out, which had been checked whilst she ran into the house.

'And the thing must be told,' sobbed the agitated girl, when she had detailed her unexpected meeting with Effingham, and its startling results; 'and father mustn't know it, or it will all be worse than ever; he'll be arming the servants and the few tenants that have got a horse left, and all the horrors will have to begin again, and he'll be killed some day, Mary, I know he will. What shall I do? What *shall* I do?'

Mary's courage always rose in a difficulty; her brow cleared now, and her head went up.

'He must not be told a word, and the King must! Leave that to me, Gracey.'

Grace looked unspeakably comforted for a moment, but the tide of her troubles surged in again irresistibly, as she thought of the suspected fisherman and the noose at the nearest tree.

'But Bosville, Mary—Bosville—think of him, close by here, and those savages hunting for him and thirsting for his blood. Oh ! Mary, I *must* save him, and I *will*. What can be done? advise me, Mary—advise me. If a hair of his head is hurt, I shall never sleep in peace again.'

'I wish we had stopped and spoken to him to-day,' observed Mary, abstractedly ; 'and yet it might only have compromised him, and done no good.'

Grace looked up sharply through her tears. 'Did you know it was Bosville, Mary, in that disguise ? So did I ! '

Notwithstanding Mistress Cave's self-command, a shadow as of great pain passed over her countenance. It faded, nevertheless, as quickly as it came. She took Grace's hand in her own, and looked quietly and sadly in the girl's weeping face.

'Do you love him, Gracey ? ' she said, very gently, and with a sickly sort of smile.

Grace's only answer was to hide her face between her hands and sob as if her heart would break.

Till she had sobbed herself to sleep in her chamber, her friend never left her. It was midnight ere she returned to her own room, and dotted the blank sheet of paper with a few short words in cipher. When this was done, Mary leaned her head upon her hand, and pondered long and earnestly.

We have all read of the pearl of great price in the holy parable, and how, when the seeker had found it, he went and sold all that he had, and bought it and made it his own. Lightly he thought of friends, and fame, and fortune, compared to the treasure of his heart. We have often imagined the weary look of utter desolation which would have overspread his features, could he have seen that pearl shivered into fragments, the one essential object of his life existent no more—the treasure destroyed, and with it the heart also. Such a look was on Mary's pale face as she sat by her bedside watching for the first flush of the summer dawn.

CHAPTER XXIX.

'THE FALCON GENTLE.'

THE sun shone bright on the level terraces of Holmby House— huge stone vases grotesquely carved and loaded with garden-flowers studded the shaven lawns and green slopes that adorned the southern front of the palace—here and there a close-clipped yew or stunted juniper threw its black shadow across the sward, and broke in some measure the uniformity of those long formal alleys in which our forefathers took such pleasure. Half-way down the hill, through the interstices of their quivering screen of leaves, the fishponds gleamed like burnished gold in the morning light; and far below the sunny vale, broken by clumps of forest timber, and dotted with sheep and oxen, stretched away till it lost itself in the dense woodlands of Althorpe-park.

Two figures paced the long terrace that immediately fronted the mansion. To and fro they walked with rapid strides, nor paused to contemplate the beauties of the distant landscape, nor the stately magnificence of the royal palace—shafted, mullioned, and pinnacled like a stronghold of romance. It was Charles and his attendant, the Earl of Pembroke, taking their morning exercise, which the methodical King considered indispensable to his health, and which was sufficiently harassing to the old and enfeebled frame of the noble commissioner. Charles, like his son, was a rapid and vigorous pedestrian. His bodily powers were wonderfully unsusceptible to fatigue; and perhaps the concentrated irritation awakened by a life of continuous surveillance and restraint may have found vent in thus fiercely pacing like some wild animal the area of his cage. Poor old Lord Pembroke, on whom the duty of a state-gaoler to his Sovereign had been thrust, sorely against his will, and for whom ' a good white pillow for that good white head ' had been more appropriate than either steel headpiece or gilded coronet, had no such incentive to exertion, and halted breathlessly after the King, with a ludicrous mixture of deference and dismay, looking wistfully at the stone dial which stood midway in their course every time they passed it, and ardently longing for the time of his dismissal from this the most fatiguing of all his unwelcome duties.

The King, whose lungs, like his limbs, were little affected by his accustomed exercise, strode manfully on, talking, as was his wont, upon grave and weighty subjects, and anon waiting with gentle patience for the answers of the lagging courtier. His Majesty was this morning in a more than usually moralizing mood.

' Look yonder, my Lord Earl,' said he, pointing to the beauteous scene around him—the smiling valley, the trim pleasure-grounds, the sparkling waters, with the lazy pike splashing at intervals to the surface, and the blossoms showering pink and white in the soft summer breeze. ' Look yonder, and see how the sun penetrates every nook and cranny of the copsewood, even as it floods

the open meadows in its golden glory. That sunlight is everywhere, my lord, in the lowest depths of the castle-vaults, as on
yon bright pinnacle, around which the noisy daws are wheeling
and chattering even now. 'Tis that sunlight which offers day,
dim though it be, to the captive in the dungeon, even as it bathes
in its lustre the eagle on the cliff. Is there no moral in this, my
lord? Is there no connexion, think you, between the rays which
give warmth to the body, and the inner light which gives life to
the soul?'

Lord Pembroke was out of breath, and a little deaf into the
bargain. 'Very true, your Majesty,' he assented, having caught
just enough of the King's discourse to be aware that it related in
some measure to the weather. 'Very true, as your Majesty says,
we shall have rain anon!' And the old Earl looked up at the
skies, over which a light cloud or two were passing, with a sidelong glance, like some weatherwise old raven, devoutly hoping
that a shower might put an end at once to the promenade and the
conversation.

'Ay! it is even so,' proceeded the King, apparently answering
his own thoughts, rather than the inconsequent remark of his
attendant. 'There is indeed a cloud athwart the sun, and yet he
is shining as brightly behind it upon the rest of the universe, as
though there were no veil interposed between our petty selves and
his majestic light. And shall we murmur because the dark hour
cometh and we must grope in our blindness awhile, and mayhap
wander from the path, and stumble and bruise our feet, till the
day breaks in its glory once more? Oh man! man! though
thou art shrinking and shivering in the storm, the sun shines still
the same in its warmth and dazzling light; though thou art
cowering in adversity, God is everywhere alike in wisdom, power,
and goodness.'

As the King spoke, he turned and paced the length of the
terrace once more. The clouds passed on, and the day was bright
as ever. It seemed a good omen; and as the unhappy are prone
to be superstitious, it was accepted as such by the meditative
monarch. In silence he walked on, deeply engrossed with many
a sad and solemn subject. His absent Queen, from whom he had
been long expecting tidings, whom he still loved with the undemonstrative warmth of his deep and tender nature—his ruined
party and proscribed adherents—his lost Crown, for he could
scarce now consider himself a Sovereign—his imperilled life, for
already had he suspected the intentions of the Parliament, and
resolved to oppose them if necessary, even to the death—lastly,

his trust in God, which, weak, imprudent, injudicious as he may
have been, never deserted Charles Stuart even in the last extremity—which never yet failed any man who relied upon it in
his need, from the King on the throne to the convict in the
dungeon.

But the Monarch's walk was doomed to be interrupted, and
Lord Pembroke's penance brought to an earlier close than usual,
by a circumstance the origin of which we must take leave to
retrograde a few hours to explain, affecting as it does the proceedings of a fair lady, who, in all matters of difficulty or danger, was
accustomed to depend on no energies and consult no will but her
own.

We left Mary Cave in her chamber at Boughton, watching
wearily for the dawn, which came at length, as it comes alike to
the bride, blushing welcome to her wedding-morn, and to the pale
criminal, shrinking from the sunlight that he will never see more
—which will come alike over and over again to our children and
to our children's children, when we are dead and forgotten, but
which shall at last be extinguished too, or rather swallowed up
in the Eternal Day, when Darkness, Sin, and Sorrow shall be
destroyed for evermore.

Pale and resolute, Mary made a careful toilet with the first
streaks of day. Elaborately she arranged every fold of her riding-
gear, and with far more pains than common pinned up and secured
the long tresses of her rich brown hair. Usually they were
accustomed to escape from their fastenings, and wave and float
about her when disordered by a gallop in provokingly attractive profusion; but on this occasion they were so disposed that
nothing but intentional violence was likely to disturb their shining
masses. Stealthily she left her apartment, and without rousing
the household sought the servants' offices—no difficult task, as
bolts and bars in those simple times were usually left unfastened,
except in the actual presence of some recognised danger; and
although such an old-fashioned manor-house as that of Boughton
might be fortified securely against an armed force, it was by no
means so impregnable to a single thief who should simply use the
precaution of taking off his shoes. Not a single domestic did
Mary meet, as she took her well-known way towards the stables;
and even Bayard's loud neigh of recognition, echoed as it was by
the delighted sorrel, failed to disturb the slumbers of Dymocke
and his satellites. With her own fair hands Mary saddled and
bridled her favourite, hurting her delicate fingers against the
straps and buckles of his appointments. With her own fair hands

she jessed and hooded 'Dewdrop,' and took her from her perch
in the falconer's mews, without leave asked of that still unconscious functionary; and thus dressed and mounted, with foot in
stirrup and hawk on hand, Mary emerged through Boughton-
park like some female knight-errant, and took her well-known
way to Brampton-ford.

We are all more or less self-deceivers, and this lady was no
exception to the rule of humanity. Secresy was no doubt
judicious on such an expedition as that which she had now resolved to take in hand; yet it is probable that Dymocke at least
might have been trusted so far as to saddle her horse and hood
her falcon; but something in Mary's heart bid her feel shame
that any one, even a servant, should know whither she was
bound; and although other and unacknowledged motives besides
the obvious duty of warning Charles of his danger prompted her
to take so decided a step, she easily persuaded herself that zeal
for the King's safety, and regard for his person, made it impera-
tive on her to keep religiously secret the interview she proposed
extorting from his Majesty; and that in so delicate and dangerous
a business she ought to confide in no one but herself.

So she rode gently on towards Brampton-ford, Bayard stepping
lightly and proudly over the spangled sward, and 'Dewdrop'
shaking her bells merrily under the inspiriting influence of the
morning air. A few short years ago she would have urged her
horse into a gallop in the sheer exuberance of her spirits; nay,
till within the last twenty-four hours, she would have paced along
at least with head erect, and eye kindling to the beauties of the
scene; but a change had come over her bearing, and her brow
wore a look of depression and sadness, her figure stooped listlessly
on her saddle; her whole exterior denoted that weary state of
dejection which overcomes the player in the great game of life,
who has thrown the last stake—and lost!

As she neared the river, she looked anxiously and furtively
around, peering behind every tree and hawthorn that studded the
level surface of the meadow. In vain: no fisherman disturbed
the quiet waters of the Nene—no solitary figure trampled the
long grass, wet with the dews of morning. There was no chance
of a recognition—an explanation. Perhaps he avoided it on purpose—perhaps he felt aggrieved and wounded at her long silence
—perhaps he had forgotten her altogether. Two years was a long
time. Men were proverbially inconstant. Besides, had she not
resolved in her own heart that this folly should be terminated
at once and for ever? Yes, it was providential he was not there.

It was far better—their meeting would have been painful and awkward for both. She could not be sufficiently thankful that she had been spared the trial. All the time she would have given her right arm to see him just once again.

With a deep sigh she roused Bayard into a gallop, and the good steed, nothing loth, stretched away up the hill with the long, regular stride that is indeed the true ' poetry of motion.' A form couching low behind a clump of alders watched her till she was out of sight, and a shabbily-dressed fisherman, with sad brow and heavy heart, then resumed his occupation of angling in the Nene with the same studious pertinacity that he had displayed in that pursuit for the last two days.

It would have required indeed all the instincts of a loving heart, such as the sorrel, in common with his generous equine brethren, undoubtedly possessed, to recognise in the wan, travel-stained angler the comely exterior of Humphrey Bosville. The drooping moustaches had been closely shaved, the long lovelocks shorn off by the temples to admit of the short flaxen wig which replaced the young Cavalier's dark, silky hair. His worn-out beaver too, slouched down over his eyes, and his rusty jerkin, with its high collar devoid of linen, completed the metamorphosis, while the small feet were encased in huge, shapeless wading boots, and the hands, usually so white and well kept, were now em-browned and stained by the influence of exposure and hard usage. His disguise, he flattered himself, was perfect, and he was not a little proud of the skill by which he had escaped suspicion in the port at which he landed, and deceived even the wary soldiers of the Parliament as to his real character, at several military posts which they occupied, and where he had been examined. Humphrey Bos-ville, as we know, had passed his parole never again to bear arms against the Parliament; but his word of honour, he conceived, did not prohibit him from being the prime agent in every hazard-ous scheme organised by the Royal Party at that intriguing time. True to his faith, he missed no opportunity of risking life in the service of his Sovereign, and he was even now waiting in the heart of an enemy's country to deliver an important letter from the Queen to her wretched and imprisoned husband.

For this cause he prowled stealthily about the river Nene, wait-ing for the chance of Charles's crossing the bridge in some of his riding expeditions, and the sport of fishing in which he seemed to be engaged enabled him to remain in the same spot for several hours, unsuspected of aught save a characteristic devotion to that most patience-wearing of amusements.

Though he saw his ladye-love ride by alone in the early morning, a feeling of duty, still paramount in his soldier nature, prevented his discovering himself even to her. So he thought and persuaded himself there was no leaven of pique, no sense of irritation at long and unmerited neglect, embittering the kindly impulses of his honest heart. He watched her receding form with aching eyes. 'Ay,' thought poor Humphrey, all his long-cherished love welling up in that deep tide of 'bitter waters' which is so near akin to hate, 'ride on as you used to do in your beauty and your heartlessness, as you *would* do without drawing rein or turning aside, though my body were beneath your horse's feet. What care you that you have taken from me all that makes life hopeful and happy, and left me instead darkness where there should be light, and listless despair where there should be courage, and energy, and trust? I gave you all, proud, heartless Mary, little enough it may be, and valueless to you, but still *my all*, and what have I reaped in exchange? A fevered worn-out frame, that can only rest when prostrated by fatigue, a tortured spirit that never knows a respite save in the pressure of immediate and imminent danger. Well, it will soon be over now. This last stroke will probably finish my career, and there will be repose at any rate in the grave. I will be true to the last. *Loyalty before all.* You shall hear of him when it is too late, but of his own free will, proud, heartless woman, he will never look upon your face again!'

Our friend was very much hurt, and quite capable of acting as he imagined. These lovers' quarrels, you see, though the wise rate them at their proper value, are sufficiently painful to the poor fools immediately concerned, and Major Bosville resumed his sport, not the least in the frame of mind recommended by old Izaak Walton to the disciple who goes a-fishing.

Meanwhile Mary Cave stretched on at Bayard's long easy gallop till she came in view of the spires and chimneys of Holmby House towering into the summer sky, when, with a gleam of satisfaction such as she had not yet displayed kindling on her beautiful face, she drew rein, and prepared for certain active operations, which she had been meditating as she came along.

Taking a circuit of the Palace, and entering the park at its westernmost gate, she loosed Dewdrop's jesses, and without un-hooding her, flung the falcon aloft into the air. A soft west wind was blowing at the time, and the bird, according to the nature of its kind, finding itself free from restraint, but at the same time deprived of sight, opened its broad wings to the breeze and soared

away towards the pleasure-grounds of the Palace, in which
Charles and the Earl of Pembroke were taking their accustomed
exercise.

Mary was no bad judge of falconry, and the very catastrophe
she anticipated happened exactly as she intended. The hawk,
sailing gallantly down the wind, struck heavily against the
branches of a tall elm that intervened, and fell lifeless on the
sward almost at the King's feet. Mary at the same time urging
Bayard to his speed, came scouring rapidly down the park as
though in search of her lost favourite, and apparently unconscious
of the presence of royalty or the proximity of a palace, put her
horse's head straight for the sunken fence which divided the
lawns from the park. Bayard pointed his small ears and cleared
it at a bound, his mistress reining short up after performing this
feat, and dismounting to bend over the body of her dead falcon
with every appearance of acute and pre-occupied distress.

The King and Lord Pembroke looked at each other in mute
astonishment. Such an apparition was indeed an unusual variety
in those tame morning walks, and the drooping figure of the lady,
the dead bird, and the roused, excited horse, would have made a
fit group for the sculptor or the painter.

'Gallantly ridden, fair dame!' said the King, at length breaking the silence, and discovering himself to the confused equestrian.
'Although this is a somewhat sudden and unceremonious intrusion on our privacy, we are constrained to forgive it, in consideration of the boldness of the feat, and the heavy nature of your loss.
Your falcon, I fear, is quite dead. Ha!' added the monarch,
with a start of recognition; 'by my faith it is Mistress Mary
Cave! You are not here for nothing,' he proceeded, becoming
visibly pale, and speaking in an agitated tone; 'are there tidings
of the Queen?'

Mary was no contemptible actress; acting is, indeed, an accomplishment that seems to come naturally to most women. She
now counterfeited such violent confusion and alarm at the breach of
etiquette into which her thoughtlessness had hurried her, that the old
Earl of Pembroke began to make excuses for her impetuosity, and
whilst Mary, affecting extreme faintness, only murmured 'water,
water,' the old courtier kept urging upon the King that 'the lady
was probably ignorant of court forms—that she did not know she
was so near the palace—that her horse was running away with
her,' and such other incongruous excuses as his breathless state
admitted of his enumerating.

The King lost patience at last.

'Don't stand prating there, man,' said he, pointing to Mary, who seemed indeed to be at the last gasp; 'go and fetch the lady some water—can you not see she will faint in two minutes?'

And while the old Earl hobbled off in quest of the reviving element, Charles raised Mary from her knees, and repeated, in a voice trembling with alarm, his previous question, 'Are there tidings from the Queen?'

'No, my liege,' replied Mary, whose faintness quitted her with extraordinary rapidity as soon as the Earl was out of ear-shot. 'This business concerns yourself. There is a plot to carry off your Majesty's person, there is a plot to lead you to London a prisoner, this very day. I only discovered it at midnight. I had no means of communicating unwatched with my Sovereign, and I took this unceremonious method of intruding on his privacy. Forgive me, my liege, I did not even know that I should be so fortunate as to see you for an instant alone; had you been accompanied by more than one attendant, I must have taken some other means of placing this packet in your hands.'

As Mary spoke she unbound the masses of her shining hair, and taking a paper from its folds, presented it to the King, falling once more upon her knees, and kissing the royal hand extended to her with devoted loyalty. 'I have here communicated to your Majesty in cipher all I have learned about the plot. I might have been searched had I been compelled to demand an interview, and I knew no better method of concealing my packet than this. Oh, my liege! my liege! confide in me, the most devoted of your subjects. It is never too late to play a bold stroke; resist this measure with the sword—say but the word, lift but your royal hand, and I will engage to raise the country in sufficient force to bring your Majesty safe off, if I, Mary Cave, have to ride at their head!'

The King looked down at the beautiful figure kneeling there before him, her cheek flushed, her eyes bright with enthusiasm, her long soft hair showering over her neck and shoulders, her horse's bridle clasped in one small gloved hand, whilst the other held his own, which she had just pressed fervently to her lips; an impersonation of loyalty, self-abandonment, and unavailing heroism, of all the nobler and purer qualities which had been wasted so fruitlessly in the Royal cause; and a sad smile stole over his countenance, whilst the tears stood in his deep, melancholy eyes, as he looked from the animated living figure, to the dead falcon that completed the group.

'Enough blood has been shed,' said he; 'enough losses sustained by the Cavaliers of England in my quarrel. Charles Stuart will never again kindle the torch of war—no, not to save his crown—not to save his head! Nevertheless, kind Mistress Mary, forewarned is forearmed, and your Sovereign offers you his heartfelt thanks, 'tis all he has now to give, for your prompt resolution and your unswerving loyalty. Would that it had cost you no more than your falcon—would that I could replace your favourite with a bird from my own royal mews. Alas! I am a King now only in name—I believe I have but one faithful subject left, and that is Mistress Mary Cave!'

As the King spoke, Lord Pembroke returned with the water, and Mary, with many acknowledgments of his Majesty's condescension, and many apologies and excuses, mingled with regrets for the loss of her falcon, remounted her horse, and leaving the pleasure-grounds by a private gate or postern of which the Earl had the key, returned to Boughton by the way she had come, pondering in her own mind on the success of her enterprise and the impending calamities that seemed gathering in to crush the unhappy King.

Much to the relief of the aged nobleman, this adventure closed the royal promenade for that morning, and Charles, giving orders for his attendants to be in readiness after dinner, as it was his intention to ride on horseback and indulge himself in a game of bowls at Lord Vaux's house at Boughton—an intention which may perhaps have accounted for his abrupt dismissal of Mary Cave—retired to the privacy of his closet, there to deliberate, not on the stormy elements of his political future, not on the warning he had just received, and the best means of averting an imprisonment which now indeed threatened to be no longer merely a matter of form; not on the increasing power of his sagacious enemy, who was even then taking his wary, uncompromising measures for his downfall, and whose mighty will was to that of the feeble Charles as his long cut-and-thrust broadsword to the walking rapier of a courtier; not of Cromwell's ambition and his own incompetency; not of his empty throne and his imperilled head—but of an abstruse dispute on casuistical divinity and the unfinished tag of a Latin verse!

Truly in weaker natures constant adversity seems to have the effect of blunting the faculties and lowering the whole mental organisation of the man. The metal must be iron in the first instance, or the blast of the furnace will never temper it into steel.

CHAPTER XXX.

'A RIDE ACROSS A COUNTRY.'

ON the day during which the events recorded in our last chapter were taking place, the good sorrel horse, with the instinctive sagacity peculiar to his kind, must have been aware that some trial of his mettle was imminently impending. Never before in the whole course of his experience had the same care been bestowed on his feeding, watering, and other preparations for an appointed task; never before had Dymocke so minutely examined the soundness of every strap and buckle of his appointments, inspected so rigidly the state of his shoes, or fitted the bit in his mouth, and the links of his curb-chain with such judicious delicacy. Horses are keenly alive to all premonitory symptoms of activity, and the sorrel's kindling eye and dilated nostril showed that he was prepared to sustain his part, whatever it might be, in the impending catastrophe. Dymocke, too, had discarded the warlike air and pompous bearing which he usually affected; he had considerably shortened his customary morning draught, and as he was well known to be a man of few words and an austere demeanour, none of his fellow-servants dared take upon themselves to question him when he left the stable-yard in a groom's ordinary undress, and rode the sorrel carefully out as it were for an airing.

'Patrolling!' quoth Dymocke to himself, as he emerged from the park-gates, and espied at no great distance two well-mounted dragoons pacing along the crest of a rising ground, and apparently keeping vigilant watch over the valley of the Nene below. 'A picket!' he added with a grim leer, and a pat on his horse's neck, as the sun glinted back from a dozen of carbines and the same number of steel breastplates drawn up near a clump of trees, where the officer in command flattered himself he was completely hidden from observation. 'Well, they've no call to say nothing to me,' was his concluding remark as he jogged quietly down towards the river-side, affecting as much as possible the air and manner of a groom training a horse about to run for some valuable stake—a process sure to meet with the sympathies of Englishmen, whatever might be their class and creed, and one which even the most rigid Presbyterian would be unwilling to embarrass or interrupt.

It was a good stake, too, that the sorrel was about to run for—

a stake of Life and Death, a match against Time, with the course marked out by Chance, and the winning-post placed by Destiny. The steed was sound and trim, his condition excellent, his blood irreproachable ; to use the language of Newmarket, would he *stay the distance and get home* ?

There was a marshy meadow by the river's brink, which even at this dry season of the year was moist and cool, grateful to the sensations of horse and rider. As the sorrel approached it, he snorted once or twice, erected his ears, and neighed long and loudly. The neigh was answered in more directions than one, for dragoons were patrolling the road in pairs, and no less than two outposts of cavalry were distinctly visible. It seemed as though the war had broken out afresh. Dymocke rode quietly round and round the meadow, apparently attending solely to his horse, and an indefatigable angler, who ought ere this to have caught every fish in the Nene, looked up in a startled manner for an instant, and resumed his sport with redoubled energy and perseverance.

Meanwhile a goodly cavalcade was approaching the half-ruined bridge of Brampton, which here spanned the Nene, and which, although impassable to carriages, admitted of the safe transit of equestrians riding in single file. Bit and bridle rang merrily as the troop wound downwards to the river side; feathers waved, scarfs and cloaks floated gaudily in the breeze, and gay apparel glistened bright in the summer sun. It was the King and his courtiers bound for their afternoon's amusement at Boughton, discoursing as they rode along on every topic save the one that lay deepest in each man's heart, with that mixture of gay sarcasm and profound reflection which was so pleasing to the sovereign's taste, and hazarding opinions with that happy audacity stopping short of freedom which always met with encouragement from the kindly disposition of the Stuarts.

It seemed to be no captive monarch surrounded by his gaolers that reined his good horse so gallantly in front of the trampling throng; not one of his royal ancestors in the plenitude of his power could have been treated with greater outward show of respect than was Charles by the attendants who spied his most secret actions, and the commissioners who were employed by the Parliament to deprive him of his personal liberty. Old Lord Pembroke, riding on his right hand a little in rear of the King, bowed his venerable head to his horse's mane at every observation of his sovereign. The Lords Denbigh and Montague, with the ceremonious grace which they had acquired years before at Whitehall, remained at the precise distance prescribed by etiquette from the person of royalty, and conversed when spoken to with the ready wit of courtiers and the frank bearing of English noblemen. Dr. Wilson as physician, and Mr. Thomas Herbert as groom of the bedchamber in waiting, made up the tale of the King's personal attendants, whilst servants with led horses, and one or two yeomen of the guard, completed the cavalcade.

No armed escort surrounded the King, no outward display of physical force seemed to coerce his will or fetter his actions; yet the Parliament had chosen their emissaries so well that for all their decorous observances and simulation of respect, with the exception of Herbert, not an inhabitant of Holmby House, from the earl in the presence to the scullion in the kitchen, but was more or less a traitor to his sovereign.

Charles beckoned his groom of the bedchamber to ride up alongside, and old Lord Pembroke fell respectfully to the rear. It might have been remarked, however, that Montague immediately spurred on and remained within earshot. Herbert was a favourite with the monarch. His affectionate disposition was not proof against that fascination which Charles undoubtedly exercised over those with whom he came in daily contact, and a similarity of tastes and habits, a congeniality of disposition between master and servant, each being of a speculative temperament deeply imbued with melancholy, laid the foundation of a friendship which seems to have been a consolation to the one in the darkest hours of adversity, the pride and glory of the other to the latest day of his life.

'What sayest thou, Master Herbert?' said Charles, laying his hand familiarly on the neck of his servant's horse as he paced slowly down towards the bridge. 'Did not the Stoics aver that the wise man is alone a king? and was not their ideal of wisdom the *nil admirari* of the satirist? Did they not hold that it was a quality which made its possessor insensible to pain or pleasure, pity or anger; alike impervious to the sunshine of prosperity as immovable by the storms of adversity; that the wise man knew neither hope nor fear, neither tears nor laughter; that he was essentially all-in-all to himself, and from his very nature equally a prophet, a priest, a cobbler, and a king?'

'Even so, your Majesty,' answered Herbert; 'and it has always appeared to me that the ox browsing contentedly in his pasture, satisfied to eat and drink, and ruminate and die, approaches more nearly to the philosopher's ideal of wisdom, than

Socrates with his convictions of the future, and Plato, with his speculations on the soul.'

'Right, Master Herbert,' answered the King, readily losing himself as was his wont in the labyrinth of abstract discussion which he delighted to provoke. 'The two schools of ancient philosophy arrived, but by different paths, at the same destination. "Eat and drink," urges the Epicurean, "for to-morrow you die." "Rest and ponder," quoth the Stoic, "for there is no reality even in life." Either maxim is directly opposed to the whole apparent scheme of the natural world. The one would impress you with the uselessness of sowing your grain ; the other convince you of the absurdity of reaping your harvest. Did either really prevail among men, the world could scarce go on a year.

'Doth it not show us that without the light of Revelation, our own intrinsic blindness leads us but farther and farther into error ? That man, with all his self-sufficient pride, is but a child in leading-strings at his best; that he must have his hopes and fears, his tears and smiles, like a child ; and that though he wince from the chastening Hand, it deals its stripes in mercy, after all. Yet, Herbert, have I often found it in my heart to envy these callous natures, too. Would that I could either place complete reliance on Heaven, or steel myself entirely against the anxieties and affections of earth. Would that I could keep down the turbulent heart that rises in wrath against the treatment it feels it has not deserved ; that longs so wearily for the absent, that aches so painfully for the dead, that cannot stifle its repinings for the past, nor cease to hope in a future, which becomes every day darker and more threatening. No tidings, and yet no tidings,' proceeded the King, in a lower voice, and musing as it were aloud, whilst his large eyes gazed far ahead into the horizon ; 'and yet letters may have been sent, may have been intercepted. I am so watched, so surrounded. Still there might be means. There are loyal hearts left in England, though many are lying cold. Alas, it is a weary, weary world ! Yonder is a happy man, Herbert, if you will,' added Charles, brightening up, and once more addressing his conversation to his companion. 'He has not a care for aught but the business in hand. He is a Stoic, a king, a cobbler—what you will. Good faith ! he should be a successful fisherman at the worst : I have watched him for the last ten minutes as we rode along. Doth he see kings and courts every day that he hath not once lifted his head from his angle to observe us, or is he indeed the sage of whom we have been talking—the " *sutor bonus et solus formosus, et est rex?*"'

As the King spoke he pointed to an angler who, having taken up a position on Brampton-bridge, had been leaning there immovable, undisturbed by the noise of the approaching cavalcade, and apparently totally devoid of the two sentiments of admiration and curiosity which the neighbourhood of a sovereign is accustomed to provoke.

The man seemed deaf or stupid. He remained leaning against the broken parapet, apparently unconscious of everything but his rod and line, which he watched vigilantly, with his hat drawn over his brows, and his cloak muffling his face to the eyes.

Lord Montague pressed forward to bid the angler stand out of the way, and leave room for Royalty to pass; but the King, who was an admirable horseman, edged his lordship so near the undefended brink of the half-ruined bridge, that Montague was fain to fall back with a bow and an inward thanksgiving that he was not overhead in the river. Etiquette forbade any one else to ride in front of the Sovereign, and Charles was consequently at the head of the party, who now defiled singly across the bridge.

The angler's back was turned, and he fished on without looking round.

' By your leave, good man,' quoth Charles, who, though somewhat haughty, particularly since his reverses, with his nobility, was ever courteous and good-humoured to those of humbler birth : ' there is scant room for us both, and the weakest, well we know, must go to the wall.' While the King spoke, his knee, as he sat in the saddle, touched the back of the preoccupied fisherman.

The latter started and turned round; quick as thought he thrust a small packet into his Majesty's hand, and almost with the same movement flung himself upon his knees at the royal stirrup in a paroxysm of pretended agitation and diffidence as unreal as the negligence for which it affected to atone.

Rapid as was the movement, it sufficed for Charles to recognise his trusty adherent. He crumpled the paper hurriedly into his glove.

' Faithful and true !' he whispered, ' save thyself!' and added aloud, for the edification of his attendants, ' Nay, good man ! we excuse thy rudeness on account of thy bodily infirmity. Look that thou be not trodden down by less skilful riders and less manageable steeds.'

As he spoke the King passed on to the other side, followed by all his attendants save only the Lord Montague, who had turned back to give directions to a patrol of the Parliamentary cavalry which

T

had arrived at the bridge at the same moment as the Royal cavalcade, and had drawn up to pay the military compliments due to
a sovereign.

The patrol, consisting of two efficient-looking dragoons, were
remarkably well-mounted, and armed, in addition to swords and
pistols, with long deadly carbines. They listened attentively to
Lord Montague's directions ; and while his lordship rode off in
pursuit of the King and his party, scanning the fisherman as he
passed him with a strange look of malicious triumph, each soldier
unslung his carbine, and shook the powder carefully up into its pan.

The King looked back repeatedly, as he rose the hill in the
direction of Boughton. Once he beckoned Lord Montague to
ride alongside of him.

' We thought we had lost your good company, my lord,' quoth
his Majesty; 'what made you turn back down yonder by Brampton Mill ?'

' I dropped my glove, your Majesty,' replied the nobleman,
scarcely concealing a smile.

' Whoever picks it up, my lord, will find a bitter enemy ! '
answered Charles ; and he spoke not another word till he reached
the great gates of Lord Vaux's hospitable hall.

Meanwhile the angler, resuming his occupation, fished steadily
on, glancing ever and anon at the retreating troop of horsemen
who accompanied the King. When the last plumed hat had disappeared over the verge of the acclivity, he took his rod to pieces
with a deep sigh of relief; and exchanging his slow listless
demeanour for one of resolution and activity, strode briskly away,
with the air of a man who has performed a good day's work, and
is about to receive for the same a good day's wages.

He thought, now that he had accomplished his task, he
would linger about her residence and see Mary Cave once more
—just once more—ere he went into exile again. He trusted
none but the King had recognised him ; and he had delivered
his packet with such secrecy and rapidity that he could not conceive it possible for any other eye to have perceived the movement. He little knew Montague's eagle glance. He little knew
that, in spite of his disguise, he had been suspected for more than
four-and-twenty hours, and that measures had already been taken
for his capture. He would know it all time enough. Let him
rest for a moment on the thought of his anticipated meeting with
his ladye-love. The wished-for two minutes that were to repay
the longings and misgivings of as many years, that he must live
upon perhaps for another twelvemonth, and be grateful that he

has had even such a crumb of comfort for the sustenance of his
soul. Strange hunger of the heart, that so little can alleviate, so
much fails to satisfy ! He walked swiftly on through the fragrant
meadows, waving with their long herbage, and bright with but-
tercups and field-flowers ; his head erect, his eye gazing far into
the horizon, as is ever the glance of those who look forward
and not back. Bosville had still a future ; he had not yet
thoroughly learned the bitterest of all life's lessons—to live
only in the past. No ; he was a man still, with a man's trust
and hope, a man's courage and self-reliance, a man's energy
and endurance. He would want them all before the sun went
down. Suddenly a shout smote upon his ear ; a voice behind
him called on him to stop and surrender. Halting, and turning
suddenly round, he beheld a mounted trooper, the tramp of whose
horse had been smothered in the long grass, close upon him ; another was nearing him from the river side. Both had their carbines unslung, and even in the confusion of the moment he had
time to perceive an expression of calm confidence on each man's
countenance, as though he was sure of his prey. For an instant
his very heart seemed to tighten with a thrill of surprise and keen
disappointment ; but it was not the first time by a good many
that Humphrey had looked a catastrophe in the face, and in that
instant he had time to think what he should do. Twenty yards
in front of him grew a high luxuriant hedge ; in that hedge was
a gap fortified by a strong oaken rail. The foremost horseman's
hand was almost on his shoulder when he dashed forward and
cleared it at a bound. Accustomed to make up his mind in
a moment, his first idea was to run under shelter of the fence
down to the river, and place the stream between himself and his
pursuers, trusting that neither heavily-armed trooper would choose
to risk man and horse in deep water. Alas ! on the opposite bank
he spied another patrol gesticulating to his comrades, and watching for him should he attempt to land. In the mean time his first
pursuers, both remarkably well mounted, had ridden their horses
boldly over the fence, and were once more close upon his tracks.
In another stride he must be struck down and made a prisoner !
But, as is often the case, at the supreme moment succour was at
hand. Not twenty yards in front of the fugitive stood Hugh
Dymocke, holding the sorrel by the bridle. The wily old soldier
had anticipated this catastrophe the whole morning, and was not
to be taken unawares at the crisis. He had been watching the
movements of the fisherman and the patrol, nor, except for a
chance shot, had he much fear of the result. With a rush and

a bound, like that of some stricken wild deer, Humphrey reached the sorrel and vaulted into the saddle. As he turned the horse's head for the open meadow with a thrill of exultation and delight, Dymocke let go the bridle and hurriedly whispered in his ear, 'God speed ye, master! Never spare him for pace; he had a gallop yesterday, and he's fit to run for a man's life!'

Ere the sentence was finished they were a hundred yards off, and the good horse, flinging his head into the air and snatching wildly at his bridle, indulged in a few bounds and plunges in his gallop ere he settled down into the long sweeping stride his rider remembered so well.

With a bitter curse and a shrewd blow from the butt of his carbine, which Dymocke avoided like a practised tactician, the foremost trooper swept by the old soldier, calling to his comrade in the rear to secure him and take him to head quarters. Both were, however, so intent on the pursuit that Dymocke, greatly to his surprise, found himself totally unnoticed, and walked quietly home with his usual air of staid gravity, reflecting, much to his own satisfaction, on the speed and mettle of his favourite and the probable safety of his young master.

And now the chase began in serious earnest. It was a race for life and death, and the competitors were well aware of the value of the stakes dependent on their own skill and the speed of the horses they bestrode.

Each trooper knew that a large sum of money and speedy promotion would reward his capture of the Royalist, whom they had now succeeded in identifying. Each was mounted on a thoroughly good horse whose powers he had often tested to the utmost, and each was moreover armed to the teeth, whilst the fugitive possessed no more deadly weapon than the butt of his fishing-rod, which he had retained unconsciously in his hand. Being two to one they had also the great advantage of being able to assist each other in the pursuit, and like greyhounds coursing a hare, could turn the quarry wherever opportunity offered into each other's jaws. Despite of broken ground, of blind ditches choked with grass, and high leafy hedges rich in Midsummer luxuriance, through which they crashed, bruising a thousand fragrant blossoms in their transit, they sped fiercely and recklessly on. All along the low grounds by Brampton, where the rich meadows were divided by strong thorn fences, the constantly recurring obstacles compelled Humphrey, bold rider as he was, to diverge occasionally from a straight course, and this was an incalculable advantage to his two pursuers, who, by playing as it were into each other's hands, were enabled to keep within sight and even within shot of the pursued, though the pace at which they were all going forbade any appeal to fire-arms, or indeed to any weapons except the spurs.

But on emerging from the low grounds into a comparatively open country and rising the hill towards Brixworth, the greater stride and speed of the sorrel began to tell. His condition, moreover, was far superior to that of the troopers, and it was with a glow of exultation not far removed from mirth, that Humphrey, finding at last a hand to spare with which to caress his favourite, looked back at his toiling pursuers, whose horses were now beginning to show undoubted symptoms of having had enough.

Even in mid-winter, when the leaves are off those formidable blackthorns, and the ditches, cleared of weeds and grass, yawn in all their naked avidity for the reception and ultimate sepulture of the horse and his rider, it is no child's play to cross one of these strongly-fenced Northamptonshire valleys. Ay, with all the fictitious excitement produced by the emulation of hunting, and the insatiable desire to be nearer and nearer still to that fleeting vision which, like happiness, is always just another stride beyond our reach; though the hounds are streaming silently away a field in front of us; though the good horse between our legs is fresh, ardent, and experienced; though we have already disposed of our dearest friend on his best hunter at that last 'double,' and are sanguine in our hopes of getting well over yonder strong rail, for which we are even now 'hardening our heart' and shortening our stride; though we hope and trust we shall go triumphantly on, from fence to fence, rejoicing, and at last see the good fox run into in the middle of a fifty-acre grass field,—yet for all this we cannot but feel that when we have traversed two or three miles of this style of country, without prostration or mishap, we have effected no contemptible feat of equitation, we have earned for the nonce a consciousness of thorough self-satisfaction intensely gratifying to the vanity of the human heart. And so perhaps it was one of the pleasantest moments of Humphrey's life when he pulled the sorrel into a trot and looked back upon the vale below. The horse snorted and shook his head. He was only breathed by the gallop that had so distressed the steeds of the two Parliamentarians. His master patted him fondly and exultingly once again. What a ride he had enjoyed! how the blood coursed through his veins with the anxiety, and the excitement, and the exercise. For two years he had not mounted what could be called a horse, certainly not one that could be compared with the sorrel. How delightful it was to feel his favourite bound under him as he used to do, once more! What a sensation to speed along those rich meadows, scanning fence after fence as he approached it, and flying over the places he had marked out, like a bird on the wing, to the unspeakable discomfiture of the dragoons toiling in his track. How gallantly he had cleared the rivulet that the two soldiers had been forced to flounder through. Well for them that it had shrunk to its summer limits, or they would have been there still. And now in another mile or so he would be safe. His pursuers' horses were too much exhausted even to continue on his track. They would soon lose all traces of him. Near Brixworth village was a cottage in which he had already passed two or three nights whilst waiting to fulfil his mission. Its owner was a veteran who had fought in his own troop at Edge-hill and Newbury, who would think little of imperilling his life for his old officer and King Charles. Arrived at the cottage, he would disguise himself again, and sending the sorrel out of the way, would lie hid till the search was past; he might then venture a few miles from his hiding-place, and at last reach the seashore and embark scatheless for the Continent. In this manner, too, he would have a chance of seeing Mary once more before he departed.

Trotting gently along, he was thus busily weaving the thread of his schemes and fancies, his hopes and fears, when alas! the web was suddenly dispelled by a shot! The crafty Parliamentarians finding themselves completely outstripped by the sorrel, and aware of a picket of their comrades stationed close under the village of Brixworth, had turned their attention to driving their quarry as much as possible towards the hill. In this they had been successful, and Humphrey's line of flight had already brought him within a few hundred yards of the enemy's post. As is often the case, however, their strict anxiety to preserve themselves unseen, had somewhat abated the vigilance of their look-out, and Bosville, accidentally changing his direction, narrowly escaped passing the negligent picket without observation or interruption.

But the veterans who pursued him were skilled in all the various practices of war; the leading horseman, quietly dismounting from his jaded steed, slowly levelled his carbine, and took a long roving shot at the fast diminishing figure of the fugitive. The bullet whistled harmlessly over Humphrey's head, but the report roused the inattentive sentry in advance of the picket, and the well-known sound of a trumpet rang out within musket range, whilst a dozen horsemen emerging from a clump of trees not two hundred yards to his right, dashed forward at a gallop, with the obvious intention of intercepting or riding him down.

Unarmed as he was, and notwithstanding the number of his foes, Humphrey never lost heart for a moment.

'Not trapped yet, my lads!' he ground out between his teeth, as with a grim smile he caught the sorrel fast by the head, and urged him once more to his speed, reflecting with fierce exultation on the mettle and endurance of his favourite, still going fresh and strong beneath him, and on the 'neck or nothing' nature of the chase, in which his only safety lay in placing some insurmountable obstacle between himself and his pursuers.

They, for their part, seemed determined to make every effort for his capture, dividing into parties so as to cover as large an extent of country as possible, and so prevent any attempt at turning or dodging on the part of the quarry, and forcing him by this means into a line of difficult and broken ground, such as must at last tell even on the power and stride of the indefatigable sorrel. The two original pursuers, moreover, whose horses had by this time recovered their wind, laboured on at a reduced pace along the low grounds, so that a diversion in that direction was impossible.

There was nothing for it but to go straight ahead, and straight ahead he went, laughing a strange wicked laugh to himself, as he thought of the Northern Water, no mean tributary to the Nene, which was even now gleaming in the distance a mile or so in front of him, and reflecting that if he were once well over such a 'yawner' as that, he might trot on and seek safety at his leisure, for not a dozen horses in England could clear it from bank to bank!

He trusted, nevertheless, that the sorrel was one of them. So he spared and nursed him as much as possible, choosing his ground with the practised eye of a sportsman, and bringing into use every one of the many methods which experience alone teaches, and by which the perfect horseman can assist and ease his steed. At the pace he led his pursuers, he cared but little to be out of musket-shot, and he reserved all the energies both of himself and his horse for a dash at the Northern Water.*

* A fair leap in the present day, when, under its later appellation of the 'Brixworth Brook,' it spoils many a silk jacket, as the flower of the British army can testify, who, in their modern substitute for Tilt and Tournament, yclept 'The Grand Military Steeple-Chase,' plunge into its profound with a reckless haste truly edifying to the less adventurous civilian.

Down the hill they come at headlong pace: the troopers, espying Bosville's object, now tax all their energies to catch him ere he can reach the brook, and spurs are plied and bridles shaken with all the mad recklessness of a neck-and-neck race.

Humphrey's spirits rise with the situation. He longs to give vent to his excitement in a wild 'hurrah!' as a man does in a charge, but he is restrained from the fear of maddening his horse, already roused by the shouts and clatter behind him, and pulling harder than his wont. Were he to get the least out of his hand now it would be fatal.

He steadies him gradually till within a hundred yards of the brink, and, regardless of his followers' close vicinity, pulls him back almost into a canter—then tightening his grasp on the bridle, and urging him with all the collective energies of knee, and thigh, and loins, he sets him going once more, the horse pointing his small resolute ears, the rider marking with his eye a sedgy patch of the soundest ground from which he intends their efforts shall be made.

Straining on his bridle, the sorrel bounds high into the air, the waters flash beneath them, and they are landed safe on the far side with half a foot to spare! Humphrey gives a cheer now, and a hearty cheer it is, in answer to the yell of rage and disappointment that rises from the baffled Parliamentarians.

Was there ever man yet that could 'leave well alone?' Alas! that we should here have to record the only instance of bravado on the part of our hero during the whole of his perilous and adventurous career. What demon prompted him to waste the precious moments in jeering at a defeated foe? Humphrey could not resist the temptation of pulling up to wave an ironical 'farewell' to his pursuers. The movement was fatal; in making it, he turned his broadside to the enemy, and half a dozen carbines were discharged at him on the instant. One bullet truer than the rest found its home in the honest heart of the good sorrel. The horse plunged wildly forward, fell upon his head, recovered himself—fell once more, and rolling over his rider, lay quivering in the last convulsions of death.

When Humphrey had extricated himself from the saddle and risen to his feet, he had no heart to make any further effort for his escape. He might perhaps have still had time to elude his enemies even on foot, but the strongest nature can only resist a given amount of difficulty and disappointment. 'Tis the last drop that bids the cup brim over, the last ounce that sinks the labouring camel in the sand.

He was weak, too, from mental anxiety as from bodily privation, from the conflict of his feelings as from the harassing nature of his task. Brave, generous, hopeful as he was, something seemed to give way within him at this last stroke of fortune, and when his captors, after making a long circuit to cross over by a ford, arrived to take him prisoner, they found him sitting on the ground, with the sorrel's head upon his knees, weeping like a woman or a child over the dead horse he had loved so well.

CHAPTER XXXI.

'FOR THE KING!'

WE left our honest friend Dymocke, with the sweep of the trooper's carbine still whistling in his ears, sauntering quietly homewards, his grim visage bespeaking more than usual satisfaction, his mental reflections sometimes rising into soliloquy, and taking much such a form as the following.

'Ah! Hugh! Hugh!' quoth the old soldier, apostrophizing the individual whom of all in the world he should have known best, 'there's few of them can hold a candle to thee, old lad! when the tackle's got fairly in a coil. Brave!—there's plenty of 'em brave enough—leastways there's plenty of 'em afraid not to seem so—but it's discretion, lad, it's discretion that's wanting; and thankful ought thou to be, that thou'st gotten enough for thyself and the whole household. There's not a man of 'em, now, could have managed this business, and not made a botch of it! Take the old lord to begin with. He'd have gone threatening and petitioning, and offering money, and what not, till the Major was blown just the same as if he'd had him cried in the market. That's the way with your quality; they can't abide to see a thing stand simmering; they must needs go shaking the frying-pan, and then they wonder that all the fat's in the fire! The women! I'll not deny but the women are keen hands at plotting and planning, and many's the good scheme they hit upon, no doubt, but where *they* fail is in the doing of it. It's "not now," or "I'm so frightened!" or a fit of crying just in the nick of time; and then the clock strikes or the bell rings, and it's too late. For the women must either wait too long, or else they'll not wait long enough, so it's as well they wasn't trusted to have anything to do with it. As for the steward, it's my opinion he's a rogue! and a rogue was never good for anything yet that wanted a bit of "heart" to set it straight; and the rest of 'em's fools one bigger than another, there's no gainsaying *that*.

'No! there was just one man that *could* do it, and he's gone and *done* it. To think of the sense of the dumb animal, too! Never but once did he neigh the whole blessed morning, though there was his master fishing within a pistol shot of him; and every time he came by the turn of the meadow, he laid his ears back, as much as to say, "I see you! I am ready for you when you want me." Ready! I believe he *was* ready. I should know a good horse when I'm on him; but the way he came round the park with me yesterday afternoon—— Oh! it's no use talking. A hawk's one thing, and a round shot's another; but he's the fastest horse in Northamptonshire at this blessed moment, and well he need to be. St. George! to see the example he made of those two! and the Major sitting down upon him so quiet, the way I always told him I liked to see him ride, popping here and popping there, with the horse as steady as a psalm-singer, and every yard they went the soldiers getting farther and farther behind. Well, the ladies will be best pleased to hear the Major's safe off, no doubt of that; and my pretty Faith, she won't cry her eyes out to see *me* come back in a whole skin—poor little woman! she hasn't the nerves of a hen. It was a precious coil, surely, and precious well I've got 'em all out of it. There's few things that can't be done by a man of discretion, 'specially when he's got the care of such a horse as *that*!'

Dymocke had arrived at home by the time he reached this conclusion. His self-satisfaction was unbounded. His triumph complete. It was well for him that his powers of vision were limited by distance—that he possessed no intuitive knowledge of the events of the day. It would have broken honest Hugh down altogether to know that the good sorrel was lying within four miles of him, down there by the Northern Water, with a bullet through his heart.

But the news he brought was right gladly received by every one of the anxious inhabitants of the old house of Boughton.

'Safe!' shouted Sir Giles with a loud 'hurrah!' that shook the very rafters of the hall. 'Ay! safe enough, no doubt, with that good horse beneath him, if he did but get a fair start! We'll drink the sorrel's health, my lord, this very night, after the King's.'

'Safe!' echoed Lord Vaux: 'delivered out of the jaws of death. Blood has been shed more than enough in these disastrous times, and I thank a merciful Providence that his young life has been spared.'

'Safe!' repeated Grace Allonby, with a sparkling glance at her father, and the old smile dimpling her triumphant face. 'Far out of danger by this time, and perhaps not recognised, after all.'

'Safe!' whispered Mary Cave, keeping out of observation as much as possible, her hands clasped tight upon her bosom, and her eyes looking up to heaven, filled with tears.

When the intelligence thus reached them, the party were assembled in the great hall immediately subsequent to the King's departure. Whilst honoured by the presence of Royalty, Dymocke had no opportunity of communicating with any of the family, and being, as he himself opined, a particularly discreet individual, he wisely abstained from dropping the slightest hint of his errand that might in any way compromise his employers, or afford a clue to his connexion with the fugitive fisherman.

Even Faith was not esteemed worthy of his confidence till he had made his report to her superiors; and to do her justice, that deserving damsel was so much taken up by the presence of Royalty, and her own multifarious duties of assisting to provide refreshments for the attendants who waited on the King, that the only notice she vouchsafed her admirer was a saucy inquiry as to whether 'he had been courting all the morning?' to which Hugh replied with a grim leer, ' It was like enough, since he confidently expected to be married next month;' whereat she blushed, and bade him ' go about his business,' returning with much composure to the prosecution of a demure flirtation, on which she had even now entered, with a solid and sedate yeoman of the guard.

The King's visit was short and ceremonious enough. His manner to Lord Vaux and Sir Giles Allonby was as gracious as usual, the few words he addressed to the young ladies kindly and paternal as his wont; but his Majesty was evidently pre-occupied and ill at ease ! The intelligence he had that morning received from Mary harassed and disturbed him, though indeed, somewhat to her surprise, he had made no further allusion to it, and indeed addressed but a few commonplace remarks to that lady.

It was evident to her that he was brooding over the threatened violation of his personal liberty, which was in effect about to take place that same night, and that this apprehension united with other causes to make him very anxious and unhappy. The letter from the Queen, which Humphrey had delivered at such risk, was also unsatisfactory and distressing. He had looked for this epistle for weeks, and when it came at last, behold! he had been happier not to have received it.

It is often thus with subjects as well as kings.

Under these circumstances, Charles was unable, according to his custom, to forget all other considerations in the trifles on which he was immediately employed—could not as usual throw himself heart and soul into the fluctuations of the game, as though life offered no other interests than a bowl and bias—did not, even for the short half-hour of his relaxation, succeed in stifling the bitter consciousness that he was a prisoner, though a king.

With his usual grave demeanour and mild dignified bearing, he played one set with the old Earl of Pembroke and a few others of his *suite*, Lord Vaux and Sir Giles Allonby standing by to hand his Majesty the implements of the game, and then taking his leave with sad and gentle courtesy, the Monarch called for his horses to depart, resisting his host's humble entreaties that he would re-enter the house and partake of a collation ere he rode.

Walking down the terrace to the gate at which his horses awaited him, accompanied by Lord Vaux and the two ladies, and followed at the prescribed distance by his personal attendants, a damask rose-tree, on which Mary had expended much time and care, caught the King's attention, and elicited his admiration, tinged as usual with the prophetic melancholy that imbued his temperament.

'Tis a fair tree and a fragrant,' observed Charles, stopping in his progress; 'grateful to those who, like myself, love the simple beauties of a garden better than the pomps and splendours of a Court. In faith, the husbandman's is a happier lot than the King's. Yet hath he, too, his anxieties and his disappointments. Frosts nip the hopes of his earliest blossoms; and the pride even of successful maturity is but the commencement of decay.'

As the King spoke, Mary, from an impulse she could not resist, plucked the handsomest flower from its stem, and presented it to her Sovereign. He accepted it with the grave courtesy peculiar to him.

'If we ever meet at Whitehall, Mistress Mary,' said Charles, with his melancholy smile, 'neither you nor I will forget the blood-red rose presented to me this day by the most loyal of all my loyal subjects. Had other hearts been true as yours,' he added, in a low solemn voice, 'I had not been a mimic king, soon to lose even the shade and semblance of royalty.' As he spoke, with a courtly obeisance he mounted his horse and departed, riding slowly and dejectedly, as though loth to return to his

palace, where he already anticipated the insults and humiliations
to which he was about to be subjected.

She coloured deeply with gratified pride, and a sense of duty
strenuously and consistently fulfilled. Poor Mary ! it was the
last act of homage she was destined ever to pay the Sovereign in
whose cause she would cheerfully have laid down her life.   The
damask-rose was fresh, and bright, and fragrant—the very type
of beauty and prosperity, and a worm was eating it away, silently
and surely, at the core.

After the King's departure, however, Dymocke's intelligence
was imparted to rejoice the hearts of the somewhat dejected
Royalists.   When people are thoroughly ' broken in,' so to speak,
and accustomed to misfortune, it is wonderful how small a gleam
of comfort serves to shed a light upon their track, and dissipate
the gloom to which they have become habituated.   Everything
goes by comparison, and a scrap of broken meat is a rich feast to
a starving man; nevertheless, the process of training to this
enviable state is painful in the extreme.

So the ladies sauntered out into the park, and enjoyed the
balmy summer afternoon, and the luxuriant summer fragrance of
leaf and blossom, and the hum of the summer insects all astir in
the warmth of June.   Grace laughed out merrily, as she used to
do years ago; and Mary's step was lighter, her cheek rosier
than it had been of late as they discoursed.   The King's visit,
and the peculiarities of the courtiers, formed their natural topics
of conversation ; but each lady felt a weight taken from her heart,
and a sensation of inexpressible relief which had nothing to do
with kings or courtiers, save in as far as the actions of those important personages affected the fortunes of one Major Humphrey
Bosville.

We must now return to that adventurous gentleman, gradually
awakening to a sense of his situation as he sat on a raw-boned troop-
horse between two stern-visaged Roundhead dragoons, his elbows
strapped tight to his sides, his feet secured beneath his horse's
belly ; and notwithstanding such impediments to activity, his
attempts to escape, if indeed any were practicable, threatened
with instant death by his rigorous custodians.

The Major accepted it as a compliment that not less than eight
men and a sergeant were esteemed a sufficient force to secure the
person of the unarmed fisherman.   This formidable escort was
commanded by his old acquaintance, ' Ebenezer the Gideonite,'
who still slung his carbine across his back in the manner that had
once saved his life; and who, to do him justice, bore his old

antagonist not the slightest malice for his own discomfiture on that occasion. It was composed, moreover, of picked men and horses from the very flower of the Parliamentary cavalry.

Humphrey rode in the midst of them, and tried to recal his scattered senses, and realize the emergency of his present position.

Weak and worn-out, we have already said that after his horse was shot he had fallen an easy prey to his pursuers. When brought before the officer in command of the party that had captured him, he was neither in a mood nor a condition to answer any questions that might be put. The subaltern's orders, however, seemed sufficiently peremptory to absolve him from the vain task of cross-examining a fainting and unwilling prisoner. In the event of capturing a certain mysterious agent described, he was strictly enjoined to forward him at once to the Parliament, with as much secrecy and despatch as was consistent with the security of the captive. So after providing Humphrey with the food and drink of which he stood so much in need, and suffering him to take a short interval of repose, whilst men were mustered and horses fed, the officer started prisoner and escort without delay on the road to London.

Thus it came to pass that while Grace Allonby and Mary Cave were taking their afternoon stroll through the park at Boughton, Humphrey Bosville and his escort were winding slowly down the hill on the high road to the metropolis.

The Major's eye brightened as he caught sight of their white dresses, and recognised the form of the woman he had loved so long and so dearly. He started with an involuntary gesture that brought the hands of his guardians to trigger and sword-hilt. Although at a distance, it was something to see her just once again.

The ladies were turning homewards when, startled by the tramp of horses, both were aware of an armed party advancing in their immediate vicinity. An unconscious presentiment prompted each at the same moment to stop and see the troop pass by. The captive's heart leapt within him as he rode near enough to scan every lineament of the dear face he might never hope to look upon again.

'They have a prisoner!' exclaimed Mary, turning as white as her dress. 'God's mercy! it is Humphrey.'

Not another word did either speak. They looked blankly in each other's faces, and Grace burst into a flood of tears.

CHAPTER XXXII.

'THE BEGINNING OF THE END.'

THE soft June night sank peacefully upon Holmby Palace, with all its conflicting interests, all its complications of intrigue and treachery, as it sank upon the yeoman's adjoining homestead, and the shepherd's humble cottage in the vale below. The thrush had finished the last sweet tones of her protracted even-song, and not a sound disturbed the surrounding stillness, save an occasional note from the nightingale in the copse, and the murmur of a fountain playing drowsily on in the garden. Calmly the stars shone out in mellow lustre, looking down, as it seemed, mild and reproachful on the earth-worms here below. What are all the chances and changes, all the sorrows and struggles, of poor grovelling mortality in the sight of those spirit eyes? Age after age have they glimmered on, careless as now of man's engrossing troubles and man's predestined end. They shone on Naseby field, whitening in their faint light, here a grinning skull, there a bleached and fleshless bone turned up by the hind's careless ploughshare, or the labourer's busy spade, as they shone on Holmby Palace, stately in its regal magnificence, sheltering under its roof a circle of plotting courtiers, with a doomed King; and their beams fell the same on both, cold, pitiless, and unvarying. What are they, these myriads of flaming spheres? Are they worlds? are they inhabited? are they places of probation, of reward, of punishment? are they solid anthracite, or but luminous vapour? material masses, or only an agglomeration of particles? Can their nature be grasped by the human intellect, or defined in the jargon of science? Oh for the child's sweet simple faith once more, that they are but chinks in the floor of Heaven, from which the light of eternal day shines through!

The King was preparing to retire for the night. Notwithstanding all the anxieties and apprehensions that had arisen from the warning he had that morning received, notwithstanding the reception of his Queen's letter—a document by no means calculated to soothe his feelings or alleviate his distress—the force of habit was so strong that the numerous preparations for his Majesty's 'coucher' were made with as scrupulous an attention to the most trifling minutiæ as when he was indued with all the pomp of real royalty and conscious of actual power long ago at Whitehall.

After 'the word for the night' had been given, a word which

it seemed a mockery to ask the prisoner himself to select, and the
other attendants had been dismissed, after Doctor Wilson had paid
his customary visit and received to his respectful inquiries the
customary answer that nothing was amiss with the royal health,
preserved as it was by rigid and undeviating temperance, Mr.
Herbert, as groom-in-waiting, presented the King with an ewer
and cloth, making at the same time the prescribed obeisance, and
setting a night-lamp, consisting of a round cake of wax in a silver
basin, on a chair, proceeded himself to retire to the couch prepared
for him in a small anteroom opening into the apartment occupied
by his Majesty, so that the King might not, even in the watches
of the night, be left entirely alone.

We have often thought that this habit of being constantly, to a
certain extent, before the public, may account in a great measure
for the fortitude and dignity so often displayed in critical moments
by sovereigns who have never before been suspected of possessing
these Spartan virtues. Never, like a humbler individual, in his
most unguarded hours of privacy entirely throwing off the character which it is his duty to sustain, a sovereign, even a weak-
minded one, acquires a habit of reticence and self-command which
becomes at last second nature; and he who is every day of his
life obliged to appear a hero to his *valet de chambre,* finds little
difficulty in sustaining the part to which he is so well accustomed
under the gaze of a multitude, even in a moment of general confusion and dismay.

As Herbert backed respectfully from the room, the King recalled him, as though for a few minutes' confidential conversation.

'Herbert,' said he, taking up at the same time his jewelled
George and Garter, which, with his customary attention to trifles,
he insisted should be placed near his bed-head, 'Herbert, you are
becoming negligent; you have omitted to lay these gauds—empty
vanities that they are!—in their accustomed place. Also this
morning you neglected to observe the command I gave last night.'

His Majesty spoke with a grave and somewhat haughty air,
which concealed a covert smile.

The attendant, in some confusion and no little surprise at the
unusual displeasure of the King's tone, admitted that he had
aroused his Majesty five minutes too late, and pleaded in extenu-
ation the usual excuse of a discrepancy amongst the clocks. The
King preserved an ominous frown.

'You are aware,' said he, 'that I never pardon a fault, nor
overlook even the most trifling mistake. Have you not often heard
me called harsh, vindictive, and exacting? I have prepared your

punishment; I trust it will admonish you for the future. Here is a gold watch,' he added, his assumed displeasure vanishing at once in a hearty burst of laughter at the scared expression of his attendant's countenance, 'a gold alarm-watch, which as there may be cause shall awake you. Wear it for Charles Stuart's sake; and years hence, perhaps when he is no more, may it remind you of the stern, unkindly sovereign, who, albeit he valued to the utmost the affection and fidelity of his servant, could not pass over the slightest omission without some such token of his displeasure as this.'

So speaking, and good-humouredly pushing Herbert from the room, he bade him a cordial 'good-night,' leaving his groom of the bedchamber more devoted to his person, if possible, than before.

Such was one among many instances of Charles's benevolent disposition; such little acts of kindness as this endeared him to all with whom he came in daily contact, and the charm of such a temperament accounts at once for the blind devotion on the part of his followers, commanded by one who was the most amiable and accomplished of private gentlemen, as he was the most injudicious and inefficient of kings.

Musing upon the fortunes of his master, and regretting in his affectionate nature his own powerlessness to aid the sinking monarch, Herbert fell into a broken and disturbed slumber, from which, however, he soon awoke, and observed, somewhat to his dismay, that the King's chamber was in perfect darkness. The door of communication being left open, in case his services should be required during the night, the attendant's first impulse was to rise and re-light the lamp, which he concluded had been accidentally extinguished. He was loth, however, to disturb the King's rest, and whilst debating the point in his own mind, fell off to sleep. After a short slumber, he was again aroused by the King's voice calling to him, and was surprised to see that the lamp had been rekindled.

'Herbert,' said his master, 'I am restless, and cannot sleep. Thou wilt find a volume on yonder table; read to me, I prithee, for a space. It may be the good bishop's discourses will lull me to repose. Thou, too, art wakeful and watchful. I thank thee for thy vigilance in so readily rekindling my light, which had gone out.'

Herbert expressed his surprise.

'I have not entered your Majesty's chamber,' said he. 'I have never left my couch since I lay down; but being restless, I observed your Majesty's room was dark, and when I woke even now reproached myself that your Majesty must have risen to perform a duty that should have devolved upon your servant.'

'I also awoke in the night,' replied the King, 'and took notice that all was dark. To be fully satisfied, I put by the curtain to look at the lamp. Some time after I found it light, and concluded then that thou hadst risen and set it upon the basin lighted again.'

Herbert assured his Majesty it was not so.

Charles smiled, and his countenance assumed that mystical and rapt expression it so often wore.

'I consider this,' said he, 'as a prognostic of God's future favour and mercy towards me and mine—that although I am at this time so eclipsed, yet either I or they may shine out bright again!'

Even as he spoke a loud knocking was heard at the outer door, communicating as it did with a back staircase that led to a private entrance into the court. Sounds of hurry and confusion at the same time pervaded the palace, and the tramp of horses mingled with the clash of steel was distinctly audible outside the walls. Major-General Browne's voice was heard, too, above the confusion, calling on the few yeomen of the guard and other officials who formed the garrison to 'stand to their arms,' exhorting them at the same time to preserve the King's person from injury, and the majesty of the Parliament, as represented by the Commissioners, from insult. Meantime, Mawl, Maxwell, and Harrington, all personal attendants of the Sovereign, rushed to his bedchamber, scared, pale, and half-dressed, but ready, if need were, to sacrifice their lives in defence of the King.

Charles alone preserved his usual composure. The knocking at the door of his private apartments being violently repeated, he desired Maxwell to hold converse with this unmannerly disturber of his repose. Reconnoitring the assailant through a panelling in the door, the old courtier was horrified to observe a Cornet of the Parliamentary dragoons standing at the head of the stairs in complete armour, with a cocked pistol in his hand, and clamouring for admittance.

The dialogue was carried on with a military sternness and brevity shocking to the prejudices of the Gentleman-Usher, more accustomed to the circumlocutions of diplomacy and the compliments of a court.

'What would you?' inquired Maxwell, through the panelling. 'Who are you, and by whose orders do you come here?'

The Cornet was a stout, resolute-looking man, with all the appearance of having risen from the ranks. His voice was deep and harsh, his countenance of that dogged nature which sets argument and persuasion alike at defiance. His answers were short and categorical.

'I would see Charles Stuart,' he replied. 'My name is Joyce, Cornet in the service of the Parliament. I am here on my own responsibility.'

'Have you the authority of the Commissioners for your intrusion?' gasped out Maxwell, totally aghast at the unheard-of breach of etiquette, in which he felt himself aiding and abetting.

'No!' thundered the Cornet; 'I have placed a sentry at the door of every man of them. Keep quiet, old gentleman—I take my orders from them that fear neither Commissioners nor Parliament.'

In effect, the Cornet's entrance into Holmby House, and his rapid occupation of every post in its vicinity, as of the palace itself, had been achieved in a masterly manner that showed him to be no inexperienced practitioner in war.

With a numerous body of cavalry at his disposal, he had been all day occupied in concentrating them silently and stealthily around the beleaguered palace. His main body had that afternoon bivouacked on Harleston Heath, strong pickets had been placed in every secluded spot which admitted of concealment within a circuit of a few miles, and constant patrols had been watching every road by which an escape from Holmby was practicable. As darkness fell he had pushed forward his several posts to one common centre, and by the hour of midnight a summer moon shone down on the court-yard of Holmby Palace, filled with a mass of iron-clad cavalry, whose numbers rendered resistance hopeless and impossible.

Colonel Graves and General Browne, however, two old Parliamentary officers, seemed to have had some inkling that an attack was meditated: for without any apparent reason they had doubled the guards around the King's person, and contrary to their wont had remained astir till midnight. When the first files of the approaching cavalry marched into the court, they had called upon the handful of soldiers and yeomen that formed the garrison to resist to the death, and had themselves held a parley with the redoubtable Cornet. When asked his name and business, he had replied, with the same bluntness that so discomfited Maxwell, that 'his name was Joyce, Cornet in Colonel Whalley's regiment of horse, and his business was to speak with the King.'

'From whom?' said Browne, with rising indignation.

'From myself!' replied the Cornet, with provoking coolness.

The two old soldiers burst into a derisive laugh.

'It's no laughing matter,' said the unabashed intruder; 'I came not hither to be advised by you, nor have I any business with the Commissioners. My errand is to the King, and speak with him I must and will.'

'Stand to your arms,' exclaimed Browne, to the handful of soldiers inside the palace : but these had in the meantime held some conference with the intruders, and finding that they all belonged to the same party, and that several were old comrades who had charged together many a day under the same banner, they refused to act against their friends, and drawing bolts and bars, admitted them without further parley, bidding them welcome, and shaking them cordially by the hand.

Thus it was that the Cornet obtained admittance even to the very door of his Majesty's bedchamber. A certain sense of propriety, however, which almost always accompanies the responsibility of a command, forbade him from offering any further violence, and with a most ungracious acquiescence he consented to leave the King undisturbed till morning, stipulating, however, that he should himself take up a position for the night on the staircase, which in effect he did, being with difficulty persuaded to lay down his firearms and return his sword to its sheath.

Charles sought his couch once more in that frame of placid helplessness which seems usually to have taken possession of him when in the crisis of a difficulty. He slept soundly, and awoke with characteristic regularity, little before his ordinary hour. His toilet was performed with elaborate care, his devotions not curtailed of a single interjection, his poached egg and glass of fair water leisurely discussed, and then, but not till then, his Majesty expressed his readiness to hold an interview with the personage who seemed to have power of life and death over his Sovereign.

The King's simplicity of manner and quiet dignified bearing overawed even the rough and low-born officer of the Parliament. Half-ashamed of his insolence, half bullying himself into his naturally offensive demeanour, Cornet Joyce was ushered into the presence with a far different aspect from that which he had assumed the night before. Such is the innate dignity afforded by true nobility of soul, that Charles and his captor seemed to have changed places. The King appearing to be the offended though placable judge, the Cornet wearing the sullen, apprehensive, and abashed look of a guilty prisoner.

Charles's good-nature, however, soon restored the official to his self-possession, and by an easy transition, to a large portion of his original insolence. In reply to the monarch's gentle interrogative as to the cause of the last night's outrage, he answered boldly, ' My orders are to remove your Majesty at once, without further delay.'

This frank avowal created no small dismay in the little circle then assembled in his Majesty's outer apartment. Herbert turned pale, and trembled. Maxwell, as red as fire, seemed to doubt the evidence of his senses; whilst General Browne, stepping aside into the recess of a window, swore fearfully for five consecutive minutes in tones not loud but deep.

The King remained totally unmoved.

' Let the Commissioners be sent for,' said he, with a dignified air, ' and let these orders be communicated to them.'

The Cornet was fast recovering his former audacity. ' I have taken measures with them already,' said he ; ' they are in watch and ward even now, and must return, will they, nill they, to the Parliament.'

' By whose authority ? ' demanded the King, sternly, but with visible uneasiness.

The Cornet shook his head, laughed rudely, and pointed with his forefinger to his own coarse person.

' I would ask you, sir, as a favour,' said the King, ' to set them at liberty ; and I demand, as a right,' he added, drawing himself up, and flushing with a sense of impotent anger and outraged dignity, ' to be permitted a sight of your instructions.'

' That is easily done,' answered Joyce, ' if your Majesty will take the trouble to step as far as this window.'

And opening the casement, he pointed into the court-yard below, where indeed was drawn up as goodly a squadron of cavalry as the whole Parliamentary army could boast, well armed, well mounted, bold, and bronzed, with stalwart frames and stern, unflinching faces, possessed, moreover, of the self-confidence and disciplined valour inspired by a career of hard-won victories. They were the same material, some of them the same men, that confronted Charles at Edge-hill, routed him at Marston Moor, and finally vanquished him at Naseby. The finest cavalry in the world, and, bitterest thought of all, his own subjects. The King's heart was sore as he looked down into the court, but he had played the part of royalty too long not to know how to dissemble his feelings, and he turned to the Cornet with a smile as he said,

' Your instructions, sir, are in fair characters, and legible without spelling. The language, though somewhat forcible, is sufficiently intelligible, and admits of no further argument. I am ready to attend your good pleasure, with this proviso, that I stir not unless accompanied by the Commissioners. You have had your audience, sir ; you may withdraw.'

The Cornet, somewhat to his own surprise, found himself making a respectful obeisance and retiring forthwith; but the King's coach was ordered to be got in readiness without delay, and that very day Charles Stuart, accompanied, as he had stipulated, by the Commissioners, commenced the journey which led him, stage by stage, to his final resting-place—the fatal window at Whitehall—the scaffold and the block.

CHAPTER XXXIII.

' THE BEACON AFAR.'

'Ebenezer the Gideonite' was no bad specimen of the class he represented—the sour-visaged, stern, and desperate fanatic, who allowed no consideration of fear or mercy to turn him from the path of duty ; whose sense of personal danger as of personal responsibility was completely swallowed up in his religious enthusiasm ; who would follow such an officer as George Effingham into the very jaws of death ; and of whom such a man as Cromwell knew how to make a rare and efficient instrument. Ebenezer's orders were to hold no communication with his prisoner, to neglect no precaution for his security ; and having reported his capture to the general in command at Northampton, to proceed at least one stage further on his road to London ere he halted for the night.

Humphrey's very name was consequently unknown to the party who had him in charge. As he had no papers whatever upon his person when captured, the subaltern in command of the picket at Brixworth had considered it useless to ask a question to which it was so easy to give a fictitious answer ; and Ebenezer, although recognising him personally as an old acquaintance, had neglected to ascertain his name even after their first introduction by means of the flat of the Cavalier's sabre. Though his back had tingled for weeks from the effects of a blow so shrewdly administered ; though he had every opportunity of learning the style and title of the prisoner whom he had helped to bring before Cromwell at his head-quarters ; yet, with an idiosyncrasy peculiar to the British soldier, and a degree of Saxon indifference amounting to stupidity, he had never once thought of making inquiry as to who or what was this hard-hitting Malignant that had so nearly knocked him off his horse in the Gloucestershire lane.

Erect and vigilant, he rode conscientiously close to his prisoner, eyeing him from time to time with looks of curiosity and interest, and scanning his figure from head to heel with obvious satisfaction. Not a word, however, did he address to the captive; his conversation, such as it was, being limited to a few brief sentences interchanged with his men, in which Scriptural phraseology was strangely intermingled with the language of the stable and the parade-ground. Strict as was the discipline insisted on amongst the Parliamentary troops by Cromwell and his officers, the escort, as may be supposed, followed the example of their superior with stern faces and silent tongues; they rode at 'attention,' their horses well in hand, their weapons held in readiness, and their eyes never for an instant taken off the horseman they surrounded.

Humphrey, we may easily imagine, was in no mood to enter into conversation. He had indeed enough food for sad forebodings and bitter reflections. Wild and adventurous as had been his life for many weeks past—always in disguise, always apparently on the eve of discovery, and dependent for his safety on the fidelity of utter strangers, often of the meanest class—not a day had elapsed without some imminent hazard, some thrilling alternation of hope and fear. But the events of the last few hours had outdone them all. To have succeeded in his mission !—to have escaped when escape seemed impossible, and then to fail at the last moment, when safety had been actually gained !—it seemed more like some wild and feverish dream than a dark hopeless reality. And the poor sorrel ! How sincerely he mourned for the good horse; how well he had always carried him; how gentle and gallant and obedient he was; how he turned to his master's hand and sprang to his master's voice. How fond he was of him; and to think of him lying dead yonder by the water-side ! It was hard to bear.

Strange how a dumb animal can wind itself round the human heart ! What associations may be connected with a horse's arching crest or the intelligent glance of a dog's eye. How they can bring back to us the happy 'long, long ago;' the magic time that seems brighter and brighter as we contemplate it from a greater and greater distance ; how they can recal the soft tones and kindly glances that are hushed, perhaps, and dim for evermore : perhaps, the bitterest stroke of all, estranged and altered now. 'Love me, love my dog ! '—there never was a truer proverb. Ay ! love my dog, love my horse, love all that came about me ; the dress I wore, the words I have spoken, the very ground I trod upon,—but do not be surprised that horse and dog, and dress and belongings, all are still the same, and I alone am changed.

So Humphrey loved the sorrel, and grieved for him sincerely. The rough Puritan soldiers could understand his dejection. Many a charger's neck was caressed by a rough hand on the march, as the scene by the Northern Water presented itself vividly to the dragoons' untutored minds; and though the vigilance of his guardians was unimpeachable, their bearing towards Humphrey was all the softer and more deferential that these veteran soldiers could appreciate his feelings and sympathise with his loss.

He had but one drop of comfort, one gleam of sunshine now, and even that was dashed with bitter feelings of pique and a consciousness of unmerited neglect. He had seen Mary once again. He liked to think, too, that she must have recognised him; must have been aware of his critical position; must have known that he was being led off to die.

'Perhaps even her hard heart will ache,' thought the prisoner, 'when she thinks of her handiwork. Was it not for her sake that I undertook this fatal duty—for her sake that I have spent years of my life in exile, risked that life ungrudgingly a thousand times, and shall now forfeit it most unquestionably to the vengeance of the Parliament? Surely, surely, if she is a woman, she must be anxious and unhappy now.'

It was a strange morbid sensation, half of anger, half of triumph; yet through it all a tear stole to his eye from the fond heart that could not bear to think the woman he loved should suffer a moment's uneasiness even for his sake.

Silently they rode on till they reached Northampton town. The good citizens were too much inured to scenes of violence, too well accustomed to the presence of the Parliamentary troops, to throw away much attention on so simple an event as the arrival of an escort with a prisoner. Party-feeling, too, had become considerably weakened since the continued successes of the Parliament. Virtually the war was over, and the Commons now represented the governing power throughout the country. The honest townsmen of Northampton were only too thankful to obtain a short interval of peace and quiet for the prosecution of 'business'—that magic word, which speaks so eloquently to the feelings of the middle class in England—and as their majority had from the very commencement of the disturbances taken the popular side in the great civil contest, they could afford to treat their fallen foes with mercy and consideration.

Unlike his entry on a previous occasion into the good city of Gloucester, Humphrey found his present plight the object neither of ridicule nor remark. The passers-by scarce glanced at him as he rode along, and the escort closed round him so vigilantly that a careless observer would hardly have remarked that the troop encircled a prisoner.

In consequence of their meditated movement against the King's liberty, the Parliament had concentrated a large force of all arms at Northampton, and the usually smiling and peaceful town presented the appearance of enormous barracks. Granaries, manufactories, and other large buildings were taken up for the use of soldiers ; troop-horses were picketed in the streets, and a park of artillery occupied the market-place ; whilst the best houses of the citizens, somewhat to the dissatisfaction of their owners, were appropriated by the superior officers of the division. In one of the largest of these George Effingham had established himself. An air of military simplicity and discipline pervaded the general's quarters : sentries, steady and immovable as statues, guarded the entrance ; a strong escort of cavalry occupied an adjoining building, once a flour-store, now converted into a guard-house. Grave upright personages, distinguished by their orange scarfs as officers of the Parliament, stalked to and fro, intent on military affairs, here bringing in their reports, there issuing forth charged with orders ; but one and all affecting an austerity of demeanour which yet somehow sat unnaturally upon buff coat and steel head-piece. The general himself seemed immersed in business. Seated at a table covered with papers, he wrote with unflinching energy, looking up, it is true, ever and anon with a weary abstracted air, but returning to his work with renewed vigour after every interruption, as though determined by sheer force of will to keep his mind from wandering off its task.

An orderly-sergeant entered the room, and, standing at 'attention,' announced the arrival of an escort with a prisoner.

The general looked up for a moment from his papers. 'Send in the officer in command to make his report,' said he, and resumed his occupation.

Ebenezer stalked solemnly into the apartment : gaunt and grim, he stood bolt upright and commenced his narrative :

'I may not tarry by the way, General,' he began, 'for verily the time is short and the night cometh in which no man can work ; even as the day of grace, which passeth like the shadow on the sun-dial ere a man can say, Lo! here it cometh, or lo! there.'

Effingham cut him short with considerable impatience. 'Speak out, man,' he exclaimed, 'and say what thou'st got to say, with a murrain to thee! Dost think I have nought to do but sit here and listen to the prating of thy fool's tongue?'

Ebenezer was one of those preaching men of war who never let slip an opportunity of what they termed 'improving the occasion;' but our friend George's temper, which the unhappiness and uncertainty of the last few years had not tended to sweeten, was by no means proof against such an infliction. The subordinate perceived this, and endeavoured to condense his communication within the bounds of military brevity, but the habit was too strong for him : after a few sentences he broke out again—

'I was ordered by Lieutenant Allgood to select an escort of eight picked men and horses, and proceed in charge of a prisoner to London. My instructions were to pass through Northampton, reporting myself to General Effingham by the way, and to push on a stage further without delay ere I halted my party for the night. With regard to the prisoner, the captive, as indeed I may say, of our bow and spear, who fell a prey to us under Brixworth, even as a bird falleth a prey to the fowler, and who trusted in the speed of his horse to save him in the day of wrath, as these Malignants have ever trusted in their snortings and their prancings, forgetting that it hath been said—'

' Go to the devil, sir !' exclaimed George Effingham, with an energy of impatience that completely dissipated the thread of the worthy sergeant's discourse; 'are you to take up my time standing preaching there, instead of attending to your duty? You have your orders, sir; be off, and comply with them. Your horses are fresh, your journey before you, and the sun going down. I shall take care that the time of your arrival in London is reported to me, and woe be to you if you "tarry by the way," as you call it in your ridiculous hypocritical jargon. To the right—face !'

It was a broad hint that in an orderly-room admitted of but one interpretation. Ebenezer's instincts as a soldier predominated over his temptations as an orator, and in less than five minutes he was once more in the saddle, wary and vigilant, closing his files carefully round the captured Royalist as they wound down the stony street in the direction of the London road.

George Effingham returned to his writing, and with a simple memorandum of the fact that a prisoner had been reported to him as under escort for London, dismissed the whole subject at once from his mind.

Thus it came to pass that the two friends, as still they may be called, never knew that they were within a hundred paces of each other, though in how strange a relative position; never knew that a chance word, an incident however trifling, that had betrayed the name of either, would have brought them together, and perhaps altered the whole subsequent destinies of each. George never suspected that the nameless prisoner, reported to him as a mere matter of form, under the charge of Ebenezer, was his old friend Humphrey Bosville ; nor could the Cavalier Major guess that the General of Division holding so important a command as that of Northampton, was none other than his former comrade and captain, dark George Effingham.

The latter worked hard till nightfall. It was his custom now. He seemed never so uneasy as when in repose. He acted like a traveller who esteems all time wasted but that which tends to the accomplishment of his journey. Enjoying the confidence of Cromwell and the respect of the whole army, won, in despite of his antecedents, by a career of cool and determined bravery, he seemed to be building up for himself a high and influential station, stone by stone as it were, and grudging no amount of sacrifice, no exertion to raise it, if only by an inch. The enthusiasm of George's temperament was counterbalanced by sound judgment and a highly perspicuous intellect, and consequently the tendency to fanaticism which had first impelled him to join the Revolutionary party, had become considerably modified by all he saw and heard, when admitted to the councils of the Parliament, and better acquainted with their motives and opinions. He no longer deemed that such men as Fairfax, Ireton, even Cromwell, were directly inspired by Heaven, but he could not conceal from himself that their energies and abilities were calculated to win for them the high places of the earth. He knew, moreover, none better, the strength and the weaknesses of either side, and he could not doubt for a moment which must become the dominant party. If not a better, the ci-devant Cavalier had become unquestionably a wiser man, and having determined in his own mind which of the contending factions was capable of saving the country, and which was obviously on the high road to power, he never now regretted for an instant that he had joined its ranks, nor looked back as Bosville would have done under similar circumstances, with a wistful longing to all the illusions of romance and chivalry which shed a glare over the downfall of the dashing Cavaliers. Effingham's, we need hardly say, was a temperament of extraordinary perseverance and unconquerable resolution. He had now proposed to himself a certain aim and end in life. From the direction which led to its attainment he never swerved one inch, as he never halted for an instant by the way. He had determined to win a high and influential station. Such a station as should at once silence all malicious remarks on his Royalist antecedents, as should raise him, if not to wealth, at least to honour, and above all, such as should enable him to throw the shield of his protection over all and any whom he should think it worth his while thus to shelter and defend. Far in the distance, like some strong swimmer battling successfully against wind and tide, he discerned the beacon which he had resolved to reach, and though he husbanded his strength and neglected no advantage of eddy or back-water, he never relaxed for an instant from his efforts, convinced that in the moral as in the physical conflict, he who is not advancing is necessarily losing way. Such tenacity of purpose *will* be served at last, as indeed it fully merits to be, and this Saxon quality Effingham possessed for good or evil in its most exaggerated form.

The weaknesses of a strong nature, like the flaws in a marble column, are, however, a fit subject for ridicule and remark. The general, despite his grave appearance and his powerful intellect, was as childish in some matters as his neighbours. Ever since the concentration of a large Parliamentary force around North-ampton, and the investment, so to speak, of Holmby House by the redoubtable Cornet Joyce, it had been judged advisable by the authorities to station a strong detachment of cavalry at the village of Brixworth, a lonely hamlet within six miles of head-quarters, occupying a commanding position, and with strong capabilities for defence. This detachment seemed to be the general's peculiar care; and who should gainsay such a high military opinion as that of George Effingham? Whatever might be the press of business during the day, however numerous the calls upon his time, activity, and resources, he could always find a spare hour or two before sundown, in which to visit this important outpost. Accompanied by a solitary dragoon as an escort, or even at times entirely alone, the general would gallop over to beat up Lieute-nant Allgood's quarters, and returning leisurely in the dark, would drop the rein on his horse's neck, and suffer him to walk quietly through the outskirts of the park at Boughton, whilst his master looked long and wistfully at the casket containing the jewel which he had sternly resolved to win. On the day of Hum-phrey's capture, the very eagerness on the part of Effingham to fulfil his daily duty, or rather, we should say, to enjoy the only relaxation he permitted himself, served to render him somewhat impatient of Ebenezer's long-winded communications; and by cutting short the narrative of that verbose official, perhaps prevented an interview with his old friend, which, had he believed in its possibility, he would have been sorry to miss.

A bright moon shone upon the waving fern and fine old trees of Boughton Park as George returned from his customary visit to the outpost. He was later than usual, and the soft southern breeze wafted on his ear the iron tones that were tolling midnight from Kingsthorpe Church. All was still, and balmy, and beautiful, the universe seemed to breathe of peace, and love, and repose. The influence of the hour seemed to soothe and soften the ambitious soldier, seemed to saturate his whole being with kindly, gentle feelings, far different from those which habitually held sway in that weary, careworn heart; seemed to whisper to him of higher, holier joys than worldly fame and gratified pride, even than successful love—to urge upon him the beauty of humility, and self-sacrifice, and hopeful, child-like trust—the triumph of that resignation which far outshines all the splendours of conquest, which wrests a victory even out of the jaws of defeat.

Alas! that these momentary impressions should be transient in proportion to their strength! What *is* this flaw in the human organization that thus makes man the very puppet of a passing thought? Is there but one rudder that can guide the bark upon her voyage, veering as she does with every changing breeze? but one course that shall bring her in safety to the desired haven, when all the false pilots she is so prone to take on board do but run her upon shoals and quicksands, or let her drift aimlessly out seaward through the night? We know where the charts are to be found—we know where the rudder can be fitted. Whose fault is it that we cannot bring our cargo safe home to port?

The roused deer, alarmed at the tramp of George's charger, sprang hastily from their lair under the stems of the spreading beeches, blanched in the moonlight to a ghastly white. As they coursed along in single file under the horse's nose, he bounded lightly into the air, and with a snort of pleasure rather than alarm broke voluntarily into a canter on the yielding moss-grown sward. The motion scattered the train of thought in which his rider was plunged, dispelled the charm, and brought him back from his visions to his own practical, resolute self. He glanced once, and once only, at the turrets of the hall, from which a light was still shining, dimly visible at a gap in the fine old avenue; and then with clenched hand and stern, compressed smile, turned his horse's head homeward, and galloped steadily on towards his own quarters in Northampton town.

CHAPTER XXXIV.

'PAST AND GONE.'

PERHAPS had Effingham known in whose room was twinkling that light which shone out at so late an hour from the towers of the old manor-house; could any instinctive faculty have made him aware of the council to which it was a silent witness; could he have guessed at the solemn conclave held by two individuals in that apartment, from which only a closed casement and a quarter of a mile of avenue separated him, even his strong heart would have beat quicker, and a sensation of sickening anxiety would have prevented him from proceeding so resolutely homewards, would have kept him lingering and hankering there the livelong night.

The solitary light was shining from Grace Allonby's apartment. In that luxurious room were the two ladies, still in full evening costume. One was in a sitting posture, the other, with a pale, stony face, her hair pushed back from her temples, and her lips, usually so red and ripe, of an ashy white, walked irregularly to and fro, clasping her hands together, and twisting the fingers in and out with the unconscious contortions of acute suffering. It was Mary Cave who seemed thus driven to the extremity of apprehension and dismay. All her dignity, all her self-possession had deserted her for the nonce, and left her a trembling, weeping, harassed, and afflicted woman.

Grace Allonby, on the other hand, sate in her chair erect and motionless as marble. Save for the action of the little foot beneath her dress, which tapped the floor at regular intervals, she might, indeed, have been a statue, with her fixed eye, her curved, defiant lip and dilated nostril expressive of mingled wrath and scorn.

Brought up as sisters, loving each other with the undemonstrative affection which dependence on one side and protection on the other surely engenders between generous minds, never before had the demon of discord been able to sow the slightest dissension between these two. Now, however, they seemed to have changed natures. Mary was writhing and pleading as for dear life. Grace sat stern and pitiless, her dark eyes flashing fiercely, and her fair brow, usually so smooth and open, lowering with an ominous scowl.

For five minutes neither had spoken a syllable, though Mary continued her troubled walk up and down the room. At last Grace, turning her head haughtily towards her companion, stiffly observed,

' You can suggest, then, no other method than this unwomanly and humiliating course ? '

' Dear Grace,' replied Mary, in accents of imploring eagerness, ' it is our last resource. I entreat you—think of the interest at stake. Think of him even now, a prisoner on his way to execution. To execution ! Great Heaven ! they will never spare him now. I can see it all before me—the gallant form walking erect between those stern, triumphant Puritans, the kindly face blindfolded, that he may not look upon his death. I can see him standing out from those levelled muskets. I can hear his voice firm and manly as he defies them all, and shouts his old battle-cry —" God and the King ! " I can see the wreaths of white smoke floating away before the breeze, and down upon the greensward, Humphrey Bosville—dead !—do you understand me, girl ? *dead* —stone dead ! and we shall never, *never* see him more ! '

Mary's voice rose to a shriek as she concluded, towering above her companion in all the majesty of her despair ; but she could not sustain the horror of the picture she had conjured up, and sinking into a chair, she covered her face with her hands, and shook all over like an aspen leaf.

Grace, too, shuddered visibly. It was in a softened tone that she said, ' He *must* be saved, Mary. I am willing to do all that lies in my power. He shall not die for his loyalty, if he can be rescued by any one that bears the name of Allonby.'

' Bless you, darling, a thousand, thousand times ! ' exclaimed Mary, seizing her friend's hand, and covering it with kisses; ' I knew your good, kind heart would triumph at the last. I knew you would never leave him to die without stretching an arm to help him. Listen, Gracey. There is but one person that can interpose with any chance of success on his behalf—I need not tell you again who that person is, Gracey ; you used to praise and admire my knowledge of the world ; you used to place the utmost faith in my clearsightedness and quickness of perception. I am not easily deceived, and I tell you George Effingham loves the very ground beneath your feet. Not as men usually love, Grace, with a divided interest, that makes a hawk or a hound, a place at court, or a brigade of cavalry, too dangerous and successful a rival, but with all the energy of his whole enthusiastic nature, with the reckless devotion that would fling the world, if he had it, at your feet. He is your slave, dear, and I cannot wonder at it. For your lightest whim he would do more, a thousand times more, than this. He has influence with our rulers (it is a bitter drop in the cup, that we must term the Roundhead knaves *our* rulers at last); above all, he has Cromwell's confidence, and Cromwell governs England now. If he can be prevailed on to exert himself, he can save Bosville's life. It is much to ask him, I grant you. It may compromise him with his party, it may give his enemies the means of depriving him of his command, it may ruin the whole future on which his great ambitious mind is set. I know him, you see, dear, though he has never thought it worth his while to open his heart to *me*; it might even endanger his safety at a future period, but it *must* be done, Grace, and you are the person that must tell him to do it.'

'It is not right,' answered Grace, her feminine pride rousing itself once more. 'It is not just or fair. What can I give him in exchange for such a favour? How can I, of all the women upon earth, ask him to do this for *me*?'

'And yet, Grace, if you refuse, Humphrey must die!' said Mary, in the quiet tones of despair, but with a writhing lip that could hardly utter the fatal word.

Grace was driven from her defences now. Conflicting feelings, reserve, pride, pity, and affection, all were at war in that soft heart, which so few years ago had scarcely known a pang. Like a true woman, she adopted the last unfailing resource—she put herself into a passion, and burst into tears.

'Why am I to do all this?' sobbed Grace. 'Why are my father, and Lord Vaux, and you yourself, Mary, to do nothing, and I alone to interfere? What especial claim has Humphrey on me? What right have I, more than others, over the person of Major Bosville?'

'Because you love him, Grace,' answered Mary, and her eye never wavered, her voice never faltered, when she said it. The stony look had stolen over her face once more, and the rigidity of the full white arm that peeped through her sleeve showed how tight her hand was clenched, but the woman herself was as steady as a rock. The other turned her eyes away from the quiet searching glance that was reading her heart.

'And if I did,' said poor Grace, in the petulance of her distress, 'I should not be the only person. You like him yourself, Mary, you know you do—am I to save him for your sake?'

The girl laughed in bitter scorn while she spoke, but tears of shame and contrition rose to her eyes a moment afterwards, as she reflected on the ungenerous words she had spoken.

Mary had long nerved herself for the task, she was not going to fail now. She had resolved to *give him up*. Three little simple words ; very easy to say, and comprising after all—what ? a mere nothing ! *only* a heart's happiness lost for a life-time—*only* a cloud over the sun for evermore—*only* the destruction of hope, and energy, and all that makes life worth having, and distinguishes the intellectual being from the brute. *Only* the exchange of a future to pray for, and dream of, for a listless despair, torpid and benumbed,—fearing nothing, caring for nothing, and welcoming nothing but the stroke that shall end life and sufferings together. This was all. She would not flinch—she was resolved—she could do it easily.

'Listen to me, Grace,' she said, speaking every word quite slowly and distinctly, though her very eyebrows quivered with the violence she did her feelings, and she was obliged to grasp the arm of a chair to keep the cold, trembling fingers still. ' You are mistaken if you think I have any sentiment of regard for Major Bosville deeper than friendship and esteem. I have long known him, and appreciated his good qualities. You yourself must acknowledge how intimately allied we have all been in the war, and how stanch and faithful he has ever proved himself to the King. Therefore I honour and regard him, therefore I shall always look back to him as a friend, though I should never meet him again. Therefore I would make any exertion, submit to any sacrifice to save his life. But, Grace, *I do not love him.*' She spoke faster and louder now. ' And, moreover, if you believe he entertains any such feelings on my behalf, you are wrong—I am sure of it —look at the case yourself, candidly and impartially. For nearly two years I have never exchanged words with him, either by speech or writing—never seen him but twice, and you yourself were present each time. He may have admired me once. I tell you honestly, dear, I think he did, but he does not care two straws for me now.'

Poor Mary ! it was the hardest gulp of all to keep back the tears at this; not that she quite thought it herself, but it was so cruel to be obliged to *say* it. After all, she was a woman, and though she tried to have a heart of stone, it quivered and bled like a heart of flesh all the while, but she went on resolutely with a tighter hold of the chair.

I think you and he are admirably suited to each other. I

think you would be very happy together. I think, Grace, you
like him very much—you cannot deceive me, dear. You have
already excited his interest and admiration. Look in your glass,
my pretty Grace, and you need not be surprised. Think what
will be his feelings when he owes you his life. It requires no
prophet to foretell how this must end. He will love you, and you
shall marry him. Yes, Grace, you can surely trust *me*. I swear
to you from henceforth, I will never so much as speak to him
again. You shall not be made uneasy by me of all people—only
save his life, Grace, only use every effort, make every sacrifice to
save him, and I, Mary Cave, that was never foiled or beaten yet,
promise you that he shall be yours.'

It is peculiar to the idiosyncrasy of women that they seem to
think that they have a perfect right to dispose of a heart that
belongs to them, and say to it, 'you shall be enslaved here, or
enraptured there, at our good pleasure.' Would they be more
surprised or angry to find themselves taken at their word?

Grace listened with a pleased expression of countenance. She
believed every syllable her friend told her. It is very easy to
believe what we wish. And it was gratifying to think that she
had made an impression on the handsome young Cavalier, for
whom she could not but own she had once entertained a warm
feeling of attachment. Like many another quiet and retiring
woman, this consciousness of conquest possessed for Grace a
charm dangerous and attractive in proportion to its rarity. The
timid are sometimes more aggressive than the bold; and Grace
was sufficiently feminine to receive considerable gratification from
that species of admiration which Mary, who was surfeited with it,
thoroughly despised. It was the old story between these two:
the one was courteously accepting as a trifling gift that which
constituted the whole worldly possessions of the other. It is
hard to offer up our diamonds, and see them valued but as
paste.

'There is no time to be lost, Mary,' observed Grace, after a
few moments' reflection. 'I will make it my business to see
General Effingham before twenty-four hours have elapsed. If, as
you say, he entertains this—this infatuation about me, it will
perhaps make him still more anxious on behalf of his old friend,
to provide for whose safety I should think he would strain every
nerve, even if there were no such person as Grace Allonby in the
world. We will save Major Bosville, Mary, whatever happens,
if I have to go down on my bended knees to George Effingham.
Not that I think such a measure will be needful,' added Grace,

with a smile; 'he is very courteous and considerate, notwith-standing his stern brows and haughty manner. Very chivalrous, too, for a Puritan. My father even avows he is a good soldier; and I am sure he is a thorough gentleman. Do you not think so, Mary?'

But Mary did not answer. She had gained her point at last. Of course it was a great comfort to know that she had succeeded in her object. Had the purchase not been worth the price, she would not surely have offered it; and now the price had been accepted, and the ransom was actually paid, there was nothing more to be done. The excitement was over, and the reaction had already commenced.

'Bless you, Grace, for your kindness,' was all she said. 'I am tired now, and will go to bed. To-morrow we will settle every-thing. Thank you, dear, again and again.' With these words she pressed her cold lips upon her friend's hand; and hiding her face as much as possible from observation, walked quietly and sadly to her room. It was an unspeakable relief to be alone, face to face with her great sorrow, but yet *alone*. To moan aloud in her agony, and speak to herself as though she were some one else, and fling herself down on her knees by the bed-side, burying her head in those white arms, and weep her heart out while she poured forth the despairing prayer that she might die, the only prayer of the afflicted that falls short of the throne of mercy. Once before in this very room had Mary wrestled gallantly with suffering, and been victorious. Was she weaker now that she was older? Shame! shame! that the woman should give way to a trial which the girl had found strength enough to overcome. Alas! she felt too keenly that she had then lost an ideal, whereas this time she had voluntarily surrendered a reality. She had never known before all she had dared, if not to hope, at least to dream, of the future with *him* that was still *possible* yesterday—and now—

Lost, too, by her own deed, of her own free will. Oh! it was hard, *very* hard to bear!

But she slept, a heavy, sound, and exhausted sleep. So it ever is with great and positive affliction. Happiness will keep us broad awake for hours, to rise with the lark; gladsome, notwith-standing our vigils, as the bird itself, refreshed and invigorated by the sunshine of the soul. 'Tis an unwilling bride that is late astir on her wedding-morn. Anxiety, with all its harassing effects, admits of but feverish and fitful slumbers. The dreaded crisis is never absent from our thoughts; and though the body may be prostrated by weariness, the mind refuses to be lulled to rest. We do not envy the merchant prince his bed of down, especially when he has neglected to insure his argosies; but when the blow has actually fallen, when happiness had spread her wings and flown away, as it seems, for evermore, when there is no room for anxiety, because the worst has come at last, and hope is but a mockery and a myth, then doth a heavy sleep descend upon us, like a pall upon a coffin, and mercy bids us take our rest for a time, senseless and forgetful like the dead.

But there was a bitter drop still to be tasted in the full cup of Mary's sorrows. Even as she laid her down, she dreaded the moment of waking on the morrow; she wished—how wearily!—that she might never wake again, though she knew not then that she would dream that night a golden dream, such as should make the morning's misery almost too heavy to endure.

She dreamed that she was once again at Falmouth, as of old. She walked by the seashore, and watched the narrow line of calm blue water and the ripple of the shallow wave that stole gently to her feet along the noiseless sand. The sea-bird's wing shone white against the summer sky as he turned in his silent flight; and the hushed breeze scarce lifted the folds of her own white dress as she paced thoughtfully along. It was the dress *he* liked so much; she had worn it because he was gone, far away beyond those blue waters, with the Queen, loyal and true as he had ever been. Oh that he were here now, to walk hand-in-hand with her along those yellow sands! Even as she wished he stood by her, his breath was on her cheek, his eyes were looking into hers, his arm stole round her waist. She knew not how, nor why, but she was his, his very own, and for always now. ' At last,' she said, putting the hair back from his forehead, and printing on the smooth brow one long, clinging kiss, ' at last! dear. You will never leave me now?' and the dream answered ' Never, never-more!'

Yet when she woke, she did not waver in her resolution. Though Mary Cave looked ten years older than she had done but twenty-four hours before, she said to her own heart, ' I have decided: it *shall* be done!'

CHAPTER XXXV.

'THE LANDING-NET.'

Faith had excited Dymocke's jealousy. This was a great point gained; perhaps with the intuitive knowledge of man's weaknesses, possessed by the shallowest and most superficial of her sex, she had perceived that some decisive measure was required to land her fish at last. Though he had gorged the bait greedily enough, though the hook was fairly fixed in a vital spot, and nothing remained—to continue our metaphor—but to brandish the landing-net, and subsequent frying-pan, the prize lurked stolidly in deep waters. This state of apathy in the finny tribe is termed 'sulking' by the disciples of Izaak Walton; and the great authorities who have succeeded that colloquial philosopher, in treating of the gentle art, recommend that stones should be thrown, and other offensive measures practised, in order to bring the fish once more to the surface.

Let us see to what description of stone-throwing Faith resorted to secure the prey, for which, to do her justice, she had long been angling with much craft, skill, and untiring patience.

Dymocke, we need hardly now observe, was an individual who entertained no mean and derogatory opinion of his own merits or his own charms. An essential article of his belief had always been that there was at least one bachelor left, who was an extraordinarily eligible investment for any of the weaker sex below the rank of a lady; and that bachelor bore the name 'Hugh Dymocke.' With such a creed, it was no easy matter to bring to book our far-sighted philosopher. His good opinion of himself made it useless to practise on him the usual arts of coldness, contempt, and what is vulgarly termed 'snubbing.' Even jealousy, that last and usually efficacious remedy, was not easily aroused in so self-satisfied a mind; and as for hysterics, scenes, reproaches, and appeals to the passions, all such recoiled from his experienced nature, like hailstones from an armour of proof. He was a difficult subject, this wary old trooper. Crafty, callous, opinionated, above all, steeped in practical as well as theoretical wisdom. Yet, when it came to a trial of wits, the veriest chit of a silly waiting-maid could turn him round her finger at will.

We have heard it asserted by sundry idolaters, that even 'the *worst* woman is better than the best man.' On the truth of this axiom we would not venture to pronounce. Flattering as is our opinion of the gentle sex, we should be sorry to calculate the amount of evil which it would require to constitute *the worst* of those fascinating natures which are so prone to run into extremes; but of this we *are* sure, that the *silliest* woman in all matters of *finesse* and subtlety is a match, and more than a match, for the wisest of mankind. Here was Faith, for instance, who, with the exception of her journey to Oxford, had never been a dozen miles from her own home, outwitting and outmanœuvring a veteran toughened by ever so many campaigns, and sharpened by five-and-twenty years' practice in all the stratagems of love and war.

After revolving in her own mind the different methods by which it would be advisable to hasten a catastrophe that should terminate in her own espousals to her victim, the little woman resolved on jealousy as the most prompt, the most efficacious, and perhaps the most merciful in the end. Now, a man always goes to work in the most blundering manner possible when he so far forgets his own honest dog-like nature as to play such tricks as these. He invariably selects some one who is diametrically the opposite of the real object of attack, and proceeds to open the war with such haste and energy as are perfectly unnatural in themselves, and utterly transparent to the laughing bystanders. When he thinks he is getting on most swimmingly, the world sneers; the fictitious object, who has, indeed, no cause to be flattered, despises; and the real one, firmer in the saddle than ever, laughs at him. It serves him right, for dabbling with a science of which he does not know the simplest rudiments. This was not Faith's method. We think we have already mentioned that in attendance upon the King at Holmby was a certain yeoman of the guard on whom that damsel had deigned to shed the sunshine of her smiles, in which the honest functionary basked with a stolid satisfaction edifying to witness. He was a steady, sedate, and goodly personage; and, save for his bulk, the result of little thought combined with much feeling, and his comeliness, which he inherited from a Yorkshire mother, was the very counterpart of Dymocke himself. He was nearly of the same age, had served in the wars on the King's side with some little distinction, was equally a man of few words, wise saws, and an outward demeanour of profound sagacity, but lacked, it must be confessed, that prompt wit and energy of action which made amends for much of the absurdity of our friend Hugh's pretensions.

He was, in short, such a personage as it seemed natural for a woman to admire who had been capable of appreciating the good qualities of the sergeant; and in this Faith showed a tact and discerument essentially feminine. Neither did she go to work 'hammer-and-tongs,' as if there were not a moment to be lost; on the contrary, she rather suffered than encouraged the yeoman's unwieldly attentions; and taxed her energies, not so much to captivate him as to watch the effect of her behaviour on the real object of attack. She had 'but little time, it is true, for her operations, which were limited to the period of the King's short visit at Boughton; but she had no reason to be dissatisfied with the success of her efforts, even long before the departure of his Majesty and the unconscious rival.

Dymocke, elated with his last exploit, and full of the secret intelligence he had to communicate, at first took little notice of his sweetheart, or indeed of any of the domestics; and Faith, wisely letting him alone, played on her own game with persevering steadiness. After a time she succeeded in arousing his attention, then his anxiety, and lastly his wrath. At first he seemed simply surprised, then contemptuous, afterwards anxious, and lastly un-doubtedly and unreasonably angry, with himself, with her, with her new acquaintance, with the whole world; and she looked so confoundedly pretty all the time! When the yeoman went away, Faith gazed after the departing cavalcade from the buttery-window with a deep sigh. She remarked to one of the other maids 'that she felt as if she could die for the King; and what a becoming uniform was worn by the yeomen of the guard.' Dymocke, who had approached her with some idea of an armistice, if not a treaty of peace, turned away with a smothered curse and a bitter scowl. All that night he never came near her, all the next morning he never spoke to her, yet she met him somehow at every turn. He was malleable now, and it was time to forge him into a tool.

It was but yesterday we watched two of our grand-children at play in the corridor. The little girl, with a spirit of unjust acquisitiveness, laid violent hands upon her brother's toys, taking from him successively the whole of his marbles, a discordant tin trumpet, and a stale morsel of plum-cake. The boy, a sturdy, curly-headed, open-eyed urchin, rising five, resented this whole-sale spoliation with considerable energy; and a grand quarrel, not without violence, was the result. The usual declaration of hostility, ' *then I won't play,*' was followed by a retreat to different corners of the gallery; and a fit of 'the sulks,' lasting nearly twenty minutes, afforded a short interval of peace and quiet to the household.

A child's resentment, however, is not of long duration; and we are bound to admit that in this instance the aggressor made the first advances to a reconciliation. 'You began it, dear,' lisped the little vixen, a thorough woman already, though she can hardly speak plain. 'Kiss and make up, brother : *you began it!*' And we are persuaded that the honest little fellow, with his masculine softness of head and heart, believed himself to have been from the commencement wholly and solely in the wrong.

So Faith, lying in wait for Dymocke at a certain angle of the back-yard, where there was not much likelihood of interruption, stood to her arms boldly, and commenced the attack.

'Are you never going to speak to me again, sergeant?' said Faith, with a half-mournful, half-resentful expression on her pretty face. 'I know what new acquaintances are—the miller's daughter's a good girl and a comely ; but it's not so far from here to Brampton Mill that you need to be in such a hurry as not to spare a word to an old friend, Hugh!'

The last monosyllable was only whispered, but accompanied by a soft stolen glance from under a pair of long eyelashes, it did not fail to produce a certain effect.

'The miller's daughter! Brampton Mill!' exclaimed Hugh, aghast and open-mouthed, dumbfoundered, as well he might be, at an accusation so devoid of the slightest shadow of justice.

'Oh! I know what I know,' proceeded Faith, with increased agitation and alarming volubility. 'I know where you were spending the day yesterday, and the day before, and the day before that! I know why you leave your work in the morning, and the dinner stands till it's cold, and the horse is kept out all day, and comes home in a muck of sweat; and it's "where's the sergeant?" and "has anybody seen Hugh?" and "Mistress Faith, can you tell what's become of Dymocke?" all over the house. But I answer them, "I've nothing to do with Dymocke ; Dymocke don't belong to me. Doubtless he's gone to see his friends in the neighbourhood; and he knows his own ways best." Oh! *I* don't want to pry upon you, sergeant; it's nothing to *me* when you come and go : and no doubt, as I said before, she's a good girl, and a comely ; and got a bit of money too ; for her sister that married Will Jenkins she's gone and quarrelled with her father; and the brother, you know, he's in hiding ; and they're a bad lot altogether, all but *her*; and I hope you'll be happy, Sergeant Dymocke ; and you've my best wishes; and (sob) prayers (sob), for all that's come and gone yet (sob), *Hugh!*'

To say that Dymocke was astonished, stupefied, at his wits' end, is but a weak mode of expressing his utter discomfiture ; the old soldier was completely routed, front, flanks, and rear, disarmed and taken prisoner, he was utterly at the mercy of his conqueror.

'It's not much to ask,' pursued Faith, her cheeks flushing, and her bosom heaving as she wept out her plaint; 'it's not much to ask, and I *should* like to have back the broken sixpence, and the silver buckles, and the—the—bit of sweet marjoram I gave you yesterday was a fortnight, if it's only for a keepsake and a remembrance when you're married, Hugh, and you and me are separated for ever!'

With these desponding words, the disconsolate damsel buried her face in her apron and moaned aloud.

What a brute he felt himself! how completely she had put him in the wrong—how his conscience smote him, innocent as he was concerning the miller's daughter, for many little instances of inattention and neglect towards his affianced bride, who was now so unselfishly giving him up, with such evident distress. How his heart yearned towards her now, weeping there in her rustic beauty, and he pitied her, *pitied* her, whilst all the time, with his boasted sagacity and experience, he was as helpless as a baby in the little witch's hands.

'Don't ye take on so, Faith,' he said, attempting an awkward caress, from which she snatched herself indignantly away, 'don't ye take on so. I never went *near* the miller's daughter, Faith— I tell ye I didn't, as I'm a living man!'

'Oh! it's nothing to me, sergeant, whether you did or whether you didn't,' returned the lady, looking up for an instant, and incontinently hiding her face in her apron for a fresh burst of grief. 'It's all over between you and me now, Hugh, for evermore!'

'Never say such a word, my dear,' returned Dymocke, waxing considerably alarmed, as the possibility of her being in earnest occurred to him, and the horrid suspicion dawned on his mind that this might be a *ruse* to get rid of him in favour of the comely yeoman, after all; 'and if you come to that, lass, you weren't so true to your colours yourself yesterday, that you need to turn the tables this way upon me.'

She had led him to the point now. Then he *was* jealous, as she intended he should be, and she had got him safe.

'I'm sure I don't know what you mean, Sergeant Dymocke,' answered Mistress Faith, demurely, sobbing at longer intervals, and drying her eyes while she spoke. 'If you allude to my conversation with one of his blessed Majesty's servants yesterday, I answer you that it was in the presence of yourself and all my

lord's servants; and if it hadn't been, I'm accountable to no one.
A poor lone woman like me can't be too careful, I know; a poor
lone woman that's got nobody to defend her character, speak up
for her, or take care of her, and that's lost her best friend, that
quarrels with her whether she will or no. Oh! what shall I do?
—what shall I do?'

The action was very nearly over now. Another flood of tears,
brought up like a skilful general's reserve, in the nick of time,
turned the tide of affairs, and nothing was left for the sergeant
but to surrender at discretion.

'It's your own fault if it be so,' whispered Hugh, with that
peculiarly sheepish expression which pervades the male biped's
countenance when he so far humiliates himself as to make a *bonâ
fide* proposal. 'If you'll say the word, Faith, say it now, for indeed I love you, and I'll never be easy till you're my wife, and
that's the truth!'

But Faith wouldn't say the word at once, nor indeed could she
be brought to put a period to her admirer's sufferings, in which,
like a very woman, she found a morbid and inexplicable gratification, until she had well-nigh worried him into a withdrawal of
his offer, when she said it in a great hurry, and sealed her submission with a kiss.

On the subsequent festivities held both in the parlour and the
hall—for Sir Giles drank the bride's health in a bumper, and the
ladies of the family thought nothing too good to present to their
favourite on the happy occasion of her marriage—it is not our
province to enlarge. In compliance with the maxim that 'happy's
the wooing that's not long in doing,' the nuptials took place as
soon as the necessary preparations could be made, and a prettier
or a happier-looking bride than Faith never knelt before the altar.

The sergeant, however, betrayed a scared and somewhat startled
appearance, as that of one who is not completely convinced of his
own identity, bearing his part nevertheless as a bridegroom bravely
and jauntily enough.

At his own private opinion of the catastrophe we can but guess
by a remark which he was overheard to address to himself immediately after his acceptance by the pretty waiting-maid, and her
consequent departure to acquaint her mistress.

'You've done it now, old lad,' observed the sergeant, shaking
his head, and speaking in a deliberate, reflective, and somewhat
sarcastic tone. 'What is to be must be, I suppose, and all things
turn out for the best. But there's no question about it —*you've—
done—it—now!*'

CHAPTER XXXVI.

'YES OR NO.'

OLD SIR GILES never refused his daughter anything now. He had always been an indulgent parent, but it seemed that of late years Grace had more than ever wound herself round his heart. The old Cavalier was getting sadly broken and altered of late. Day by day his frame became more bent and more attenuated; the eye that used to gleam so bright was waxing dim and uncertain; the voice that had rung out so clear and cheerful above the tramp of squadrons and the din of battle, now shook and quivered with the slightest exertion, and the once muscular hand that used to close so vigorously upon sword and bridle-rein, had wasted down, thin, white, and fragile like a girl's. The spirit alone was unaltered—bold, resolute, and unyielding as of old; the stanch Cavalier drank the King's health as unshrinkingly every night as was his wont; and lacked opportunity only to lead the King's troops into action as undauntedly as ever. Ay, although too feeble to sit upright in a saddle, he had waved them on to certain death from a sick man's litter. It is glorious to think how the spirit outlives the clay. But with Grace it seemed as if he could not be tender and gentle enough. Whether it was an instinctive feeling that his child was not happy, or an inward presentiment that they must soon take leave of each other in this world, something seemed to prompt him to lavish all the affection of his warm old heart on his darling, and bade him grant her all she asked, and anticipate her lightest wish while it was yet in his power. Thus it befel that to Grace's unexpected proposal, 'Father, may I write in your name to bid General Effingham to the Hall?' he answered feebly in the affirmative, and the young lady found herself in consequence sitting down for the first time in her life to pen a formal letter to the Parliamentary General.

Now this invitation, albeit unnatural and unexpected enough, scarcely did as much violence to Sir Giles's feelings as might have been supposed. Years before, at Oxford, he had imbibed a strong personal liking for George Effingham; and although the latter's desertion of his colours had been a grievous offence to the loyal old Cavalier, he could not but respect the successful and distinguished soldier, who had won such laurels on the side he had espoused too late; he could not forget that he owed his life to Effingham on the fatal field of Naseby, nor could he be insensible to the many kindnesses conferred upon him and his by the General since he had entered upon his high command at Northampton. It was bitter, truly, thus to be beholden to a renegade, and a Round-head to boot; but then the rebel, though a political enemy, was a personal friend, and it was doubtless pleasant to be exempt from the fines, penalties, domiciliary visits, and other inconveniences to which those Cavaliers were liable who were not so fortunate as to possess a protector on the winning side. So Sir Giles answered in the affirmative, though a little testily, considering it was Grace to whom he spoke.

'As thou wilt, wench, as thou wilt. Let him come and see the two poor old cripples, an' he choose. Vaux is a-bed, and I'm little better, but the time has been that he's ridden alongside of us in buff and steel, the renegade. 'Slife, he's seen us front, and flanks, and rear, and all,' laughed the old knight, grimly, reverting to the defeats at Marston Moor and Naseby. 'Let him come and have a look at us, now we're laid upon the shelf and he's got the sun his own side o' the hedge, with a murrain to it! But write him a civil cartel, Gracey, too, for we're beholden to the black-muzzled varlet, Roundhead though he be.'

And thus it came to pass that Grace sat alone in the great hall at Boughton, with her colour coming and going, and her heart beating a very quick march the while George Effingham's orderly led his horse from the door, and the General himself walked into her presence, trembling in every limb, and in a state of nervous alarm sufficiently contemptible for a man who could face a battery without wincing. The usual ceremonious observances were gone through. Grace presented a cold cheek to her visitor's salute as she bade him welcome. And the latter dropped the hand extended to him as if it were some poisonous reptile, instead of the very treasure on earth for which he would have given every drop of blood in his body. They did not speak much of the weather, but according to the custom of the time, the gentleman made the most minute and circumstantial inquiries as to the state of health enjoyed by each separate member of her family, and the lady answered categorically, and by rule. Then there was a dead silence, very awkward, very painful, apparently interminable. Grace began almost to wish he hadn't come.

She broke it at last with an effort.

'I have to thank you, General Effingham, for so promptly attending to my request. Were you not surprised to receive my letter?' she added, with an attempt to lapse into a more playful vein.

George muttered something unintelligible in reply. He was no carpet-knight, our honest friend, and the last man on earth to help a lady either out of, or into, a difficulty.

She was obliged to go on unassisted. It was not so formidable as she fancied, now that the ice was broken, and she had recovered the alarm of hearing her own voice.

'I can count upon you as a friend, General,' she said, one of her frank, cordial smiles lighting up the whole of her pretty face; 'and I am about to put your friendship to the test. You can do me a kindness that will make me the happiest girl in the world—can I depend upon you? If you promise me, I *know* I can.'

He coloured with a swarthy glow of pleasure. This frank dealing accorded well with his honest earnest nature.

'I am a plain soldier, Mistress Grace,' he replied; 'I would give my life to serve you, and you know it.'

Grace's head began to turn. Now for it—she must plead with her lover to save one whom he could not but consider his rival, and perhaps the effort would cost the mediator all that makes life most valuable. Well, she was in deep water now, and must sink or swim. She struck out boldly at once.

'Do you know that your old comrade, Humphrey Bosville, is a prisoner in London, on a charge of high treason?'

He had not heard a word of it. He was grieved beyond measure. Bosville was so devoted, so persevering, had been so stanch to the Royal cause, had been concerned in every plot and every scheme, had been pardoned once by the Parliament. It would go hard with him this time—he was very, very sorry to hear of it.

'And that is exactly what I ask you to prevent,' she broke in. 'I have sent for you that I might implore you to save him. George Effingham, you are the only man alive that I would ask to do so much. Grant me my desire as freely and frankly as I entreat it of you.'

It was exactly the way to take him. Had she beat about the bush and *finessed* and coquetted with him, he would probably have refused her sternly, although such a refusal would have forbidden him ever to see her again. He would have set up some objection of duty or principle, and hardened himself to resistance, even against *her*, but he was not proof against this open-hearted, confiding, sisterly kind of treatment, and had she asked him to ride to London incontinently, and beard Cromwell to his face, he must have yielded on the spot. Where had Grace acquired her knowledge of human nature? Surely it is by intuition that

women thus readily detect and take advantage of our most
assailable points. They need no Vauban to tell them that 'a
fortress is no stronger than its weakest part,' but direct their
attack unhesitatingly where the wall is lowest, and carry everything before them by a *coup de main.*

George saw all the difficulties in his path plainly enough. He
knew that to ask for his old comrade's life would subject him to
much suspicion and misrepresentation on the part of his colleagues.
Like all successful men, he had no lack of rivals, and now that
the fighting was over it had already begun to be whispered that
the converted Cavalier was but a lukewarm partisan after all, nay,
the fanatics averred that he was, alas! but 'a whited sepulchre,'
and little better than a 'Malignant' in his heart. Cromwell
indeed, whose religious enthusiasm was strongly dashed with
political far-sightedness, knew his valour, and to Cromwell he
trusted; but he could not conceal from himself that he was about
to stake on one throw the whole of that influence and position he
had so ardently coveted, and which it had cost him such strenuous
and unceasing efforts to attain.

But George's was a generous nature, and the instant he had
determined to make this sacrifice for the woman he loved, he had
resolved that she should be the last person to learn its value and
importance.

'Is it to save my old friend's life, Mistress Grace,' he said,
'that you think it necessary thus to entreat me? I should indeed
be grateful to *you* for informing me of his danger. I will lose no
time in making every exertion on his behalf, ay, even should I
have to give my life for his. I only wish you had proposed to
me some more unwelcome task, that I might have shown you how
ready I am to comply with your every wish.'

He spoke with a playful, for him, even with a courtly air. He
marked the glistening eye and the flush of pleasure with which
she listened, nor did he wince for a moment, and though his lip
trembled a little, the brave face was as firm as marble.

Did he think he could blind her? Could he believe she did
not calculate his danger, and appreciate his unselfishness? Did
he not feel how her woman-nature must respond to a generosity
so akin to its own? If ever you would win her, George Effingham, open your arms now, and take her to your heart!

The tears were coming to his eyes, but he drove them back
with a strong effort, as, seeing she was too much moved to speak,
he proceeded—

'I will bring him back to you without a hair of his head being harmed, Mistress Grace. Perhaps in happier days you will both think kindly of the renegade Cavalier.'

She put her hand in his, smiling sweetly through her tears.

' Do this,' she murmured, ' and ask me what you will in recompense.'

He was too proud to understand her.

' There is not a moment to be lost,' he said ; ' make my excuses to Sir Giles and good Lord Vaux, that I must take my leave without waiting on them. Farewell, Mistress Grace; fear not. Farewell ! '

Without another word, without even touching her hand, he made a profound obeisance and left the room.

Grace's knees were knocking together, and she shook in every limb. She sank into Sir Giles's huge arm-chair, and there she sat and pondered the momentous question that some day or another presents itself to every woman's heart. ' How noble,' thought Grace, ' how generous, how chivalrous, and how good ! Never to show that he was conferring a kindness, never to place me under the sense of an obligation ; and all the time he is willing to give up his fame and his command and his position ; nay, a dearer, fonder future still, and for my sake.' Grace blushed up to her temples though she was alone. ' This is indeed true affection—the affection I have heard of and dreamt of ; that I never thought any one would be found to feel for me. For me !—what am I that that brave, determined, goodly man should thus be at the disposal of my lightest word ? ' Grace went to the end of the hall, peeped in the glass, and sat down again, apparently a little more satisfied and composed. ' If their positions were reversed, would Humphrey have acted so ? I trow not. Has he the firmness and the energy and the strength of mind of this one ? Oh ! why did I not love George Effingham instead ? Stay ! do I not love him now ? Shame, shame !—and I almost told him so. And perhaps he sees how wavering and unworthy I am, and despises me after all.' Grace sat back in her chair, in a most unenviable frame of mind—provoked with the past, impatient of the present, and undecided as to the future. George stepped calmly along the terrace, with the sad composure of a man who has nothing more to fear on earth. He had long known it must come to this at last ; had long anticipated the moment when the frail cobwebs of self-deception which weave themselves insensibly around the human heart must be swept away in a breath ; when the vain imitation of Hope that had beguiled its loneliness must be surrendered once for all ; and he accepted his lot with a proud, quiet resignation. At least he would make her happy, ay, though it cost him every treasure he had in the world; and when he could bear it he would see her again, and in her welfare should be his reward.

The rustle of a lady's dress behind him caused him to start and stop. Could she have followed him for one more last word? Could his self-sacrifice have touched and softened her? No; as he turned his head it was Mary Cave that hurried up to him with trembling steps, and accosted him in the faltering accents of extreme anxiety and distress.

She was so altered he hardly knew her. She whose manner used to be so composed and queenly, dashed it may be with a little too much self-confidence and assumption, was now nervous and pre-occupied; apparently humbled in her own estimation, and abrupt, almost incoherent, in her address. She had lost her rich colour, too, and there were lines on the brow he remembered so smooth and fair; while the soft blue eyes that formerly laughed and sparkled, and softened all at once, had grown fixed and dilated, even fierce in their expression of defiance and endurance.

'One word with you, General Effingham,' she said, without waiting to go through any of the common forms of salutation; 'have you seen Mistress Allonby?'

He answered in the affirmative with a bow. She seemed to know it, for she scarcely waited for a reply.

'You have heard it all,' she hurried on, speaking very fast and energetically, with a certain action of the hand and wrist that was habitual to her, but never (and this was so unlike her), never looking her companion in the face. 'Grace has made no subterfuge, no concealment; she has told you everything—everything? And you are going to London immediately?—this very day? You will not lose an instant? He will be saved, Effingham—don't you think he will?'

'I shall be on the road before the sun goes down,' he replied courteously, affecting to ignore her agitation; 'I have already promised Mistress Allonby that I will leave no stone unturned to save Humphrey Bosville. I think I can answer for his life being spared.'

She could not help it; she burst into tears. Alas! they came easier every time, and she had so often cause to weep now! But it relieved her, and after this display of weakness she relapsed into something of her old air of composure and superiority.

'He is a very dear friend,' she said, the colour gradually stealing over her pale face; 'a very dear friend to us all. You will command Grace's eternal gratitude, and Sir Giles's and Lord Vaux's—and mine.'

He was only too happy to serve them, he said; and he, too, valued Humphrey as much as any of them—so brave, so kindly; above all, so gentle and true-hearted.

'Hush!' she stopped him, quite eagerly, the while she laid her hand in his with a frank cordial pressure, but her face worked as though she would fain burst out crying once more. ' There is not a moment to lose; I must detain you no longer. There is one thing more I had to say. You will see him; you will tell him how anxious we have all been for him, and you will give him this packet yourself,' she drew it from her bosom as she spoke, ' and you will entrust it to no hand but his own. It is only a matter of—of—business,' she faltered out, ' but I wish it to arrive safe at its destination. Thank you—God bless you.'

She would not have been a woman had she not reserved this one little bit of concealment. Effingham must not know, no one must ever know, how she had loved Humphrey Bosville. The packet was but a matter of *business*—business, forsooth!—exchange and barter, and dead loss and utter bankruptcy; but none must fathom it. They are all alike; reeling from a death-blow they can find a moment to dispose their draperies decently, nay, even tastefully, around them. And whilst on the subject of drapery we may remark, that even in the deepest affliction they preserve no slight regard to the amenities of dress. Though Mary's heart was breaking, her robe was not disordered, neither was her hair out of curl.

As Effingham ordered out his horses and betook himself to the saddle, he little thought how he had created so deep an interest in the two gentle hearts he left behind him. Grace was already studiously comparing him with a previous idol, a comparison which generally argues the dethronement of the prior image from its pedestal in the female breast; and Mary, of all people, could most thoroughly enter into his feelings, pity his loneliness, and appreciate his self-sacrifice.

Humphrey's case was indeed one of extreme peril. Heavily manacled, and committed to Newgate like a common malefactor, his only prospect of release was when he should be brought before the Parliament and placed on trial for his life. Scant mercy, too, could he expect from that conscientious assemblage. A confirmed Malignant, a brave and zealous officer, an adherent of the Queen; lastly—setting at naught his previous pardon—an emissary from

Y

the French Court to the imprisoned King, nothing was wanting
to prove him guilty of high treason against the majesty of the
Commons House of Parliament by law assembled,—nothing but
an extraordinary reversal of the usual sentence could prevent his
paying the extreme penalty attached to that heinous offence.

In vain he pleaded the innocence of the letters with which he
was charged; in vain he urged that they contained a simple
application to his Majesty from the Prince, his son, for permission
to accompany the Duke of Orleans to the wars. In vain he
pleaded his own position as a mere domestic functionary attached
to the person of the Queen. His well-known character for loyalty
and reckless daring, accompanied by his steady refusal to sign his
name to a written statement embodying the above explanations,
utterly nullified all that could be said in his defence, and left him
nothing to anticipate but an adverse verdict, a short shrift, and a
speedy end.

It was evident, however, that some strong influence was at
work below the surface in favour of the Royalist prisoner. Powerful debaters in the House of Commons itself urged the policy of
clemency, and the antecedents of the culprit, as arguments for a
mitigated sentence, if not a free acquittal. Shrewd lawyers
reserved points of law in his behalf. One eminent patriot boldly
expressed his admiration of such devoted constancy even in an
enemy; and although the case was too clear to admit of doubt,
and Lenthall (the Mr. Speaker of his day) was compelled to do
his duty and commit the prisoner for trial on the capital charge,
he was not even then abandoned by friends, who must indeed
have felt *themselves* secure to make such exertions in his behalf.

On his return to Newgate from Westminster, the coach in
which he sat was curiously enough upset. Two of his guards
appeared strangely stupefied, a third was drunk, and the fourth,
slipping a note into his hand, bade him run for his life the while
he extricated the horses and rated the driver soundly for their
misfortune. Perhaps Humphrey was not so surprised as he might
have been, had he not previously held an interview with Effingham in his prison, whose writing he recognised in the slip of
paper in his hand. Its contents were short and pithy :

' Keep quiet and in hiding,' it said, ' for a few months. You
will be purposely overlooked, but remain where you are not
known, and above all—keep still.'

There was no signature, but Humphrey wisely tore it into
shreds as he made his escape through the increasing darkness.

And now Effingham was anticipating his reward. As he journeyed rapidly back to Northampton, riding post, and urging the good horses beneath him to their swiftest pace, he was thinking of Grace's grateful smile when he should assure her that her lover had been saved by his exertions; and his own gratification, in which indeed there was no inconsiderable leaven of pain, at her delight.

He was to see her just *once* again—that once which, contrary to all the rules of arithmetic, is multiplied by itself into so many, many times—to witness her happiness with his own eyes, and feel that henceforth he was never so much as to think of her again. For this he had worked and fawned, cajoled and promised, intrigued and threatened; done constant violence to his stern, true nature, and lost that position with his party which it had cost him so much to attain. And for this he would have done as much and twice as much again, because, you see, he was going to have his Reward.

How even this consolation was denied him, we must detail in another chapter.

CHAPTER XXXVII.

' WELCOME HOME.'

THERE was hurrying to and fro in the old house at Boughton; a hushed confusion seemed to pervade the establishment, and though the servants rushed here and there in aimless anxiety, everything was done as noiselessly as possible, and they did not even venture to express in words that which their scared faces and white lips told only too well.

Horses had been saddled hastily, and ridden off at speed in search of medical assistance. With the strange piteous earnestness to do *something* which pervades us helpless mortals when we feel that *nothing* can avail, mounted messengers had been dispatched in needless repetition. There was little to be done but to wait for the leech and summon fortitude to endure his confirmation of their worst fears. The sick man said himself there was no hope. He seemed less affected than any in the household by the recent catastrophe.

Sir Giles was down under a mortal stroke. He preserved his senses and his speech; the rest of the man was a mere helpless shell; but his mind was as vigorous as ever, and the old knight's courage had not given way even now—no, not an inch.

He had often looked on Death before, and fronted him in the field, spurring his good horse against him, with a jest on his lips, and told him that he feared him not, to his face. He had seen all he loved best on earth fast in the skeleton's embrace, and he had not quailed even then. Would he shrink from him now? Pshaw! let him do his worst.

We have said it before, and we say it again, that the mind which has never prepared itself for the great change, is usually incapable of doing so when that change is actually present. Far be it from us to aver that it is ever too late whilst there is life; we only remark that it seems ill-advised to make no preparation for a long, what if it be an endless, journey? till the foot is actually in the stirrup.

Grace was weeping by his bedside, her hand in his, her face turned from him to hide the big drops that coursed each other down her cheeks. Poor Gracey! Many a true friend loves you well, many a heart leaps to the glance of your kind eyes, and warms to your gentle voice; but where will you find an affection so constant, so unwavering, so regardless of self, so patient of ingratitude, as his who lies gasping there on his death-bed? Where will you find another love that shall be always willing to give everything and receive nothing? that shall pour on you its unceasing stores of care and tenderness, nor ask even for a word of thanks in return?

'I've been a kind old father to thee, lass,' said the dying man, 'and thou'st been a rare daughter to me; but I must leave thee now.'

What could Grace do but bow her head down upon the poor thin hand she held, and weep as if her heart would break?

He folded the pretty head to his bosom as he used to do when she was a little child, stroking the hair down, and fondling and consoling her.

'Don't ye cry so, my darling,' said the old warrior. 'What! Gracey, little woman, cheer up! 'tis not for long, lass, not for long.'

She seemed to be the dying one of the two. She lay motionless, her head buried in his breast. She was praying for him to *his* Father and hers.

He was still for a time. Conscious of his failing powers, he was gathering himself, as it were, for an effort. When he spoke again she looked up astonished at his strength of voice.

'Is Mary here?' he asked—'Mary Cave? bid her come round here. God bless thee, Mistress Mary.'

She had been sitting afar off at the window, quietly waiting, as was her custom, till she could be of use. She came to the bedside now, and put her arm round Grace, and looked down upon the helpless knight with a calm, sad face. The greater grief absorbs the less, and constant pain will make callous the most sensitive nature. Poor Mary! two short years ago she would hardly have stood so composed and statue-like at good Sir Giles's death-bed.

'Care for her, sweet Mistress Mary,' he resumed, with something of his old energy of voice and manner; 'take charge of my pretty one when I am gone. I thought sometimes to see her married to you good lad, him that rode the sorrel horse so fairly —my memory fails me now, I think—how call you him? Ay, I thought to have seen her married and all; but she's young, very young yet. I am failing fast, Mistress Mary; don't ye speak to Gracey about it; she loves her old father, and it might disturb the child; but I'm not for long here. I know not if my senses may be spared me. I must speak out whilst I can. Gracey, are you there? Where is Gracey?'

She was close to him still, pressing her wet cheek to his.

'Here, father,' she whispered, '*dear* father;' and her voice seemed to revive him for the time.

'Mary will take care of thee, my little lass,' he said, feebly stretching his hand to hers, and trying to place it in that of her friend. 'Thou wilt not leave her, Mary; never leave her till she's married to some good man—not a rebel, Gracey, never a rebel, for the old father's sake. I loved that bold lad well; why doth he never come to see us now? Kiss me, Gracey. I shall see thee again, my child. God forgive my sins! I have never sinned by thee. I shall see thee again, and thy mother too. God bless thee, Gracey!'

He sank into a stupor. The leech had not arrived yet. Something told their hearts that all the leechcraft on earth would be of no avail, and the two women sat noiselessly weeping in the silence of the death-chamber.

He spoke again after a while; but his eyes shone with a strange brightness, and the indescribable change was on him—the change which we cannot but instinctively acknowledge, and which pervades the dying, like a gleam of pale light from the land beyond the grave.

He spoke of the old times now. Anon he was charging once more at the head of his brigade on Naseby field; the tramp of squadrons and the rattle of small arms were in his ears, and Effingham's steel-headed pikes lowered grimly in his front. Alas! the battle shout was but a hoarse labouring whisper, yet the two pale listeners could recognise the tactics of an action and the stirring old war-cry, 'God and Queen Mary ! For the King! for the King! '

Then he prayed for his Sovereign, fervently, loyally, prayed that he might recover his power and his throne, intermingling short pithy phrases from the ritual of his Church, and expressing himself proud, happy, privileged, that he might die for his King.

Yet a thread of consciousness seemed to run through these fitful wanderings of departing reason. It was pitiful to hear him urge on his fancied retainers to ease his saddle and curb his good horse tighter, as he flew his hawk once more in the green meadows under the summer sky.

'He was getting infirm,' he said, 'and the days were long at this time of year; but it was evening at last, and he was glad, for he was tired, very tired. It would be dark before they got home. It was very dark even now.'

There was a dead silence. The startled women thought he was gone; but he breathed yet, though very faintly, and with parted lips. His eyes were closed, but he was wandering still. He called to his hawk, his horse, and his hounds. He must see Gracey, too, he said, 'before he took his boots off'—'She was very little, surely, *very* little to run alone ; ' and he spoke fondly and tenderly to another Grace—a Grace that had been treasured up many a long year in the depths of his stout old heart, a Grace that would almost weary expecting him, even in heaven—that was surely waiting for him now on the other side.

He opened his eyes once more, but they rolled aimlessly around, fixing themselves at last feebly upon his daughter. Grace felt to her heart's core that his last look was one of consciousness upon *her*—that he knew *her* even while that look was glazing into death—that the 'God bless thee, Gracey ! ' which he gasped out with his last breath, was the same old fond familiar farewell with which he was always used to depart upon a journey.

So he went upon his way, and surely when he reached the promised land he found a fond face there, waiting to welcome him home.

Ere the surgeon arrived in hot haste there was nothing left on earth of the stout old Cavalier but a goodly war-worn frame, a fixed marble face, smooth and placid, renovated, as it were, to the sculptured beauty of its prime. He shook his head as he acknowledged himself to be too late, and left the mourners to the sacred indulgence of their grief. Grace Allonby wept in her friend's arms, clinging to her in her distress with the helpless abandonment of a child, and Mary, roused from her own sorrows by the necessity for exertion, soothed her gently and pitifully like a mother. Lord Vaux was by this time a helpless invalid, and both women felt they had at last lost their only protector, as well as their best and kindest friend.

' You must never leave me, Mary,' sobbed out Grace again and again, as a fresh burst of grief broke wildly forth, ' never leave me now, for I have but you in the world.'

It was a goodly funeral with which they did honour to the brave old Cavalier. Many a stout yeoman came from far and near to see him laid in his last resting-place, and told, not without pride, as he quaffed the ale which ever flowed freely on such occasions, how he had charged to the old knight's battle-cry at Naseby, or followed him through serried columns and levelled pikes at Edgehill or Roundway-down. Not a brave heart within three counties but when he heard of Sir Giles's death said, ' God rest him ! he *was* a bold one.' The King himself, the harassed, careworn Charles, wrote a letter of condolence with his own royal hand to the daughter of his faithful servant; and Prince Rupert, pining in exile, vowed that ' the last of the real old Cavaliers was buried with Sir Giles.'

But better than troopers' admiration, prince's approval, and king's autograph, there was more than one poor friendless widow that came with her orphans in her hand, whilst the turf was fresh and ere the stone was up, to weep over the grave of her kind friend and benefactor. Epitaphs may lie, monuments may crumble, deeds of arms and mortal fame may pass away, but the tears of the widow and the fatherless are treasured up as a lasting memorial in a certain. stronghold, where ' neither moth nor rust doth corrupt, and where thieves do not break through nor steal.'

CHAPTER XXXVIII.

' WESTMINSTER HALL.'

' WRAP thy cloak well round thee, Gracey; the wind strikes chill to the very marrow.' It was Mary Cave who spoke, and suiting the action to the word, drew with a tender hand the folds of a large dark mantle round the form of her companion.

Grace shivered from head to foot, her teeth chattered, and she tottered as she walked, supported by her friend, who, faithful **to** the trust he left her, seemed to take a maternal charge of Sir Giles's orphan daughter.

'I never thought they would have dared to do it,' observed Mary, pursuing the train of her own reflections, 'but it has come at last. He was brought from Windsor last night. I saw him myself by torchlight as he descended from the coach—so altered, Grace, so altered, in a short eighteen months!'

The expression of Grace's countenance was as that of one who sees some horrible deed of sacrilege committed, which the witness is powerless to prevent. She hurried on nervously, and without answering a word.

More than a year had elapsed since the events recorded in the preceding chapter—a year of trouble and anxiety to the nation—a year of sorrow and seclusion to these two hapless mourners. Lord Vaux, whose failing health had long been a subject for alarm, seemed utterly unable to recover the shock occasioned by his old friend's death. His kinswomen had brought him to the capital in search of the best medical assistance, and the two Royalist ladies were naturally anxious to be near the centre of those desperate measures which agitated the politics of the day. A powerful hand, too, seemed to protect this Malignant family. They came and went unquestioned where they would, and were free from the annoyances to which so many of their friends were subjected. It is possible that Grace may have been able to guess the shield which thus guarded her; but if so, gratitude did but add another painful ingredient to the total of her sufferings. Her father's kind old face was ever before her eyes as she saw it last, and the dying whisper, 'not a rebel, Gracey, never a rebel, for the old father's sake!' seemed to ring in her ears day and night.

She shivered again as she drew the dark heavy folds tight around her: it was so cold—so bitter cold.

A keen black frost, very different from his gladsome brother who comes sparkling down upon us, his stiff crisp raiment glittering with diamonds in the sunshine, bound the shrinking earth in a churlish embrace. A cutting north-easter, sweeping over her surface in fitful gusts, whirled up clouds of dust that stung and irritated the unprotected face like pin-points, and a dull leaden sky, against which the leafless trees of the Mall seemed to wave their skeleton branches as it were in mockery, lowered over all. London wore her blackest, her most forbidding look, and the pinnacles and spires of proud old Westminster frowned hard and threatening in the dense cold atmosphere.

Yet people were standing about in groups, some talking in

whispers with suppressed though eager gestures; others waiting patiently, as if for some show or pageant. As is usual in a crowd, the women slightly predominated, yet was there but little sarcastic questioning and shrill reply, while the gambols of the London urchin—a race never on any public occasion to be sought in vain—failed to excite more than a transient smile in the grave and preoccupied multitude.

As Mary and Grace passed rapidly on they heard many an ominous whisper and broken phrase respecting the great event which was thus collecting the agitated citizens. Strange improbable rumours flew from lip to lip; hints of impossible combinations and contradictory circumstances obtained implicit credence. Here a sedate-looking personage assured his auditors that 'his Majesty was never firmer on the throne; that he was coming in state to Westminster to open his faithful Parliament in person; that the Lords at Windsor, the greatest personages in the kingdom, served him daily on their knees; and that he knew this to be a fact, he who now spoke to them at the present time, for his sister's son, a gardener by trade, had the King's own commands for the sowing of certain Spanish melons at Wimbledon. And is it likely,' added the orator, looking up to the gloomy sky, 'that his Majesty would be sowing melons, especially Spanish ones, and in this weather too, unless he felt confident of seeing them ripen?' 'God bless him!' he would have added, but he caught the scowl of a wild fanatical-looking personage glaring so fiercely at him that the words died upon his lips.

Then a little dirty man, a cobbler by trade, something of a demagogue by profession, and a drunkard by choice, gave it as his own opinion, with much unnecessary circumlocution, that 'Charles,' as he called him, was about to place himself unreservedly in the hands of his Parliament. 'Do we not know,' said the little man, brandishing aloft a pair of much-begrimed hands, and steadying his whole person by fixing his lack-lustre eye on a quiet individual in the crowd, who thus found himself, much to his annoyance, an object of considerable interest—'do we not know that the people, under God, are the original of all just power? that the Commons, chosen by and representing *us*' (the little man smote his shabby breast violently with his dirty hands) 'are the fountain of all power and authority, so that what the Commons declared law *is* law and nothing *but* law? and all the people of this nation are concluded thereby, although the consent and concurrence of the King and the House of Peers be not had thereunto!'

The little man had got the last clause of the Parliament's

proclamation carefully by rote, and used the same for his peroration with considerable skill, much to the delight of his auditors, who very generally expressed themselves satisfied with the soundness of his reasoning and the correctness of his principles.

But still, amongst all the conflicting reports alluded to, all the different opinions expressed by this motley assemblage, not a whisper was breathed as to the dreadful event which was really impending, not a suspicion seemed to exist even amongst the strongest partisans of the Parliament, that the people of England would exact the penalty of a king's blood.

It was only the well-educated and the far-seeing—those, in fact, who might be said to be behind the scenes—that could anticipate the worst; those who knew that the Commons had declared themselves independent of the Lords, that a commission had already been nominated for the trial of Charles Stuart on the charge of high treason, and that out of the hundred and thirty-five members appointed, scarce eighty consented to act, might indeed acknowledge the signs of the coming storm—the blast that was so soon to level the loftiest head in England with the dust.

As the hour of noon approached the crowd thickened considerably, and as it drew into its vortex more and more of the lowest rabble, the feeling against the King seemed to gain greater strength. Coach after coach rolled by, bearing the magnates of the country to the important scene in Westminster Hall, and as these were mostly well known to the populace, it might be remarked that such as were suspected even of a leaning towards royalty were assailed with groans and execrations, sometimes even with missiles of a more injurious nature, whilst those whose levelling principles were beyond doubt received a perfect ovation of cheers and congratulations, sometimes ridiculously personal, but always intended to be complimentary in the highest degree.

Amongst the rest one equipage in particular aroused a perfect tumult of applause: it was the coach of General Fairfax, containing his lady, seated alone in all the pomp of her native dignity and her robes of state. Like every successful man for the moment, Fairfax was at that period an immense favourite with the mob, and they clustered round the carriage that conveyed his wife with coarse and boisterous expressions of goodwill. The face inside was a study of strong suppressed feeling. Sitting there in the majesty of her beauty, she could scarce restrain the overpowering sentiments of hatred and contempt with which she regarded those who now surrounded her with such demonstrations of affection. The blood of the Veres boiled within her as she thought of her husband's forfeited loyalty, and the scene from which she had persuaded him to be absent, but to which she was herself hurrying. Her face turned red and white by turns, she bit her lip and clenched her hand as she bid her coachman lash his horses recklessly and drive on. Like the proud Tarquin's prouder wife, she would scarce have stopped had a human form been down beneath her feet.

Jostled by the crowd, notwithstanding her haughty step and imperious gestures, Mary could scarce make her way, and Grace's visible agitation increasing more and more, rendered her position one of peculiar annoyance and discomfort.

They narrowly escaped being run over by the rapidly approaching carriage, but as it passed so close that its wheels brushed Mary's garments, a well-known face appeared at the window, a familiar voice she had not heard for many a year called to the coachman to stop, and Lady Fairfax bade them enter and come with her, in her usual accents of command.

' Mary Cave ! I thought it was you,' she exclaimed. ' What are you doing amongst this *canaille* ? Jump in, and your friend too. Let us see the end of this shameful business in Westminster Hall.'

The unconscious *canaille* gave her ladyship and friends three hearty cheers as they drove off.

Under such protection as that of Lady Fairfax, with whom Mary had been intimate in girlhood's brighter days, the two ladies found no difficulty in obtaining access to the Hall.

Seats had been apportioned, and what were even then termed ' boxes' partitioned off for the wives and families of the chief actors to witness the proceedings, and one of the principal of these had been reserved for the lady of the powerful Parliamentary General.

It was an awful and a solemn scene which burst upon the sight of our two devoted loyalists as they entered. The King's trial was about to commence, and already had the commissioners taken their seats, with more than the usual pomp of form and ceremony. The stern and able Bradshaw, he whose sense of duty has earned him an unenviable immortality under the title of 'The Regicide,' stood erect as President, supported by his assessors, Lisle and Say, skilful lawyers both, and bold, uncompromising men.

All heads were turned, all eyes directed towards the bar, at which was set a velvet chair of state. This inanimate object seemed to excite universal interest. It was to receive the royal prisoner, but it was still empty.

Anon the vague murmur that pervades all large assemblies in·
creased audibly, and a certain stir was apparent at the far end of
the Hall; then succeeded the deep hush of intense expectation,
and many a heart heard nothing but its own thick beating, as it
strained for a forward glimpse of but a few hours.

A sedan-chair was carried slowly up the Hall; many uncovered
as it passed them; one or two voices were even heard to murmur
a blessing. But that chair contained Charles Stuart, and his
judges sat doggedly with their hats on, neither rising nor showing
the slightest mark of respect to their unfortunate Sovereign.

When the King reached the bar he alighted, and without removing his hat, seated himself at once in the chair appointed for
him; but presently rising again, looked sternly about him, at the
president, at the court, at the people in the galleries; his nerve
was as unshaken as it had ever been in the presence of *physical*
danger. He was at bay now, and he was every inch a king.

But he was altered, sadly altered too. Mary's heart sank
within her as she traced the furrows that suffering and anxiety
had ploughed in those royal lineaments, for which she had all her
life been taught to cherish an affectionate veneration. His well-
knit figure was firm and upright as ever; nor were his locks,
though slightly tinged with grey, much thinner than of old; but
his features were sharpened, and his eyes hollowed, as if he had
been suffering acute physical pain; while the *doomed* expression
that had always been the chief characteristic of his face, had deepened to an intensity of melancholy that it was piteous to look upon.

When Bradshaw spoke, however, his features hardened into
defiance once more.

Silence was proclaimed, and a whisper might have been heard
from one end to the other of that vast hall. Then the clerk, in a
sonorous and business-like voice, read over the ordinance for the
King's trial, a formal document, couched in terms of legal obscurity.
When the ceremony was concluded, the list of commissioners was
called over by the same functionary, those present answering to
their names.

'John Bradshaw!'

'Here,' replied the President, in a loud undaunted voice, looking sternly at the King, who returned his glance with a haughty
and contemptuous frown.

'Thomas Fairfax!'

There was no response. A stir pervaded the hall as men
turned and stared, and whispered their neighbours with eager,
anxious faces.

Again the clerk called in a loud voice, ' Thomas Fairfax ! '

' He has more wit than to be here,' was answered, in distinct confident tones ; but though Bradshaw bent his brows in anger, and the commissioners made hasty inquiries, and gave peremptory orders to their officials to secure the offender, it was not easy, in the increasing confusion, to ascertain whence the bold reply had come.

It originated, however, a murmur and a disturbance which it took some minutes to quell. Signs of disapprobation were swamped by a strong inclination to applaud ; and it was evident that a powerful feeling in favour of the royal prisoner existed even in the very court in which he was to be tried.

The impeachment was then read over, accusing the monarch of ' designs to erect to himself an illimited and tyrannical power, to overthrow the rights and liberties of the people ; of high treason in respect of the levying war against the present Parliament, and the people therein represented ; ' as denoted by his appearance at York and Beverley with a guard ; by the setting up of the standard at Nottingham ; by the battle of Edgehill ; and so on in order enumerating the different battles at which the King had been present. The document then went on to say, that he had caused the death of thousands of free-born people ; that after his forces had been defeated, and himself made prisoner, he had stirred up insurrection in the country, and given a commission to the prince, his son, to raise a new war against the Parliament ; and that, ' as he was the author and contriver of these unnatural, cruel, and bloody wars, so was he therein guilty of all the treasons, murders, rapines, burnings, spoils, desolation, damage, and mischief to the nation which had been committed in the said wars, or been occasioned thereby ; and that he was therefore impeached for the said treasons and crimes, as a tyrant, traitor, and murderer, and a public implacable enemy to the Commonwealth, on behalf of the good people of England.'

The King had sat perfectly silent and composed during the reading of the above strangely-worded impeachment, save that at the terms ' tyrant and traitor ' as applied to himself, he had smiled contemptuously in the faces of the court. He raised his head, however, as the clerk paused to take breath after enunciating the last paragraph, and seemed about to make some objection or remark, but was arrested in the act, for the same female voice that had already interrupted the proceedings of the court, now rose once more, distinct and forcible through the hush of the attentive audience.

'The good people of England!' it exclaimed, in clear mocking tones. 'No! nor one hundredth part of them!'

Great was the disturbance that ensued; several members rose hurriedly from their seats, and a tumultuous rush in the body of the hall added to the general confusion. Some even thought a rescue was impending; and a few of the more timorous were already glancing about for a speedy egress. Colonel Hacker, who commanded the guard of musketeers, and to whom was confided the custody of the King's person, gave orders to fire into the box whence these sounds of disapproval had arisen; and the stern soldiers had already levelled their muskets to obey this unmilitary command. Lady Fairfax rose undauntedly and faced their muzzles with a bold imperious brow. Mary, too, rushed to the front to share the danger of her friend. Grace, trembling and weeping, shrank behind them, half paralysed with fear. For a few moments all was breathless confusion; but a voice, that even in her terror the frightened girl recognised only too plainly, was heard to exclaim, in loud reproving tones, 'Shame! shame! Recover your arms! Cowards! would you fire upon your countrywomen?' and George Effingham, in his uniform as a general of the Parliament, struck up the barrels of the muskets, and threatened to put Hacker under immediate arrest.

An usher of the court, however, came round to the box occupied by Lady Fairfax, and endeavoured to prevail upon her to withdraw. It was only under a promise that she would remain tranquil, extorted from her by the entreaties of her companions, that she was permitted to remain. With clenched hands and angry brow she sat out the remainder of the proceedings.

When order was once more restored, Mr. Cook, the Attorney-General, being about to speak, the King laid the long amber-headed cane which he usually carried, upon his shoulder, and bade him 'hold;' but the Lord President requiring him to proceed, his Majesty folded his arms, and bending his brows fixedly upon him, listened attentively to a summary of the charges against him, which was now repeated.

His Majesty then required to know by what authority he was brought hither.

'I have,' said Charles, 'a Trust committed to me by God by old and lawful descent; I will not betray it to answer to a new unlawful authority; therefore, resolve me that, and you shall hear more of me.'

'Sir,' replied the President, 'you are required to answer these charges in the name of the people of England, of whom you are the elected king.'

'I deny that,' interrupted the indignant monarch. 'England has been no elective kingdom, but a hereditary monarchy for near a thousand years. I dispute your authority. I do stand more for the liberty of my people than any here that come to be my pretended judges.'

Bradshaw in an insolent tone bade him interrogate the court with becoming deference and humility.

His pride aroused, his royal dignity insulted, Charles lost his assumed calmness and that presence of mind for which he was not always too conspicuous. With intemperate voice and gesture, he inveighed against the injustice of the proceedings, calling on Divine Providence, in no measured language, to avenge him of his enemies, and right him in the face of the whole world. Whilst thus declaiming, the amber-head of his staff fell off, and this little incident, ominous as it might have appeared to a super-stitious mind, served to change the current of his ideas, and to moderate the violence of his deportment.

Mary's loyal heart swelled with indignation as, sitting unob-served behind Lady Fairfax, she could not but remark how no obedient courtiers pressed to pick it up—how the King, with a gesture of patient surprise, was fain to stoop for it himself, and as though reminded by the very act of the friendlessness of his posi-tion, and the necessity for resignation, rose once more with the calm brow and the air of quiet long-suffering that had become habitual to that careworn face.

But Mary, too, with all her Cavalier enthusiasm and exagger-ated sentiments of the devotion due to her Sovereign, had other matters to occupy her wandering thoughts, other causes for agita-tion and excitement, apart from the great political tragedy of which she was then and there witnessing the first act. Each one of us lives an inner as well as an outer existence. How curious would it have been to have analysed the thoughts of the different individuals who thronged that spacious hall! Met there for a common object, and that an object of vital importance, not only to the destinies of their country, but to the personal safety of the lieges, how many minds amongst them were bent, to the exclu-sion of all other images, solely on the affair in hand! How many even of the judges but had a large share of their attention preoc-cupied by matters solely personal and interesting to themselves— by a farm far off in Lincolnshire, a wife sickening at Bath, a child unhappily married in Scotland; nay, even by such trifling annoy-ance as domestic difficulties with a servant, or the lameness of a favourite horse! How many but had some overpowering interest

at heart, to which the justice of the trial and the guilt or innocence of the royal prisoner was a mere gossamer, and who
could scarce withdraw their minds for a few minutes at a time
from the one engrossing object, to bend them on the paramount
duty they had sworn to fulfil!   What was Charles's condemnation or acquittal, to the idol each had privately raised up and
worshipped, as men worship false idols alone—the schemes of
selfish aggrandizement, the acquisition of wealth, the fascinating
temptations of intrigue, or the thrilling satisfaction of revenge?
Even Lady Fairfax, wrathful and defiant as she was, pitying with
a woman's pity the innocent victim, and chafing with a woman's
indignation at the palpable injustice, could not forbear a glance
into the possible future, when that royal prisoner should be no
longer the first personage in England, could not keep back a swell
of pride as she bethought her of one who had no slight prospect
of assuming the reins of power, who *might* rise from a Parliamentary General (as his comrade really did) to be a Parliamentary Dictator ; and how for such an one she was herself no
unworthy mate.

And Mary, too, no longer bent her whole attention on that
velvet chair and its hapless occupant.   In glancing wearily round
the hall, searching, as it were, for a friendly face on which to
rest, her eye had caught a glimpse of a countenance that reminded
her—oh ! so painfully—of one which even now to think of
brought the blood to her cheek, and left it paler than before.
Yes, though lost again instantaneously in the crowd, there was a
face somewhere, she was sure of it, that resembled *his*.   That it
was himself, of course, was impossible.   He was in strict hiding,
no doubt, and probably had taken refuge on the Continent ; at
all events, the last place in the world to which even *his* recklessness would bring him, was the very stronghold of his enemies in
Westminster Hall.   But weak, childish, humiliating as it was,
there would be something gratifying, something of a strange in-
definable pleasure, mixed with pain, in looking once more on
lineaments which could recall those that all the schooling in the
world had not taught her to forget; so her eyes wandered over
the Hall, and refused to rest until they had found that which they
desired.   A momentary stir amongst the group immediately surrounding the Sovereign exposed the object of her search once
more.   It was but one of the musketeers who formed the escort,
after all, that had so reminded her for an instant of one now lost
to her for ever, and on regarding him attentively, though there
was something in the air and figure that resembled Humphrey

Bosville, the colour and complexion were so totally different from those of the proscribed Cavalier, that the resemblance became every moment more indistinct, and Mary smiled to herself, a faint, heart-sick smile, as she thought how harmless in its utter hopelessness was folly such as hers.

But it beguiled her mind from the afflicting present, it led her fancy wandering away through the enamelled meadows and by the golden streams of that fairy land in which it is so dangerous to linger, and it was with a start of returning consciousness and the confused sensations of one awaking from a deep slumber, that she was aware of the general stir created by the departure of the prisoner from the Hall.

The proceedings had terminated for the day. Charles, after vainly protesting against the authority of his judges, had relapsed into the quiet dignified bearing of one who, while he feels the injustice to which he is subjected, resolves bravely and patiently to sustain his fate. As he was conducted down the hall, loud expressions of loyalty greeted him from many an unknown and unsuspected partisan even amongst those therein assembled, although a strong majority of his enemies strove to drown these ebullitions by violent cries for 'justice.'

When the King passed the sword of state, placed conspicuously in the sight of the whole assemblage, he manned himself with an air of dignity, and facing the court, pointed to the emblem of death, while he exclaimed in a loud, firm tone, 'I do not fear *that*!'

It was no empty boast. How little Charles Stuart feared the extreme moment from which poor human nature instinctively recoils, he proved nobly and resignedly on the scaffold.

CHAPTER XXXIX.

'THE MUSKETEER.'

THE Guard was strengthened more than common at St. James's. Sentries were doubled in all the principal avenues to the Palace, not only for the increase of vigilance, but for the nullifying of any attempt at tampering with those unmoved functionaries. Stringent orders were given as to the exclusion of strangers, and a watchful expression pervaded the countenance of sergeants and corporals as they visited their respective posts with unusual frequency and circumspection. Nevertheless, within the guard-room the men off duty for the time lounged and laughed and smoked as soldiers will whether they have a crowned head in ward or an enemy at the gates. Small respect did these rude men of war pay to the former consideration. Their commander, Colonel Hacker, was a stern and coarse-minded person: a leveller in politics and a fanatic in religion, he was not likely to insist on any inordinate reverence for his illustrious captive; and the private soldiers, taking their cue from their chief, lighted their pipes and laughed out their ribald jokes in the presence of patient and outraged Royalty itself.

It was the first day of the King's trial. The escort which had conducted him back to St. James's were off duty for the nonce, and the guard-room was thronged with the usual complement of idle, talking, preaching, and smoking champions who constituted the flower of Hacker's redoubtable musketeers. Here a stalwart warrior, lying at his lazy length along the coarse oaken form, and puffing forth volumes of tobacco-smoke, expressed his own opinions as to the proceedings of the day with a degree of irreverence for all concerned—judges, prisoner, and spectators—such as nothing but a guard-room could produce. There a grim war-worn corporal, with an open Bible in his hand, and a stern, dogmatic frown upon his brow, waited impatiently for a moment's silence to commence what he termed an 'exercise,' and to vilify and vituperate in every possible manner 'the man Charles Stuart,' 'for the improvement of the occasion.' Some were rubbing up their belts, inspecting the pans of their firelocks, or exploring the contents of their haversacks previous to going again on duty; whilst others, fatigued with watch and ward, and regardless alike of King and Commons, right and wrong, accusers and accused, were stretched supine in sound and snoring sleep.

One soldier, however, stood at the grated window of the guard-room, apart from the rest, seemingly immersed in thought. His eyes, fixed on vacancy, were looking back far into the Past; his dark face, strangely at variance with the light flaxen curls that stole from under his iron head-piece, wore an expression of acute pain, borne with resolute endurance—such an expression as betrays the existence of a fatal malady, bodily or mental, to which the sufferer scorns to give way.

His spare and muscular figure was cast in a more graceful mould than generally pertains to those of humble birth; and the hand, in which he crumpled a much-creased letter, though strong and sinewy, was shapely as a woman's. He seemed struggling with some powerful influence or temptation : ever and anon a soft, tender expression swept across his swarthy features, but a glance at the paper in his hand hardened them into bronze once more.

This soldier had but lately joined the corps of Hacker's musketeers. He was no raw recruit, as was soon apparent by his thorough knowledge of military details; and more than one scar on his neck and arms argued the presumption that he had been a brave front-rank man in his time. His own account was that he had served for a while in the Netherlands, and afterwards sailed as a buccaneer on the Spanish Main ; and this story tallied well with his soldierlike habits and the unnaturally dark colour of his skin where it had been exposed to the sun. He won the good opinion of the sergeant who enlisted him by one or two feats of strength and agility ; and in those days of tumult few questions were asked as to the antecedents of a soldier who brought into the ranks an iron frame and a thorough familiarity with his profession. But his comrades scarcely knew what to make of their new acquisition. With a peculiar frankness and kindliness of manner, he was more prompt than is the custom of that boisterous class to check a liberty or resent an insult. And his personal strength, added to the self-evident daring of his character, made them chary of rousing him by any of those rude aggressions or disagreeable jests which the rough musketeers loved to practise on one another. Of the soundness of his religious views there were grave suspicions. The preaching corporal opined that he was one of those predestined backsliders who fall into utter and hopeless reprobation ; but this uncharitable opinion, biassed as it seemed to be by the impatience he had frequently manifested of that worthy's long-winded discourses, was scarcely shared by his comrades in so unmodified a form. That he was a stanch anti-Monarchy man was apparent less from his words, for he seldom enlarged much upon that or any other topic, than from the anxiety he displayed to lose no opportunity of witnessing the humiliations to which Charles was subjected. For all duties of guard or escort about the person of the monarch, Henry Brampton, as he called himself, was an eager volunteer. His comrades liked him, too ; there was a nameless fascination in his pleasant manner that told on those rude, good-humoured natures ; and then—he treated one and all to liquor whenever there was an opportunity.

Undisturbed by the noise and confusion in the guard-room, Brampton stood gazing long and fixedly into the narrow paved yard which bounded his view from that grated window. Once only a large tear gathered in his eyelashes, and dropped heavily on the back of his hand. Startled, as it seemed, and bitterly shamed by the incident, he fell to one more perusal of the letter he had been crushing in his grasp—a letter that had reposed inside his buff-coat for months; that had been read and re-read day by day, again and again; that had opened the old wound afresh at each repetition; and yet a letter that now constituted all his wealth on earth. It was cold, cruel, bitterly ungrateful and un-feeling. Why did he treasure it so? We will peep over the musketeer's shoulder, and read with him the words he knew so well by heart :—

'General Effingham will bear you this paper; you will easily recognise the hand of one who has always looked upon you, who always *will* look upon you, as an esteemed and valued friend.

'The General will spare no exertions to save you from the consequences of that last rash act of yours, to which I of all people cannot but offer my tribute of admiration and approval. It is right you should know that to Grace's influence with him, and to Grace alone, you owe your life. It is right you should be made aware of her great regard and esteem for you—of the effort she has made for your sake; of the claim she must always have upon your gratitude—nay, upon a warmer, holier feeling still. As a man of honour I entrust you with her secret; as a man of honour you must feel that you owe everything to her, and that she has a right to your affection and devotion such as *no other* ever has had, or ever could have. You will do as you have always done —follow the path of duty and gratitude and loyalty; and you will be very, *very* happy together, for you know what she is, and you have proved her regard for you. Indeed, I hope and pray you have a long and happy life before you. You are still young, though old enough for the follies and illusions of youth to have passed away for evermore; and with such a companion as dear Grace, you have every cause to anticipate a bright unclouded lot. I shall perhaps not see you again—I will not pretend that it is without regret I wish you farewell; but surely friends may be parted by the force of circumstances, and yet remain true and faithful friends. My own prospects are very uncertain; you will, however, hear *of* me, though it is better that you should not hear *from* me again. You have my earnest prayers for your welfare. You will like to know that I am well, and shall be quite happy when I hear of your safety, about which we are all so anxious—quite happy. Farewell!'

It was indeed a cruel letter. Had she been a surgeon, and the recipient an insensible patient under the knife, she could scarce have laid her cuts straighter, cleaner, deeper, than she did. How his honest heart bled when he received it; how it ached afterwards in the daily self-inflicted penance of its perusal. Could she give him up so calmly, so coldly, without an effort and without a pang? Could she thus transfer to another the wealth of an affection which she could surely not calculate, not appreciate? Was *he* nothing in the compact—he whose destiny she had been, who had built the whole fabric of his life on that faithless, heartless woman? and now what was all this glorious superstructure, with the noble elevation of its hope, and the golden embellishments of its romance? A wreck—and oh, what a wreck!

Poor Humphrey!—for we need scarcely say that Henry Brampton, with his dyed skin and his flaxen curls, was none other than the disguised Cavalier—poor Humphrey! it was the first real well-delivered thrust that had ever reached his heart; he might be excused for wincing when it pierced home to the core. He was a boy in his affections still, and he felt it very keenly, like a boy. He did not know—how should he?—what it had cost the writer. He could not fathom the inscrutable depths of the female character, or comprehend the morbid satisfaction with which it can inflict suffering on those it loves, if only feeling that it is undergoing pangs tenfold more unendurable itself. He only knew that he had lost the light of his life, and he felt sorely inclined to sit him down in the darkness without an effort for evermore.

And now it was well for Humphrey that he had long proposed to himself one great object on which to direct all his energies and all his thoughts. A heart thus driven back upon itself, whether it belong to man or woman, is a fatal possession; and the better it was originally, the worse is likely to be its eventual fate. Deprive a human being of hope, and you drive that being into physical or moral suicide. What is the cause of nine-tenths of the vice and immorality in the world? The absence of a glimpse of something brighter in the future than adorns the present. The material becomes all-in-all to him for whom the ideal is a blank; and the desperate man is nearly always a sensualist. When disappointment is keen enough to upset the foundations of a reason not originally very strong, the fool who was so weak as to hang all his hopes on an earthly thread, who built, in fact, 'his house upon the sand,' slips quietly out at a side door of the tenement, with an ounce of lead to the brain, or an edge of steel to the throat; but is he much less to be pitied who drowns the whole mansion that he loathes to live in, though he dare not quit it, in

floods of wine and revelry, content to wallow in the swine's filth,
so as he may but purchase the swine's insensibility ?

It is the salvation of a noble nature to have some task of self-
denial, some motive for self-sacrifice left, when all that made the
daily burden of life endurable has passed away. Happy he who
has habituated himself to look upon his whole earthly career but
as a task of which the reward, though not given *here*, is as priceless
as it is certain.

Our Cavalier, however, had long considered that, next to his
God, he owed his whole service to his Sovereign. Whilst Charles
was a dethroned monarch, and indeed a helpless prisoner, there
was no room in Humphrey's mind for despair. 'Loyalty before
all !' was still the motto of his shield, though the blazoning that
adorned it was defaced, and the flowers that had graced and
charmed it with their sweetness were withered away. After the
first stunning effects of the blow which prostrated him had passed
off, he summoned his whole energies to return once more to the
task he had set himself in happier times. That he should feel
utterly lonely and miserable was to be expected. His was a
disposition on which a disappointment of the affections tells most
severely. Naturally confiding, where he trusted at all he trusted
entirely, ignoring, as most sincere men do, the existence of deceit.
Constant and sensitive himself, he could not conceive the possibility of change or unkindness in another ; nor, although the last
to overrate his own value, could he be blind to the merit of his
unswerving truth and fidelity. Above all, inexperienced as he
was in the ways of women, his straightforward honesty of purpose
could not understand how they delight in the generous duplicity
which, for the beloved one's welfare, feigns to yield of its own free
will all that it best delights to keep, and veils its sufferings with
a smile, the sweeter in proportion to the pain it affects to hide.

Well, come what might, as long as Charles Stuart was in
adversity, so long was Humphrey Bosville his reckless and devoted
servant. Cautiously walking in the most crowded parts of London, which then even more than now afforded the securest hiding-
place for a fugitive, he had passed a few weeks subsequent to his
interview with Effingham and release from Newgate in the enforced
inactivity which he loathed. This was the period at which he
felt most keenly the disappointment he had undergone. It was
during these long leaden weeks that Vice stretched her ghastly
arms to enfold him, not in her most alluring, but in her most
dangerous form. When she offers her treacherous goblet, sparkling with nectar and wreathed with flowers, though thirsty nature

may quaff greedily at the poison, there is yet an instinctive antipathy to the draught, a speedy reaction when its intoxicating
effects have passed away. All happiness is heaven-born, and even
its spurious copy, mere enjoyment, cannot entirely divest itself of
the reflected light shed by that which it strives to imitate; so he
who in the exuberance of youth, and health, and animal spirits,
laughs the merriest laugh, and drains the fullest cup of riot and
revelry, feels inwardly conscious the while that he is meant for
better things. But it is when she assumes the garb, not of the
garlanded Goddess, but of the dark and shrouded Fate, when she
says to her votary, 'My child, here is the deadly opiate; drink,
and feel no more! Mine is the dull trance of oblivion; come to
my arms, poor wretch, to slumber and forget!' that she offers her
most fatal temptation, that she drags the devoted sufferer headlong
into her whirlpool, to wheel a few giddy turns in vain around its
edges, and then sink into its vortex without hope for evermore.

But Humphrey was saved by his devotion to his King. While
something womanly in his nature caused him to shrink from
grosser vices, the noble ambition to serve the Stuart to the last
bade him preserve to the utmost his mental and bodily powers for
that sacred purpose; and so the while he waited his opportunity,
he led a weary life of solitude and self-denial. It was a long time
to be immured in an obscure lodging, uncheered by comrades,
forgotten by friends, with nothing but that cruel letter for a solace
and a study—a long time, but it came to an end at last.

After much consideration, it appeared to Humphrey that the
only method by which he could have a chance of assisting his
royal master was to obtain some appointment, if possible, about
his person, and then trust to accident for an opportunity either of
effecting his escape or communicating between him and his friends.
For one so well known, however, as the young Cavalier officer,
whose daring attempts had already marked him out as the most
dangerous 'Malignant' of them all, this was no such easy matter;
and he resolved at length to disguise his person and enlist in one
of the Parliamentary regiments quartered in the metropolis, by
which means he hoped at one time or another to be in immediate
attendance on Charles himself.

Fortune favoured him, as she often does those who trust in her
guidance while they make light of her favours; and it was not
long before the name of Henry Brampton was added to the roll-
call of Hacker's musketeers, that worthy commander remarking
when the recruit was brought up for inspection, that 'The Spanish
Main was no bad school for a soldier of the Parliament; and he

would scarce boggle at anything demanded of him to further the good cause here, who had stuck at nothing in the service of the devil yonder.'

So Brampton mounted his buff and bandeliers, shouldered his shining musket, took his round of fatigue duty, and tramped up and down his post on sentry, as though he had not been a few short years ago one of the most promising officers in Prince Rupert's cavalry division.

It was seldom, though, that he had an opportunity of being near the person of the monarch. It was not till the first day of the royal prisoner's trial that he was permitted to come actually into his presence. He could not but think, however, that Charles had recognised him. Like the rest of his line, the latter possessed an extraordinary memory for faces, and a wonderful facility in identifying those which he had once seen; it was not therefore surprising that he should have penetrated the disguise of one whom, indeed, he would scarce have been justified in forgetting, and whose features he had once before detected under the fisherman's slouched hat at Brampton Mill.

Yes, he felt sure the King must have known him again, but it was during a moment of great confusion, and even Humphrey's coolness had not kept his head as clear as it should have been at that trying period. It was after the keen bitter tones of Lady Fairfax had for a second time disturbed the judicial proceedings in Westminster Hall. Hacker had just delivered his brutal command to fire into the box occupied by that lady, and the musketeers were preparing to obey. Like the rest, Brampton was compelled to step to the front, and bring his firelock to the 'Present;' not that he dreamed for an instant of fulfilling so barbarous an order, but that any appearance of hesitation or unwillingness might have invited detection. It was at this moment that he caught Charles's eye fixed upon him with a peculiar and impressive glance. It seemed at once to instil caution, patience, and forbearance; but all was lost in the mist that came before his eyes and the whirl that stupified his brain, occasioned by the face that met his own as he levelled his musket in the direction of Lady Fairfax.

Standing forward in the old attitude he knew so well, looking just as she used to do, only graver and paler, but still, as his heart told him, even in that moment of surprise and confusion, as dear, as beautiful as ever, appeared the woman he had vowed he would love no longer, he had resolved he would never see again. There she was, ready to confront danger, ready to die if need be, rather than show the slightest symptom of cowardice; and hurt, angry, maddened as he had been, he felt *proud* of her even then.

As he stood at the guard-room window it required many a perusal of the fatal letter to harden him into indifference once more; and it was with a feeling of no small relief and satisfaction that he heard his name read out by the sergeant on duty as one of the permanent escort told off to guard the person of the imprisoned Sovereign.

CHAPTER XL.

' THE PROTEST.'

As a venturous swimmer striking out fearlessly from the bank finds himself carried downward by the current far lower than he intended, and discovers that all his energies, all his powers, will be severely taxed to make good his landing on the opposite shore, so doth he who embarks on the stream of political life learn to his cost that the river runs swifter still as it gets deeper, and that if he would keep his head above the surface, rather than sink into oblivion, he must consent to be borne onwards, in defiance of his own better judgment, at the mercy of the flood.

George Effingham had long ago cast in his lot with the Parliament; of what avail was his single arm to arrest the desperate measures which had now become necessary to the existence of that body, clinging as it did to the shadow of power whereof the substance was already in the iron grasp of the Dictator.

Effingham had won a position such as would have satisfied the ambition of any ordinary man, such as any ordinary man would have made considerable sacrifices of conscience and feelings to retain; but George was not an ordinary man, and his character was altered, his heart softened by the ordeal he had undergone. Long ago he had dreamt of religious freedom, of personal and political liberty, of a monarchy based on those utopian principles which form the foundations of all theoretical governments, which men will see carried out when the golden age comes back once more; and for the realisation of these visions he had been content to give up friends, party, military honour, all the hopes that make life dearest and sweetest, and to wade knee-deep in blood and guilt for the establishment of peace and holiness on earth. It was sad to find the conviction growing stronger on him day by day that he had been mistaken—that the party he had joined was no whit less ambitious, less selfish, less intolerant, and less tyrannical, than that which he had left; to see the leaven of ambition, the restless thirst for self-aggrandisement, as strong in the formal Puritan as in the dissolute Cavalier, to be forced to acknowledge that the son of the Lincolnshire grazier could be no less regardless of principles and defiant of consequences than the scion of the Stuarts, and to watch with horrified gaze the inevitable approach of that tragedy in which it was never his intention to participate.

He had been a stern pitiless man once, a man who would have hesitated at nothing in the execution of a purpose which he had determined it was his duty to fulfil, but many influences had combined to temper the strength and harshness of his original character; the habits of high command had accustomed him to a broader and consequently a more tolerant view of men and things; the practice of that true religion of which the very essence is the 'Charity that thinketh no evil,' had brought out, as it never fails to do, the kindlier impulses of his nature, and the chastening hand of sorrow had taught even proud George Effingham that he must bow resignedly to a stronger will than his own. There was little left of the haughty unbending soldier, save the gallant spirit that still could not be brought to acknowledge fear of any man that ever stepped the earth.

He had been present during the King's trial in Westminster Hall. He had loudly remonstrated against the disrespect with which his Majesty was treated during the ceremony. He had rebuked Hacker sufficiently sharply for his intemperate and un-officer-like conduct, and he had even recognised the well-known form of Grace Allonby shrinking behind the two Cavalier ladies who stood forward so proudly to vindicate their loyalty even in that moment of danger. It was painful to see her again, but George was accustomed to pain now—what did it matter? She was married to his old comrade by this time, of course, his old comrade whom he had himself saved to give her, his old comrade who was within three paces of him all the time, but whom he did not detect under the disguise of a Parliamentary musketeer. From feelings of delicacy he had kept aloof from all communication with the family of her whom he felt he had lost; it was enough that he had done all in *his* power to make her happy, and he hoped she *was* happy, and had forgotten him altogether, at least so he told himself; and yet perhaps it would not have affected him inconsolably to have known that she was pining and solitary, and that Humphrey Bosville had neither seen her nor heard from her since his release.

Each day Effingham attended the trial, and when it was concluded, contrary to his wont, he made no comment or remark upon a topic which engaged all voices and occupied all thoughts : but next morning he issued from his lodging dressed in full uniform as a Parliamentary General, and with a darker brow and more compressed lip than usual took his way, silent and preoccupied, towards the residence of the most powerful man at that moment in England, Oliver Cromwell.

It was perhaps, with one exception, the saddest day of his life. Each by each his visions had all departed from him, each by each he had given up, first his enjoyments, then his hopes, lastly his consolations. When he had resigned his command, and repudiated all further connexion with those whom he had deserted his colours to join, what would be left to him on earth ? He could see before him the weary useless life, the long leaden days, wanting even the distraction of professional occupation and the stimulus of professional exertion. He would have no position, no station in the world—he who was at that very moment one of the most important men in the kingdom ; but he never wavered : it was right, and he would do it. God would find him some task to fulfil, if it was good that he should have an appointed task, and if not, he would accept a humble lot without repining. Once only he thought how different things might have been, thought of a happy, quiet home, with domestic duties and domestic pleasures, and a smile that could make a sanded floor brighter and fairer than a palace ; but he drove these visions from him with an effort, and resolved to carry his burden, heavy as it might be, without shrinking from the labour. He had gone through the crucible at last, and had learned—bold, powerful, and successful as he was—the most difficult task of all, *to bear* humbly, resignedly, and without a murmur.

As he strode resolutely along he overtook a female figure that he seemed instinctively to recognise, although, pre-occupied as he was, he had scarcely noticed its movements or appearance. It stopped as he approached, and putting back its hood, disclosed an extremely comely face, blushing to the very edge of its cap at its recognition in the open street by so distinguished a person as General Effingham.

'No offence, General,' exclaimed Faith curtseying, for indeed it was no other than Grace Allonby's waiting-maid, grown into a sedate and matronly personage. 'No offence, I hope, but when

I looked back and saw it was you and none other, I couldn't help stopping, just for old times' sake. Ah! great changes have taken place, General, since you've seen me and my young lady; but, dear me, it's a world of change, and who'd ever have thought of my taking up at last with Hugh Dymocke! but no offence, General, I humbly hope.'

Faith dropped another curtsey, and looked very demure and pretty as she did so.

George muttered a few unintelligible words of greeting. The distinguished officer was far more agitated at this chance meeting than the humble waiting-maid. He stammered out at last a confused enquiry as to the well-being of 'Mistress Cave, and—and Mistress Grace,' he could not trust himself to add her maiden surname now, lest she should have changed it for another.

'Alack! General,' answered Faith, 'truly they are ill at ease. Indeed, the world never seems to have gone rightly with us since poor Sir Giles Allonby went to his account; and there's my Lord lying sick in his lodging down here by Whitehall, and my goodman, that's Dymocke—Hugh Dymocke—asking your pardon, General, you remember him,' quoth Faith, with another blush and another curtsey; 'he's an altered man since they took the poor young Major, and Mistress Grace, she takes on sadly to get no news of him, for dead or alive he might be, and none of us one whit the wiser; and as for Mistress Cave, it's never a word, good nor bad, she says to any one, but walks about pale and silent like a ghost; and I'm scarcely half so merry as I used to be, though that's not to be expected, of course; and indeed I never thought to see such days as these, though I'm sure, when I took Hugh Dymocke, I humbly hoped it was all for the best.'

She stopped to take breath, and George, who had by this time recovered his composure, observed with considerable simplicity,

'I thought your young lady had by this time followed your good example, Mistress Dymocke, and was married.'

'Married!' echoed Faith, with a laugh of derision; 'not she— and never likely to be; she's a sweet young lady, Mistress Grace, and a winsome, but she's been looking too long for the straight stick in the wood, and after rejecting this one and that one, here and there, she'll come out into the fields again and never find what she seeks. It was but yesterday I said to her as I was doing her hair—for leave her I never will till I see the colour in her cheeks once more—"Out of such a number," says I, "Mistress Grace, it ought not to be so hard to choose." "Never speak of

it, Faith," says she, taking me up mighty short, and turning so
pale, poor thing. "And why not?" says I, for I can be bold
enough when I like, and I was determined once for all I'd know
how and about it. "Isn't there gallants here and gallants there,
all ready to fling themselves at your feet? Wasn't there Major
Bosville, and many another of the Cavaliers, that would have gone
barefoot to Palestine and back again, only for a touch of your
hand; and now that the Parliament's uppermost, and the land is
purged, as they call it, from vanity, couldn't you pick and choose
among the saints, God-fearing men though they be?" With that
she fired up as red as scarlet. "How dare you, Faith!" says
she; "leave me this instant!" but she turned quite white again,
and was all of a tremble, and I heard her muttering-like, "Never
a Rebel, for the old father's sake," and though I was forced to do
as she bid me, and go out of the room, I made bold to peep
through the keyhole, and she had flung herself down on her knees
by the bedside, and was weeping as if her heart would break. Oh
she'll never marry now, wont Mistress Grace. And as for the
poor young Major, that they make such a talk about, it's my
belief that Mistress Cave loves him a deal better than my young
lady ever did, though I durstn't ask *her* such a question, not to
save my life!'

Having arrived at her destination and the end of her disclosures
at the same moment, Faith deemed it incumbent on her to point
out the house now occupied by Lord Vaux and his relatives,
which was indeed on the opposite side of the street, and to invite
the General on her own account to step in and see his old friends
once more. George was sorely tempted to break through all his
good resolutions; but he had a duty to fulfil, and he determined
until that task was accomplished he would suffer no human
weaknesses, no earthly considerations, to turn him aside from the
path of truth and honour. The waiting-maid's revelations had
indeed made sad havoc of the dull mental equilibrium he had
sworn to preserve. It was much to learn that Grace was still
free; much to hear that her antipathy to a rebel could create such
a turmoil in her feelings. He was no fool, George Effingham, and
who shall blame him if he drew his own conclusions, and became
conscious that hopes which he had stifled and eradicated with the
strong hand only waited a favourable opportunity to germinate
and blossom once more? Nevertheless, he would not permit
himself to dwell for more than an instant on the dream that had
so affected his outer life; but taking a courteous leave of Faith,

and forcing on her at the same time a munificent wedding-present, he pursued his walk with even a firmer step and a more resolute brow than before.

If one short hour ago he was strung to a dogged, obstinate defiance of danger, he could have faced the deadliest peril now with positive exultation and delight.

It was the 29th of January, and Lieutenant-General Cromwell's leisure was not likely to be at the disposal of the first comer; nevertheless the sentry at his door made room for Effingham to pass with a military salute, and after a very brief interval of waiting in an ante-room, a pale and agitated secretary ushered George into the presence of the Lieutenant-General, with a grave apology that so distinguished a servant of the Parliament should be kept in attendance even for a few minutes.

Cromwell was standing in the middle of the room, attired with his usual plain simplicity, but somewhat more carefully than his wont. The pale secretary reseated himself after the entrance of Effingham, and continued his occupation of writing from the Lieutenant-General's dictation, but his hand was so unsteady that it shook even the massive table on which he leaned his arm. His master took a short turn or two up and down the room, and for some minutes did not appear to notice the new arrival. George had time to scan him minutely. He had been familiar with him for a long period, had watched him in many an emergency of difficulty and danger, yet had he never seen him quite like what he was now.

In the turmoil of battle, in the critical moments on which his own destiny and that of England depended, it was a part of the man to become cooler and cooler as the plot thickened. His check would glow and his eye would brighten when leading the Ironsides to a successful charge; but should their advance be checked and the scales of victory hang doubtful in the balance, those plain heavy features seemed to settle into lineaments of iron. Now, though the orders he was enunciating were but trifling matters of military detail, a faint sallow flush came and went over his countenance, and the large lips twitched and trembled, while the broad jaw beneath them closed ever and anon with a convulsive clasp. He seemed to speak mechanically, and with his thoughts fixed on some topic far distant from the strategical movements he was directing, and he started—positively started—when in one of his short restless turns he encountered George Effingham.

There were but those three in the room—the pale secretary bowing his head over his writing; the Parliamentary officer loftily confronting his chief; and the Dictator himself, hiding an air of remorse, irritation, and perplexity under an assumption of more than military brevity and decision.

'What would you,' demanded Cromwell, his brow darkening as, with the perspicuity of all great men, he read Effingham's face like a book—'what would you with us in this press of business? Be brief, for the time is short, and lo! even now the hour is at hand.'

'I come to resign my commission into your Excellency's hands, answered Effingham in slow, steady tones, emphatic as they were sorrowful. 'I come to demand my dismissal from your Excellency's service. I come to protest against the murder of Charles Stuart.'

Cromwell's brow had grown darker and darker as the officer went on; but when he reached his climax, all the wrath he had so long repressed, all the accumulated feelings of self-reproach which had burdened him for days, broke forth in a burst of incontrollable fury. His face became purple, his features swelled, and his eyes glowed like coals, as, with a shout that made the pale secretary start out of his chair, he thundered forth—

'Out upon you, George Effingham! vile traitor and doubly-dyed renegade—will you put your hand to the plough and dare now to look back? Will you come into the Lord's vineyard, and shrink like a coward from your share of the work? God do so to me and more also if I lay not your head as low before evensong as that of Charles Stuart will lie to-morrow, to spare whom I take heaven to witness I would give my right arm—yea, the very apple of mine eye!'

George had nerve as well as courage. He remained perfectly calm and erect during this outbreak, and at its conclusion repeated, in tones if possible more distinct and accusatory than before, 'I protest against the murder of Charles Stuart!'

We have already said that a stern daring akin to his own never failed to touch the keystone of Cromwell's character. His wrath abated as rapidly as it had risen. With the inevitable self-deception of all who would fain stretch conscience too far, he was willing to vindicate his actions to his subordinate, though he felt he could not justify them to himself. Perhaps something within told him that, had he been in Effingham's position, he would have acted in the same manner.

'Nay, I do wrong thus to chafe that thou art still in darkness,' said he, with a strong effort at composure, and a countenance paling rapidly now that his natural violence of temper had expended itself. 'Thou art a tried comrade, Effingham, and a fellow-labourer in the good work; yet it may be that thine eyes have not been opened, and thou canst not see the hand of the Lord in our dealings with this man of blood. I would not be hasty with thee, my trusty friend. Take back thy resignation, and forget that thou hast thus bearded one of the Lord's appointed servants in the execution of his work.'

Cromwell turned to his secretary as if to continue the previous employment which Effingham's presence had interrupted, and made as though the subject was now concluded between them; but George was not to be thus put off. Eyeing the Lieutenant-General gravely and sternly, he once more placed his written resignation in his hands.

'I will no longer serve,' said he, 'with those who set at nought the Divine ordinance, and dip their hands in blood for the security of their temporal power. How shall I answer at the Great Day when the life of Charles Stuart, king though he be, is required at my hands, and I stand convicted of aiding and abetting in his murder—ay, his murder, General Cromwell, of whom the Scripture itself hath said, "Touch not mine Anointed?" How wilt thou answer for it thyself *there*, who canst not give an account of it that shall satisfy mankind even *here* ?'

Cromwell paced the room with rapid and irregular strides, his hands folded together, and the fingers entwining each other as of one in the extreme of perplexity. His features worked and trembled with the conflict of his emotions, and his breath came short and quick as he muttered out his vindication partly to himself and partly to the brave captain, whose defiance he could not but admire.

'It is not for me to answer it—surely not only for *me*! Do I stand alone amongst the people of England? Am I at once accuser, judge, and executioner in my own person? By the verdict of sixty just men; by the decree of a nation pronounced through its Parliament; by the laws of God and man—the head of the unrighteous hath been doomed to fall, and shall I alone be called to give account for it here and hereafter? And yet can you divide blood-guiltiness by figures, and mete out the portions of crime as one meteth out corn in a bushel? Nay, it is a just decree, and by its justice must we stand or fall—Council and Commons, Peers and Parliament, down to the meanest trooper of the army—and let none shrink from his share of the great work in which all are alike bound to take a part.'

'You can save him if you will,' said Effingham, fixing his eye calmly on the agitated countenance of his powerful superior, the pale Secretary looking at the pleader the while as one who watches a man placing his head voluntarily in the lion's maw.

'None can save him now,' answered Cromwell in grave prophetic tones, 'but He in whose hands are the issues of life and death. What am I but a sword in the grasp of the slayer—an instrument forged to do the bidding of the saints, the despised and jeered saints, that have yet triumphed in despite of their enemies? Albeit the lowest and the humblest in that goodly communion, I will not flinch from the duty that wiser and holier men than I have set me to perform. "It is expedient for us that one man should die for the people, and that the whole nation perish not." Enough of this, George Effingham—thou in whom I have trusted, who wert to me even as a brother, go out from among us, if it must be so, lest a worse thing befall thee. He that is not with us is against us. Go out from among us, George Effingham, false and unprofitable servant! Begone and see my face no more.'

Cromwell turned from him angrily and abruptly. He had lashed himself into wrath again, and the imploring looks of the Secretary warned Effingham to withdraw. He placed his resignation on the table, and keeping his eye on Cromwell, whose averted face and troubled gestures betrayed the storm within, walked steadily from the room. As he reached the door, the Lieutenant-General was heard to mutter, 'It is the Lord's doings! It is the atonement of blood!'

The Council were already assembled in the Painted Chamber, and were waiting but for him who was indeed as their very right arm and the breath of their nostrils. While Effingham walked home afoot, a ruined, and in the eyes of his own world a degraded man, Lieutenant-General Cromwell stepped from his coach amidst the clang of arms and the deferential stare of the populace, the most powerful individual in England. Which of the two looked back on the 29th of January with the most tranquil heart?

But the future Lord Protector was by this time fully nerved for the stern measures he had undertaken to carry out. If his conscience told him that the life of Charles Stuart would be required at his hands, was not the iron will powerful enough to stifle the still small voice? Could not Ambition and Fanaticism, the ambition that had originated in Patriotism, the Fanaticism that had once been piety, march hand-in-hand to their triumph, calling themselves Duty and Necessity? Was Cromwell the first who ever forced himself to believe that honour and interest pointed to the same path, or the only man who has persuaded himself he

2 A

was a tool in the hands of the Almighty whilst he was doing the devil's work? Saint or hypocrite, patriot or usurper—perhaps a mixture of all—can we judge of his temptations or realise to ourselves the extremity to which he found himself reduced? Sacrilege or justice, crime or duty, he went about it with a bold brow and a steady hand.

Small deliberation did they hold, those gloomy men who met in the Painted Chamber. Their nerves were strung, their minds made up, they had even leisure to trifle with their awful task;' and the ink that was to witness the shedding of a king's blood was flirted from one to another in ghastly mockery of sport. The Death Warrant lay before them, the merciless document that pronounced ' Charles Stuart, King of England, to stand convicted, attainted, and condemned of high treason, and other high crimes;' that sentenced him ' To be put to death by the severing of his head from his body, of which sentence execution yet remaineth to be done. These are therefore to will and require you to see the said sentence executed in the open street before Whitehall upon the morrow, being the thirtieth day of this instant month of January, between the hours of ten in the morning and five in the afternoon, with full effect. And for so doing this shall be your warrant.

' And these are to require all officers and soldiers, and others the good people of this nation of England, to be assisting unto you in this service. Given under our hands and seals.'

And then they signed their names in full, thus :—

> ' John Bradshaw.
> ' Thomas Grey, Lord Groby.
> ' Oliver Cromwell.'

(And fifty-six others.)

And the third signature was written in the steadiest hand amongst them all.

CHAPTER XLI.

' A FORLORN HOPE.'

Charles Stuart's last day was come. He had undergone his trial with a dignity and calmness which many attributed to his conviction that even at the last the Parliament dare not proceed to extremities, that at least the *person* of a sovereign must always be respected in England. If such was the reed on which he leaned, he must have found it broken in his hand. If he had cherished any expectations of a reprieve or commutation of his sentence, had been deceived by any of those visions which are so apt to take the place of Hope when Hope herself is stricken to the earth, he must have seen them now completely cleared away; and yet his courage never failed him. The King was as composed, as gentle, as majestic, in his warded chamber at St. James's on that bitter 29th of January, as though he had been the most powerful monarch in Europe seated triumphantly on a throne.

In the ante-room of the prisoner's apartment was stationed a guard of Hacker's musketeers: rough, careless soldiers were they, opposed to royalty both from interest and inclination; and yet, now that the sentence was passed, now that the prisoner whom they guarded was no longer a monarch on his trial, but a human soul that would be in eternity to-morrow, their boisterous jests were checked, their rude voices hushed, and all appeared to feel alike the influence of that majesty with which the King of Terrors clothes him whom he is about to visit.

One amongst them, indeed, seemed more restless than his comrades. Henry Brampton, with his dark face and flaxen curls, had omitted no opportunity of approaching the prisoner; and yet even now the last hour was almost come, and his duty had not yet brought him in immediate contact with Charles's person. The suspense was getting absolutely maddening; and the disguised Cavalier's feelings, outraged and lacerated by the sufferings he saw his sovereign compelled to undergo, worked upon him to a degree that it cost him all the efforts of which he was capable to hide from the observation of his companions.

Brampton had laid his plans with the energy and decision of his character. For weeks he had been ingratiating himself with the more dissolute and desperate men in the company to which he belonged. He had prayed with them, preached with them, jested with them, and, above all, drank with them, till he could count some dozen or so of choice spirits with whom he felt his influence to be all-powerful. These he had sounded cautiously and by degrees. Like most men with nothing to lose, he had found them totally without fixed principles, and perfectly ready for any undertaking which promised to conduce to their own advantage. Without committing himself to any one of them, or letting them into his confidence, he had given them to understand that he meditated some bold stroke at a fitting opportunity, in which he counted upon their adhesion, and which, if successful, would render them independent of military service for life, and give them wherewith to drink to their heart's content for the rest of their days.

These myrmidons he had contrived with infinite pains to unite in one squad, or division, which generally went on guard together, and which formed in rotation the escort of his Majesty. Could he but depend upon them at the important moment, a plan for the King's escape was practicable. Relays of horses were ready at all hours to carry his Majesty to the coast; and if the fidelity of his guards could once be seduced, it would be no impossibility to hurry him out of St. James's, and away to a place of safety under cover of night. Two obstacles stood in the way of the dauntless Cavalier. The first was so to arrange as that this escort, and no other, should guard him during the hours of darkness, a difficulty which appeared at length to be overcome, as they had been told off for duty this very evening; the second, to apprise the King of his intentions, no easy matter, guarded as was the royal prisoner, every word scrupulously noted, and every action rigidly watched.

The great stake must be played out to-day. To-morrow it would be too late; and Brampton's manifest restlessness and perturbation began to excite the remarks of his reckless companions.

'Thy conscience pricks thee, Henry,' said one rude musketeer. 'Overboard with it, man! as thou didst with the Dons yonder on the Spanish Main.'

'Nay,' quoth another, 'the time hath come at last; and Brampton's plot, whatever it be, is about hatching just now.'

'Well, I for one am tired of doing nothing,' observed a third. 'Have with thee, lad, be it to rob a church or to skin a bishop!'

'Or to put Fairfax in irons,' said a fourth.

'Or to take the New Jerusalem by escalade. Hurrah! for three hours' plunder of those streets, my boys, after the storm,' shouted a fifth. They were ripe for anything now, and the 'hurrah!' was re-echoed more than once through the guard-room, when the last speaker, the wildest reprobate amongst them all, raised his hand with a warning gesture, and a wistful look upon his dissipated war-worn face. 'Hush, lads!' he said, in a hoarse whisper! and whilst he spoke the guard-room became still as death. 'Hush, for pity's sake. His children are going into him even now. God help them, poor things! I've got young ones of my own!'

There was a tear on more than one shaggy eyelash, as the Princess Elizabeth and her little brother, the infant Duke of

Gloucester, were led by faithful Herbert through the guard-room, to see their father for the last time on this side the grave.

Charles sat at a small table on which lay a Bible, a work of controversial divinity—for even at this extreme hour he could not take his religion pure from the fountain-head—and a casket containing a few small diamond ornaments and other jewels. This casket had been sent to him the night before, in return for a signet-ring which he had forwarded to its guardian as a voucher, and had been religiously kept by that custodian, the Lady Wheeler, until such time as the King's necessities should force him to ask for it. Its contents were scarcely of royal value, being but a few dilapidated 'Georges' and 'Garters;' but as they lay spread out upon the table before him, they constituted all the worldly possessions left to Charles Stuart.

He was looking at them wistfully, and with a sad pensive expression on his brow. Many a gorgeous scene did those glittering toys recal, many an hour of royal state and courtly splendour when he who was now a prisoner waiting for his doom, needed but to lift his hand to bid the proudest heads in England bend lowly before him, when he was the centre of that charmed circle which numbered in its ranks the flower of the noblest aristocracy in the world, now, alas! scattered, exiled, ruined, and destroyed—when he was the first personage in its peerage, the first knight in its chivalry, the powerful sovereign, the happy husband, the lawgiver, the benefactor, the fountain-head of honour, and wealth, and renown. Where had it all fled? Could those times have ever been real? or was it not some vision that had melted dreamily away? Alas! those broken ornaments typified too truly the broken fortunes of him who now gazed on them for the last time. It is said that on the near approach of death, especially a death of violence undergone while body and mind are still untouched by decay, the whole of a man's life passes before him like a pageant. What a strange eventful pageant must it have been that thus glided across the spiritual vision of the doomed King! His careless boyhood, his indulgent father's kindly smile and awkward ungainly form; the romantic expedition to Madrid, the gorgeous feasts, the tournaments and bull-fights of chivalrous old Spain; the face of Buckingham, beautiful exceedingly, and the sparkling smile of his own young Bourbon bride; the assembled Parliaments, a royal figure standing out in relief as that of one with whom he was not personally identified, calling them together and proroguing them at will; Laud's stately bearing, Hampden's goodly presence, respectful even in defiance, and scapegoat Strafford's pale reproachful smile; then the Scotch progress, and the magnificence of New-castle's princely hospitality, the unfurling of the standard, the marches and counter-marches of civil warfare; the Court at Oxford, with its narrowing circle of the loyal and true, stanch Ormond's noble brow, hot Rupert's towering form, Goring's long love-locks, and stout old Astley's honest war-worn face; then the midnight bivouac and the morning alarm, the sweeping charge, the thrilling war-cry, the shattered rout of Naseby's fatal field; a prisoner, still a king, at Holmby House, Hampton Court, Carisbrooke Castle, Windsor itself; the poor bird beating its wings more and more hopelessly against the bars of each successive cage; to end in Bradshaw's pitiless frown and the final sentence read out to consenting hundreds in Westminster Hall. Ay, it *was* reality, after all, else why this sombre apartment, with its barred doors and lofty window-sills? why the sad faces of his few personal attendants? why the rude oath and jest and clang of arms in the adjoining guard-room? above all, why the chill dull foreboding, creeping and curdling even round *his* brave heart, the stunned consciousness that *to-morrow* he must be in another world.

It is a splendid pageant, truly, that of a king's life; yet perhaps at the extreme hour its scenes appear no whit more important, no whit more satisfactory to look back upon, than those which flit through the brain of a beggar, laying him down to die homeless by the wayside.

It was pitiful to see the children as they came gently into their father's presence. On each little face there was a dim prescience of evil; a dread of something felt but not understood—fear for themselves, sorrow for him, although they knew not why, mingled with childish wonderment, not altogether painful, and interest, and awe.

Charles had need of all his fortitude now. He took the Princess lovingly on his knee, and the child looked up wistfully and fondly in his face. Something that crossed it caused her to burst out a-crying, and she hid her wet cheek on her father's shoulder in a passion of tears. Her little brother, frightened at her distress, wept plentifully for company. The rough soldiers in the guard-room had rather have fronted the King's culverins at point-blank distance, than entered that chamber sanctified by sorrow. They herded together as far as might be from the door, and if they exchanged words it was not above their breath.

The King took his few diamond ornaments from the table.

'My children,' said he, 'behold all the wealth I have it now in my power to give you.'

With that he placed the gauds in their little hands, reserving only a ' George,' cut in an onyx and set with diamonds, the which he wore on his breast like a true knight, as he walked steadfastly to death on the morrow.

Then he blessed them with a father's blessing. ' My children,' said Charles, ' I shall be with you no more : you will never again see your earthly father in this world. But you have a Father in Heaven of whom none can rob you. To Him I commend you— to Him I bid you commend yourselves. Observe your duty to the Queen your mother. Swerve never in your loyalty to the Prince your brother, who is, and who always must be, my rightful successor. Fear not the face of man ; fear only to do evil in the sight of Heaven. Farewell, my children ! Be comforted, and farewell ! '

Then lifting his little son upon his knee, a boy that could scarce speak plain, he bade him for the love of his father never to supplant either of his brothers; never to believe that he could be a rightful sovereign while they lived ; never to allow wicked designing men to tempt him to the throne ; and the little one understood him, and kindled as he spoke, lisping out that he never would—

' I will be torn in pieces first ! ' said the sturdy child. So he dismissed them ; and calling them back once more folded them in one long parting embrace, and blessed them for the last time. Then he turned away to the window ; and when the door closed upon them it seemed to him that the bitterness of death was past.

Good Bishop Juxon was then admitted to the Royal presence, and Charles Stuart's last evening on earth was passed in penitence and trustful prayer.

Henry Brampton's suspense was becoming too painful to endure ; but the welcome order came at last, and our Cavalier found himself once more on the eve of one of those desperate enterprises in which it was his destiny to be continually engaged; in which, indeed, only he seemed now to live. Personal danger had for long been a stimulant of which he could ill forego the use, and it had become his normal existence to work in a perpetual plot on the King's behalf.

With a brutality which was hardly characteristic even of that stern commandant, Hacker had issued an order that two musketeers should remain in the prisoner's chamber the whole night previous to his execution ; and it was with a deep, thrilling sense of triumph that Brampton heard his assumed name read out by

the corporal of the guard as selected for this otherwise unwel
come duty. As he ran over in his own mind the arrangements
he had completed—the adherents on whom he could calculate as
sufficiently numerous to overpower any refractory sentinel; the
coach which was in waiting night after night, on some pretext or
another, in the Mall; the relays of the best horses then in England, furnished from many a nobleman's and gentleman's stable,
stationed at short intervals along a direct and unfrequented cross
country road to the coast; the raking corvette, that stood off and
on from an obscure seaport during the day, and coming into harbour at night, was kept ready at any hour to trip her anchor,
shake out her topsail, and, fair wind or foul, beat out to sea; the
disguise prepared for the well-known person of the King; nay,
the very papers which should vouch for his assumed character in
case he were stopped at any of the numerous armed posts pervading the country, and for which friends in high places had
actually procured the impression of the new Parliamentary seal,
with the English arms and the Irish harp, and the inscription, 'In
the first year of freedom, by God's blessing restored;'—as he
ran over all these well-assorted arrangements in his mind, he felt
that the moment could no longer be delayed, and that now or
never he must make proof of the inferior instruments with the
assistance of which his plan must necessarily be carried out.

One by one he sounded them in different corners of the guard-
room; one by one he found them, as he had anticipated, men
ready to undertake any measure, however desperate, for an ade-
quate consideration. All of them loved adventure for its own
sake; none of them were inaccessible to a bribe.

There was something about Brampton, too, that made its way
rapidly with men; a certain womanly kindliness which—joined
to obvious daring and reckless contempt for consequences, has an
unspeakable charm for the grosser sex—had invested him with a
high degree of interest in those untutored minds; and the stories
they told each other of his miraculous adventures and romantic
crimes on the Spanish Main and elsewhere—stories which originated solely in their own imaginations—had surrounded him with
a halo of renown and mystery by which they were completely
dazzled. He was not slow to take advantage of this spurious
fascination. Singly and collectively he bound them by an oath
to do his bidding, whatever it might be, for that one night; and
pledged himself equally solemnly to endow them severally with
sums which, to private soldiers, represented unheard-of affluence
on the morrow. His own patrimony was well nigh exhausted, it

is true, but the King's adherents had not yet been completely
rooted out of the land. Broken, dispersed, sequestered, ruined
as was the Cavalier party, he had no fear that the money would
not be forthcoming. When Brampton belted on his bandeliers
and shouldered his musket to take his post in the King's bed-
room, his heart bounded under his buff-coat to think that at last
he had saved his Sovereign.

Good Bishop Juxon had taken leave of his beloved master for
the night; faithful Herbert had prepared the pallet on which,
as an act of especial favour to the prisoner, he was permitted to
repose by the King's bedside. Charles had completed his usual
devotions, and had busied himself in the observance of all the
accustomed *minutiæ* of his toilet, as though it were but one of
the many ordinary evenings which lead up surely and successively
to the last. When he was ready to undress he seemed to indulge
in a short interval of contemplative repose—calm, resigned, nay,
even hopeful, like a man who is about to undertake a journey on
which he has long speculated, and for which, now that his departure is near at hand, he has neither repugnance nor fear. Herbert
busied himself about divers matters in the chamber, to hide
his troubled countenance and overflowing eyes, which the King
observing, spoke to him cheerfully and with a smile, bidding
him rouse himself at an early hour on the following morning,
'for,' said Charles, 'I must be astir betimes; I have a great work
to do to-morrow.'

The attached servant's fortitude here gave way completely, and
clasping his master's hand to his bosom, he burst into a passion
of grief.

'Nay,' said the King, 'be comforted; to-morrow is a day of
rejoicing rather than of sorrow. Is it not my second marriage-
day? To-morrow I would be as trim as may be, for before
night I hope to be espoused to my blessed Jesus.'

For even now, on the verge of eternity, trifling matters wrested
their share of attention from the grief of the one and the pre-
occupation of the other. Herbert asked his master what clothes he
would be pleased to wear on the morrow, and the warrior-spirit
of the old English kings flashed up for the last time, tempered,
but not extinguished, by the resignation of the Christian—

'Let me have a shirt on more than ordinary,' said Charles, 'by
reason the season is so sharp as may probably make me shake,
which some observers will imagine proceeds from fear. I would
have no such imputation. I fear not death; death is not terrible
to me. I bless my God I am prepared!' These last words the

King uttered in a low, devout, and solemn tone. He had done with everything now, on this side of eternity.

Yet is life passing sweet, even to him who has most manned himself for its loss; and one more trial was in store for the prisoner ere the gates of earthly hope were closed upon him for ever. A loud knock was heard at the door of his apartment, and without waiting for permission to enter, a file of musketeers marched steadily into the room, and stationed themselves one on each side of the King's couch.

In vain Herbert stormed and expostulated; in vain he threatened the vengeance of the Colonel, the General, the Council, and the Parliament: the soldiers had their orders, they said; and the King, calming his servant's indignation, gently bade him be still and submit with patience, as he did himself, to this last indignity.

One of the musketeers seemed stupified with drink, as was indeed the case, and remained like a statue on his post; but the door had scarcely closed upon the stir and clang of the guard-room ere the other, flinging his musket on the floor, was prostrate at the King's feet, covering his hand with kisses, and pouring forth expressions of loyalty and devotion such as the Sovereign had not heard for many a long month. Despite the flaxen curls and the dyed skin, the King recognised him at once; and to the Cavalier's hurried entreaties that he would save himself, as he poured forth a torrent of explanations and adjurations that not an instant was to be lost, did but reply—

'It was like thee, Humphrey Bosville, bold, gallant heart!—loyal to the last. It is no fault of thine that Charles Stuart must wear no more an earthly crown. But it is not to be. Listen, good Bosville; already they are changing the guard in the ante-room. Thy plot hath failed thee even at the eleventh hour. God grant they may not have suspected thee and thy comrades. Surely, ere this time to-morrow enough blood will have been shed. Fare thee well for ever, my truest, bravest servant. It is the will of God—God's will be done!'

It was indeed too true. The last chance had failed, like all the rest. No sooner had Lieutenant-General Cromwell been informed of Hacker's directions that the prisoner's last hours should be subject to intrusion, than he rescinded the brutal order; but the practised warrior at the same time commanded that the guard in the ante-room should be relieved every four hours, and that the same men should not be warned twice for this duty until after the execution—thus nullifying any attempt at tampering with the soldiers fidelity, unless the seducer was prepared to corrupt the whole regiment.

Humphrey had but time to resume his arms and his soldierlike attitude, when he was recalled to his comrades in the ante-room, and with them marched back to his regimental quarters. He carried off with him, however, one of the King's gloves, which Charles, with his accustomed kindliness in trifles, had taken from the table and slipped into his hand as he bade him farewell. That glove was treasured by Bosville's descendants as the most precious relic of their house.

At roll-call on the following morning some dozen or so of Hacker's musketeers were missing. Amongst the deserters was one Henry Brampton, of whom no further intelligence was ever obtained, though, unlike the rest, he had left his buff-coat, his arms and accoutrements, for the benefit of his successor in the ranks.

CHAPTER XLII.

'THE WHITE KING.'

WITH grave and doubting looks the people in the streets asked each other if it would really be ? In twos and threes, and small distinct groups, they conversed in low tones, glancing anxiously now towards St. James's, now in the direction of Whitehall. No crowd was collected, no circulation stopped. Ere a knot of persons, gathering like a snowball, could exceed a score, they found themselves insensibly dispersed and moving on. Compact bodies of soldiers, horse and foot, paraded to and fro in all directions, while St. James's Park was lined with a double row of musketeers, in review order, their drums beating, their colours flying, and their ranks opened. Officers and men wore a grave determined air ; there was little of triumph, much of sorrow, in their honest English faces. The day had broken gloomily enough— not a ray of sunshine lighted the lowering sky. The wind swept up the streets and across the open Mall in moaning fitful gusts, and it was bitter cold. Masons had been knocking and scraping all night long at the wall of the banqueting-house in Whitehall, and carpenters in paper caps had concluded their work in front of the King's palace. The multitude looked up at that solemn fabric with a dull stupified air. It was the scaffold.

One man amongst the crowd in St. James's Park, habited in

the dress of a plain country gentleman, and muffled in a sombre-coloured cloak, was recognised by several of the officers and men on duty. They would have accosted him, but he shunned all their greetings, and exchanged not a word with any of them. His countenance bore the impress of a deep sadness and contrition; his very gait was that of one who is bowed down by sorrow and remorse. Though he had thrown up his part, George Effingham had come to see the end of the tragedy played out.

The moments seemed to move like lead to the expectant thousands; perhaps to one they passed more swiftly, perhaps even he could have wished the agony of expectation were over at last.

Many a false alarm, many a stir about St. James's, caused every head to turn in that direction; but the drums beat up at last, the colours flew out once more, the long line of soldiers brought their firelocks to the 'shoulder,' and in the open space between their ranks a small group of persons moved slowly, solemnly, steadily, towards the place of doom.

The good Bishop on his right hand trembled like a leaf. Herbert's face was blanched and swollen with weeping; even the Parliamentary Colonel who attended him, drilled soldier though he was, marched not with so firm a step as he.

Ay, look at him well, George Effingham; you have not been so near him since he reviewed your squadron on the eve of Newbury; was his eye brighter, his mien more stately when he sat his charger, in mail and plate, before your drawn swords, than it is now? Look at him well; would you ever have deserted his service had you thought it would come to this?

As the King passed on, the musketeers on either side wheeled up behind him, closing in their ranks and forming an impassable barrier to the multitude in their rear. By favour of a stalwart sergeant who had served in his own stand of pikes at Naseby, Effingham was permitted to advance with this unbroken column. An inexpressible fascination compelled him to see out the end of that which his very soul abhorred.

On arriving at Whitehall, his Majesty passed along the galleries to his bedchamber, where he halted for a while to take a short interval of repose. Here he was served with a morsel of bread and a goblet of claret wine, upon a silver salver. Charles broke off a corner of the manchet and drank from the cup. Herbert meanwhile gave to the Bishop a white satin cap which he had in readiness for his master; he could not endure to see him under the axe of the executioner.

It was now time. Colonel Hacker, who was in attendance, and on whose stern nature the patience and dignity of the royal sufferer had made no slight impression, knocked respectfully at the chamber door. It was the signal of leave-taking. Herbert and the Bishop sank on their knees before their Sovereign, covering his hand with kisses. The latter, old and infirm, bowed down moreover with excessive grief, had scarcely strength to rise again. Gentle and kindly to the last, Charles helped the prelate up with his own hand. He bade the door be opened, and followed the Colonel out with the free step and the majestic bearing of an English King.

The galleries and banqueting-house were lined with soldiers. Firm and unwavering, they stood upon their posts, but those warlike faces bore an expression of unusual dejection : glances of pity, changing fast to admiration and even reverence, were cast upon the King from under their steel head-pieces, and the duty was evidently little to the minds of those frank bold men. They had confronted him in battle, they had fought him, and beaten him, and reviled him, but they had never thought it was to end like this !

Men and women crowded in behind them, peering and peeping under their elbows and between their heads at the doomed monarch. Fervent expressions of loyalty and goodwill greeted him from these bystanders, expressions not rebuked, nay, sometimes even echoed, by the very guards who kept them back.

'God bless your Majesty !' exclaimed George Effingham, in loud, fearless tones, baring his head at the same time with studied reverence.

The blessing was caught up and repeated by many a broken voice, and the King, returning his salutation, looked his old officer kindly and steadily in the face. Whether he recognised him or not, George was the happier for that glance during his lifetime.

He would fain have remained near him now, would fain have done him homage and returned to his allegiance even at the block, but the press became more and more resistless, and he was swept away by the crowd to a distance from which he could with difficulty watch the last actions and catch the last words of the King against whom he had rebelled.

He saw him emerge upon the fatal platform with the same dignified bearing, the same firm step. He saw him expostulate for an instant with those around him as he asked for a higher block, that he might not stoop lower than became a Stuart even in his death. He could see, though he could not hear, that the King was speaking with animated gestures in vindication of his conduct throughout the war ; but the royal voice rose audibly with the last sentence it ever spoke on earth, and every syllable struck loud and distinct as a trumpet-blast, while it declared in the face of earth and heaven—

' I have a good cause—I have a gracious God, and I will say no more !'

Had Effingham lived to a hundred, he could never have forgotten the picture that was then stamped indelibly on his brain. For many a year after he never shut his eyes that it did not present itself in all the firm strokes and glowing colours of reality. The sea of white faces upturned and horror bound, as the face of one man—the spars and props of the scaffold—the little groups that broke its level line—the sparrow that flitted across his vision and diverted his eye and his thoughts for an instant even then—the Bishop's white rochet and the Parliamentary Colonel's burnished helmet—the masked headsman's gigantic figure and the clean sharp outline of the axe—the satin doublet and the veiled head bowed down upon the block—the outstretched hand that gave the signal—

　　　　*　　　　*　　　　*　　　　*　　　　*　　　　*

Effingham was a brave stout soldier, but he grew sick and faint, and turned his eyes away. A hollow groan, more terrible, more ominous in its stifled earnestness, than the loudest shout that ever shook the heavens, told how Charles I. had been beheaded, and the reaction that placed Charles II. on the throne had already commenced. And one more scene closed the eventful drama. The faithful servants who had attended him to the threshold of eternity did not desert his mortal remains when he had passed its portal. The Parliament was memorialised and petitioned till that body, already startled at what it had done, gave permission for his burial. The decency and respect that had too often been refused the living monarch were not denied to his senseless corpse. It was brought from St. James's to Windsor in a hearse with six horses, like that of any private gentleman, and attended by four mourning coaches and the remnant of his Majesty's household. The service for the burial of the dead appointed by the Church of England was not permitted to be read ; but good Bishop Juxon, stanch to his post even when all was lost, stood ready with the Prayer Book in his hand to have used the prescribed ritual. In a vault at Windsor Castle—his own old Windsor—amongst his kingly ancestors, he was laid in his last resting-place. A few high-born Cavaliers chose the spot for his burial; a few devoted servants attended the obsequies of the master whom they loved. He lay, like a true knight, in St. George's Hall, with the banners of the noblest order of chivalry waving over him, and winter sunbeams struggling through the emblazoned windows to gild his rest. When they carried him thence to the vault wherein he was to lie, the sky that had been bright and serene clouded over ; a heavy storm of snow came on, and fell so fast that it covered coffin and hangings and pall with a pure and spotless robe—fit emblem of his innocence who slept so sound beneath.

The mourners looked significantly in each other's faces, and so they bore the White King reverently to his grave.

CHAPTER XLIII.

A GRIM PENITENT.

It is never too late to make reparation for evil, and George Effingham, although he had put it off till the eleventh hour, felt a stern satisfaction in remembering that he had thrown up his appointment on the King's condemnation, and that he at least was guiltless of Charles Stuart's death.

His case was not unlike that of other powerful champions of his party. Many a grim Puritan, though prepared to resist with the strong hand and to the death all assumption of irresponsible power, all aggressive interference on the part of the Crown, shrank with horror from so desperate a measure as the sentence of his sovereign to a criminal's death upon the scaffold, turned away with disgust from those who had completed the ghastly work when it was over. The very men who had fronted him so boldly in battle entertained a certain respect for the brave antagonist they had defeated, and the soldierlike feeling with which years of warfare had saturated their English hearts, especially revolted from the slaughter in cold blood of a vanquished foe. Fairfax himself—' *the General,*' as he was then termed *par excellence* by his party, and supposed at that juncture to be the most powerful man in England—was not aware of the execution till it was over ; but Fairfax could not have stopped it even had he known in time, for with all his *prestige* and all his popularity, the Man of Destiny was twice as powerful as he. The deed was now fairly done, and Effingham, shocked, repentant, and sick at heart, resolved to bear arms no more.

It is a serious matter for a man of middle age—by middle age we do not mean thirty or forty, or fifty, or any term of actual years, but simply that period at which the bloom is off the fruit once for all—it is a serious matter, we insist, for such an one to have lost his profession. A fortune kicked down can be built up again, like a child's house of cards; the same skill, the same labour, and the same patience, will not fail to erect a similar fabric, while those who have studied most deeply the enjoyment of wealth affirm that the pleasure of *making* money far exceeds that of spending it. Friends may fail or die, old and tried friends, but the gap they leave closes of itself far sooner than we could have supposed possible, and although we cannot quite

Go to the coffee-house and take another,

we resign ourselves to the inevitable with sufficient calmness, and go on much as we did before. Even a lost love may be replaced; or should the old wound be too deep to stanch, we cover it up and hide it away, ashamed, as well we may be, to own an incurable sore. But the profession, if *really* a profession, is a part of the man ; other privations are but forbidding him wine, this is denying him water : it is an every day want, a perpetual blank that irritates him at every turn. He would fain be in mischief rather than remain idle; be doing harm rather than doing nothing.

Effingham was very restless, very unhappy. The dull despondency of resignation that had oppressed him for so many months, that he had soothed and blunted with constant duty and unremitting labour, was indeed gone, but in its place was a feverish irritation, a morbid desire for change, an intense thirst for happiness, which is of itself the most painful of longings, and a rebellious encouragement of that discontent which asks repiningly, 'Why are these things so?' He could not forget Grace Allonby, that was the truth ; worse still, he felt that he would not if he could. To deceive another is often, as indeed it ought to be, a task of considerable difficulty ; to deceive oneself the easiest thing in the world. One knows the dupe so well, his petty weaknesses, his contemptible pliancy, his many faults, which he cultivates and cherishes as virtues. It is a poor triumph truly over a disarmed and helpless adversary, so we do it every day.

Effingham considered himself a proud man; it was the quality on which he most plumed himself. Never to bow his lofty head to human being, never to yield an inch of his self-sustaining dignity, this was his idea of manhood, this was the character he had trained himself to support. Perhaps it was for his pride that meek Grace Allonby loved him. Well she might. She had humbled it, and put her little foot upon it, and trod it into dust.

After his last interview with her, this pride forbade him ever to see her more. Even after he heard she was still free, after gossiping Faith had poured such balm unconsciously into his heart, something told him that it was not for *him* to sue again, that he must leave everything now to *her*; and that as she did not seem anxious to communicate with him, and he was determined to remain stern and immovable towards her, the probability was that they would never meet again. This point finally settled, it was no wonder that an irresistible longing came over him to visit Lord Vaux at the lodging wherein he lay on a sick bed; to request, nay, if necessary to demand, an interview with Mistress Cave, who inhabited the same house; not to shun—why should he?—the presence of any other lady who might happen to be with them at the time. That would indeed be ridiculous. It would look as though there *were* something between them, as though she could influence proud George Effingham in any one hair's-breadth of his conduct, as though he *cared* for her, which of course he did not now—not the least in the world—and this was the proof. Also a morbid desire came to possess him of justifying his conduct before these old Royalist friends, of disavowing his share in the King's death, a crime on which they must look with unmitigated horror, and of proving to them that, though a strict Puritan and a determined adherent of the Parliament in its previous resistance, he was no regicide; nay, he was now no rebel. He had but fought for liberty, not revolution; he had opposed, not the King, but the King's dishonest advisers. Under proper restrictions, he would wish to see the monarchy restored, and in the person of the late King's natural successor. Certainly he was no rebel. Sincere, earnest George Effingham was turning sophist.

He was turning coxcomb too, it seemed, else why did he linger so long over his preparations to go abroad that fine winter's morning? Why did he put on his sad-coloured raiment with so much care, and comb out those iron-grey locks and that grizzled beard with such an unpleasant consciousness that he was indeed turning *very* grey. He had not heeded his appearance for years: it set him well now, a worn and broken man, to be taking thought of his looks like a girl. He turned from the mirror with a grim sardonic smile, but he smothered a sigh too as he recalled a comely brown face that was not so bad to look at less than twenty years ago, and he wished, he knew not why, he had it back again just for to-day. Pshaw! he was not going wooing *now*. He began to think he was turning foolish. Why did his hand shake so as he tied his points, and at that early hour why so restless and eager to be off? Then, although the day was fine for walking, keen and bracing as a winter's day should be, Effingham felt very hot as he turned the corner of that street once so uninteresting and so undistinguished from the thousand and one adjacent streets, its fellows. There must have been some peculiarity in the street, too, else why should he have traversed it so often, examining its different houses so minutely ere he stopped carelessly, and quite by accident as it were, at the one he sought? It was reassuring, however, to be admitted by Faith, with her inspiriting glances and well-known smile; it was *not* reassuring to be turned loose in an empty room, to await my Lord's leisure, on whom, by a pleasant fiction, this visit was supposed to be made, and who, as an invalid, could scarcely be expected to be astir at half-after nine in the morning, the early hour, even for those early times, at which George arrived.

How the room reminded him of that other room at Oxford, of which every detail was printed so indelibly on his memory. Photography, forsooth, is no invention of this or any other century. It came with mankind fresh and perfect upon earth. When Adam left the garden and knew he should see it no more, he took with him into the dreary waste of the outer world an impression of his Paradise that had not faded when his eyes were dim and his years had numbered nine hundred one score and ten. Eve, too, carried another in her aching bosom, though she could scarcely see it through her tears. Their children, one and all, possess the art and its appliances. Effingham's 'positive' was no less vivid than that of his fellow creatures.

Men inhabit a room as an Arab pitches his tent in the desert, careful only for immediate shelter and convenience, as a place that, when they have left it and done with it, shall know them no more. Women, on the contrary—at least *some* women, and these, we think, are not seldom the gentlest and most loveable of their sex—seem to pervade it, as it were, with their influence, though for the time they may be absent indeed in the body; shedding, so to speak, an atmosphere of beauty and refinement about them which clings around the place when they are gone. 'Tis an old hackneyed quotation, though none the worse for that, about 'The vase in which roses have once been distilled;' but it describes as poetically and as adequately as language can, the charm we all know so well, the spell that a loved and loving woman casts upon the threshold of her home.

Mary Cave possessed this faculty in a high degree. Any one who knew Mary intimately could tell at a glance on entering a room whether she was in the habit of stationing herself there; and the something that George recognised here in the London lodging, which he had learned to appreciate in his Oxford experiences, was but one of the many attractions belonging to that lady of which he had never made any account. Lover-like, he attributed it all to Grace, and looked round the apartment with a softening eye, believing that it was *here* she sat and worked and pondered, thinking perhaps sometimes, and not unkindly, of *him*.

Poor Grace! she was generally too restless now to sit still anywhere. When not occupied with the invalid, to whom both the women devoted themselves as only women can, she spent most of her time in wandering to and fro about the house, looking out of all the windows that commanded the street, and turning away from them as if she expected somebody who never came, varying this dreary amusement by long political discussions with her friend, in which she sought to prove the Parliament not so far in the wrong, shocking that Cavalier lady much by the disloyalty of her opinions, which seemed to incline daily more and more towards Puritanism, and as Mary told her, almost with indignation, 'flat rebellion.'

Had George Effingham known all this, perhaps he would hardly have trembled so ridiculously as he stood bending his sheathed rapier about unconsciously in that sacred apartment. No; he was a bold man, George, and he loved her very honestly. It would have made him more nervous still.

In his stirring and eventful career he had faced as much danger as most men, not only the open dangers of the battle-field, which to one of his calibre were indeed no great trial of courage, but the more thrilling hazards of advanced outposts, night attacks, and such uncertain duties, when a moment's relaxation of vigilance, a moment's loss of coolness, might not only have destroyed himself, but imperilled the very existence of the army for whose safety he was answerable. Never in his whole life, however—as George once confessed, many a long day afterwards to a certain individual, who received the confession with happy smiles, melting into happier tears—never before, on picket, with Rupert hovering about his flanks at midnight, or detached with a handful of men to make his way in broad daylight between Goring's keen-sighted vigilance and Astley's unerring tactics, no, not even when he stood face to face with old Sir Giles at Naseby, and bore the brunt of that impetuous charge in which the stout knight fell wounded, had he felt his lips blanch and his heart leap to his mouth as they did on this eventful day simply to hear a light footfall coming along the passage, and a gentle hand lifting the latch of the door.

To him entered no more important a personage than his friend Faith, whose sense of the ludicrous, damped, yet not altogether smothered, by the grave realities of matrimony, was sorely tried by George's open-mouthed expression of countenance, denoting anything but coolness or self-command.

'My Lord prays the General will excuse his waiting on him in this apartment,' quoth Faith, demurely, ' and begs the favour of his company in the sick chamber to which his Lordship is still confined ; ' with that she bade him follow her guidance, and make as little noise as possible, in consideration of the invalid—an unnecessary injunction to a man who, though conscious of no evil intention, felt already like a convicted thief. George, however, was too experienced a soldier not to recognise the inspiriting influence of locomotion ; his courage came gradually back as he advanced to the attack.

She was in the room. He knew it somehow without seeing her. He was conscious of a presence, and a grave, formal courtesy and the old stupifying sensation, that was yet so fascinating. He was conscious also of another lady, pale and faded, who greeted him with stately coldness, and of the suffering nobleman himself reclining languidly on his couch.

Poor George Effingham ! they were drawn up in battle order to receive him, horse, foot, and dragoons. For an instant he was coward enough to wish he hadn't come !

There is nothing like a plunge at once in *medias res* to brace the nerves for an encounter. To his Lordship's distant salutation, and somewhat haughty inquiry as to the cause which had obtained him the honour of the General's visit, though he could not forbear adding, courteously enough, ' that he trusted it was to give them some opportunity of returning the many favours they had received from the Parliamentary officer,'—George replied with manly frankness at once, ' that he had come to see his old friends, in order to do himself justice. He had but few now,' he said, ' and could not afford to lose one of them. He was no longer in a position either to ask or to confer a favour. He was neither a general now, nor an officer in the service of the Parliament.'

The party looked from one to the other in some perturbation. Grace turned very red and very white again in less than a second. Lord Vaux feebly signed to the ladies to withdraw. One of them could not, and the other would not, see the signal. An embarrassing silence succeeded : the three were at what is termed a 'dead lock.'

Mary was the first to break it. He quite started at her voice ; it was so changed from the full, steady tones he remembered ; he looked attentively in her face, and was sorry to see how time and grief had altered her. It was a beautiful face still, but it had lost for ever the rounded outlines and the bright comeliness of youth.

'We are glad to know that it is so,' said Mary, assuming for the nonce the old queenly air that sat so well upon her. 'You can understand our feelings. You see our loyalty is no whit shaken even now. Mourning for him as we do, ay, even in our outward garb '—she glanced as she spoke at her own dress, for all there were in the deepest black—' how is it possible for us to forgive his murderers ? Had you come here with the King's blood on your hands, George Effingham, not one of us could have spoken a kind word to you again.'

Grace looked up at him with one rapid, speaking glance ; the next instant her eyes were fixed intently on the floor. She at least would listen to his justification with no unfavourable ear.

In a few manly, simple words George told his tale. Addressing himself to the old Cavalier nobleman, he detailed his early experiences of the royal army and the royal party, his scruples of conscience, his change of faith, the moral obligation he felt to join the champions of liberty, and the contagious enthusiasm kindled in his mind by their religious zeal. Without dwelling on his own deeds or his own feelings, he confined himself to a simple narrative of facts, relating how he had served his country and his party at once ; how he had mitigated the rigorous measures of the Parliament towards the Royalists, as indeed they themselves knew, to the utmost of his power ; and how even at the very last he had gone to Cromwell with his commission in his hand, and protesting against the sacrilege which he was powerless to prevent, had thrown it at the Dictator's feet, and stripped off the uniform which he had resolved from henceforth he would never wear again. 'And now,' said George, kindling as he spoke, and fixing his eyes unconsciously on Grace, who sat blushing and trembling, drinking in every word, ' I see, too late, the error into which we have fallen. I see that we have trusted too little to the people, too much to the sword. I see that we have ourselves built up a power we are unable to control; and that, setting aside every question of right, we must return within those limits we ought never to have overstepped, resume the allegiance that we have never intentionally shaken off, and re-establish a monarchy to save our country. I may have gone too far; but in these times there has been no middle course. I have borne arms not against my sovereign, but against those who would have persuaded him to be a tyrant. No! There is not a drop of Charles Stuart's blood on my hands, and I have never been a rebel, my Lord, never a rebel, as I am a living man ! '

Grace thanked him with a look that made Effingham's heart leap for joy.

Poor Lord Vaux, sadly weakened and broken down, had listened courteously and with a well-pleased air to a man for whom in his heart he had always entertained a high respect, and to whose kind offices he had often of late owed his own welfare and security. He bowed his head feebly, and said, ' he was glad to hear it; ' then looked wearily around as though to ask when his noonday draught would be ready, and when his visitor was going away. Mary alone remained obdurate and uncompromising.

' You have justified yourself,' she said, ' of the Blessed Martyr's blood, but you can never deny that you, and such as you, have been the unconscious instruments of this odious sacrilege. You are not *of* us, George Effingham, and you must not be *with* us. We are glad to have heard you in your defence; to have seen you once more; to thank you for the favours we have received at your hands; and to bid you farewell. We wish you no evil, we bear you no malice; but between us and *you* stands the scaffold at Whitehall. It is a barrier that can never be removed. I speak for Sir Giles Allonby's daughter as well as myself. Come, Grace, you and I have no business here ! '

How could she say such hard, such cruel words? What was this impulse that bade her do violence to her own better feelings, and trample so ruthlessly on those of her friend? Her tone, too, was unnaturally calm and constrained; and she pressed her hand upon her bosom, as if in physical pain.

He had bent his head down, down to his very sword-hilt while she was speaking, but he raised it more loftily than his wont when she had done, and Grace observed that he looked sterner than usual, and had turned very pale. Her woman's heart was rising rapidly; her woman-nature rebelled fiercely against this assumption of authority by her friend. She sat swelling with love, pride, anger, pity, a host of turbulent feelings. It wanted but little to create an outbreak.

He rose slowly, and bade Lord Vaux a courteous farewell. He bowed to the ground before Mary, who acknowledged his salutation with one of those miraculous courtesies which the dames of that period performed to such perfection. Then he turned to the door, and in doing so he must pass close by Grace's chair. How her heart beat. Once she thought he would pass without speaking. For more than a minute she had never taken her eyes off his face, and a sad, hopeless expression crossed it now that made her thrill with pain. He stopped before her chair, and took her by the hand. 'Farewell,' he said, 'a long farewell, Grace !' There was a world of quiet sorrow in the tone with which he spoke that last word; a world of hopeless love in the deep eyes that looked down so reproachfully, yet so fondly, into hers. The girl's heart was full to suffocation. She could bear it no longer; the room seemed to swim before her eyes. The next moment she was sobbing on his breast like a child.

Effingham walked out of that London lodging perhaps the happiest man that day in England. He was no accepted suitor, no affianced lover, it is true; but for the first time he knew now beyond a doubt that the blessing for which he had pined so long was his own ; that even if she might never be his, Grace Allonby loved him dearly in her heart; and the light which the poet affirms ' never was on sea or shore,' but without which both sea and shore are but dull and dreary wastes, began to shed its golden gleams on a life that only too joyfully accepted this one boon in lieu of everything else which it had lost.

Trembling, weeping, agitated, horribly ashamed, yet by no means repentant of what she had done, Grace retired to her chamber, whither, from the sheer force of habit, she was followed by her friend ; and where, in broken sentences and frequent sobs, not unmingled with smiles, she told her how she had loved their enemy so long, ever so long, ay, even before she had entreated him to save Bosville's life, only she was not quite sure he cared for her ; and how she had nevertheless always believed it was for her sake Effingham had been so kind to the Royalists ; and how proud she always was, though she knew it was very wrong, of his prowess and his successes ; lastly, how she had feared she must never see him nor speak to him again; and how to-day was the happiest day in her life; 'for, you see, Mary, he is not a rebel, after all—he says so himself—not a rebel at all; and even, if I never see him again, I shall always love him better than any one else in the world.'

And Mary listened, and soothed her, and remonstrated, like a confirmed hypocrite as she was. (All good women are, far, far more so than the bad ones.) And even urged the claim of another, with a pale smiling face too, and dissuaded her in every way she could think of from what she termed 'this wicked folly;' and Grace, cheering up rapidly, laughed at the latter argument, and said with a mocking voice, 'If ever he turns up, you will have to marry him yourself, Mary. You have taken charge of him ever since we have known him. It is very careless of you to have lost him now!'

They reached home, those unconscious friendly stabs, dealt so innocently by a loving hand—home to the very quick, every one of them. Grace could not guess why her friend bent down to kiss her so assiduously at this moment, and talked on so volubly immediately afterwards; but the conversation was resumed again and again; the argument against marriage, so resolutely urged by the elder lady, becoming weaker and weaker at every fresh attack.

The contest ended as such contests usually do when the one side is thoroughly in earnest, the other fighting against its own convictions. Lord Vaux, an easy good-tempered man, devotedly fond of Grace, and in the intervals of his malady only too glad to make every one happy about him, was soon brought to think that George Effingham would be an extremely fit person to take charge of his dear Grace, provided always they would both come and live with him in the old Hall at Boughton. With much reluctance—so much indeed as to seem more feigned than sincere—Mary withdrew her opposition, and the spring, gloomy and disastrous as it proved to the Royalist party, smiled on at least one happy heart amongst the despondent and ruined Cavaliers.

CHAPTER XLIV.

'COMING HOME.'

MASTER DYMOCKE sat basking in the beams of an early summer's sun on the terrace at Boughton. He had been left in trustworthy charge of that establishment for several months, as was indeed well known to the inferior domestics of the household, on whom his military strictness and somewhat peevish disposition, by no means improved after matrimony, had produced an impression the reverse of agreeable. The males held him in considerable awe; the females, excepting one or two of the prettiest, to whom he relaxed considerably, opined, and, womanlike, freely expressed their opinion, that he was 'a thankless old curmudgeon.' Perhaps as he was now altogether out of the game, the single ladies may have regarded him with a peculiarly unfavourable eye.

He seemed, however, thoroughly satisfied with the current of his own reflections. The family were expected to return that very day, and although he was sufficiently habituated to his pretty wife's absence to bear it with conjugal composure, he had no objection on earth to see her smiling face again. Though firmly convinced in his own mind that he had paid too high a price for that treasure, Dymocke, we need scarcely repeat, was a philosopher, and the last man to be guilty of such an absurdity as that of undervaluing a purchase because it had cost him pretty dear. No, Faith belonged to *him*, and that was of itself a very considerable merit. It is only right to add that the little woman ruled him most thoroughly, and tyrannized over him as only such a little woman can.

The afternoon was rapidly verging towards evening, and the sun was already beginning to shed that golden haze athwart the distant valleys which makes our English scenery, dotted with timber, and clothed with copse and hedgerow, like a dream of fairyland, and yet they had not arrived. Well! It was three good days' journey from London to Northampton for a horse litter, and thankful they might be that my Lord was sufficiently recovered to come home at all, and a merry home-coming it would turn out, with Miss Grace's happy face, as pleased with her dark grim lover as if he had been a bran-new gallant from the French Court; and Mistress Mary, whom the poor old folk for many a mile round had missed sadly during her absence, and his own little vixen's saucy smiles, and my Lord's calm weary approval of all that had been done whilst he was away. Dymocke had imperceptibly usurped the authority of every other functionary in the establishment, and had constituted himself butler, gardener, groom, and steward, with a grave tenacity peculiarly his own. It was now most gratifying to reflect that the house was clean, the garden trim, the stable in order, and the very pigsties arranged with military method and precision; also to be convinced that he, Hugh

Dymocke, was the only man in England who could so completely
have set everything to rights.

Thus absorbed in his self-satisfied meditations, honest Hugh
rose from the bench over which Mary's roses were already putting
forth a thousand tiny buds, and strolled into the park to catch the
first glimpse of the expected cavalcade.

Dazzled with the slanting sunbeams, he shaded his eyes with
his hand as he perceived the figure of a man in the park apparently threading the old trees so as to avoid observation.

'Something wrong,' thought Dymocke. 'Some one here for
mischief, I'll be sworn. 'Tis too tall for old Robin the mole-
catcher, and "Forester Will" is away psalm-singing at Harborow,
with a murrain to him! He'd better not come home drunk as
he did the last time, a prick-eared knave! It must be some
poaching scoundrel looking after the young fawns. I'll raddle
his bones for him if I catch him, I'll warrant; and I can run a bit
still for as old as I am, and wrestle too with here and there a one.'

Thus soliloquizing, our veteran, in whom the pugnacious pro-
pensity was still strongly developed, hastened towards the
intruder with long swift strides, craftily careful, however, to keep
every advantage of ground in case his new acquaintance should
take fright and make a run for it.

This, however, seemed to be the last thing in the stranger's
mind. He leaned his back against a tree, with his eyes fixed on
the ground, as though the young fern springing up beneath his
feet were a study of absorbing interest and importance. If he
were really a botanist, he seemed a most attentive one, and took
not the slightest notice, as indeed he was probably quite unconscious, of the sturdy sergeant's approach.

That worthy's conduct was, to say the least of it, remarkable.
On perceiving that the stranger's dress and exterior denoted a
gentleman, he had halted at a distance of about a hundred yards
and reconnoitred. Then, without further preliminary, he sent
an excellent new beaver spinning high into the air, bounded three
feet from the ground, as if he were shot, and with a howl of
mingled triumph, affection, and astonishment, ran the intervening
distance at the very top of his speed, and seizing the stranger's
hand with famished eagerness, mouthed and kissed it much as a
dog would do a bone, while down his brown cheek and on to that
hand, stole the first and only tear the stout sergeant is ever recorded to have shed.

'He's alive and well! he's alive and well!' gasped the old
soldier as if a giant's fingers were griping his throat. 'God bless

thee, Master Humphrey—my dear young master!' and he burst
out with a snatch of one of their jolly Cavalier songs in a hoarse
hysterical voice that would have tempted a bystander to laugh
had he not indeed been more inclined to weep.

It was sad to see how little Humphrey responded to the sergeant's affectionate welcome. He pressed his hand indeed kindly,
for it was not in Bosville's nature to hurt the feelings of a single
soul, but his countenance never for an instant lost the expression
of deep melancholy that had become habitual to it, and he looked
so sadly in his old servant's face that the latter's triumph soon
turned to apprehension and dismay.

' What is it, Master Humphrey?' he asked eagerly, and using
unconsciously the old familiar appellation of long ago; ' you are
safe here—quite safe; surely the bloodhounds are not after you
now? Oh, Master Humphrey, d'ye mind how we gave them the
slip, and what an example the sorrel made of 'em that blessed
day? We've got his half-brother now; goes in my Lord's coach;
and I've kept one of his hoofs. I went and cut it off myself
when he lay dead down yonder by the waterside, and it's stood
ever since over the corn-bin against you should come home !'

Humphrey smiled a forced, sad smile. ' Thanks, Honest Hugh,'
he answered; ' I have not many treasures left. I should like
the sorrel's hoof, for your sake and that of the good old horse.
Go and fetch it me now. I will wait here till you come back. I
must be in the saddle again to-night, and in a few more hours I
shall leave England for ever. Hugh, you're an old soldier; I can
trust you. Do not let any of the family know you have seen me
here to-day.'

' Why, bless you, there isn't a soul of them at home,' answered
Dymocke, and his master's face fell visibly the while. ' They're
all expected back to-night. I was out looking for them just now,
when I saw you. My Lord's getting quite hearty again, Heaven
be praised ! and you've heard the news? Our young lady's going
to be married, and to our old Captain, too. Ah, Major, there
wasn't as smart a troop in the King's army as ours. D'ye mind
what the Prince said at Newbury when he bid the whole brigade
take up a fresh alignement upon us? " Dress," says he, " upon
Captain Effingham's troop, and be d—d to ye !" He was a hearty
free-spoken gentleman, was Prince Rupert; "for they stand,"
says he, " like a brick wall," says he; and so we did, and a pelting shower we got from Essex's culverins before they'd done with
us; but we never broke our line ! Well, well, it's a world of
change; and I'm married, too, Major—married and settled and

all. Oh, my dear Master Humphrey, don't ye be in too great a hurry! But that's neither here nor there; and you've heard doubtless of Mistress Mary's good luck, and the fortune that's fallen to her?'

He had, indeed. We must be more than estranged from those we love when we cease to hear *of* them if not *from* them, to make inquiries, needlessly disguised and indirect, about their welfare—to take an interest all the keener that we are ashamed to own it in the remotest trifles that can affect them. He had heard what was indeed true, that by the death of a relative Mary Cave had become possessed of broad lands away by the winding Avon, waving woods, and smiling farms and acres of goodly pasturage; nor, though he rejoiced in aught that was likely to benefit her, could he stifle a bitter and unworthy pang to feel that this succession was but another barrier raised between himself and the woman from whom he felt he was hopelessly separated. If he had been voluntarily discarded by her before, could he condescend to sue her now that she was a wealthy heiress? Not he. That at least was a folly he had done with for evermore, and when his softer nature got the better of him, and he felt too keenly how sweet that folly was, he would fall to reading the letter once more that he still carried in his bosom, thin and almost illegible now from frequent perusals, yet perhaps scarcely so frayed and worn as the heart against which it lay. Had he known—had he only known! But such is life. Can we wonder at the bumps and knocks we receive when we think what a game at Blind-man's-buff the whole thing is!

And Mary's pleasure in her succession to this heritage was of a strangely sober nature. 'Too late—too late!' was all that lady said when she heard of it. Too late, indeed! The cause was irretrievably lost that had been with one exception the thing nearest and dearest to her heart, and he for whom alone she feared she would have been capable of abandoning that cause itself, was parted from her for ever! She could not even gain tidings that he was alive now. No wonder Mary had grown so pale and haggard! No wonder she was so altered from the proud, careless, free-spoken Mary Cave who had asserted her independence so haughtily while she flew her hawk at Holmby with stout Sir Giles not so many years ago. The wheels of Old Time run smoothly enough, but they leave their marks as surely dinted on the barren sand as on the fresh green turf, alike impartial whether they grind weed and thistle into their beaten track, or bruise the wildflower to the earth never to lift its gentle head again.

It was with no small difficulty that Humphrey could impress upon his old servant the necessity of his remaining *incog.*; could persuade him it was really his wish that none of the family should be informed of his presence; or could make him believe that he was in sober earnest in the intention he had expressed of leaving England forthwith. Dymocke was even sorely tempted to throw up his own comfortable and lucrative situation in order to follow once more the fortunes of a master to whom he had been always attached, but the thought of his lately-married wife and his fresh ties stifled this new-born impulse even as it rose. Dymocke put it in this way—' If I should once get back to my bachelor habits, I should never be able to settle down again. Perhaps I'd best stay as I am. What's done can't be undone; and maybe it's easier to keep the barrow trundling, than to stop, once and again, for a fresh start!'

' Not a word more at present, Hugh,' said the Major, after a few further inquiries and observations about old times had been made; ' I have good reasons for wishing my visit here to remain a secret. See! they are arriving even now. Meet me to-night under the cedars when they are all gone to bed. Bring the old horse's hoof with you for a keepsake, and we will wish each other a last farewell.'

As he spoke he disappeared amongst the old trees; and Dymocke, vainly endeavouring to settle his countenance into its habitual calmness, hurried back to receive his master at the hall.

It was indeed a happy party. The old lord, benefited by the advice of his London physician, and no longer harassed by the share he had so long sustained in that unequal conflict, which for the present was terminated by unequivocal defeat, had regained somewhat of his former strength and spirits, was able to alight from his litter without assistance, and gladdened Master Dymocke's heart with an appropriate jest and a kindly smile as he trod once more the threshold of his home. Happy Grace, still young enough to possess that elasticity of temperament which makes light of past suffering as though it had never been, blushed and sparkled as she did at sixteen, pressing her lover's hand with shy affection as he assisted her from her horse, but already beginning to treat him with that playful tyranny which a young wife is apt to assume over a grave and superior husband in whom she has perfect confidence, and of whom in her heart of hearts she is immensely proud. George's dark face beamed with a light which had been a stranger to it for years. Happiness is a wonderful restorative, and already the lines were beginning to fade from his rugged brow, the harsh defiant expression was changing for one of deep grateful contentment; the dark eyes, no longer glittering with repressed feelings and feverish excitement, shone with the lustre of health and strength; while the swarthy glow upon his check accorded well with his bold, frank bearing, and square, well-built frame. It was a manly, vigorous beauty still, thought Grace, and none the worse for the grizzled hair and beard. He looked joyous and light-hearted, although in the false position of a man 'about to marry.' The practice of humiliating the lords of the creation, when thus disarmed and at the mercy of their natural enemies, is by no means peculiar to the present era. From time immemorial, ay, since Father Laban imposed so cruelly upon Jacob, the bride-groom expectant has ever been discomfited as much as possible by the bride and her auxiliaries. It may be that this dishearten ing process is considered a salutary purgatory, such as shall en-hance the paradise of the subsequent honeymoon, or it may be simply intended as a judicious foretaste of conjugal discipline hereafter; but that it has existed among all civilised nations as a great social institution, we take every Benedick to witness who has found, like George Effingham, that bodice and pinners are a match, and more than a match, for doublet and hose.

Dymocke's face as he lifted his pretty wife from her horse was worth a mine of gold. There were tenderness, self-restraint, a comical consciousness of shame, and a sly glance of humour, all depicted at once on his rugged features.

'Welcome home, lass!' he whispered, winding his arm round her trim waist, 'welcome home! I can do well enough without thee; but it warms my heart like a tass of brandy to see thy bonny face again!'

This was a great deal from Hugh, and Faith stooped her pretty head and kissed him accordingly.

But 'some must work while others sleep;' and although the majority of the party were basking merrily in the sunshine, one was drooping visibly in the shade. Kindly, gentle, and forbear-ing—trying to forget her own grief in the joy of others—purified and softened by sorrow—there was yet on Mary Cave's brow a weight of care which it was sad to see in one still in the prime of life and the meridian of beauty. Her temperament, like that of many who possess abilities above the average, was impressionable enough on the surface, but hard as adamant beneath. In her younger days she was quite capable of enjoying and even recipro-cating the empty and harmless gallantries which were the fashion of the Court; but though it was always easy enough to attract

Mary Cave's attention, none save Falkland could boast that he had won her interest; and this attachment to an ideal, strong as it undoubtedly was, had in its very nature a false and morbid fascination which would too surely pass away. When it was gone it left her colder, haughtier, more inwardly reserved than ever. Then came the daily association with one possessed of many winning qualities; above all, of that which in the long run cannot fail to be appreciated—a faithful, loving heart; whom she had accustomed herself to consider as her own peculiar property; whose affection she regarded as neither obtaining nor expecting a return; whom she had taught herself to look upon as a devotee, a slave— always true, always unchanging, never to assume any other character. Little by little the unyielding disposition became saturated with an insidious and delightful sentiment. The wilful heart, so difficult to tame, found itself enclosed in meshes it had been weaving insensibly for its own subjection. In time it began to hint to her that she could ill afford to part with her secret treasure; at last it told her that it must break at once if she was to lose him altogether.

Then arose the fearful struggle out of which she came a victor indeed, but too surely conscious that *such* a victory was more crushing than any defeat. For Grace's sake, for the sake of every one—nay, for his *own* sake—she voluntarily gave him up: and while she did so she knew and felt she gave up all her hopes this side of eternity. Subsequent events added but little to her despondency. The one great fact was ever before her—that of her own free will she had discarded the man she loved; and Mary's love, once won, was no light matter. She would look at her hand—the shapely hand he used to admire and praise with a lover's childish folly, and wish it had withered to the bone ere it had penned that fatal letter. For of course he could never forgive her now. Even his kindly nature would be estranged by heartlessness such as hers. He would avoid her and forget her—nay, he *had* avoided and forgotten her. It was all over at last—he was lost to her for ever, and she had done it herself!

It was a mockery to see George and Grace so happy; to feel how utterly she had sacrificed her own future in vain. It was a mockery to hear the joyous girl prattling of her future household and her wedding-dress, and to be asked for grave matronly advice, as though she herself were indeed without the pale of the loving and the hopeful. Above all, it was a bitter mockery to have inherited broad lands, and wealth that was valueless to her now, since she might not share it with the ruined Cavalier.

It was cruel work. What could she do? There was but one resource—there never has been but one resource for human sorrow since the world began. When the burden became too heavy to bear, she knelt beneath it, and she rose again, if not hopeful, yet resigned; humbled but consoled as those alone rise who ask for comfort meekly on their knees. She was often in that position now; had she never known sorrow, she had never sought Heaven. Providence leads us like children through the wilderness, by many a devious track towards our Home. Joy brightens the path for one, and he walks on thankfully and happily in its rosy light. Grief takes another by the hand, and clutching him in her stern gripe, points with wasted arm along the narrow way. What matter for so short a distance, how we reach the goal? Brother! help me with my knapsack the while I guide thy feebler steps, and share with thee the crumbs in my homely wallet. Let us assist rather than hinder one another. Yonder, where the lights are twinkling, is a welcome for us all. Dark is the night, and sore the weary feet, and rough the way. Cheer up!—toil on!—we shall get there at last.

CHAPTER XLV.

'LOST AND FOUND.'

DYMOCKE was uneasy and full of care. 'There's something wrong,' muttered the old trooper in his beard, as he went fidgeting about the house and offices, putting everybody out under pretence of seeing things done correctly with his own eyes. A sumptuous supper was soon served in the great hall for the travellers, and Lord Vaux looked round him with an air of thorough comfort and enjoyment to be at home once more. The flush of sunset softening in the south to a pale transparent green, but edging the light clouds that roofed the meridian with flakes of fire, flooded the quaint old Hall in crimson light richer than the very hues of the stained glass above the casements, opened wide to the fragrant evening air. A solitary star twinkled already in the pure clear depths of the infinity above, while the highest twigs and branches of the old trees, not yet clothed in their summer garments to their very tops, cut clear and marked against the pale, calm sky. The rooks were drowsily cawing out their evensong, and a young moon peeping shyly above the horizon, afforded no more light to the outer world than did the needless lamp burning on the supper table to the domestic circle within. Lord Vaux was a quiet studious man of earnest temperament but of few words. He saw his fine old home preserved to him, his oaks uninjured, his fortune, though impaired, still amply sufficient for his wants; above all, his old retainers around him, and the two last of his kinsfolk left alive sitting at his board. He stretched his hand across the table to Effingham.

'God help the Cavaliers!' said he in a broken voice; 'George, I owe all this to you!'

It was the first time he had called him by his Christian name, and Grace thanked him with such a happy, grateful glance. Then she stole a look at her lover, proud, radiant, full of tenderness and trust. George blushed, stammered, looked down—and finally said nothing. It was all he had to say—would he not have given his heart's blood long ago for anyone connected, however remotely, with the name of Allonby, and never asked for thanks? There was nothing to be grateful for, he did but follow his nature. The three talked quietly, but cheerily, not laughing much, nor jesting, but in the soft, low tones of those who have a deep store of happiness within. For two indeed the cup was brim full, and running over.

Mary, too, joined in the conversation, but Dymocke, bringing in a tapering flask of Hippocras, could not but observe her absent manner and pale dejected looks.

'There's something wrong,' muttered the old soldier once more, and he fell to reflecting on all the circumstances he could think of which bore in any way on that lady's case, for whom, like the rest of the household, he felt and professed a chivalrous devotion. He had obtained a few vague hints from Faith that Mistress Mary was 'sadly changed—not herself, by any means—took the King's death much to heart,' and 'was over-anxious also about absent friends;' but Faith, besides holding the person of whom she spoke in considerable awe, was one of those women who are far more discreet in entrusting secrets to their husbands than to their own sex, and Dymocke's conjectures, whatever they might be, were but little assisted by the penetration of his wife. True to his profession, however, his ideas naturally reverted to the sorrel, as indeed they were apt to do whenever the old trooper fell into a despondent mood. He bethought him how, although the two ladies had both been in the habit of petting and fondling so good and handsome an animal, Mistress Mary's attention to that chestnut favourite were paid much more secretly than her friend's -how, going in and out of the stable at odd times, he had come unexpectedly on the latter lady making her accustomed visit when the servants were at meals or otherwise engaged, and how upon one occasion, noiselessly descending a ladder from the hay-loft during the important hour of dinner, he had seen her with his own eyes lay her soft cheek against the horse's neck, and he could have sworn he heard her sob, though she walked away with a statelier step than ever when she found herself disturbed, and as the stout soldier confessed to himself, he dared not have looked in her face for a king's ransom. Then he remembered sundry little weaknesses of the Major's, which, being his personal attendant and valet, he had not failed to remark. How he had often been surprised at the value that careless young officer seemed to attach to the most insignificant trifles. What a fuss he made about a worn-out riding-glove, which had been unaccountably lost by one of the ladies on a journey to Oxford, and as unaccountably found with the thrust of a rapier right through the palm, a few hours after the duel with Goring; also how his master's usually sweet temper had been ruffled, and he had sworn great oaths totally unwarranted by the occasion, when Dymocke, in his regard for cleanliness and order, had emptied a vase of a few roses, which had been kept there in water till indeed by any other name they could scarcely have smelt less sweet. All these matters he revolved and pondered in his mind, till at last, having, as he termed it, 'put stock and barrel together,' he came to his own conclusions, and resolved to act, soldier-like, on his own decision. It required, however, a good deal of courage to carry out his undertaking. The affection with which Mary inspired her subordinates, and indeed her equals, was tempered with awe. There are some natures with which no one ever presumes to take a liberty, some persons, often the most amiable and best-tempered of their kind, who, without the least effort or self-assertion, inspire general respect. It required no little courage and effrontery even for an old soldier to go up and tell Mary Cave, if not in so many words, at least in substance, that she was over head in love with a ruined Cavalier, and that if she didn't go out to-night and meet him under the cedars, she would probably never set eyes on him again !

Dymocke manned himself for his task. After supper, Effingham and Grace, lover-like, strolled out upon the terrace to look at the young summer moon : much of her they saw—neither of them found out she rose the other side of the house ! Lord Vaux, fatigued with his journey, hobbled quietly off to bed. Mary, with her head upon her hand, seemed lost in thought. She had

no heart for her embroidery to-night, to-morrow she would begin
new duties, new tasks; she must not sink, she thought, into a
useless apathetic being, but this one night may surely be given to
remembrance and repose. Dymocke made two efforts to speak to
her, but each time his courage failed him. She thought the man
lingered somewhat about the room, but she was in that mood
which we have all of us known, when the spirit is so weary that
any exertion, even that of observation, becomes a task; when we
are too much *beat* even to be astonished or annoyed. She rose as
if to go away, and Dymocke felt that now or never he must take
his plunge. He coughed with such preposterous violence that
she could not but lift her sad eyes to his face. She might
reasonably have expected to see him in the last stage of
suffocation.

'Mistress Mary,' said the sergeant, blank and gaping with
agitation, and there he stopped.

She thought he was drunk, and eyeing him with a calm,
sorrowful contempt, passed on to leave the room.

'Mistress Mary!' gasped the sergeant once more, 'good
Mistress Mary—no offence—he's here—I've seen him!'

No need to tell her *who*. Her limbs trembled so that she was
fain to sink into a chair, and she grasped its arms in each hand
like an old palsied woman, as, true to her mettled heart, she
turned her face to Dymocke, and tried to steady her voice to
speak. Not a sound would come save a husky stifled murmur in
her throat—not a sound, and the soldier in very pity hurried on
with what he had got to say.

'He's to meet me to-night in the Park—under the cedars—
he's there now—he's going away at once, for good and all—going
over sea—we'll never see him more. Oh! Mistress Mary, for
pity's sake!'

She smiled on the honest sergeant, such a wild, strange smile.
Never a word she spoke, but she rose steadily to her feet, and
walked away with her own proud step; only he noticed that her
face was deadly white, and she kept one hand clasped tight about
her throat.

Humphrey sat under the cedars in the misty moonlight, and
mused dreamily and sadly enough on his past life, which indeed
seemed to be gone from him for evermore. A man's strong
heart is seldom so hopeful as a woman's; it is harder for his
more practical nature to cling, like hers, to a shadow; perhaps he
has not so studiously reconciled himself to suffering as his daily
lot; perhaps his affections are less ideal, but his despondency is

usually of a fiercer and less tractable kind than her meek sorrowing resignation. Humphrey had gone through the whole ordeal, the trial by fire, which scorches and destroys the baser metal, but from which the sterling gold comes out purified and refined. He had suffered bitterly ; he sometimes wondered at himself that he could have endured so much ; but his faith had not wavered : to use the language of that old chivalry which has never yet died out in England, though it might cover his death wound, his shield was bright and spotless still.

After the King's martyrdom, as the Royalists termed the fatal execution at Whitehall, Bosville, a deserter and a conspirator, was fain to hold himself concealed in one of the many hiding-places provided by the Cavaliers for their more conspicuous friends. It took time, and cosmetics too, for the dye to wear itself out of his natural skin. It took time for his comely locks and dark moustache to grow once more, and thus efface all resemblance to the flaxen-haired Brampton, whilome a private in Hacker's redoubtable musketeers. Although when he was at length able to go abroad again, it was a nice question whether the proscribed Cavalier major did not incur as much peril by being recognised in his own real character, as in that of the sentinel who had plotted for the King's rescue, and then absconded from the ranks of the Parliamentary army. Many long weeks he remained in hiding, and it was during this interval of inaction that he heard of Effingham's proposed marriage to Grace, and of Mary's succession to her goodly inheritance. It was bitter to think how little she must have ever cared for him, that she should have made not the slightest effort to discover his lurking-place. He judged her, and rightly, by his own heart, when he reflected that she ought to know he could not sue to her now—that if ever they were to become even *friends* again, the advances must come from her. His spirit sank within him when he thought that heartlessness such as this affected even the past, that she never could have loved him for five minutes to forget him so easily now, and that he had bartered his life's happiness for that which was more false and illusive than a dream. God help the heart that is sore enough to say of the loved one, ' I had rather he or she *had died* than used me thus ! ' and yet poor Bosville had thought so more than once.

As is often the case with blind mortality, much of this self-torture was wholly uncalled-for and unjust. While Humphrey was blaming her with such bitter emphasis, Mary busied herself day by day and hour by hour in endeavouring to find out what

had become of him. Without compromising his safety, she was
bringing into play all her abilities, all her experience of political
intrigue, all her new wealth and old personal influence for this
purpose, but in vain. The Cavalier party was so completely
broken-up and disorganised, that it was almost impossible to
obtain information concerning any one of the proscribed and
scattered band. Mary was fain to give up her search in despair,
concluding that he had either fled the country or was dead. The
latter possibility she combated with a reasoning all her own. She
was not superstitious, only very fond and very sorrowful.

'It was all my fault, I know,' she used to think, that humbled,
contrite woman; 'and yet he loved me so once, he could not surely
rest in his grave if he knew how anxious and unhappy I am.' She
would rather have seen him thus than not at all.

After a time, his pride came to his assistance, and he resolved
to seek in other lands, if not forgetfulness, at least distraction and
employment. His fortunes were nearly ruined with the ruined
cause he had espoused. He had little left save his brave empty
heart and the sword that had never failed him yet. In the golden
tropics there were spoils to be won and adventures to be found.
Many a bold Cavalier who, like himself, had been more used to
bit and bridle than bolt-sprit and mainstay, was already afloat for
the Spanish Main, with a vague thirst for novelty and a dim hope
of romantic enterprise. Fabulous accounts were rife of those en-
chanted seas, with their perfumed breezes and their coral shores,
their palm trees and their spice islands, their eternal summers and
their radiant skies. Nothing was too extravagant to be credited
of the Spanish Main, and many an enthusiast, gazing at sunset on
the flushing splendour of the Western heaven, was persuaded that
he might realize on earth just so gorgeous a dream far away in
yonder hemisphere to which his eyes were turned.

So the Cavaliers clubbed their diminished means together, and
chartered goodly brigantines, and loaded them with merchandise,
looking well to their store of arms and ammunition the while, and
launched upon the deep with mingled hopes of trade and conquest, barter and rapine; the beads to tempt the dusky savage
in the one hand, the sword to lay him on his golden sands in the
other.

And Bosville had a share in one of these pirate-ships, lying,
with her fore-topsail loosed, in the Thames. She was well found,
well manned, well freighted, and ready to sail at a moment's
notice. Before he left England for ever, he thought he would go
and take one more look at the old haunts that had always been so

dear, that had witnessed the one great turning-point of his life ;
and thus it came to pass that Humphrey had met his former
servant that afternoon in the park at Boughton, and sat at nightfall under the cedar, musing dreamily in the misty moonlight.

He was not angry with her now. The bitterness had all passed
away. He could no more have chid her than one can chide the
dying or the dead. Already they were parted as if the past had
never been. He could never again suffer as he had done. The
worst was over now. Ay, there was the light glimmering in her
chamber ; he could see it through the trees. Well, well ; he had
loved her very dearly once. It was no shame to confess it, he
loved her very dearly still. Large tears welled up in his eyes.
He knelt upon the bare turf, with his forehead against the gnarled
trunk of the old cedar, and prayed for her from his heart, God
bless her ! God in heaven bless her ! He should never see her
more !

A dark figure rushed swiftly across the park. She stood before
him in that pale moonlight, white and ghastly like a corpse in
those mourning garments she had worn ever since the King's
murder. As he rose to his feet she grasped his hand. How long
those two stood there without speaking, neither ever knew. It
might have been a moment, it might have been an hour. Each
heart beat thick and fast, yet neither spoke a syllable.

She broke the silence first.

'You would not go without bidding me good-bye ?' she said,
and he felt her grasp tighten ; then the proud head sank lower,
lower still, till it rested upon his hand, and the hot tears gushed
over it as she pressed it to her eyes, and she could say never
another word than 'Forgive me, forgive me, Humphrey !' again
and again.

These scenes are all alike. Most of us have dreamt them ; to
some they have come true. None dare ignore them from their
hearts. The moon rose higher and higher in the sky, and still
they stood, those two, under the cedar, her wet face buried in his
breast, his arm around her waist. They must have had much to
tell each other, yet is it our own opinion that but little was said, and
that little sufficiently unintelligible ; but Humphrey Bosville never
sailed for the Spanish Main, and that he had good reasons to forego
his departure, we gather from the following reply to one of his
whispered interrogatories under the cedar, murmured out in soft
broken tones by weeping, blushing, happy Mary Cave—

'My own, you never knew it, but I loved you so fondly all the
time.'

CHAPTER XLVI.

'THE FAIRY RING.'

ONCE more we gather the friends, from whom we are about to part, in a fairy-ring under the old oak-tree at Holmby. More than two lustres have elapsed, with their changes, political and private, since we saw them last,—lustres that have stolen on insensibly over many a birth and many a burial, over much that has been brought gradually to perfection, much that has wasted silently to decay. The Man of Destiny has gone to his account. The Man of pleasure reigns, or rather revels, on his father's throne. All over England bells have rung, and barrels been broached, to cele-brate the Restoration. A strong reaction, to which our countrymen are of all others in Europe the most subject, has set in against Puritanism, propriety, everything that infers moderation or re-straint. Wine and wassail, dancing and drinking, quaint, strange oaths, and outward recklessness of demeanour, are the vogue; and Decency, so long bound hand and foot in over-tight swaddling clothes, strips off her wrappers one by one, till there is no saying where she may stop, and seems inclined to strike hands and join in with the frantic orgy, nude and shameless as a Bacchanal. As with boys fresh out of school, there is a mad whirl of liberty all over the playground ere each can settle steadily to his peculiar pleasure or pursuit. And the old oak looks down on all, majestic and unchanged. There may be a little less verdure about his feet, a few more tender chaplets budding on his lofty brows, a few less drops of sap in the hardening fibres of his massive girth, but what are a couple of lustres to him? He stands like a Titan, rearing his head to heaven, and yet *his* time too will come at last.

He spreads his mighty arms over a happy party; not so noisy perhaps (with one exception), as most such parties are in these roaring times, but one and all bearing on their countenances the stamp, which there is no mistaking, of a destiny worked out, of worthy longings fulfilled, above all, of a heart at peace with itself. They are well mounted, and have had to all appearance an excel-lent afternoon's sport; a brace of herons lie stricken to death on the sward, and Diamond herself, that long-lived child of air, proud, beautiful, and cruel, like a *Venus Victrix*, perches on her mistress's wrist, unhooded, to gaze upon the spoils. Grace Effingham takes but little notice of Diamond beyond an unconscious caress to her father's old favourite; for her attention, like that of the others, is taken up by an addition to this familiar party, who seems indeed, as doubtless he esteems himself, the most important personage of the whole.

He is a bright laughing child, of frank and sturdy bearing, not without a certain air of defiance. He has his mother's soft blue eyes and rich clustering hair, with something of the wilful tones and playfully imperious gestures which sat so well on the loveliest lady that adorned Henrietta's court, but his father's kindly disposition is stamped on his open, gentle brow, and his bonny, rosy mouth. He has his father's courage, too, and physical delight in danger, as Mary often thinks with a glow of pride and happiness, while she watches him riding his pony hither and thither over fortuitous leaps, and galloping that obstinate little animal to and fro with reckless and uncalled-for speed.

A tall old man, his visage puckered into a thousand wrinkles, his spare form somewhat bent, but active and sinewy still, bends over the boy with assiduous tenderness, adjusting for the twentieth time the pony's saddle, which is always slipping out of its place. Hugh Dymocke has no children of his own—an omission on the part of Faith which does not, however, disturb their married harmony—and of all people on earth he is most devoted to the urchin, who never allows him to have a moment's peace. The two are inseparable. The child knows the whole history of the Civil War, and the details of each of its battles, as furnished with considerable embellishments by his friend, far better than his A B C. He believes stoutly that his father and Hugh are the two greatest and bravest men that ever lived, inclining to award the superiority, if anything, to the latter, and that his own destiny must be necessarily to do precisely as they have done. Besides all this, Dymocke has taught him to ride, to fish, to play balloon, to use his plaything sword, and a host of bodily accomplishments; also he has promised to give him a crossbow on his seventh birthday. Wherever little Master Humphrey is seen (and heard too, we may be sure), there is Dymocke not very far off. Faith, grown stout, easy, and slipshod, having moreover deteriorated in good looks as she has improved in amiability, gives her husband his own way on this single point and no other. 'Indeed, he's crazed about the child, and that's the truth,' says Faith; generally adding, ' I'm not surprised at it, for you won't see such another, not on a summer's day !'

They are all proud of him. Uncle Effingham, as the boy persists in calling George, with half-a-dozen little black-eyed darlings of his own, spoils him almost as much as Grace does. He is not a man of quips and cranks, and such merry conceits; but he has one or two private jests of their own with the little fellow, in which, judging from the explosions of laughter by which they are followed, there must be something irresistibly humorous, apparent only to the initiated. George's beard is quite white now, and the snowy locks which peep from under his beaver form no unpleasing contrast to his coal-black eyes, glittering with fire and intellect, and the swarthy glow on his firm healthy cheek. He is very happy, and obeys Grace implicitly in the most trifling matters. The only fault to be found in his strong sensible character is, that he defers too much to the whims and fancies of his pretty wife. Need we observe she has plenty of them ready for the purpose. The neighbours say she 'rules him with a rod of iron,' that she 'bullies him,' and 'worries his life out,' and 'abuses his good-nature;' that 'his stable contains a grey mare better than any horse,' &c. &c.; but George knows better. He knows the depths of that fond true heart; he knows that a word of tenderness from him can at any time bring the tears into those fawn-like eyes, which he still thinks as soft and beautiful as ever. What though he does give her her own way in everything? Does he not love her, and is she not his own?

So he works on manfully and fearlessly, doing his duty in that public life to which he has returned. His fanaticism has been disciplined to piety, his enthusiasm toned to patriotism; he is an able statesman and a valuable member of society. Probably little Humphrey is the only person in the world who thinks George Effingham 'the funniest man he ever saw in his life!'

The young gentleman is an only child; need we say what is his parents' opinion of their treasure? Need we say how his father watches every turn of his countenance, every gesture of his graceful, childish limbs, and loves him best—if indeed he can be said to love him at any one time more than another—when he is a little wilful and a little saucy, when the blue eyes dance and sparkle, and the rosy lip curves upward, and the tiny hand turns outward from the wrist, with his mother's own gesture and his mother's own beauty blooming once more, and radiant as it used to be, long, long ago? He is Sir Humphrey Bosville now, knighted at Whitehall by his Sovereign's hand; for prone as was the Second Charles to forget faithful services, he could not for very shame pass over such devotion as Bosville's unnoticed and unrewarded.

'Odd's fish, man!' said the Merry Monarch, as he gave him the *accolade* with hearty good-will; 'many a shrewd blow have you and I seen struck in our time, but never was one given and received so deservedly as this!'

But Sir Humphrey is all unchanged from the Humphrey Bosville of the Queen's household and the King's guard-room. He rides maybe a stone heavier or so upon his horse, but he rides him still like a true knight, fearless and loyal to his *devoir*, faithful and devoted to his ladye-love—yes, she is his ladye-love still—as dear, as precious now after years of marriage as when he took leave of her at Falmouth, and watched for the very glimmer of her taper to bid her his tacit farewell from under the cedar at Boughton. He has got the foolish sleeve-knot still, he has got one or two other equally trifling absurdities; perhaps they represent to him a treasure that is beyond all value here; that, unlike other treasures, he may peradventure take away with him hereafter.

And Mary, riding by her husband's side with calm contented face, is no longer the proud imperious Mary of the Court—the spoiled beauty, whose intellect no statesman was to overreach, whose heart no gallant was to be able to touch. She has known real sorrow now, ay, and real exquisite joy—such joy as dries up the very memory of pain with its searching beams. They have each left their traces on her countenance, and yet it is beautiful still with the placid and matronly beauty of the prime of womanhood. There may be a line or two on the sweet fair brow—nay, a thread of silver in the glossy rippling hair; but there is a depth of unspeakable tenderness in the comely mask through which the spirit beams with more than its pristine brightness; and the love-light in her eyes as she looks in her husband's face is unquenched, unquenchable.

Mary laughs, and says 'she has grown into a fat old woman now;' and no doubt the graceful figure has become statelier in its proportions, and the Court dresses of Oxford and Exeter would scarcely be induced to meet round the still shapely waist; but Humphrey cannot yet be brought to consider her as a very antiquated personage. He says, 'She has always been exactly the same in his eyes;' and perhaps indeed the face he has learned so thoroughly by heart will never look like an old face to him.

She spoils him dreadfully—watches his every look, anticipates his lightest whim, and follows him about with her eyes with a fond admiration that she does not even try to conceal. She is always a little restless and out of spirits when away from him if only for a few hours; but she brightens up the moment they come together again. It seems as if she could never forget how near she once was to losing him altogether. She would not say a wry word to him to save her life; and she is angry with herself, though she cannot but confess its existence, at her jealousy of his lavishing too much affection even on her boy.

With all a mother's fondness she knows she loves the child ten times better that he is so like his father.

So the little fellow shoots out from amongst the group upon his pony, careering away over the upland like a wild thing, amidst the laughter and cheers of the lookers-on ; and they too move off at a steadier pace behind him, for the sun is already sinking, and the old trees' shadows are creeping and lengthening gradually to the eastward. They move off, and the old oak stands there, as he did in King James's time, when Sir Giles Allonby was young; as he will when that bright-haired child shall become a feeble grey-headed man ; when the actors and actresses in our historical drama shall be dead and buried and forgotten.

He is standing there now, though the scenes which we have shifted are scenes of full two hundred years ago. He will be standing there, in all probability, two hundred years hence, when we shall assuredly be passed away and gone—passed away from this earth and gone elsewhere—Where ?

PRINTED BY BALLANTYNE AND COMPANY
EDINBURGH AND LONDON